One Knight Only

PETER DAVID

ACE BOOKS, NEW YORK

This is a work of fiction. Names, characters, places, and incidents either are the product of the author's imagination or are used fictitiously, and any resemblance to actual persons, living or dead, business establishments, events, or locales is entirely coincidental.

ONE KNIGHT ONLY

An Ace Book / published by arrangement with
Second Age, Inc.

PRINTING HISTORY
Ace hardcover edition / July 2003
Ace mass market edition / July 2004

Copyright © 2003 by Second Age, Inc.
Cover art by Tristan Elwell.
Cover design by Rita Frangie.
Interior text design by Kristin del Rosario.

ISBN: 0-441-01174-8

ACE®
Ace Books are published by The Berkley Publishing Group,
a division of Penguin Group (USA) Inc.,
375 Hudson Street, New York, New York 10014.
ACE and the "A" design
are trademarks belonging to Penguin Group (USA) Inc.

PRINTED IN THE UNITED STATES OF AMERICA

10 9 8 7 6 5 4 3 2 1

*Dedicated to those who survived,
those who didn't,
and the heroes who made all the difference.*

"The shortest and surest way to live with honor in the world is to be in reality what we would appear to be."

—SOCRATES, PHILOSOPHER (470–399 B.C.)

YE OLDE PRELUDE

✝

THE HIGH KING is happy.

The stag has given him quite a run, and required an entire day of tracking, across the length and breadth of the island. Naturally the High King could have had as much help as he'd desired. Any number of individuals would have considered it the greatest of honors to accompany him on a hunt. They would have beaten the bushes for him, carved the way through the forest, scouted ahead. They would have gladly run the stag to ground for him, attempted to bring it down with bow and arrow or spear, or even assailed it barehanded, as the High King himself had done. They would have, in point of fact, broken their bodies on his behalf, crawled across broken glass, taken a brace of arrows, all to please the High King.

That was all fine for them. But what fun was that for the High King, really?

Then again, had that not been one of the recurring themes of his existence? Had there not always been those, walking the earth or stalking the heavens, who had seemed to exist primarily to prevent the High King from taking any joy in his life at all?

Immediately he pushes his thoughts away from such moribund musings. He knows himself all too well. He knows that if he continues to dwell upon it, the anger will come, followed as always by the righteous indignation. He will stew upon it, and his stomach will bubble in turmoil, and slowly the anger will build with volcanic intensity until either it explodes outward into open demonstrations of fury . . . or else be turned inward, to devour him and send him spiraling into a depression that could last weeks, even months.

It has taken him a long time, ever so long a time, to find the balance and equanimity that now governs his life. He has learned many hard and bruising lessons along the way to reach this point, and he has resolved never to forget any of them . . .

T HE HIGH KING moved among his people, looking as nonchalant as one can with a mighty stag slung over one's shoulders. He cut an imposing figure and he knew it all too well. He was bare-chested this day, as he customarily was when he hunted, and bare-legged as well. A simple breechcloth, which he would just as easily have tossed aside had he been of a mind to, was all that served to protect modesty. His body was so uniformly tanned and so firm that he looked as if he had been carved from teak. His musculature was perfectly defined, and when he walked he looked like nothing so much as a giant cat uncurling with every stride. His skin seemed to shine with the glow of matchless health. Even had he not been physically taller than everyone else, he would still have seemed to loom over them just from the sheer majesty of his presence. His shoulders were so wide that his torso almost seemed triangular as it narrowed to his waist, and his powerful legs were like knotted tree trunks. He was holding the stag over his shoulders with one hand; his other arm swung in a leisurely fashion at his side, and the muscles rippled and played against one another. His long, black hair—dotted with brambles and clods of dirt from the hunt—hung straight about his shoulders, with a section of it tied off in a lengthy tail down his back. His eyes were close-set and dark, dark as a storm, dark as death. Dark as blackness that could swallow an entire peoples whole and not even blink. He had a straight nose, with nostrils that tended to flare whenever he was in a hunt. Although he was normally clean shaven, the strong lines of his jaw sported a shadow of stubble, since he had not gone out of his way to attend to personal grooming while tracking the stag, and his facial hair tended to grow quite quickly.

He exuded power and confidence and the wisdom of the ages, and every so often as he walked past his subjects, he would toss off a brief nod of acknowledgment, which seemed to please them greatly. He could only wonder, in a distant and oblique fashion, what it was like to be them. Then again, there were times he wondered what it was like to be he himself, and he was not entirely certain of the answer to that question either.

The High King strode up the short flight of stairs to his palace, his sandals scraping on the concrete steps. The guards who were posted, two on each step, bowed sequentially as he passed them. They were each dressed somewhat similarly to him, but wore tunics as well as loincloths, and boots rather than sandals. Each of them held a single spear, points gleaming as sunlight sparkled off the gold trim. This was amusing to the High King. What was there in the world, after all, that the High King needed to fear, that he would require guards? But it was of little consequence to the High King. It gave the natives pleasure to serve him in this fashion, so there seemed no harm in it. Nor did any of his other subjects seem to mind. In fact, they seemed to derive some old-world pleasure from it. And who was he to deny anyone pleasure? After all, one had to find it where one could.

Courtiers and servants bowed and nodded to him. "Good hunt, High King," they would say. "Well done, High King." "The beast never stood a chance, High King."

Well, that was the truth of it, wasn't it? As his sandalshod feet padded across the polished floor, he pondered the fact that the beast, indeed, never had stood a chance. It was something of a paradox to him. He wanted to take pride in his accomplishment, to revel in the praise that his followers heaped upon him. On the other hand, really . . . was there much point to it? To anything?

He quickly withdrew from such musings, forcing himself to take a mental step back. He knew that if he followed that train of thought to its logical conclusion, it would plunge him into yet another one of his dark and dreary depressions. No one needed to endure that: not his people, and certainly not he himself. But it bothered him; that was twice now, in a relatively short period of time, that he had needed to force himself back to the realm of equanimity in which he dwelt for so long. That which had been so simple for him after long practice, he was now having to impose upon himself with an effort of will. Something was bothering him, gnawing away at him. But he didn't have the faintest idea what it could be.

He walked through his private chambers to out behind the palace, where the mighty river ran. It was as clear and pure and unsullied as it had been when he had first seen it, and for a moment he gazed with satisfaction at his reflection. Standing there as he was, streaked with dirt, his hair matted, his prey slung over his shoulders, he felt as if he was staring across centuries to mankind in its earliest, most primeval days. He regarded himself for a time longer, and then eased the beast's carcass off his shoulders and into the narrow river. It splashed down into the water and simply lay there, its dead eyes staring at nothing. The water burbled and splashed around it, as if toying with the stag's body, and then the High King turned away and walked back to his private chambers.

He could have had the most opulent furnishings, but he had preferred instead to keep things simple, yet elegant. All the furniture was carved from wood, glistening brown much as he himself was. Tapestries, woven centuries before, decorated the walls, depicting mighty deeds from times gone by. Here upon the wall, Ulysses again eluded the Sirens, while Robin Hood valiantly sliced one arrow with another, and Jason felt the glory of the golden fleece between his fingers for the first time. Other heroic moments, captured by skilled artisans, all belonging to the High King. Sometimes he could gaze upon them for hours, speculating, dreaming, remembering.

The High King draped himself over a chair with an ornately carved back that gave it the appearance of the head of a bull leaning over him, guarding him. As he pulled thoughtfully at his lower lip, he heard a splash from outside. He glanced through the open doors, and saw the river where he had deposited the corpse of his prey. The stag's body was no longer there. He gave the creature no further thought, but turned back instead to his own musings.

"I am bored," he said out loud, but softly. He didn't want his voice to carry, for if it did, he would undoubtedly have dozens of courtiers descending upon him, all endeavoring to entertain him in various ways. He wasn't remotely interested in that. The problem was, he wasn't sure what he *was* remotely interested in.

He rose and went to his bath. The servers were waiting there for him, of course, and they poured the warm, soothing waters for him as the High King slipped off his sandals and loincloth and eased his powerful body into the shallow pool. He leaned back, allowing the water to come up to his shoulders. The nubile women who were his bath servers slid into the water with him, washing his hair and cleansing the dirt of the hunt from him. One of them smiled at him in a manner that was both shy and knowing, cautious and inquiring. He smiled back, nodding in acquiescence. She removed the few vestments she was wearing, climbed upon his lap to face him while wrapping her legs around his middle, and he took her. She cried out, gasping, calling out his name, burying her face in the nape of his neck, and when he finished and she lay back in the water, sated, he waited a few minutes and then took the other girl as well. Not only was she no less eager than the first, but she felt she had something to live up to. She performed more than well, as did he, which was to be expected, and when she joined the first in blissful stupor, he sat there and regarded the two of them and wondered why he was still bored. He continued to wonder that even as he drifted to sleep . . .

He has not had Seeing Dreams in quite some time.

Oh, they had been there, floating about in his subconscious, teasing and taunting him with the faintest visions of things to come. But there has been nothing absolute, nothing concrete. For that matter, there has been nothing to worry about. The High King does not like the Seeing Dreams, for they are invariably sent by the gods who live to torment him. Indeed, in many ways it seems that these days they live for little else. Most of their followers are long, long dead, and most of their power is gone along with them. The High King can't help but feel that the gods bedevil him lest they fade from memory and power completely.

Apparently they have chosen to torture him now, and even the High King has to admit, grudgingly, that they have not lost their touch . . .

The dream came to him, and it was so unsettling, so disturbing, ending so violently, that the High King was propelled from his slumber with enough force to let out a yell that could well have awoken the dead. Since there were no dead around in his vicinity, and had not been for quite some time, it awoke instead the bathing servants, who let out startled yelps as the High King splashed about in alarm.

Immediately they started babbling out apologies, even though they hadn't the faintest idea what they might actually be apologizing for. The High King barely heard them, his head still whirling with the sights he had seen. It took him long moments to remember who and where he was, and when he finally managed to compose himself, he turned to the cowering women and rumbled, "Summon the Aged One." He did not wait for them to emerge from the pool before him, to prepare the towels to rub him down or the powders or scented oils. Instead he simply splashed out of the pool, picked up his blue robe from where it lay draped over a chair, and pulled it on even though his body was still soaked. A large wet stain spread across the back of the robe, but he paid it no mind. Instead he walked away quickly, smoothing out the tangles in his hair with his thick fingers even as his mind raced, trying to sort out the images and make sense of them before they slipped away, victims to his wakefulness.

He went to his receiving room without bothering to change out of his robe. He was, after all, the High King. Who would dare look disapprovingly at whatever he chose to attire himself in? Many dared not look upon him at all, and that suited him just fine.

He sat upon his great chair and waited for what seemed an interminable time. Finally he heard the soft, steady tap of a cane upon the floor, one that he knew as well as the sound of his own heartbeat. He drummed his fingers impatiently upon the armrest as he waited for the Aged One to enter. There was no use complaining or demanding that the old fellow hurry up. Of all the residents upon the isle, there were only two who did not treat the High King with due deference. One of those treated him as an equal . . . and the other as a subordinate. It was the latter of the two who approached him now, and the High King kept his peace until the Aged One was finally in front of him. His hair and beard were long and white, his face so creased with years that it was hard to believe he once had any features other than wrinkles. His clothing was loose and shapeless, and the High King suspected that beneath it he was not much more than a skeleton with some stringy meat upon him.

Still . . . he lived. And he knew things.

"I am an old man," said the Aged One without even an attempt at a politic greeting. "I need my sleep."

"You sleep all day and all night," replied the High King. "I fail to see your point."

There was no purpose whatsoever in bandying words

about. Instead he leaned forward, exuding power, as he interlaced his fingers and rested his chin atop them. "I had a Seeing Dream," he said gravely.

"Ah."

The High King blinked in annoyance. "You have nothing of more moment to say than that? Have you any idea of the importance of what I've just told you?"

"No," the Aged One replied pointedly. "I have no idea of anything. You have told me the means by which a message was conveyed, but not the message itself. It could be trivial."

"Trivial?" The High King practically spat out the word. "The gods wouldn't waste their time with trivialities."

The Aged One did not seem the least bit impressed over the High King's indignation on the gods' behalf. Instead he rapped his cane on the floor several times, as if trying to snag the attention of a recalcitrant child. The High King slumped back, looking sullen. In a faintly scolding tone, the Aged One said, "You seem to be under the impression that because you are two-thirds a god, you know of what the gods will. Well, High King, I may not share your patrimony, but I am older than you by far, and I can tell you that no one can predict the gods. We are in their image, and they in ours, and if we can be petty, cruel, and foolish in our ways, then they can be more so if they're so inclined. Do not ascribe great depth to everything the gods give you, for that way surely lies madness."

"I would have thought the continuation of this conversation would lead to madness even more quickly," grumbled the High King, shifting in his chair. "Must you always lecture me? Must you always try to make me feel as if I am less than I am?"

"Of course," said the Aged One with a shrug. "If not I, then who?"

The High King took that in for a moment, and then a slow smile spread across his face. It made him look even more handsome, because it made him seem a bit more human, rather than the icon of perfection he ordinarily resembled. "Well spoken, Aged One," he allowed. "Very well spoken. I would be the less for it, were I not accompanied by someone who existed to put me in my place."

Snorting at that, the Aged One said, "And are we not full of ourselves. I exist at your sufferance, you say? Faw." He made a dismissive, guttural noise. "I exist at the sufferance and pleasure of the gods, and will do so for as long as it amuses them to keep me about. And when they feel it is time to dispose of me—which cannot come soon enough for me, I assure you—then will I be gone, whether you have need of me or not. Gods, but if this insufferably dull conversation continues, it will seem that I have lived more than twice the span I've already consumed. Out with it, High King. What of this dream, then, for I've much to do and important naps to take that I'd prefer not to be kept from."

"The dream, then," said the High King. He suddenly felt most uneasy discussing it, for he was not one to let down his guard or speak of that which disconcerted him. It implied weakness, and was not appropriate for one who was, as the Aged One said, two-thirds god. But there was really no avoiding it. "I saw a sword . . . a sword like no other. A wide, black pommel, and a guard with runes upon it that looked as if they were ancient at a time when even you first walked the earth. And the blade, by the gods, it gleamed, Aged One, as if it was forged in the very cauldron of creation itself. It hung before me, suspended in the air, and I tried to reach for it. I touched it briefly, and heat seemed to explode from it, heat of such ferocity that it near to burned me alive." His voice filled with dread, for recounting it now chilled him to his marrow. "Then the sword spiraled through the air, and lit in the hand of another man. He swept it through the air, back and around—"

"In a shape?" the Aged One said quickly. "A pattern?"

The High King frowned, trying to recall. "A . . . figure eight, I believe. Sideways. Is that significant?"

"Go on," said the Aged One, not committing himself to any observations yet.

"There is not much more. In his other hand, the man was clutching a black rock. It was rather large. He did not attempt to throw it; he simply held it. He came toward me, swinging his sword in that same way, and then he said . . . the oddest thing." Before the Aged One could ask, he continued, "He said . . . 'I'm sorry.' But he didn't say what he was sorry for. And then . . ." He gave a small shrug. "I woke up."

The Aged One nodded slowly then, pausing to take it all in. Then he rocked back and forth slowly on his heels, humming softly to himself. The High King sat patiently, waiting. It had been a long time since he had sought the Aged One's counsel on a Seeing Dream, and he was not about to rush him.

"The sword you saw," the Aged One finally told him, "may or may not be known to me. If it is the sword I think it to be . . . it is the blade known, in its misted origins, as 'Calad Bolg' . . . ."

" 'Hard Lightning,' " the High King translated.

The Aged One nodded once in what appeared to be approval. The High King took some pleasure in that; it seemed so rare that the Aged One acknowledged, in a positive manner, just about anything he ever said. That should not have mattered to the High King . . . and yet, annoyingly, it did. "Yes. The blade of hard lightning. There are many explanations as to its origins. The most likely, as I've heard the tale, is that an Elfin smithy, or perhaps a dwarf, fashioned it, with a forge stoked by the flaming breath of the first dragon of them all, the very reptile that the Norse claimed wrapped itself around the middle of the world. The blade was first wielded by an Irish hero named Cu Chulainn, and then it disappeared upon his death. Some said it returned on its own to the Elf folk that made it; others say that a human returned it to them."

"And what happened to Calad Bolg after that?" asked the High King.

The Aged One once again lapsed into silence. The High

King's patience began to wane a bit, and it took a physical effort not to shout at the old man. When he spoke once more, it was as if he had not heard the High King's question. Instead he said, "The eight is significant. It is a time. It could be eight days . . . eight weeks, or months, or years from now . . . but at the end of that span, Calad Bolg will confront you. What is also significant is that an eight, sideways, represents infinity. Endlessness."

"So?"

Regarding the High King with a stare that could only be considered pitying, the Aged One reminded him, "You, High King . . . are endless. As am I. The sword, and its wielder, represents a threat to that endlessness."

He drew in a sharp breath. "Impossible," he spat out. He felt angry, not so much at the old man, as he did at the very notion that the way of life that they had carved out for themselves was in any way endangered. He was up off his throne, pacing, fuming, virtually outraged at the concepts he was being forced to address. When he walked, each foot came down with such force that the room seemed to shake slightly with every step. "Impossible, I say. Nothing can threaten us. Nothing can defeat me," and he thumped his fist on his chest. "I am the High King! None would dare! Even this sword, forged in a dragon's breath, cannot stand against that which protects us! For the old magic guards us."

"For now. Yes. The black stone—"

The High King stopped his pacing. He had completely forgotten about that other part of the dream. "The black stone, yes. And what will this wielder of Calad Bolg do? Pelt us with rocks in his frustration as he fails to lay us low?"

"It is not a rock. It is a symbol," said the Aged One patiently. "It is in his hand, and so it represents a servant of his. A black servant. Hard as stone, patient as stone, unyielding as stone, eternal as stone. This servant will come first. When he departs, he will bring the master. He will bring the one who bears the sword . . ."

At that, the High King laughed, loudly and dismissively. "Is that all there is to it, then?" And, sounding quite jovial, he clapped a hand on the Aged One's shoulder.

The Aged One was obviously puzzled at the abrupt change in the High King's demeanor. "Is that . . . not enough?" he asked. "The warnings of the gods could not be more dire . . ."

"They could not be more helpful!" replied the High King. "This is simplicity itself. When this black servant of the stone appears . . . all we need do is detain him here forever. If he cannot go to summon his master, the master will not come, and the Land will be safe from this Calad Bolg. You have set my mind at ease, Aged One!"

"I was hoping," the Aged One said pointedly, "that I would serve to alert you."

"You have indeed. You have alerted me to the generosity of the gods." He clapped his hands together briskly. "I know exactly what I should do. I should make a sacrifice to the gods." His grin widened as he contemplated it. "Yes! Yes, I shall hunt down a magnificent beast, capture it, and sacrifice it to the gods in thanks for this vision of warning they have given me!"

"Have you not just returned from a hunt?" asked the Aged One. "Are there not other matters you should be attending to?"

"They can wait!" said the High King cheerily. "Because thanks to the gods, we are once again assured of having all the time in the world. Will you join me in the hunt, little father?"

"Number one, I am not your father and would terminate my own immortal life were I so, provided I could find a way to do so," the Aged One said with such acid in his voice that the words alone threatened to tear the High King's skin off. "And number two . . ."

The High King wasn't listening. As if he had totally

forgotten the Aged One was still there, he strode past him and, cupping his hands to his mouth, called out, "Summon my hunting brother!" He spun and, almost as if it was an afterthought, bellowed, "Thank you, Aged One, for all your fine counsel! Here I had felt a certain despondency, but now . . . now I feel more alive than I have in ages! And I have you to thank for it! Thank you!" Newly invigorated, he turned and ran out of the room.

"You're welcome," said the Aged One. "And by the way . . . Calad Bolg is also known as Excalibur . . . and is now wielded by the Pendragon, who—last I heard—was president of the United States of America. A pity you didn't stay around to hear that. It could have saved all of us a great deal of time and aggravation, not to mention quite a few lives."

Unfortunately, the High King was not around to hear that.

And somewhere, the gods were laughing.

PARTE THE FIRST:
Wheels

CHAPTRE
THE FIRST

✚

NELLIE PORTER LOOKED at her boss with guarded bemusement. "I'm sorry, ma'am, what did you say?"

"I just asked if it would be possible to make a slight detour over to Belvedere Castle."

One could tell just by looking at Porter that she was an intelligent woman, with a strong chin, snapping blue eyes, and a straightforward, no-nonsense manner. But now she simply sat there slack-jawed, clearly befuddled, as if someone had just slapped her in the face with a large vaudevillian powder puff. She was in the rear of the limousine, her long legs tucked up and feeling a bit cramped as she tried to balance her notepad on her knees, facing her boss, who was seated opposite her. Her back was up against the closed privacy partition that separated them from the driver. Porter was old-fashioned and preferred to stay on top of things using traditional writing implements instead of computer pads and such. Now, however, she had stopped writing.

"Well, ma'am," she said cautiously, "you're running the show, of course, but we do have schedules to keep . . ."

"Five minutes, Nellie. That's all it would take."

"It would take fifteen," Porter corrected her, calculating the additional travel time with the efficiency of a well-oiled piston engine. "The plane will be waiting . . ."

"It could wait another fifteen minutes, couldn't it?" asked her boss, and even though it was framed as a question, it was actually more of a statement. Porter, smart woman that she was, naturally picked up on that, and realized that she was not being asked *if* it was possible, but instead was gently being informed that she should find a way to *make* it possible. She gave a world-weary sigh and then rapped on the privacy partition. It rolled down and the Secret Service man in the passenger seat turned and looked at her, eyebrows raised.

"We're making a detour," said Porter.

The Secret Service man, a heavyset black man named Cook who started out as a linebacker for the Lions and looked it, stared at her, and the thick eyebrows went even higher. Any higher, they'd have been skidding over the top of his shaved head. He had a headset wrapped around the top of his skull, with a microphone perched an inch from his mouth. "A detour?" he said, sounding unenthusiastic.

"Belvedere Castle."

"And we're doing that . . . why?"

"Because the First Lady asked us to."

The First Lady, in the far seat, waggled her fingers and even managed to feign an apologetic look. "I hope that won't be a problem," she said.

"In point of fact, Mrs. Penn, it will be . . ."

She leaned forward, smoothing the skirt of her simple blue power dress. "Guys . . . tomorrow's the State of the Union. That's where all the media and attention is. Since I happen to be in the area, and the place holds nostalgic value for me, I'd like to swing by it. On a slow news day, the press makes hay of it. They make a big thing out of it even though it's not a big thing. But today, they're not going to give a damn. So indulge me, okay?" And once again, there was nothing about that "Okay?" that gave any indication that she was looking for permission so much as she was issuing instructions.

Porter sighed, and reasoned that she should have been used to such things by now. "Consider yourself indulged, Mrs. Penn. Should we inform your husband?"

Her boss smiled in that way she had when speaking of the President. It seemed to Porter that the First Lady had a dazzling variety of smiles, each carefully practiced and developed for different occasions. But when mention was made of her husband, then and only then did she sport a smile that seemed . . . almost shy. Girlish.

Porter thought about all the times when she had seen series of photographs of men who had been the president, and marveled at the physical toll that the job apparently took on people. The year-by-year aging was just an amazing thing to see (except for Nixon, she recalled, who didn't appear to grow older at all while in office, as if he somehow fed off the power like some sort of vampire.) But no one ever did such studies of first ladies . . . and yet the position could be just as stressful. After all, one shared in all the grief and aggravation that one's husband had to endure, without the personal authority to do anything about it.

Mrs. Penn had not been immune from those effects. Her strawberry blonde hair now had a few streaks of premature gray in it, which she resolutely refused to dye. She actually seemed pleased about them, once confiding to Porter that she'd always been very self-conscious about her looks.

"But . . . there's nothing wrong with you!" Porter had exclaimed.

Mrs. Penn had grunted acknowledgment of the assessment. "Yes, exactly. If there were, my face would be more memorable. As it is, it has nothing interesting about it at all."

Porter had thought that Mrs. Penn was being entirely too hard on herself, but had not pushed the issue, other than chalking it up to people's amazing ability to have skewed self-perceptions. In any event, when Mrs. Penn had noticed the gray hairs coming in, she had practically burst into cries of rejoicing, and had firmly countered even the slightest suggestion that she do anything about it.

Now Mrs. Penn smiled as she considered Porter's question. "Inform my husband that I'll be a half hour later than previously anticipated? I wouldn't even insult him by thinking that such a thing would be of the remotest importance."

At that moment, the car phone rang. Porter picked it up promptly and said, "Yes." She blinked once, said, "Yes, Mr. President," and handed the phone to her boss.

Mrs. Penn took the phone and said, "Yes, Arthur?" She paused and then let out an annoyed sigh. "Yes, I'm going to be about half an hour late. Cook"—she turned her voice away from the phone—"you ratted me out, didn't you?"

In the front seat, the Secret Service man looked resolutely ahead, obviously not wanting to own up to it.

Turning her attention back to the phone, Mrs. Penn said, "I'm just visiting an old site. . . Yes. . . Yes. *That* old site. Call it nostalgia. I just feel, considering that tomorrow you're going to be focusing on where we're going, I wanted to remind myself about where we've been. It won't take long." There was a firmness in her tone that indicated that, as far as she was concerned, the discussion was over. She paused and then obviously got the answer she wanted, because she said, "Thank you, love. See you in a few hours."

She ended the connection and flipped the phone casually through the air to Porter, who caught it easily. "Men," she said lightly. "No matter what office they hold, they're still men."

"I've noticed that about them," Porter replied. Since they were having some additional time as a result of their unexpected detour, Nellie began scanning through her notes to see what other matters needed attending to. "Ah. Fred Baumann from the New York *Daily News* has been rather insistent," she said, "about a one-on-one for a State-of-the-State-of-the-Union interview."

Gwen moaned and tilted her head back, thumping it

softly on the back of the seat. Porter tried not to smile: Mrs. Penn was never exactly subtle when something was irritating her. "Baumann a problem?" asked Nellie.

"Ohhhh, we go way back." Gwen sighed. "Baumann has been covering my husband since the mayoral days. I think he feels his coverage helped Arthur get his start in politics . . . and who knows, maybe it did a little. And Baumann has been getting up there in years, so we try to help out, give him exclusives whenever we can, but still . . ." She shook her head. "Sometimes he just . . . he just acts as if he feels we owe him. As if he's somehow entitled to our time whenever it'll benefit his deadlines or get him in good with his boss. Maybe I should just cut him off at the knees and be done with it . . ."

"Well, now, wait," Nellie replied. "I mean, if he's been supporting you since way back . . . it could be argued that you do owe him. Besides, don't they always say you should be nice to the people you meet on the way up . . . ?"

"Yes, I suppose you're right," agreed Gwen. "Still . . . if I could only get some breathing space . . ."

"How about I talk to him," she offered. "I'll get a little tough with him. That way you can stay nice and sweet, and I'll be the evil witch."

"Trust me," Gwen assured her, "you're definitely no evil witch."

Nellie laughed at that. "Seen many, have you?"

But there was no smile on Gwen's face as she said rather quietly, "Just one. That was more than enough."

And she turned and stared out the window, and didn't seem to be listening to anything else Nellie was saying.

THE WALLS OF Belvedere Castle were just as Gwendolyn DeVere Queen Penn remembered them.

Gwen Penn . . .

She laughed softly to herself. One would have thought that, considering how long she had sported the moniker, she would have stopped wincing every time she thought of it. And she had. Now she only winced every other time.

The environment, the situation, was, of course, quite different. Surrounding the perimeter of the castle were Secret Service agents, several of them unable to hide the confusion in their faces as to just what the hell they were doing here. Porter was standing there, stiff and dependable as always, occasionally looking pointedly at her wristwatch. Late-night joggers, who tended to travel in packs for obvious reasons, slowed and stopped and watched from a distance, trying to figure out what was going on.

Gwen managed to ignore them all . . . or, if not ignore them, at least push them to the recesses of her attention.

To anyone else, Belvedere Castle—situated in the middle of the park around Seventy-ninth Street—was a Central Park landmark. It was not a true medieval castle; it had been constructed in the middle of the nineteenth century on Vista Rock, next to the Shakespeare Gardens. The United States Weather Bureau had instrumentation there, so whenever one heard what the weather was in Manhattan, Belvedere was likely the source.

But to Gwen, it was something far, far more. It had been the place that Arthur, years ago, had taken her as a refuge from her abusive boyfriend . . . when he had "rescued" her from a horrendous situation, and revealed the reality of his background to her.

Until that moment, Arthur Penn had simply been a boss to her, a man who was running for political office. To be specific, he had seemed bound and determined to become mayor of New York City. Even from the first, though, there had been so much more about him. His strength, his fortitude, his quiet dignity, his vision. He hadn't been a particularly tall man, nor widely brawny, although he was strong. The muscle that he did have was compact and sinewy rather than showy, but she hadn't known that at the time. Still, for all that, there had been something about him. When he walked into a room, he had commanded instant attention even if he'd said nothing. She'd once jokingly said that if one looked up the word "charisma" in the dictionary, Arthur Penn's face would be pictured next to it.

But she had not imagined the half of it. The imagination—the reality, rather—made itself apparent the night that Gwen's former significant other, Lance, had been abusing her terribly . . . the latest in a series of such events and, as it turned out, the last. For Arthur had kicked open the door to the dingy apartment, and that was when she had had a firsthand view of the strength in Arthur Penn's arms as he had tossed Lance around as if he were weightless. No . . . as if he was utterly insignificant.

As Gwen moved around Belvedere Castle, her questing fingers came upon a small, innocuous hole in the wall of one corner. That was it. She recognized it instantly. That was the "keyhole" into which Arthur had inserted a glowing sword, opening an entrance to . . .

Well, she'd never really understood it.

It had been an entire suite of rooms, furnished as only the best medieval castle could be. It had not seemed remotely possible to her that such a thing could exist. Was it rooms hidden within the castle, but somehow forgotten until now? Was it some bizarre tunnel through time and space, transporting them to another reality right next to their own? All the attempted explanations had tumbled around within her mind, and she had kept coming back to the same answer over and over: Magic.

And then Arthur had sat her down and explained it to her.

He was Arthur.

The Arthur.

Arthur as in King. Arthur as in Pendragon (shortened into "Penn" for the purpose of modern audiences). Arthur as in the guy who had pulled a sword from the stone and was declared king of all the Britons. Arthur as in Richard Burton and Richard Harris and Sean Connery and just about every other classy actor with a United Kingdom accent.

Arthur, who had miraculously survived a near-death experience at the hands of his bastard son, Modred, and had been in a cave for half a millennia, kept alive by his friend and mage, Merlin, through . . . well . . . magic again. It had all been most miraculous to her, even though he had pointed out that—to primitive people—something as utterly mundane as a lightbulb coming on at the flick of a switch would be attributed to magic. Still, to Gwen, the idea of a chamber of rooms transdimensionally connected to a castle in the middle of Central Park went somewhat beyond electricity and chandeliers. Arthur, however, saw no difference in terms of degrees, and that was just one of the many things she found so endearing about him.

He had continued his run for mayor, they had fallen in love, and many things had happened during that time, some of them pleasant, many of them far less so. But they had endured, and they had triumphed.

As she regarded the full moon hanging in the sky overhead, dancing along the top of the fortress, she thought about their life since then. About his political career, and how he had handled his stewardship of the city. Initially he had found politics wearying. After all, as king he was accustomed to simply being able to issue orders, to accomplish things through royal fiat rather than constant dickering and bargaining. Many was the time when Gwen and Arthur would quietly take leave of Gracie Mansion through a portal Merlin installed there that brought them straight to their castle hideaway, and there and only there, Arthur son of Uther would vent. He would pace furiously, tremble with righteous indignation, and say, "When I was king, I was accustomed to dealing with lords, barons, other kings. Each of them held their own provinces, their own shires and interests. Ultimately, though, they knew who the ruler was. It always gave me the leverage I required to accomplish what needed to be done. But these people, Gwen"—he swept an arm as if he could encompass the entirety of New York—"they all act as if they're my equals!"

"You're dealing with New Yorkers, Arthur," she would say patiently. "They don't defer to anyone."

"Such an arrogant lot!"

"Yes, as I said, New Yorkers. You're not making any new or novel observations, my love."

And then he would fume and fret, and claim that he was just going to toss aside the entire thing because he'd never really wanted to rule anyway, it had all been Merlin's idea. If Merlin had just left him in the damned cave, none of this would have happened.

"That's right," she would say, "and among the things that wouldn't have happened would have been that you would not have met me. Me, the reincarnation of your beloved queen . . . except, this time, the story ends happily instead of tragically."

"Yes, well . . ." He grumbled and shuffled his feet and sulked a bit, but in a charming way, and then said, "Well, the fates owed me that much, at least."

Then he would complain and worry about how he could possibly accomplish anything in this cursed environment, and the next morning he would go out and meet with people and find a compromise that suited everyone. It was a cycle that was repeated any number of times, and Gwen never minded it for a moment because she knew that she was needed, and not by just anyone, but by a truly great man.

Still, Arthur had his detractors, and they were loud and vehement, so much so that although he felt he was doing a good job, he was considered simply an adequate mayor, nothing special.

That was until the terror hit home.

For years, the pundits had warned of how unsafe the United States truly was, of how the belief that "it could never happen here" was a pleasant fantasy to which Americans lulled themselves to sleep at night. As caught up in the day-to-day routine of trying to improve life in the city, inch by frustrating inch of progress at a time, it never occurred to Arthur to worry about the big picture. And then,

one day, totally without warning, he was caught up in the
big picture . . .

FIRE TRUCKS ARE *everywhere, and there are people
screaming, and Gwen doesn't know where to look first.*
*This is madness, this is madness, this is not happening, I'm
going to wake up any moment, echoes and reechoes through her head.
They are not supposed to be here, in front of the fallen remains of
one of the city's greatest landmarks. They are supposed to be clear
across town, attending a taping of a popular late-night talk show
on which Arthur has agreed to make an appearance.*

*People run past the windows of the limo, a few of them pausing
to try and glance in, the rest of them not giving a damn, caring
only about trying to put as much distance as possible between themselves and this place of death. The streets are becoming thick with
people; in moments it's going to be difficult for the limo to go anywhere at all.*

*Suddenly there is a banging on the limo roof. Through the open
front window of the driver, she sees Arthur's grim face, streaked
with ash. She can see behind him the sky thick with gray smoke,
drifting upward in leisurely fashion as if God is exhaling pollut-
ants. "Get her out of here," Arthur says.*

*"No, Arthur!" she cries out. They had been rerouted here upon
hearing of the emergency, and she will be damned if she is suddenly
shunted away once more.*

*"It's too dangerous," he tells her, and to the driver, in a tone
that will brook no discussion, he says, "Go."*

*The limo starts to roll forward, but before it gets three feet, Gwen
shoves open the door on the side opposite from where Arthur is. They
look at each other across the rooftop, his face darkening with a
scowl, and then she spots elderly people, struggling to walk or even
stand. "Here!" she calls to them, and without a word of question
or protest they ease themselves into the limousine. Five of them are
able to fit, including one with a walker, and Arthur keeps speaking
her name to her in growing frustration, but she ignores him. Going
quickly to the passenger-side window, she calls through to the*

driver, "Hit the siren, Clancy. Take them to the nearest hospital, make sure they're checked for smoke inhalation."

Clancy, caught between two masters, looks from Arthur's face to Gwen's and back, and quickly decides whom he is less interested in arguing with. He hits the siren, and as crowded as the streets are, as shellshocked as the refugees may be, they still make way for the limo as it rolls away from the scene of the catastrophe.

Arthur stares at her, shaking his head. Under ordinary circumstances, he would have allowed a smile to appear in recognition of her annoying pluck, but these are far from ordinary circumstances. "So be it," he snaps, and then promptly hurls himself into conference and aid with the senior emergency officers on the spot.

Gwen pitches in everywhere she can. Within minutes she is so covered with filth that she's not immediately recognizable. It doesn't matter. She's smart, she's willing to work, and she's breathing; at that point in time, that's absolutely all that matters. She sees the human misery, she sees the heroism all around her, she sees the suffering and the scattered body parts and the numb looks on the faces of everyone involved, and whenever she thinks it's more than she can bear, she thinks of the building as it had been mere hours before, and how those who destroyed it would like nothing better than to break the spirit of all Americans, and then she redoubles her efforts and gets back to work.

As for Arthur, God, he's everywhere. One minute he's directing operations, the next he is speaking to the TV cameras, assuring anyone watching that the city's finest and bravest are on top of the situation, the next minute he's helping to haul out rubble. His jacket is long gone, and his shirtsleeves are rolled up. His necktie he has tied off around his head, like a bandana, to keep strands of his brown hair out of his eyes and soak up the sweat from his forehead. His white shirt is thick with dirt and perspiration, the pants legs torn. The suit's pretty much unusable, and yet somehow that seems extraordinarily trivial right about then.

Already the words are being bandied about, first in whispers and then in full-voice growls of anger: Terrorists. This was no explosion from a gas main leak. This was a series of carefully placed bombs, laid at the foundations of the building, undetected over a

*lengthy period, and then detonated. Fortunately the great structure
had collapsed straight down; if it had fallen to the side, any side,
the death toll would be beyond calculation.*

*Arthur and Gwen labor ceaselessly, long into the night. At one
point Gwen collapses from exhaustion onto a Red Cross bed, just to
close her eyes for a few moments. It is several hours later when she
comes to. Arthur has not stopped working in all that time. She has
no idea how he's doing it. He may be many things: a thousand
years old, a former king, a warrior born, but superhuman in terms
of strength and stamina he is most definitely not. Yet there he is,
everywhere, determined not to stop standing until he literally can
stand no longer, and considering his efforts thus far, it seems just
barely possible that he can manage it.*

The journalists take notice.

*Although it is not his intention, and even though he doesn't
really give a damn about the media, nevertheless he benefits from it
immensely. Arthur is on the front page of all the daily newspapers,
full-color pictures depicting Arthur and Gwen in assorted altruistic
moments. But that initial coverage pales beside what happens in
the glow of the next morning sun . . .*

"**M**RS. PENN. . ." GWEN blinked, like an owl hit with
a spotlight, and brought herself back to reality.
"Yes?"

"Nothing, it's just," said Porter, clearly a bit uncomfortable, looking rather out of place there with her beautifully
tailored suit and very modern manner, surrounded by an
environment that seemed plucked out of centuries agone,
"it's just that you'd been staring at that wall for fifteen
minutes without saying anything. Is there something particularly significant about that wall . . . if you don't mind
my asking?"

"No," Gwen said softly, her breath misting in front of
her as the temperature dropped precipitously. It had been
an unseasonably warm January afternoon, but now she was
really starting to feel the chill. She noticed Porter shivering

slightly and felt guilty. "No, nothing particularly significant about it at all. I was just thinking about . . . things. This is a piece of the past, after all. What better place to think about the past?"

"Well . . . if you're asking my opinion . . . the inside of a warm limo seems much better," Porter ventured.

Gwen chuckled at that, and then nodded. She headed for the car and Cook was all too pleased to be holding the door open for her. She noticed that, even in this relatively sedate and safe setting, he was looking back and forth, his great head resembling a conning tower. He was trying to spot the slightest hint of danger, from any direction, of any kind. She had no idea how he managed to do the job; if it were her, she would have gone insane.

She slid into the car, Porter directly behind her, and the door slammed decisively shut. But the sound was a distance away, for her mind was elsewhere . . .

*T*HE PRESIDENT OF *the United States arrives.*
It is, more or less, over the figurative dead bodies of his Secret Service men, who are insisting that this is a gargantuan mistake on his part. The area is not secure, they tell him. They cannot guarantee his safety. But the President is an old warhorse of a man, a veteran who spent time in a prison camp, and he makes his position clear through word and deed: He will not be hunkered down somewhere while a U.S. city is under siege. Furthermore, he is an old-school hard-liner, and has made a war on terrorism one of the centerpieces of his presidency. So he is not about to let the actions of terrorists dictate where he will go and when he will go there.

There are the cynics, of course. There are those who say that he is seeking to have the photographers and press snap pictures of him walking amongst the rubble, head held high, a flag raised in one hand and an arm draped around the shoulders of a tired but inspiring fireman. There are those who say that he is so obsessed with mindless machismo that he is putting himself at risk rather than listening to the advice of his handlers, who know best and would keep him out of harm's way. His presence in New York, it is said, will accomplish nothing on any sort of practical level.

He does not care. He will not be reasoned with, because he knows what is right and true and best.

He is accompanied by enough Secret Service men to take down the entire offensive line of the Denver Broncos. High overhead, United States Air Force fighter pilots cut through the air in patrol, locking down New York airspace, while all flights from JFK, LaGuardia, and Newark are shut down for the duration of the President's visit.

Gwen is not on hand. Exhausted and spent, she has returned to Gracie Mansion, practically collapsing onto the bed as fatigue overwhelms her. She is unaware of the President's visit until she opens her eyes drowsily and—through some sixth sense—decides to turn on the television. Fumbling for the remote, she snaps on the set and stares across the bedroom, her mind not quite registering what she's seeing at first. There's Arthur, her husband, and there's the President of the United States. Slowly she sits up, rubbing the sleep from her eyes. This is totally unexpected. She's a big admirer of the President, even if she didn't vote for him. She hadn't held much hope for him originally, but he seems to have grown into the job and developed a streak of independence that had prevented him from turning into the tool and spokesman for arch conservatives, which she'd feared he would become. She's annoyed that she's missing the opportunity to meet him, and wonders if there's time to change and get down there.

She starts to reach for the phone to speak to her personal aide, and there, live, on the screen, she sees the bomb go off.

She is not expecting it. No one is expecting it. There will be a lengthy investigation later, and the only thing that anyone will be able to come up with is that it had been planted in the street, weeks previously, by terrorists disguised as street workers who blatantly, in full daylight over a period of two days, used a jackhammer to chew up a small section of the street, plant the bombs, tar them over, and leave them there to be detonated later by remote control. The stone-cold planning and ingenuity is chilling; the audacity of the scheme is stunning; the fact that policemen routinely passed the "workers" without bothering to check whether they had any right or permit to be there or any sort of valid identification will cause several high-placed heads to roll.

Gwen does not know any of that. All she knows is that one moment her husband and the President are walking around, news cameras recording every moment, and the next there is nothing but chaos. There is smoke and rubble everywhere. Vehicles have been blown sky high, Secret Service men are running all around like blind madmen. A water main has broken, sending water fountaining high into the air, and the newsmen can be heard shouting about bombs. No one can see anything. The air is impenetrable with smoking haze, and Gwen is screaming "Arthur! Arthur!" at the TV screen as if he could somehow hear her and respond. Flames are springing up, more black fumes curling thickly through the air, and there is the frantic face of the newscaster on the screen, trying to explain the inexplicable. Gwen's aide dashes into the room hearing her scream, and together they watch the TV screen, transfixed, spellbound by the horror of what they're seeing. Although naturally they have no way of knowing for sure, Gwen is positive that people throughout New York are watching while calling their neighbors and saying, "Are you watching this? Do you have the TV on? They've killed the President! They've killed the Mayor!"

"Arthur, oh my God, Arthur," Gwen is moaning, and she doesn't know whether she's mourning more the loss of her husband or the world's loss of a man who could have done so much for it.

That's when she sees it at the same time that everyone else watching does. A form staggering through the smoke, carrying a burden, hazy at first as the TV camera covering the debacle has trouble focusing. But then it zooms in, the picture coming in clear, and there is an image that will be on the front page of every newspaper in the country the following morning.

Arthur Penn, emerging from the smoke with no less showmanship than would accompany the Second Coming, his clothes burned from where the flames had been licking at him, his face singed, and he is visibly gasping. And cradled in his arms is the President of the United States.

Months earlier, during his run for mayor, he had wound up saving children from a burning apartment building, a rescue thoroughly recorded by the TV news and which aided greatly in increasing his citywide profile. The drama of that rescue, however, is nothing compared to this. Another explosion, this time from flames hitting a gas main, it is believed, propels Arthur, but he does not drop the chief executive even as he is hurled forward, hitting the ground and absorbing the impact with his own body. Then an instant later the Secret Service has charged in, hauling both Arthur and the President into waiting ambulances and speeding away from the site to an undisclosed location where both will be pronounced suffering from shock and smoke inhalation, but otherwise in sound health. Opinion is also uniform: with the Secret Service men scattered by the blast, if Arthur had not hauled him out from the midst of the disaster area, the President would have been a dead man.

"Profile in Courage," the headlines will blare, and nevermore will Arthur Penn be simply considered a New York institution. Instead, in many ways, he will belong to the world, having earned the gratitude of the President and plaudits from a grateful nation.

The President will continue his war on terrorism, a war that will focus on a man named Sandoval, and Arthur will receive commendations and the congressional medal of honor, which he will graciously turn over to the firefighters and rescue workers of New York, stating that he is simply accepting it as a token on all of their behalf.

From then on, it is only a matter of time until Arthur's own run at the presidency, and his own victory, and his own battles with the elusive terrorist . . .

All of which is in the future. For now, Gwen gasps in relief, laughing and crying at the same time, and she hugs her aide and thanks God for giving her husband back to her when all seemed lost.

"Of course he survived," says a confident young voice.

She turns. Merlin is standing there. Even after all this time, she still cannot get over him. Gwen dismisses her aide, telling her to spread the good news to the rest of the staff, as Merlin saunters into the bedroom. She cannot get over the fact that this boy . . .

this skinny boy, with his hands too large for his arms, his feet too large for his legs, his silken brown hair longish in the back, and his ears virtually stuck out at right angles to his head. . . . is a centuries-old sorcerer who happens to be aging in the wrong direction. "He'd survive anything, I'm starting to believe," Merlin continues. "Cockroaches have nothing on him."

"It's easy to say after the fact," she retorts. "He gave you some bad moments there."

"He always does." Then his face suddenly grows serious. "I will not always be there for him, Gwen."

"What?" She is surprised by the shift in conversation. She wants to celebrate the fact that Arthur is still alive, not dwell on curious and ominous comments about the future from the mage. "What are you talking about, Merlin?"

"I did not like you, Gwen. I never have," he says candidly, which was the only way he ever spoke. "But I have come to the realization that, sooner or later, I will likely be gone, and only you and Percival will be there for him. He will need you. Arthur, for all his adherence to principles, does far better believing in people than those same principles. He needs you to believe in, or he will not be able to function. Be there for him, and for Mab's sake, be careful."

"Yes, all right, but . . . why are you saying these things?"

"Because," he tells her, blunt as ever, "they are the things you can understand," and with that he exits the room.

It will be years later when Merlin is taken from him, and his loss is devastating to Arthur. It is all Gwen can do to pull him through emotionally.

She never liked Merlin any better than he liked her. But she misses him because Arthur misses him . . .

G WEN BOARDED THE plane to Washington, D.C., in preparation to be with her husband for the State of the Union address. She imagined, as the plane arced into the air, that she could see Belvedere Castle below her in Central Park, a silent sentinel and reminder of days that she hadn't

realized back then were simpler times. It was the day before
the beginning of the end of Arthur Penn's presidency.
Gwen's thoughts turned to picking out the right shoes to
wear.

Chaptre
the Second

✛

ARTHUR LOOKED UP from the desk in the Oval Office, feeling a swell of appreciation for the interruption. Spread out before him was the fifteenth draft of the treaty with Trans-Sabal. "You know, Ron," he sighed heavily, "for the life of me, I can't determine how this draft is substantially different from the fourteenth or the thirteenth."

Once upon a time, Ron Cordoba had been addressed as "Ronnie," but since becoming the White House chief of staff, he had announced that he preferred the more formal "Ron" since it was somehow more in keeping with the dignity of the office. Cordoba had kept himself in splendid physical shape since that time, still zealously playing racquetball, maintaining a whipcord slim body, and claiming that such exercise enabled him to preserve the ability to think on his feet. His impressive head of blond hair, however, had proceeded to abandon him a year or so later.

Cordoba had been with Arthur since his days of the mayoral race. At the time, Cordoba had no idea of the truth behind Arthur's background. Eventually he had been brought into the loop. It had seemed rather necessary; he was one of the only staffers to have any sort of continuous interaction with Merlin, and considering that the "young boy" was not only not aging, but in fact starting to look even younger than before, that would certainly have garnered comment and confusion from Cordoba.

All things considered, he had taken the revelation rather well. Nevertheless, there were still some uncomfortable moments preceding Arthur's run at the presidency. Cordoba had sat down with Merlin and Arthur, one dark and stormy night. "You do realize that in order to be president, you have to have been born in this country," he had told them.

"The fact that I wasn't is hardly my fault," Arthur had said mildly. "After all, when I was born, the United States of America didn't exist yet. Certainly I shouldn't be penalized for that. Shouldn't there be a . . . ?"

"A grandfather clause?" suggested Merlin, his face carefully neutral.

"Yes, exactly. Thank you, Merlin. A grandfather clause."

"Perhaps," Cordoba had admitted, "there should be . . . so that those candidates who are capable of celebrating a personal tricentennial shouldn't be excluded from the pool. Unfortunately, it doesn't exist."

"No, it doesn't," Merlin had said, not sounding particularly concerned about the situation. "However, papers do exist that more than provide Arthur with absolutely bulletproof evidence that he was, in fact, born in this country. Home-schooled as a child, an admittedly not especially memorable undergraduate."

"Nice picture in the yearbook, though," Arthur remarked.

Cordoba had studied Arthur and Merlin, trying to see if they had the slightest idea of the severity of what they were discussing. "Gentlemen . . . it's fraud. I need you to understand that, to realize what we're about to embark upon. You prize highly, Arthur, your determination always to tell the truth. Should you win the presidency, you will be swearing a sacred oath to uphold the Constitution of the United

States . . . a document that you're already knowingly violating, because the Constitution specifically states in Article Two, Section One, and I quote—"

Arthur interrupted. " 'No person,' " he had said calmly, " 'except a natural born citizen, or a citizen of the United States, at the time of the adoption of this Constitution, shall be eligible to the office of president; neither shall any person be eligible to that office who shall not have attained to the age of thirty-five years, and been fourteen years a resident within the United States.' "

"Yes. Exactly," Cordoba had said. "So . . . don't you see? You would be building your presidency upon a foundation of hypocrisy."

The thunder rumbled outside the suite of offices, as if lending divine emphasis to Cordoba's cautions. Arthur said nothing, his face impassive and controlled. Cordoba was reasonably sure that all of this had occurred to Arthur already, and that he wasn't telling the Man Who Would Be President anything he didn't already know and hadn't already wrestled with.

"Would it help you if I told you," Merlin had said slowly, "that papers were filed for citizenship for Arthur back in the year 1777 . . . rendering him an official, naturalized citizen of this country before the Constitution was put in place? So that, although he was not born here, he would in fact be eligible to run since he was a citizen at the time that the Constitution was adopted?"

Cordoba had been stunned. Such a notion had literally never occurred to him. But it was certainly possible, he supposed. Merlin had, after all, been around for centuries, or so he'd been told. Then the phrasing of the question caught his attention, and his eyes narrowed. "Are you saying," he had asked, "that you actually did that? Or are you just asking me whether I would have peace of mind if you told me that you had?"

"The question is the question," Merlin had replied, taking

on that infernal know-it-all enigmatic wizard attitude he occasionally liked to display.

Cordoba sighed, realizing that the conversation had gone about as far as it was going to. Leaning back in the chair, tacitly admitting defeat, he had said, "Yes, that would give me peace of mind."

"All right then," Merlin had said with finality. "Consider it said."

And that was that.

So here they were, all these years later, and Merlin was gone, and Arthur and Cordoba were still here. Cordoba had never thought for a moment that he would miss the little wizard, for Merlin had been a royal pain in the ass many a time, but if nothing else he missed him because he had been such a rock for Arthur to lean upon. Cordoba, in his position of trust as chief of staff, had endeavored to model himself upon the example Merlin set, because he was reasonably sure that was what Arthur needed. And if Arthur needed it, then that was what the country needed.

"There are some subtle differences in the language, Mr. President," Cordoba said in regard to the treaty, entering the office and closing the door behind him. "They don't have any real impact on the substance of the treaty. They're more to pacify the religious fundamentalists in the Trans-Sabal government."

"And of course, we wouldn't want to upset any religious fundamentalists," Arthur commented wryly.

"It's a remarkable achievement, Mr. President," Cordoba reminded him. "Two years ago, the government of Trans-Sabal was the single greatest supporter of Sandoval in the world. Now there's a new government in place, they're allies of ours, and they're not protecting him."

"So they say. Yes, there's a new government," said Arthur, standing up and smoothing his tie as he did so. It was remarkable to Cordoba how little Arthur had changed over the years. Although Arthur had sworn that—now that he was out of his cave of healing and residing in the real world—he was aging normally, Ron simply couldn't see it. It suggested to him that Merlin might have worked a little magic that he hadn't even told Arthur about, or else there was a painting of Arthur somewhere that was starting to deteriorate.

Despite what the treaty represented, Arthur seemed bothered. Even someone who had known him for a fraction of the time that Ron had would have been able to see it. "A new government that we helped put into place, and that is dependent upon us. Here's the odd thing about that, Ron: Those governments that depend upon us for their existence sooner or later seem to start resenting the hell out of us. Have you noticed that? Even Sandoval . . . he was once a CIA ally, remember? Enlisted to help oppose an oppressive government. His tactics were acceptable when they served our interests." Arthur sighed. "You know what happens when you embrace monsters, Ron? They just transform into different monsters."

"Not always, Mr. President."

"Not always, no, but certainly enough times to give us cause for concern."

"Sir, with all respect," Cordoba pointed out, "if and when the government of Trans-Sabal turns against us . . . you won't be in office by that point, most likely. It'll be the next guy's problem. All you can do is all you can do."

"A trite and meaningless phrase," Arthur said with the barest touch of a smile, "and yet, oddly, I draw some small comfort from it." He leaned against his desk. "What did you need to see me about? Is it the cabinet meeting already?"

"No, no . . ."

Arthur looked suddenly irritated. "Not the dairy farmers again. I make one passing comment about milk making me belch, and you'd think I'd told a class of kindergartners that there's no Santa."

"It's Bob."

"What's Bob?" he asked, frowning, and then his face cleared. "Our Bob?"

"Right. Bob Kellerman. Your head speechwriter."

"What about him?" asked Arthur with concern. "Is he all right?"

"Not at the moment, no." Cordoba folded his arms and tried to sound just slightly stern, while maintaining enough of a respectful tone considering whom he was addressing and where he was standing. "Did you tell him that you were going to toss the text of the State of the Union address and just 'wing it'?"

"I might have done," Arthur said, trying to recall.

"That would be the speech he's been working on twenty-four/seven for the past month," he said, as if trying to ascertain just which State of the Union they were discussing.

"That's as may be," said Arthur, "but why? I was just joking. He must have known that."

At that, Cordoba moaned, not believing that he needed to spell it out. "Sir, you know Bob. He takes everything literally. He's been lying on the couch in his office for the last hour with an ice pack, moaning that his life is pointless."

"Oh, dear," Arthur said. "That won't do. Ron, be a good lad and tell him that I was kidding, would you? On second thought . . ." He walked back behind his desk, picked up the phone, and tapped in the intercom connection. He paused a moment, waiting for it to be made, and then said, "Bob? This is your commander in chief. Bob, I was simply making a sporting jest about the speech. The latest draft was a thing of beauty, and therefore—by extension—a joy forever. You have done credit to yourself and your family going back five generations. Now get off the bloody couch, go home to your wife, and celebrate the praise from your president in a manly fashion." He hung up and spread his hands in a *"How was that?"* manner.

"Thank you, Mr. President," said Cordoba.

There was a sharp knock at the door and Arthur's personal aide, Mrs. Jenkins, a brisk, no-nonsense woman of indeterminate years, stuck her head in and said, "Mr. President, the First Lady is here."

"Tell the faithless trollop she is never to darken my door again," Arthur instructed.

"Yes, sir, I'll send her right in," Mrs. Jenkins replied without missing a beat.

"How marvelous to command that level of respect," Arthur said to Cordoba.

Cordoba shrugged. "We serve at the pleasure of the President."

Mrs. Penn entered briskly, her eyes lighting up in that way she had whenever she saw the President again after a lengthy absence. However, they had developed a very reserved, formal means of embracing since he had been elected, and they employed it now as she crossed the room to him, placed her hands on either arm, and lifted her face to his lips as he sedately brushed her right cheek with a kiss. "Faithless trollop?" she asked.

"I meant that with the greatest respect. How did your trip go?"

"As well as can be expected, considering it was busywork."

Cordoba and Arthur exchanged glances, with Ron silently dreading the direction the conversation was about to go. "Perhaps I'd better . . ."

"No, stay, Ron," Gwen said firmly, turning to Arthur, her arms folded. She had a stern look on her face . . . not annoyed so much as she was determined to discuss something that she obviously suspected wasn't going to go over especially well. "It was busywork, Arthur. You know it, I know it."

"I know no such thing," Arthur replied sharply, "and frankly, I resent the implication. That you believe I think so little of you."

She dropped into one of the chairs facing the desk. Cordoba could still remember the first time that Gwen had entered the Oval Office. She had squealed in disbelief, sat in every piece of furniture, and wondered who might have sat there before her. She had literally been bubbling over with joy. Now she just looked tired. Arthur had been President for two years. What the hell were they going to be like in another two? Or if he ran for reelection?

"It's not that you think little of me, Arthur," she sighed.

"Then perhaps you think little of your work. The people adore you, Gwen . . ."

"Yes, I know," said Gwen, crossing her legs and resting her hands on her knees. "And I go to different cities, and I talk to the soccer moms about their problems, and the B'nai B'rith, and the Mothers Against Drunk Driving, and on and on, but don't you see? I feel segregated. As if the only thing you think I'm suited for is 'women's work.' "

"Gwen, my dear, perhaps we should discuss this later . . ."

"Don't you trust me, Arthur?"

Well, there it was, the worst question a woman could ask a man. Cordoba shifted uncomfortably in his spot, wishing for all the world that he was anywhere else.

Slowly Arthur walked over to her, knelt, and took one of her hands between his two. "Gwen," he said firmly, "of course I trust you. The things you've been involved with until now have been vital. If we're going to be pragmatic about it, the simple fact is that the women's vote carried the day when I ran, and it's important to keep a very, very active presence with that group. And you are better suited to that task than am I."

"So you get to do what benefits the country and the world," Gwen said, eyes flashing challengingly, "and I get to do what benefits you. Is that how it is?"

His head slumped as if he was presenting it onto a block for a headsman to dispatch. "May I ask, just out of morbid curiosity, what brought this on? Does this have anything to do with the delay in your returning, and your visit to the castle?"

"In a sense," she said with a small shrug. "When I was there, it just reminded me of a time when absolutely anything seemed possible. That's how it was when I was there with you, Arthur. You freed me from a restricted life, one of abuse and denial, and opened up an existence filled with potential. Now I want to live up to that potential, and I feel as if I'm not being allowed."

"All right, Gwen," Arthur said, sounding very reasonable. "What is it that you would wish to do?"

"Well . . . trying to reorganize and streamline health care might be a start . . ."

Ron made no attempt to hide his very loud moan. "Ohhh, trust me, Mrs. Penn, you definitely do *not* want to get involved with that."

She smiled indulgently. "You're probably right, Ron."

"Thank you, Mrs.—"

Gwen then snapped open the purse she'd kept carefully balanced on her lap, and extracted a sheet of paper from it. "As it so happens, however, I've been making a list."

Ron Cordoba and the President of the United States exchanged looks. This was suddenly shaping up to be a very, very long night.

ARTHUR FELT THE need to talk to Merlin.

It was late at night, Gwen having already gone to bed after an extremely lengthy discussion in the Oval Office. Cordoba had gone back to scrape Bob Kellerman off the wall and take him out for a drink, or possibly many drinks. Arthur had continued to study the treaty, assuring Gwen that he would be along shortly. He had very much meant it when he had said it, but time had passed and he was still not the least bit drowsy.

The late-night staff, the Secret Service . . . they were used to Arthur's occasional meandering. No one commented upon it, though. He was, after all, the President, and certainly wandering about in the middle of the night was hardly a violation of his oath of office.

He made his way to the Rose Garden. There was a small

greenhouse set off to the side, carefully maintained. Roses continued to bloom here even though they were out of season. Arthur laughed softly to himself at the thought; it was like stepping into the Garden of Eden, a place of quiet reflection and paradise on earth . . . as if such a place still existed.

He dwelt on that for a long, pleasant moment. The notion of Eden on earth was a cheerful, quaint myth. On the other hand, to most people . . . so was he. Oh, certainly he had publicly stated that he was King Arthur of Camelot. Circumstances had arisen during the mayoral race that left him no choice. But the public had seized upon that in a fit of amused fancy. They thought it a marvelous joke that they were all in on. For a time, all of New York indulged itself, turning itself into one big renaissance fair. It was ridiculous to Arthur, but he had gone along with it because it had served his purposes so perfectly, and because Merlin had told him to.

Merlin . . .

There he stood, in the far corner of the Rose Garden.

Arthur drew close to him, moving noiselessly across the small, meticulously watered lawn. He was, of course, just as Arthur had remembered him, as he would be for all time. There was that typical Merlin expression of barely masked annoyance, coupled with whimsical detachment, as if his last words had been: "Do you seriously think this will hold me?" Several strands of his hair were hanging in front of his face, and he was frozen in mid-spell cast, his hands poised for all eternity to inflict some sort of mystical damage that would never be delivered.

Merlin the Magician, Merlin the Demonspawn, Merlin son of none . . . a statue of polished granite, half hidden in shadows, half bathed in moonlight. Somehow that seemed symbolic.

Arthur placed one hand upon the smooth stone; it was as cold to the touch as ever, just as dead as it always was. Arthur had long since given up hope that he would feel some sort of distant warmth, some sign that this was something other than a lifeless sculpture. For the first months he had convinced himself that this condition was only temporary. That, somehow, Merlin would fight through it and come back: that he was asleep, that he was in some kind of stasis . . . *something*. But slowly Arthur had come to the conclusion that such was not the case. That Merlin was, in fact, lost to him, and this statue—this statue that had once been a living, breathing being—was all that remained of him. Not for the first time, he cursed under his breath the name of the individual who had done this horrific thing.

Should it ever come to pass, Arthur, you will take no vengeance on my behalf, Merlin had warned him. *I knew what I was getting into, and I'm far too old to start fobbing the blame off on others.* He wondered if Merlin had known what was going to be coming. Perhaps if Merlin had indeed had the slightest inkling of his fate, he would have done more to stave it off, or maybe come up with a way . . .

"And sometimes," Arthur sighed, "you just run out of ways, don't you, Merlin." He allowed one hand to remain upon the statue's shoulder, a gesture of familiarity in which he likely would never have indulged during Merlin's life. "When a thousand challenges face you, and you have to pull the thousand and first trick out of your hat . . . sometimes you find the hat empty."

Slowly he circled the statue, as he had so many times before. He always made sure it was kept meticulously clean. He knew that some on his staff thought his devotion to this particular piece of artwork to be somewhat . . . peculiar. But on the rare occasions that someone happened to voice curiosity as to what drew the President to this immobile young boy, Arthur would simply invite them to stare into the polished, unmoving features for a few minutes. They would do so, willing to accommodate him since he was, after all, the President. When they came away, however, some of them looked thoughtful, others shaken, and they would go back to Arthur and say, "I understand now, thank you, sir." The truth was, of course, that they could never completely understand. They simply thought they did.

"But isn't that the way of things, Merlin?" he asked. His breath floated away from him in small puffs of mist. "Didn't you always tell me that people could never distinguish between the concept of being entitled to their opinion, versus being entitled to their *informed* opinion? No one understands that, do they? They believe that, because they think something, it has validity just because it's their own thought. They feel that their rights are being threatened if someone points out that to hold a worthless opinion is like holding a fistful of sand: It means nothing whether you've got it in your hand or not.

"And 'rights' . . . everyone is so obsessed about those, Merlin. These people,"—he inclined his head as if he could take in the entirety of America with the gesture—"these people make such noises about their rights . . . but so few of them have actually *fought* for those rights. Their being born American simply entitles them, or at least makes them feel they're entitled. 'That they are endowed by their creator with certain unalienable rights.' " He rolled his eyes. "It's a nice turn of phrase, but I almost wish that Jefferson hadn't put it into the Declaration. People always treasure much more those things that they have to earn than those things that they feel are theirs by divine right. Don't you think so, Merlin?"

"Yes, I do."

Arthur jumped back three feet, gasping, hand to his heart, not believing what he had just heard, and then he perceived light, musical laughter behind him. With a grimace and look of utter chagrin, he turned and knew what he was going to see even before he saw it: Gwen standing there, trying to stifle her laughter, putting her hands to her mouth to stem the noise. But her shoulders and chest were bouncing up and down from the suppressed laughter.

"Very funny, very funny," said Arthur with the air of someone who didn't think it was the least bit funny at all, even though he had to admit to himself that it was a rather worthy little prank.

She lowered her hands, her mouth still in a thin and amused smile as she said, "I'm sorry."

"No, you're not."

"All right, I'm not. But I guess I should have resisted."

"Yes, you should have. And it's a cruel lady you are, to have such a jest at Merlin's expense, especially when he cannot defend himself."

"I'm sorry," she said again, and this time sounded as if she meant it. Holding his hand, her own robe drawn tightly around herself, she walked purposefully back to the statue, and looked it up and down. Then she looked back to her husband, who stood there with a somber expression. "You still blame yourself, don't you?"

"Well, of course," said Arthur matter-of-factly. "Who else could there possibly be to blame, if not myself? Truman was quite right: The buck stops here."

"But, Arthur, Merlin was a big boy ... . well . . . relatively speaking," she amended, glancing at the statue. "He knew the risks. He knew what could happen. And I really don't think that he would have wanted you to continue to mourn his fate."

Arthur considered that. "You know . . . I'm not so certain that he wouldn't have wanted that. Indeed, he might have actually enjoyed it, knowing I was tormented so. He could be a vindictive little cretin when he was so inclined. It's truly difficult to know which way he would have gone on it."

"But, Arthur, you knew him better than any man living."

"And yet," he admitted, "in many ways, it's as if I never knew him at all."

"So what you're saying," Gwen reasoned, "is that either he wouldn't have wanted you to blame yourself . . . in which case you'd be acting contrary to his wishes. Or he *would* have wanted you to blame yourself, thus certifying that he was in fact a selfish little shit. Does that pretty much cover the range of possibilities?"

"Yes," said Arthur thoughtfully. "Yes, I suppose it does."

"So you've more or less got a no-win scenario on your hands."

"It certainly wouldn't be my first, and very probably won't be my last."

They said nothing for a long moment, instead just basking in the quiet. Even though Arthur knew that elsewhere in the world, much was going on, here—just for that brief period—he felt as if everything was utterly still. That the entirety of the planet earth had joined him in this moment of silence.

"Arthur," Gwen said finally, and even though her voice was barely above a whisper it made him jump slightly just the same. "Arthur . . . you have a busy day tomorrow. You're delivering the State of the Union. And I'm freezing." And he saw that, indeed, she was lightly bouncing up and down in place in order to keep her circulation going. "Can we please . . . ?"

"Of course," he said solicitously, and putting an arm around her, he guided her back into the White House. Behind him, falling silently, gentle snowflakes drifted in on the night air, frosting the ground and covering Merlin the magician with a blanket of white.

CHAPTRE
THE THIRD

✝

THE PERUVIAN AIR hung heavily around him, and had he not been standing in the middle of a hospital ward, the broad-shouldered black man would have been inclined to pull out his machete and try to hack his way through it. He knew it was a ridiculous notion. One couldn't carve a path through something that wasn't there. Still, it would have made a nice symbolic gesture.

Some years earlier, he had been found in an alleyway by a young boy who claimed to be—and actually turned out to be—a centuries-old magician named Merlin. For all his eldritch talents, Merlin would likely never have recognized the black man now. He was wearing a green tank top, sweated through, which revealed sizable arms and broad shoulders. Since he'd taken to shaving his head, removing all hint of the graying hair he'd once had, his indeterminate age became even more difficult to fathom. To the casual viewer, he might have been twenty, he might have been sixty. It would have been impossible to say . . . except that anyone guessing in the vicinity of a thousand would have been far closer to the mark.

His bald head glistened with perspiration. He was wearing army utility slacks, the pants pockets bulging with various necessities ranging from small bottles of fresh water to bug lotion. The machete he kept in a holster slung over his back. A Colt was hanging from a holster on his right hip. He would have preferred a dependable broad sword, unable to shake the feeling—even after all these centuries—that taking down a foe while standing a good twenty, thirty feet away just wasn't fair somehow. If you're going to take a man's life, be close enough to do him the courtesy of seeing the light depart from his eyes. Still, he was realistic enough to admit that he was very likely old-fashioned in that regard.

In general deportment, he looked like a mercenary who had just wandered in from the jungles, which suited him fine. He wasn't about to cause trouble with anyone, but he wasn't inclined to paint himself as an easy target, either.

The hospital itself was a very primitive affair. Understaffed and overwhelmed, it served the needs of a populace that had been through an absolutely abysmal year. Several acts of God, including an earthquake, a flood, and—worst of all—a particularly virulent plague, had prompted some to wonder just what the hell the people of this country had ever done to deserve this kind of treatment. A fake memo from the United States Attorney General's office, which had made the rounds on all the computer nets, had suggested a class action suit be filed against the Almighty since all these "acts" attributed to him amounted to either extreme neglect or intense malevolence on his part. Either way, it seemed actionable.

Obviously the United States had not embarked upon legal remedies, but President Penn had been front and center in spearheading a global relief effort. The black man who was now walking through the hospital had the nominal and vague title of presidential aide, which suited him just fine. He had the freedom to come and go as he pleased, and be wherever his king—that was to say, his president—needed him to be.

At that moment, where he happened to be was Camana. Camana, situated on the South Panamerican Highway, 830 kilometers from Lima, was on the South American coast in a fairly agricultural valley. It was a popular coastal getaway, and was renowned for the "camarones," or shrimp, that the rivers in that region produced. At the moment, however, Camana—population approximately 35,000—was hardly a getaway for anything, unless one was anxious to get away to a scene of devastation. Even though it had not been the epicenter of the quake, the damage had nevertheless been catastrophic.

The black man had volunteered to go down and participate in the rescue and salvage operations, and the President had allowed him to go. That was the black man's way; he liked to go where he felt he was needed, where he could do some good. Not for him were endless meetings and discussions with people whose primary job seemed to be preventing anything from being accomplished in a remotely expeditious manner. He liked to be hands on, to just go in and get things done.

So down he had gone to South America. He was trying to allow for all possibilities; should he find himself in a jungle situation, the machete would come in handy. Should he find himself facing looters or similar vermin who took it upon themselves to prey on individuals in their darkest times, the firearm would attend to them. He was prepared to offer his services wherever and whenever they were needed, and at the same time could report back to the President over how the multinational rescue effort was going.

He had not, however, expected to stumble upon a very old scent.

It is said that when one is looking for something and cannot find it, the best thing to do is stop looking. Go on about one's life, attend to business. And while in the process of doing that, all unexpectedly, one winds up stumbling over that which one had been searching for in the first place.

Such was the case now.

In his travels around Peru, he had heard rumors floating around about . . . a man. A strange, mysterious man, who had supposedly washed up on the shore nearby a Camana resort (a resort that, as it so happened, was now a pile of rubble.)

A man who was young.

A man who wasn't young anymore.

A harried-looking doctor with a white coat flapping around him approached the black man suspiciously, but the quick flashing of an ID halted the doctor in his tracks. He seemed confused as to what the black man was doing there, and clearly wanted to be polite, but he also was far more concerned with attending to the needs of his patients. All around him, people were moaning and bleeding and dying, and he looked as if he hadn't slept in seventy-two hours.

"Who are you looking for again?" asked the doctor.

The black man was about to reply, when suddenly his nostrils flared, and he was nearly rocked back on his heels.

"Are you all right?" the doctor inquired with concern. He was probably less worried about the black's condition than he was nervous over the notion of having to deal with yet another patient. Every bed in the place was occupied, as was just about every morsel of free space.

"I'm . . . fine. I'll find him. Don't worry." With that the black man turned, leaving the confused doctor behind.

The black man made his way through the ward, his shaved head swiveling back and forth as if he was sending out radar. He looked more than anything like a great cat on a hunt, and then slowly he approached one particular bed.

No one else would have noticed anything extraordinary about the occupant of the bed. To any observer, it would have seemed simply an old man, gaunt, tired, clinging to life by the most tenuous of strings. His skin had the consistency of parchment, and his lips were drawn back to reveal yellowing teeth with several notable gaps between them. His eyes were fluttering rapidly, like trapped butterflies, as if they were fighting to retain the delicate soul that was on the verge of being pulled away. His hair had once been black, but was now entirely white and mostly missing. His breathing was a loud hiss between his graying lips.

But the black man looked upon him, and felt a certain type of excitement stirring within him for the first time in many, many years. Instantly he felt a connection to this . . . this heap of skin and bones lying helpless on a bed. The dying man was hooked up to tubes, but it was painfully obvious to the black man that the patient wasn't going to be around much longer, despite whatever devices they hooked him up to. He was beyond all means of salvation that the world had to offer . . .

All means but one. And he had the scent of that one on him, and it was so plain to the nose of the black man that it was all he could do not to tremble with excitement in the presence of the dying man. He could smell it upon the man; he could even see a faint glow around him. He looked around in wonderment. No one else was reacting as he was. How could they not see? How could they not realize, not understand, that someone who had basked in the sustained presence of holiness was among them?

The dying man looked up at the black man, and his gaze—which had been wandering about since the black man had arrived—now focused clearly for the first time. He looked rather surprised. "A Berber?" he asked, and despite his extreme age, his voice sounded strong.

The black man was slightly surprised, although he realized he shouldn't have been. Who knew what age this man was from? "Close. A Moor," he corrected.

"Same thing," the dying man said with a disdainful shrug. "What would you have of me, Moor? Do you derive some enjoyment from watching an old man sicken and die?"

Taking a step toward him, in a low voice, the black man said, "My name . . . is Percival." Then he searched the man's face carefully for some sign of recognition.

There was nothing at first. Just that sort of warily blank expression that people sport when they think they're supposed to have an idea of whom they're meeting, but can't quite place it. Then, very slowly, a vague suspicion began to grow. "Not . . . *the* Percival."

Percival nodded.

"The Grail Knight?"

Percival nodded once more.

He just stared at him for a long moment. "Hunh. I'll be damned," he said finally. "I never read anywhere you were a man of color."

"Yes, I know. Somehow that little fact always seems to be dropped from the books," Percival said dryly. "And my understanding is that your name is Joshua."

Joshua nodded.

"The one who fought the battle of Jericho?"

At that, the old man started to laugh. This set off a ferocious round of coughing, and it went on for several minutes. Percival made no effort to offer him anything for it; he didn't much see the point. Finally Joshua's coughing fit eased up and he managed to gasp in a few lungfuls of air. "No. No, nothing so biblical. I'm just someone from . . . from long ago."

"How long?"

"How long do you think?" he fenced.

Percival shook his head. "I've no idea," he admitted. He also didn't like what he was seeing; the man was aging still. It was happening slowly, but inexorably. He wasn't sure how much longer the old man had.

And then Joshua said something utterly unexpected: "Are you going to try and take it back?"

At first Percival didn't understand what he was talking about, but then he did. "You mean the Grail?"

Joshua managed a nod, and forced a mostly toothless smile. "I will . . . do you the courtesy of not playing games. Of not pretending that we both don't know what this is all about. You're here because you somehow 'sensed' . . . what? That I was associated with the Grail somehow?" When Percival nodded, the smile spread wider. "I believe it. When you're near it, it's like . . . like . . ."

"Like touching the earth, when it was new," Percival said reverently.

More slowly than before, Joshua nodded, and Percival saw a single tear work its way down his face. "Yes. Yes." Then he refocused on Percival. "You have not . . . answered the question. Are you going to take it back?"

"It does not belong to me," Percival admitted. "If I were to take it back . . . it would be to my liege lord, and truthfully, I am not even sure what he would do with it. I don't know what I would do with it. Not really. But I know this: It was taken from me, long ago. I would like to see it again. Maybe if I see it . . . I'll know what to do."

"Oh, I can tell you what to do."

"Really?"

Joshua bobbed his head and, although it was clearly a tremendous effort for him, he gestured for Percival to draw closer to him. Percival did so. The feeling, the aura, the "scent" of the Grail was beginning to fade from him, to be replaced by a nearly overwhelming aroma of rot. He bent his ear toward Joshua's lips and then Joshua hissed, *"Destroy it."*

He said it with such venom, such pure fury, that Percival was utterly taken aback. He regarded the dying man with astonishment. "Destroy it? But . . . it is holy."

"It is unnatural. It is unnatural, and it has long outlived its use . . . just as I have. But I, at least, realized it."

"I don't understand," Percival said, speaking faster because he sensed that time was slipping away. "Did you drink of the Grail? Because if you did . . . I don't understand why you're aging now. I drank of it, and I am still here, still very much as I was when I first downed its contents." He braced himself, asking the question he had not wanted to ask. "Is what's happening to you going to happen to me? Does the Grail delay the effects of age for only so long, and then it all catches up with you at one time? When did you drink from it? Are you far older than I? Where—"

"Skeleton Keys."

The response was, to Percival, a complete non sequitor. "What? Skeleton Keys? What about them? Is it locked somewhere? Do you need a Skeleton Key to open it?"

Joshua took a deep breath and, when he exhaled, the rattling was frightening, and Percival thought for a moment that it was in fact his death rattle. But then Joshua opened his eyes, and there was fire in them, as if his soul was going to consume his body in one, final desperate burst of energy. "I left," he whispered. "He never thought I would. He's quite mad. He fears death . . . fears it so much. The others do, too. But I realized . . . realized we were dying there. Our souls were dying, even if we weren't. It's a perversity. It's wrong. It's not what God intended. Had to get away. He'll be furious . . ."

"He who?"

Joshua started coughing again, his body flailing about. But there were so many people in misery in the hospital ward, and the doctors stretched so thin in their endeavors to attend to them all, that it went unnoticed. He said something that sounded to Percival like "Beware . . . hiking," and he reached up and gripped Percival's hand with one of his bony ones. "Skeleton Keys," he said again, and then . . . incongruously, bizarrely . . . he said—very clearly, very articulated—"Pus."

"Pus?" asked a bewildered Percival. "Like . . . from an infection? What does that have to do with anyth—?"

And that was when Percival heard it, unmistakably this time: the rattle of death, the sound of a tortured and pained soul departing its mortal shell. Joshua slipped back onto his pillow, his eyes fixed on some far distant point, and the light left them.

In his extended life, Percival had witnessed more deaths than he once would ever have thought possible. Yet in all that time, he had never beheld a soul so eager to slip away.

Centuries—perhaps eons—of memories escaped with it, and he knew he should be mourning, but instead all he could be was happy for this single-named being, this "Joshua," about whom he would very likely never learn anything else.

He wasn't entirely sure what to expect next, and yet somehow he knew there would be something. And he was right. Slowly the body began to collapse in upon itself. He knew that something like eighty percent of the human body was made up of fluids; these dissipated now from Joshua, the body dwindling and shrinking as if incredibly anxious to leave. As if it felt that its mere existence, so long after it should have by rights been gone, was an abomination.

Percival forced himself to sit and watch and wonder whether it was his own future he was seeing. These were, after all, semi-mystical forces that were being dealt with. Who knew what would happen to him? Who knew the ways of God, even as they manifested themselves through such objects of power as the Holy Grail?

And Percival realized that he was not afraid of whatever pain might be involved nor was he the least bit concerned about the prospect of death. He was just . . . overwhelmingly curious, that was all. Curious as to what sort of fate awaited him. Then again, he mused, in that respect he was certainly no different than any other man who walked the earth.

The distracted-looking doctor approached at that point, looking at a chart rather than at Percival, and said, "Sir, I will have to ask you to leave. This is a—" Then he stopped and stared at the bed. "Where's the patient who was here?"

"What patient?" asked Percival innocently.

The doctor took a step back, eyeing Percival suspiciously, clearly wondering if some sort of foul play was involved. But there was no exit door nearby the bed, nor even a window. Nor, obviously, had Percival slipped the patient into his hip pocket or in some other less ludicrous way attempted to hide him. Yet plainly the patient was gone. His hospital gown was lying upon the bed, and there was a fine film of dust upon it, but otherwise there was no sign of him.

Rallying, the young doctor demanded, "Where's the man who was here?"

Percival stood and recited, "Last night I saw upon the stair . . . a little man who was not there . . . he was not there again today . . . oh, how I wish he'd go away." With a slight flourish he bowed, said, "E. E. Cummings," and walked away.

Utterly bewildered, the doctor said to Percival's departing back, "Good-bye, Mr. Cummings," and then turned to stare in puzzlement at the little man who wasn't there.

CHAPTRE
THE FOURTH

TERRANCE STOCKWELL HAD never been all that fond of Arthur Penn. Stockwell, a former Arizona governor—and a formidable quarterback in his college days—had considered Penn to be too much of a showboat. Oh, there was no denying that Penn talked a good game, but for Stockwell's tastes, it was all "pie and blue sky," as he liked to call it.

Stockwell was not the most photogenic of men. His face was almost triangular, his dark eyes a bit too closely set together and a bit too recessed. His black hair was cropped closely, nearly to a buzz cut, and a sharp widow's peak extended down past the edge of his otherwise receding hairline. When someone was speaking to him, he tended to lean forward, anxious not to miss a single word. His intelligence, his leadership abilities, were beyond dispute. But he left a number of voters rather cold, because he did not suffer fools gladly, and that put him on the outs with a disturbingly large percentage of the American electorate. His college career as a football hero at Arizona State had helped him considerably when he'd turned to politics, but his transition to the national level had not been an easy one. A lifelong Democrat, he'd been left in the dust during the primaries.

He had been astounded when Arthur Penn, running for the presidency as an Independent, had picked him up off the scrap heap and offered him the opportunity to be his running mate. The idea had seemed insane to Stockwell . . . at first. But Penn's numbers were doing nothing but soaring, and despite his personal problems with the way Penn did business, there was no denying the man's raw charisma and the distinct possibility—remote, but distinct—that Penn might indeed wind up in the White House someday. So Stockwell swallowed his considerable pride, hooked up with Penn . . .

And now, here he was, sitting in the East Wing of the White House, watching television.

It was not at all where he wanted to be. He should have been seated in the Senate, in his capacity as Chairman, perched in a seat directly behind the President on a podium when the President delivered the State of the Union address to Congress.

Instead he was in the residence wing, bristling with annoyance, even though he knew that there was nothing to be done for it. That certain laws had been put into place some years ago that forbade—absolutely forbade—any circumstance in which the president and the vice president were publicly together.

The room was comfortable enough; about as luxurious as they came, really, in the White House. There was food laid out, and even though Stockwell wasn't especially hungry (having had an unusually large dinner), he indulged himself by nibbling on a few carrot sticks. But he was shaking his head even as he did so, and the moment Ronnie Cordoba walked into the room, Stockwell was verbally assailing him.

"You realize we've let the terrorists dictate our actions once again, don't you, Ronald?"

Cordoba shrugged in the manner of someone who had had this conversation many times in the past, and wasn't seeing the upside of going around one more time. "There's no harm in being cautious."

"Cautious. Cautious." He laughed with low derision at the concept. He had gone to a window that looked over the Front Lawn, and he pointed to it. "Once upon a time," Stockwell informed him, "people would bring their farm animals right up to the lawn to graze. Can you believe it? There was virtually no security in the whole place. You could practically walk up to the front door and ask to speak to the president. Things have changed, Ronald, and not for the better . . . and it's pigs like Sandoval and his ilk that have made it that way."

Cordoba had heard the argument more times than he cared to count. "Mr. Vice President," he said, "the White House was made a far more secure place long before the Trans-Sabal war, long before Sandoval, long before any of it."

"So your defense of my saying that the world is a wretched place," observed Stockwell, "is to point out that it's been a wretched place far longer than any of us wants to admit. Is that about right?"

"Whatever you say, sir."

Stockwell was on his feet, pacing about. He was not one for sitting still if he didn't have to. "Save the patronizing tone for those who deserve to be patronized, Ronald."

Cordoba stepped in close then, his eyes narrowed, and he said sharply, "All right, Terry. Then how about just for one night we drop the bitching about how the world is unfair, so that we can sit back and enjoy the President making his constitutionally mandated yearly speech, before I have to kick your ass into the Potomac."

They locked gazes for a long moment, and then Stockwell let out the short, guttural bark that passed for his laugh. "That's more like it," he said. "That's the Ron Cordoba I knew back in my college days."

"I doubt it," retorted Cordoba. "That guy you knew would have knocked you flat long before this."

Obviously satisfied with having gotten Cordoba to drop—even for a few moments—his carefully nurtured mask of infinitely patient civility, Stockwell eased into the chair in front of the wide-screen television. The TV was already focused on the outside of the Capitol building. Stockwell glanced at his watch.

Cordoba, in clear anticipation of what was going through Stockwell's mind, said, "They're scheduled to arrive in two minutes."

"Is the area secure?" Stockwell asked.

"Yes, it's secure."

"Because something doesn't smell right."

Cordoba walked across the room to the liquor cabinet, from which he withdrew a bottle of very old, very fine Scotch. Carefully, as if he was unwrapping a fine porcelain statue, he unstoppered the bottle and poured himself a shot into a shot glass that bore the emblem of an American eagle on it. "Ben Franklin wanted the national bird to be a turkey, you know," he said conversationally.

"Yes, Ronald, I am aware of that, as is just about every schoolchild in the country," retorted Stockwell, shaking his head when Cordoba silently offered him a shot of his own. "I notice you're ignoring my concerns."

"It's the same concerns as always, sir. You always say it smells bad."

"It always does. Have you ever considered," he said in all seriousness to Cordoba, "that the other times I was worried something might happen, it might have been that I was right? That the terrorists were in place, everything ready to go, and there was just some sort of last-minute happenstance."

"When it comes to the protection of the President of the United States," Cordoba said firmly, "there's no such thing as happenstance. Everything is planned too carefully, thought out too far in advance."

"Yeah. I'm sure that's what they told Kennedy right before his brains decorated the inside of his car. And I'm warning you"—he stabbed a finger at Cordoba—"if you point out that Lincoln died at the Ford, while Kennedy died in a Lincoln, I *will* have to hurt you."

"I appreciate the warning." He took another shot of the Scotch, turned, and refilled himself.

The President's motorcade pulled up on screen. Secret Service men were already spread out, keeping crowds securely behind police barriers and making sure that no one would get too close. So it was on that basis that Stockwell groaned as he watched President Penn—instead of heading in to speak to Congress—work the crowd. He went right up to them, reaching around his agents or over their shoulders, shaking hands, signing autographs. "My God, you'd think he was running for reelection," he said.

"You've said it yourself, sir, any number of times: a president is running for reelection from the moment he swears the oath of office. Besides," and he sat on the edge of the couch facing Stockwell, "you were just busy talking about how there's been this distance growing between the White House and the electorate thanks to fear. So there's the President walking right up to people, any of whom might have weapons on them, and shaking their hands. He's not being the least bit afraid . . . and you're complaining. I thought you guys were supposed to be on the same side."

"We are on the same side, and don't patronize me, Ronald."

"I'll try not to, sir; but you make it very easy."

Stockwell smiled mirthlessly at that, and then focused his attention back onto the TV. He saw Gwen, dressed rather elegantly . . . a bit too much so, he would have thought. She was wearing an evening dress rather than something sensible, like a woman's business suit. It was a dark blue dress with a scooped neck, a provocative—but not too provocative—slit along the right side, and a wrap that he knew beyond question was fake fur. That made sense: Gwendolyn Penn was the fake fur spokeswoman. In that outfit, he thought, she was making it look more like some sort of awards ceremony or banquet than a serious, constitutionally mandated speech to the citizens of the United States of America.

As if reading his thoughts again, Cordoba said, "The First Lady looking a bit too glamorous for you, sir?"

Stockwell shrugged. "She's not my wife."

"You don't have one, sir."

That was certainly true. Stockwell was divorced, and it had been a very acrimonious and vicious parting of the ways . . . so much so that it had left him permanently burned in regard to the state of matrimony. He didn't have any intrinsic problem with it as far as others were concerned; he just had no care to dabble in it himself. Still . . . Gwendolyn was a damned fine attractive woman, he had to admit that. She seemed a touch flighty to him on a personal level, but there was no denying that she was quite, quite fetching. And there was something in her attitude, her voice, her every mannerism, that just made you want to like her. To hold her tight, to . . .

He cleared his throat and said softly, "Ronald . . . I think I'll have that drink now, if it's still available."

Without a word, Cordoba poured him a shot. Stockwell downed it in a heartbeat and extended the shot glass for more. Cordoba obliged him.

As the evening progressed, various aides came in and out, asking Stockwell questions, making inquiries about his schedule for the next day, asking if he needed anything. Stockwell answered all of them in terse, no-nonsense terms. Every time the door opened and closed, he could see the ever-present, ever-vigilant Secret Service men in the hallway. He knew it should make him feel safe, give him some degree of security. He wondered why it never did.

The President's entrance was announced, and Congress rose to its collective feet as Arthur made his way down the main aisle. He stopped to shake hands, speak a few words here and there to congressmen who would invariably smile or laugh or nod their heads in apparent approval. *And half of them would be perfectly happy to stab you in the back*, Stockwell thought grimly. Arthur was, after all, an Independent, which earned him exactly no party loyalty from either side of the GOP or the Democrats. The only thing he had going for him—and it was an impressive advantage, Stockwell had to admit—was his remarkable personal popularity. The cynic in Stockwell had always made him wonder whether Arthur's decision to step up the war on terrorism was motivated by genuine belief in the importance of the project, or hopes of political gain since personal safety from terrorism had become a major concern for most Americans.

"You're embarking on a slippery slope, Mr. President," Stockwell had warned him privately during one summit meeting. "Americans have a short attention span and are notoriously impatient. They want results. Fighting terrorists underground doesn't get any media attention because it can't, so you lose that advantage. And since Sandoval is effectively public enemy number one, if you don't get him, you run the risk of looking impotent and losing your support base."

Arthur had just stared at him and said quietly, "I am less interested in my support base than in doing what is right." It had almost convinced Stockwell. Almost. But he was too much the politician—and therefore too much the cynic—to believe in anything or anyone one hundred percent.

On the TV screen, Arthur said, "Distinguished members of Congress . . . Mister Speaker of the House . . ." Then he looked right into the camera and, with a half smile, said, "Mr. Vice President . . ."

Cordoba chuckled softly behind him, and even Stockwell had to suppress a smile at that. In the long run it meant nothing, but he appreciated the acknowledgment nevertheless.

"As I stand before you," Arthur continued, "I ask you now the same question that I asked of you the previous year: Are you happier than you were this time last year? For as Benjamin Franklin said, despite the fine words of the Declaration of Independence . . . we are not actually entitled to happiness, but rather instead merely to the right to pursue it. And we have been going at it full tilt, have we not."

Stockwell suddenly turned to Cordoba and said, "Does he really believe he's King Arthur?"

The question caught Cordoba off guard, as Stockwell knew it would. He choked slightly on the Scotch, which he'd been in mid-swallow on. "Uhm . . . shouldn't we be watching the speech, sir?"

"As if I haven't read it already," sniffed Stockwell. "I'm just curious. All that business during the mayoral race years back. The 'King Arthur' theme that emerged . . . even the jousting and swordplay. Humiliating, trite foolishness. But he went along with it and became a man of the people, so I suppose I've no right to be snide about it. Still . . . does he truly believe it? Is it some psychosis that he's simply learned to turn to productive means? Or was it an act?"

Arthur was speaking about the economy. Cordoba cleared his throat. "Sir, I'm not sure why you're asking me this . . ."

"I'm asking because you were with him since his mayoral campaign." He leaned forward in his chair, staring intently at Ron. "I'm asking if he genuinely has a delusion that he is King Arthur. And don't lie to me, Ronald. I'm very, very good at telling when people are lying to me, so don't even try it. Just tell me. I have a right to know, not only as the Vice President, but as an American citizen."

Cordoba took a long, deep, steadying breath and then looked Stockwell in the eyes and said, with utter calm, "I've known Arthur for quite some time, and I can personally assure you: He is not suffering from a delusion about being King Arthur."

The congressmen were on their feet, applauding something Arthur had said about job opportunities. Stockwell ignored it, focusing instead on Cordoba, searching for some hint of duplicity. He got nothing off him in that regard, which meant either Cordoba was being honest, or he was so brilliant in concealing the truth that Stockwell never wanted to play poker with him. "So it's image making, then, is what you're saying," he said guardedly.

"You're saying that, sir. Me, I'm just agreeing with you."

Then the mention of Trans-Sabal caught both of their attention and brought their focus back to the TV screen.

"Our concentration on foreign affairs—particularly the revolution in Trans-Sabal—has been wearying, I know," Arthur said. "No one is more painfully aware of the difficulties we still face at home than I. The road to eliminating terrorism in our lifetime has been a long and rocky one." His hands rested firmly on the podium, his gaze fixed upon the people before him. Stockwell shook his head, still not believing that Arthur had once again disdained the use of a TelePrompTer or notes. "The problem," continued Arthur, "is that because America is a great country, filled with such wonder, such opportunity . . . we have always had the inclination to put America first. That is a laudable goal, an understandable one . . . as far as it goes. But in our formation of an international coalition with the intent of making the world a safer place, we have had to look beyond our borders and think about putting the world first. We look upon our own difficulties and think, 'Why should we be so concerned with what's happening in other countries?' But the lesson we have learned over these trying months has been that we must think from the greater to the smaller. To consider the greater problem—in this case, a world at the mercy of terrorist activities—and solve that so that smaller difficulties can be attended to. By bringing to the world a sense of global community, so that instead of matters being viewed simply as that we are helping everyone else . . . it is seen that we are all helping one another. Terrorists are cowards, no more, no less. We have taken the measure of these terrorists . . . and found them wanting.

"And that point of view has paid off. I am pleased to announce that our peace treaty with Trans-Sabal, the last country that gave willing haven to Arnim Sandoval, has been finalized. All assets of his operation have been frozen.

Furthermore, as an act of good faith, Trans-Sabal intelligence agencies have turned over to us massive records that have given us a broader picture of Sandoval's organization than we have ever had before. We know who his agents are, his lieutenants, his field operatives. We know where they are. And, I am pleased to announce . . . we believe we know where he is, as well." There was an audible gasp, and Arthur, with a fierce smile, said, "According to latest intelligence, he is—apparently—in several hundred pieces."

There was an uproar on the floor of the Congress, but for all the deafening and thunderous ovation that Arthur received with that utterly unexpected announcement, it was as nothing compared to the infuriated bellow from Stockwell. He was on his feet as was everyone else, but it was not in appreciation.

"That's not confirmed!" he fairly howled. "That is not confirmed! We do not have confirmation on that!" He leaned forward to the TV as if Arthur could hear him and shouted once more, *"We do not have confirmation!"* Then he whirled toward Cordoba, his face alight with barely controlled fury. Picking up the remote, he punched the Mute button and the sound went off, to be replaced by captioning. But his attention was entirely upon Cordoba. "Did you know about this? Did you know he was going to say this?"

Cordoba shook his head, looking ashen. "No . . . no, I didn't . . ."

"Son of a bitch," and louder, *"Son of a bitch!* That was a preliminary intelligence report!" He paced furiously around the room, at one point in such a rage that he punched the wall, scraping his knuckles fiercely. "That information is barely two hours old! Delta Force is still picking up the pieces! We know we hit Sandoval's main bunker, but we don't know for sure he was in it! The President was told it was only seventy percent certain! He was told this! I know because I was told this, and I'm reasonably sure I was told the same thing he was! Wasn't I? I'll kill him! I swear to

God, I'll kill Penn for this! And if it was her idea, I'll kill her, too!"

Cordoba had pulled out his cell phone and he was talking urgently to one of his aides, trying to find out what had happened. But he paused a moment to comment, "Sir, may I point out that threatening the life of the President of the United States and the First Lady, within hearing distance of the Secret Service standing just outside the door, may not be the brightest of maneuvers, even if you're the Vice President."

Stockwell growled in annoyance, and as Cordoba went back to his conversation, the Vice President paced past the screen, staring at it with cold and growing anger. "You smug son of a bitch," he snarled at Arthur's image. "Had to go for the big show, didn't you? Had to go for something that would knock them flat."

"I just spoke to Nellie Porter," Cordoba said, flipping shut his phone.

"Porter? She's the First Lady's woman! What does she—?"

Trying to steady the incensed Vice President, Cordoba put his hands up in a placating manner, which only irritated Stockwell even more. "She's who I was able to get on the phone and she was in the limo with the President. She said Mrs. Penn was concerned that CNN was going to air the story first. Break it before any of us said anything, and we'd be playing catch-up. Mrs. Penn suggested that he say something during the State of the Union, emphasizing that it wasn't definite. You heard him. He put in qualifiers."

"Qualifiers?" He pointed at the TV screen. The congressmen were still on their feet, applauding. He had a feeling it was going to be a record for length of an ovation. "You mean just because he said 'apparently.' You think 'apparently' is going to mean a damned thing to *that*? That stupid—"

"All right, that's enough!" Cordoba said so sharply that it brought Stockwell up short. "He made a judgment call! And

since he's the goddamn President, he gets to goddamn do that! You want to vent? You want to call him an asshole for making a decision that you don't agree with? Fine. Then you do it here, or you do it in private with him, but the moment we walk out there, or you find cameras stuck in your face, you smile and you suck it up and you keep your feelings to yourself, you got it?"

"How dare you . . ."

"Yeah, how dare I. I'm the chief of staff," said Ron sarcastically. "That's what I do. I dare. And that ass kicking is still available."

Stockwell glared at him, then turned his back, but didn't want to look at the screen, either. He moved through the room, shaking his head, saying, "Damn fool thing" over and over again. Cordoba simply stood there, apparently deciding that the best thing to do was let Stockwell vent and get it out of his system.

The State of the Union went on for another forty-three minutes, and eventually Stockwell's anger lapsed into frustrated muttering. When he finally sat on the couch, he simply crossed his arms tightly, looking for all the world like an oversized five-year-old who was incensed because he wasn't getting candy.

"It was damned stupid," he finally said. "And I just hope to hell we don't wind up with more damage control than we can handle if it turns out Sandoval is still sucking oxygen."

"So do I," Cordoba said neutrally.

Having concluded the State of the Union, Arthur was drinking in the ovation that greeted him as he slowly made his way back up the way he'd come in. Gwen was waiting for him on the aisle, and he put out an arm to her. She wrapped her arm around his, and Stockwell, for all his annoyance at the situation, had to admit reluctantly that they were a handsome couple.

"He doesn't understand, Ronald," Stockwell said finally, as the coverage switched to outside the Capitol building.

All things considered, he thought he was sounding rather calm. It might have been that the shots he'd been consuming were helping to take the edge off as well. "After all this time, he still goes in for spectacle. Still goes in for the big gesture, the big moment. He doesn't fully understand what governing is. The small compromises, the little moments. He still orders people around as if he was . . ."

"King?" suggested Ron.

"Yes, that's exactly right. And it just makes you wonder about the long-term health of his presidency—"

That was when they heard the shrieks.

On the screen, Arthur and Gwen were heading for the limo, ringed as always by their protectors, and suddenly there was screaming on the TV screen. Arthur seemed to be looking around, and Gwen fell against him, and everyone was shouting at once and the Secret Service men had drawn in, obscuring them from view, hustling them toward the limo. Cordoba was on his feet, eyes wide, his cell phone ringing, and there was a faint buzz in Stockwell's head because he hadn't fully processed what he'd seen yet . . .

Then there was a brief flowering burst of red from the middle of the ring of Secret Service men on the television screen, and Stockwell realized that it was blood fountaining, perhaps from an artery, and oh my God, it was shots, someone had been shot . . .

The door to the study exploded inward, and for a split second Stockwell thought that it was assassins. He threw his hands over his head, surrendering, and then the study was alive with Secret Service men. "We have to go, sir," one of them said briskly, and Stockwell—who hadn't had his feet leave the ground since the tackling injury in college that had ended his football career—was suddenly airborne. Cordoba was gone from his view, the room blurring around him, and he barely had time to think, *I didn't* really *mean I'd kill them, oh my God, they're going to blame me for it*, before he was whisked away.

* * *

HE IS SMILING, *greeting the people, and they're cheering his name. He thinks,* This was for you, Merlin, this whole presidency, it was for you. For you and for Gwen . . .

He glances over at her as she squeezes his arm tightly, affectionately, and she is smiling, her eyes alive with light and joy and love. And then she staggers, and for a moment Arthur thinks that she has broken a heel on her shoe, or perhaps snagged the hem of her gown, because the shouting and cheering obscure any other sounds.

She looks up at him, and her mouth moves but no sound emerges. Instead blood comes out, trickling down as if she's a vampire in a horror movie who's just fed off a victim. The love and joy evaporate from her eyes to be replaced by bewilderment, and the whole thing takes barely two seconds between the first confusion and the second time she staggers, except this time it's far more pronounced. This time she is actually thrown against him, propelled by an outside force even as Cook, the burly Secret Service man, shouts, "Gun! Go go go!"

Arthur is shoved forward, Gwendolyn next to him, and just like that, she is not supporting herself at all. Instead she's little more than a meat sack, a collection of blood and muscle, bones and organs no longer working in unison, and Arthur hauls her forward with his powerful arms even as the Secret Service men come in from behind. Everything is a blur to him. He is in the limo, and Gwen is there and there's blood everywhere. He is not afraid of blood, not daunted by it. He has waded hip deep through it in his time. He has seen grown men carved to bits, women and children savaged by vicious soldiers seeking to expand the holdings of some petty warlord. He's seen people hung, drawn and quartered, eviscerated, decapitated. There is no atrocity that can possibly be committed to the human body that Arthur has not witnessed and, in some cases, inflicted with his own hand.

But this . . .

This . . .

Gwen is slumped against him, and Nellie Porter is screaming, and then Gwen is pulled away, pulled to the far side of the limo, and an oxygen mask is being strapped over her face. A paramedic (where the hell did he come from?) is trying to staunch her wounds, but there's more blood, and it's as if it's flowing from her by the gallon. Cook's hands are all over Arthur, and it seems bizarre until he realizes that Cook is checking him for wounds. Arthur shoves his hands away. "I'm fine, I'm fine!"

"The First Lady to the hospital, the President to the lockdown at the White House!" Cook orders.

"I'm staying with her," says Arthur.

"Mr. President—"

"I'm staying with her!" he thunders, and that is really all there is to it.

The limo's siren kicks into overdrive and the long black car, like a great metal dragon, roars toward the hospital.

Don't let her die, don't let her die, Merlin, save her, and it is only later on that Arthur realizes that he is praying to a statue rather than to God. But somehow, at that moment, God seems farther away than ever he has before . . .

CHAPTRE
THE FIFTH

†

"**M**ISS BASIL! YOU'RE back!"

Miss Basil was sitting on her customary bar stool at the Jamaican resort wherein she had taken up semipermanent residence. The bar was situated outside, down toward the beach, so thirsty hotel guests didn't have to pad far from their towels to obtain liquid refreshment. Furthermore there were waitresses and servers eagerly scuttling up and down the beach, making sure to accommodate everyone who looked the least bit parched. Miss Basil was wearing a skimpy green two-piece bathing suit with a pattern on it that looked a bit like a reptile's scales, and a printed skirt tied around her middle that was settled comfortably around her lengthy legs. Her hair was long and blacker than would have seemed natural, her neck extraordinarily long and her jaw well-rounded. Her eyebrows were thin and arched, and when she looked out toward the rolling water with her dark green eyes, it would have seemed to any passerby that she was able to discern things beneath the waves that no other living creature would have been able to.

Despite the fact that she was dressed so lightly, the night

air did not bother her. She wasn't especially fond of the cold; she far preferred the warmth to bathe her old bones, but she had learned to tolerate much in her time.

"Yes, Carlos, I'm back," she said. She tapped the bar in front of her and within moments Carlos, the heavyset bartender who could mix a drink faster than anyone on the island (or so he liked to boast), had a rum placed in front of her. "I was off attending to some business for the boss . . . but it's good to be home."

He was looking at her with open curiosity. "What sort of business, Miss Basil?" he asked.

"The sort that smart bartenders don't ask about, Carlos," she said wanly.

He clearly did not take the least offense. "You are absolutely right, Miss Basil. I should remember that. Welcome back, then. It's good to have you back . . . because life here is good."

"Yes," she said slowly and thoughtfully. "It hasn't been a bad life here, Carlos."

"No, it hasn't, Miss Basil," he said agreeably.

"This wasn't my first favor for the boss . . . and likely won't be the last. That's why he lets me stay here, as his permanent guest. I do him . . . favors. You've heard about that, haven't you, Carlos?"

"Yes, Miss Basil." He turned his concentration to cleaning glasses.

"Have you ever wondered about the nature of my favors?"

"No, Miss Basil."

She fixed a stare at him, and smiled to herself, for she knew that he was uncomfortable beneath her gaze, and she knew why he was uncomfortable, even if he didn't. "Really. And why is that?"

"Because," he said, fixing his attention even more attentively upon the glasses, "you appear to me to be someone about whom the less is wondered, the better."

She laughed lightly at that. Then she took a deep breath

and let it out slowly, with a very faint hiss. "The wheels are turning, Carlos."

"Wheels?"

"The wheels. A storm is rolling in on them."

Carlos looked in the direction that she was looking. Although it was a night sky, it was still quite obviously cloudless. "I don't think so, Miss Basil, but I don't want to contradict you," he said, doing his level best to be accommodating. "If you think there is . . ."

"Not that kind of storm, Carlos," she assured him. "The wheels of fate are turning. They do so all the time, but sometimes with greater force and more inexorably than usual. They're like great cogs, as you would see in a watch, Carlos. And every so often, those cogs come together and crush anyone who happens to get in between them."

"I see," said Carlos, who didn't. "And . . . how would you know that this is happening?" He had ceased polishing the glass, instead focusing his full attention on his very curious late-night drinker.

"Because, Carlos," she said patiently, "when you have been around for a long enough time—as I have—you learn to intuit these things. I have attended to the advice of Santayana, and listened to the lessons of history so that I am not doomed to repeat them." Her glass was devoid of rum. Without having to be asked, Carlos reached over and filled it, and she gave him a grateful inclination of her head. "I smell it in the air, Carlos, just as a sailor can smell a storm. Those ever turning wheels." She ran her finger around the rim of her glass. "So . . . I have been out of touch with the news as of late. Anything interesting going on in the world? I notice you don't have the television on," and she nodded toward a small TV with an eight-inch screen that was mounted along the upper section of the bar.

"Yes," said Carlos, the edges of his chapped mouth turning downward. "The guests would just sit here and watch it and get upset, with all the coverage of . . ." He paused, his eyes wide. "You haven't heard?"

"Heard what?" She couldn't quite keep the boredom out of her voice. Considering how long she'd been around, she found it hard to believe that anything could possibly occur in the world that would seize her interest. "Something going on that's out of the ordinary?"

"President Penn. His wife was shot. They say it's very bad."

Immediately Miss Basil snapped to full attention, her green eyes narrowing. "Gwen?"

He nodded. "Several days ago. She is in the hospital. Shot here"—he tapped his chest—"and here," and he put a finger to the side of his head.

"That's terrible," she said, doing her best to keep the amusement out of her voice. She had never been particularly enamored of Gwen; her antipathy for her was one of the few things she'd had in common with Merlin. Still, the little queen had never done her any harm personally, and she'd even shown a bit of spunk now and then that Miss Basil would never have ascribed to her upon first meeting her. But the whole thing struck her as ironic. All the things that Arthur had done for her, the sacrifices he had made, the risks he had taken throughout the ages . . . and now, here they were, reunited—he through Merlin's magic, she through the oddities of reincarnation—with the world at their feet, and boom. Fate had conspired to deprive him of her yet again. She couldn't help but wonder whether Arthur was finally going to take the hint. "Will she survive?"

"No one knows. Do you want to see? The news station speaks of nothing else these days."

"Yes. Yes, by all means," she said thoughtfully. She stuck her finger in the rum and swirled the liquid around a bit.

She smelled the young man approaching her from behind before she saw him. Carlos didn't notice him, since he was busy tuning in the television. The set operated off a satellite dish, and it wasn't always cooperative in picking up broadcasts. But Miss Basil was aware of him without even having to look at him. Her sensitive nose cut through the cheap cologne he was wearing and detected the heightened stimulus coming from the hormonal odor he was unconsciously emitting. She sighed deeply and didn't bother to look at him as he sat on the stool next to her.

"Hey, there," he said. From his voice and scent, she pegged him as being mid to late twenties. He twanged like a Texan, and also had that smell of oil and cattle and pollution adhering to him with a permanence that no amount of bathing could ever erase. She shifted in her seat and leveled her gaze on him. He was lantern-jawed with two days' worth of light blond stubble and hair that hung partly in his face. He was wearing Bermuda shorts and a blue flowered shirt that was unbuttoned, revealing a tanned and hairy chest. "Can I buy you a drink?"

She held up the rum.

"A refill, then?"

She shrugged.

He leaned forward, the alcohol floating off his breath. "Name's Ricky. How you doing?"

"I'm doing fine, Ricky." Her gaze flickered to his hand. "And you're married."

"Heh." He glanced down at his ringed finger. "Well . . . it's a funny thing about that. See . . . this here trip, well . . . it was the in-laws' idea. See, they don't wanna accept the fact that the marriage is over, so they offered to send the wife and me on a second honeymoon. Hoped it might 're-kindle something.' " Ricky shook his head, obviously doing his best to try and look sorrowful. "Some people . . . they just don't get it. But you . . . you look like a woman of the world. You look"—he rested a hand on her thigh—"you look like someone who gets it."

"Oh, I get much more of it than I could possibly want," she replied, and put her own hand on his leg. She squeezed it, found it a bit muscular, but probably not stringy. "So let me see if I understand this, Ricky. . . You're down here on a second honeymoon, with your wife, on your in-laws' dime, and you're hitting on me."

He laughed, his large Adam's apple bobbing up and down as he did so. "You're direct! I like that in a woman! What's your name?"

"Miss Basil."

"My my. Keeping it awful formal, aren't we?"

"Well," she said easily, sipping her rum, "if one lives long enough, one tends to appreciate that too much informality is never a good thing."

Then her attention was drawn to the television.

Carlos had been absolutely right. The news station was talking about nothing but the shooting, and inside of ten minutes, she'd seen film of it twice. She watched with fascination as Gwen went down, saw the blood jetting onto Arthur's suit, except he didn't seem to realize it at first.

"Terrible thing," Ricky said, shaking his head. "Crazy world. Goddamn crazy world."

Miss Basil looked to Carlos. "Did they get the shooter?"

But Ricky interrupted before Carlos could respond. "Oh, they found him, all right. What was left of him. From the tenth floor of an office building with a high-powered rifle. They had the building surrounded in no time. By the time they got to him, he'd already blown the top of his skull clean off."

She took that in. "Obviously he didn't want to be captured. Afraid of being forced to name his connections or employer."

Carlos started to speak and again Ricky cut him off. "Hell, everyone knows it was that sumbitch Sandoval. The President thought he was dead—announced it and everything. This was the sumbitch's way of announcing that he was alive and kicking and just as mean as ever. He sent out a press release about it. People think he's still hiding in Trans-Sabal . . . that the whole treaty thing is just a ruse. Everyone's screaming war; that we should just bomb the place back into the Stone Age."

"I've been to Trans-Sabal," Miss Basil said. "They're not all that much advanced beyond the Stone Age now."

Ricky smiled in what he obviously thought was a winsome manner. "My, my. You get around, don't you. So do I. Why don't you tell me more about yourself?" He slid his hand farther up her thigh.

Carlos stepped forward and said to Ricky in a low voice, chancing a quick glance in Miss Basil's direction, "Sir, I don't think you want to be doin' that."

"Oh, now Carlos," Miss Basil said, her voice faintly scolding. "You shouldn't be so concerned. Ricky's a big boy. You are a big boy, aren't you, Ricky?" And she brushed her fingers lightly over his crotch, causing him to jump slightly on the bar stool. "A big man, in fact. Probably too much man for his wife, aren't you?"

"Well . . . Rhonda *is* kinda holding me back." Ricky sighed. He leaned forward, looked right and left, and said, "Truth to tell . . . I wasn't all that keen on getting married. But it's what my folks wanted, and Rhonda's dad's loaded, and she frankly ain't too bad to look at."

"And does she love you, Ricky?"

He shrugged. "Way I see it, that don't really matter. If it ain't two ways, what's the point?"

"Indeed."

Carlos rested a hand on his arm. "Mister . . . I gotta tell you, you might be sorry—"

But Ricky yanked his arm away, and with obvious anger he snapped back, "Look, buddy, your job is to pour drinks. You just mind your own business or you're the one who might be sorry, okay?"

Carlos stepped back, putting his hands palms up in an "I give" manner. Ricky returned his focus to Miss Basil. "You know what I like about you, Miss Basil? A man knows where he stands with you."

"Oh, he does indeed, Ricky, he does indeed. Tell you what," and she rested a hand on his. He shivered slightly; although her leg was warm, her hand was cold, and he probably noticed that. Or perhaps it was the sudden sense that he was in trouble and just didn't quite know why or how yet. She could tell that a fight-or-flight instinct was seizing hold of him, but fortunately enough, he was far too civilized to be aware of it for what it was. "Tell you what," she said again, "how about we go someplace"—she ran a fingernail along the curve of his jaw—"somewhere . . . private."

He rallied. He had no idea why his courage was faltering, because the notion of reacting on a gut basis to unrecognized primal evil was alien to him. "Well, that sounds . . . that sounds really great to me."

She eased herself off her stool, turned, and winked lazily to Carlos. "Keep the set on," she said. "I'll be back in just a few minutes." And she and Ricky walked off into the night.

Carlos sighed and finished cleaning the glasses. The night air seemed more still, and the breeze that had been blowing steadily had ceased. He waited to hear a scream, but knew there would be none. There never was.

Miss Basil returned a few minutes later, easing back onto her stool. Carlos slid a fresh glass of rum to her without comment, and she took it and bobbed her head slightly in appreciation. On TV, there was a news conference with a doctor—the one who apparently had been working on Gwen. He looked tired and careworn, and he had nothing new to report, but the reporters didn't appear to know how to handle lack of news and were acting as if they wanted him to manufacture something, accurate or not.

"You, uhm," and Carlos touched the side of his own mouth, "you got something . . . right here."

Miss Basil reached up and pulled a piece of thin blue cloth, with the hint of a flower on it, from between her teeth. "Thank you, Carlos," she said. The breeze had returned, and she tossed the cloth carelessly into it, letting the tropical zephyr carry it away.

Then Miss Basil looked up with renewed interest, because they were running a statement that Arthur had made earlier. It didn't indicate exactly when he had spoken, but that didn't matter to her. What she was fascinated by, instead, was the fact that she had never seen him look so scared. She couldn't begin to count the number of times she had seen him thrust into battle, and never had he hung back. Arthur was simply not that sort of king; as far as he was concerned, it was the leader's job to lead. She didn't think the man had any concept of fear. Certainly personal jeopardy held no terror for him. He would risk his life in a heartbeat for what he thought was right, and if he should fall in the endeavor, then he would go to his grave confident that he had done well.

But now she saw it in his eyes, for Miss Basil was more attuned to the eyes of others than anyone else who walked or crawled the earth. He spoke bravely, his words were strong, his demeanor was confident . . . but the concern was there, in his eyes, for her—if not anyone else—to see.

The scene was clearly at the hospital, for there was no sign of the Presidential seal or some such behind him that would have indicated a White House location. Arthur was standing behind a podium, his manner grave, and he spoke softly but firmly while the words "recorded earlier" ran along the screen. "I want to assure the people of this great country," he said, "that the First Lady is receiving the best care humanly possible. I have every confidence in these fine men of medicine," and he nodded to the physicians on either side of him, "to do all they can for my wife. Furthermore, I have received letters and telegrams of support from thousands of you, and all of them are very . . . very much appreciated. In addition . . ."

He stopped. There was something in his voice that made Miss Basil sit up and watch the screen with rapt attention. Suddenly the concern was gone from his eyes, to be replaced by quiet, burning anger and more . . . a deep resolution, as if he'd made a decision. Again, it was subtleties that only a master of reading eyes could discern, but Miss Basil was one such.

"In addition," he said, and instead of looking at the reporters he was staring straight out of the TV screen, or so it seemed, although naturally he was just looking right into one of the cameras that was positioned dead center. "In addition, I received a very nice note from the Pope . . . who even now is praying in Saint Peter's Basiliskos . . ."

Miss Basil's jaw dropped, even as an astounded smile touched her lips.

"I'm sorry," Arthur said in that same formal tone. "I meant to say 'Basilica' . . . not *Basiliskos* . . ."

"I'll be damned," said Miss Basil.

Carlos looked over to her. "What is it?"

She chuckled softly. "Just . . . something I was not expecting to hear."

"Excuse me," came a young female voice from behind them.

Both Miss Basil and Carlos looked over to see a young woman approaching, looking rather concerned. She was not overly pretty, but not ugly, either. Just average. Average hair, average face, average average. "I was looking for my husband. He's about this tall." She indicated with her hand out, flat, and indicating a height of close to six feet. "He was wearing a—"

"Ricky?" asked Miss Basil quietly.

She blinked in surprise. "Yes!"

"And you would be Rhonda."

Rhonda looked extremely pleased. "Yes! Yes, that's right. He was by here? Was he . . . telling you about me?"

For the briefest of instants, Miss Basil felt a slight wave of regret, but she quickly dismissed it from her mind. Regret was for mortals. The reason mortals ever regretted anything was because their time on earth was limited, and they were always concerned that—if they had done something wrong—they were not going to have the opportunity to get it right before shuffling off the mortal coil. Someone like Miss Basil, on the other hand, needn't worry about such things. She had the luxury of undertaking every single permutation of any situation, and seeing what suited her best.

"Yes. Yes, he was telling us about you." She paused, and

then patted the bar stool next to her. "Rhonda . . . sit down a moment."

"Is . . . is something wrong?" Rhonda started looking around, apparently under the impression that Ricky was nearby. Which, in a sense, he was; just not in any condition to respond to anyone.

"Nothing's wrong. Sit down." She patted the bar stool once more. This time Rhonda did sit, but she was clearly puzzled as she cocked her head slightly and stared at Miss Basil.

"Rhonda," she said, and her head was moving from side to side ever so slowly. It was such a subtle move that Rhonda began imitating it without realizing it. "Rhonda, I need you to understand something: Ricky's gone and he's not coming back."

"*What?*" Rhonda's voice was high with alarm, but the force of Miss Basil's gaze kept her fixed in place.

"If Ricky had stayed with you," continued Miss Basil as if Rhonda had said nothing, "you would have had a life of nothing save for pain and misery." Her green eyes became darker, and there was a flatness to them, but a hypnotic quality as well. "He was going to cheat on you, time and again. He was going to do so because he had no respect for you. And because he had no respect, he was going to abuse you in other manners. He was going to strike you, beat you. And you were going to lack the inner strength or resolve to do anything about it, because you have grown up believing that any man is better than no man. You likely would have had children with him—boys, with your luck—who would have followed their father's example, seen how he treated you, and grown up not only feeling contempt for you, but for women in general. This is what your world would have been. You have been saved from it. Do not ask how, nor why. You will have the opportunity to begin a new life. Use the opportunity wisely, for it may not come again."

Rhonda's mouth was moving, but no words were coming

out. Finally she managed to say, "I . . . I don't understand . . ."

"You need not understand. Just accept."

"But where's Ricky?!" Her voice rose in alarm. "Where is he?"

Miss Basil fought a smile. "He fell victim to a consuming passion."

Rhonda stared at her for a long moment, then pitched back her head, cupped her hands to her mouth, and called out, *"Riccccccky! Riiiiickkkkkyyy!"* With one final, angry glance at Miss Basil, she jumped off the bar stool and headed away.

"No gratitude," sighed Miss Basil. "Simply no gratitude in the world. Carlos, I hate to drink and run, particularly since the former often precludes the latter . . . but please let the boss know I have to leave."

Carlos was dumbfounded. The business with Rhonda had already been forgotten, mostly because he was reluctant to dwell on it for too long. "But . . . didn't you just get back?"

"Yes, yes, I did. But someone has asked for my help, and frankly I'm so amazed that he did, I can't pass it up."

The bartender didn't bother glancing at Arthur's image on the screen, because of course he didn't realize that was who was being referred to. "But why would it be so amazing that he would ask for your help?"

"Because," said Miss Basil matter-of-factly, tossing the reply over her shoulder, "I killed his best friend." And she headed off to her luxurious suite of rooms to pack.

A RNIM SANDOVAL HAS *been drinking heavily for the past several days.*

It is not something his lieutenants are accustomed to seeing. Actually, it is very much a surprise. They have seen him coordinate multilayered, multileveled strikes, pulled off with clockwork precision, and never show the slightest hint of strain or stress. But they do not question. They have sworn to live and die on the word of Arnim Sandoval, because they believe him the anointed of God.

Among his men, he is called the Glowing One, for it is said, in certain lights, that one can actually see the celestial holy glow that surrounds him. It is his gift from on high.

Arnim Sandoval knows that he will cease drinking soon. It is an indulgence, a luxury that he can ill afford. Matters have come to a head in Trans-Sabal, but he was aware that would happen. It is not by coincidence that Arnim Sandoval is a master chess player. Indeed, it is becoming impossible for him to be challenged in a chess game, for he has long accustomed himself to thinking seven, eight moves ahead of his opponent.

This American President, though . . . he has been different. Of all those walking the global stage, only this Arthur Penn has outthought him on several occasions. Thrown him off guard, drawn his attention in one direction while striking from another. Arnim Sandoval feels as if he should befriend him . . . or admire him . . . or kill him. He has not yet decided the ultimate direction the relationship will take.

However, Arnim Sandoval needed to hurt him. And he has hurt him. The hurt does not ease the suffering of Arnim Sandoval himself, but he has at least been able to repay in kind some of what was done to him.

Sleep has not come to him. Numbness has not come to him. Nothing except the emptiness, which all the hardship brought upon Arthur Penn cannot hope to erase.

Arnim Sandoval endeavors to crawl inside the bottle.

In years, he is a young man. In appearance, he looks far more aged than he is. The pressure has been building upon him. He knows he is right in what he does, and he trusts his god to guide him and succor him, and yet the losses he has experienced sting just as sharply.

He stings back.

The losses still throb.

Arnim Sandoval rises from his desk. Muffled in the distance are the sounds of missiles. He does not know which country drops them, nor does he care. They are no threat to him. After he gets some rest, he will record a new video message and release it. He will make his followers proud.

He staggers, braces himself, crosses the room, and rests his hands upon an urn.

"I cannot rest," he says to the urn. "Help me rest."

He finishes the bottle, staggers to his chair, and slumps back. He does not sleep.

CHAPTRE
THE SIXTH

✝

UNDER THE CLOAK of night, the water lapping gently against the bow of his boat, Percival anchored his schooner in what he believed to be a fairly secluded part of the island. Certainly he didn't see any lights or signs of civilization. He checked his charts one more time, trying to make certain that he had indeed found the correct place, and hoping—not for the first time—that he had not been sold a bill of goods. The information had certainly *seemed* genuine, but those from whom he purchased it had not been the most reliable of sorts. Frankly, they seemed a bit shady, and he could just imagine his liege, Arthur, scolding him severely for bothering to waste any time (much less money) on such riffraff.

But Percival had looked his primary source full in the eye and, concentrating the considerable force of his not-inestimable personality and strength of character, said, "If you are lying to me, I will come back for you, and I will find you, and I swear it will not go well for you at all."

His source had simply nodded his head, not seeming the least bit put off, and replied, "May I die if I am lying to you."

There are, of course, ways around such epithets, not the least of which is that people die whether they lie or not. It just happens. Well . . . not to everyone. But to most. Still, the sincerity and fervency was enough to marginally convince Percival, and so with considerably less money left in his pocket—but even more resolve—he had obtained the small but sturdy craft and set out. And now he had arrived at his destination . . .

". . . wherever that may be," he said out loud with self-directed scorn. He surveyed the distance between the boat and the shore, and it really wasn't much of anything. Percival wrapped his guns and gunbelt tightly in waterproof material and tucked them into his pack, which he then eased onto his back. He was wearing a wetsuit over his clothes as well for added protection, and within moments Percival had slid over the side of the boat and into the water. The water was warm, as befit the tropical environment, and with quick, sturdy strokes he paddled toward shore. Within moments he was on land, trying everything he could not to make any noise. The moon had darted behind clouds and didn't seem the least bit interested in emerging from hiding. That didn't bother Percival; he simply slid his night-vision goggles over his eyes, blinked a few times to adjust his sight, and then soldiered on. Percival then removed the pack from his back, holstered his guns, and slid the machete from its sheath strapped on to his back.

Even though he was seeing his way through the red tint of the night-vision goggles, that couldn't begin to disguise the beauty of the land through which he was passing. The verdure around him was thick and teaming with life, so dense that it was practically a jungle. He would have wagered that there were parts of the undergrowth that never saw sunlight, so covered were they by a canopy of branches.

But it was inhabited, that much was for certain. It did not require any great leap of intuition, because Percival was making his way down a trail that had unquestionably been carved by human hands. However, he had to admit it was possible that the island had been inhabited at some point in the past, but no longer was. Although he kept the machete gripped firmly in his right hand, he thus far had no need to carve through the brush with it. The paths remained consistent and clear.

He went on for some time like that, wrestling with his confusion and inner frustration, unsure of whether he was wasting his time or not. Wasting one's time didn't much matter when one has all the time that one could possibly require. Nevertheless, it was the principle of the thing that counted, and Percival felt that he was entirely too busy an individual to chase about on foolish outings.

That was what he kept thinking until the path ahead of him opened up, the jungle ending . . . or at least the section of it that he was traversing was ending. To his surprise, he saw what appeared to be a small amphitheater, ringed by stone pillars. They were not carved or ornate in any way, but flat and featureless, standing anywhere from seven to ten feet high. It reminded him a bit of Stonehenge.

With warrior's senses honed by centuries of experience, Percival approached slowly, on the balls of his feet, ready to fight or fly as the case required. Still holding on to his blade with his right hand, his left hand hovered at the level of the gun hanging from his left hip, to be able to draw it as needed. Percival was an accomplished shot with either hand.

Then he stopped. He started to feel something, a light-headedness, almost a giddiness. Instantly he recognized it, for it was a sensation like no other. It was the feeling, the very spoor, of the Grail. He had felt it coming off the dead man named Joshua, back in Peru. He felt it again here, only a hundred times stronger.

It seemed to be coming from everywhere, all at once. Every cell in his brain was screaming at him to run now, to get out while he still could, and yet he not only did not flee, but instead continued his path forward on wavering legs. It was as if he had utterly lost control of his motor skills, as if he were being both pulled and pushed by some unholy . . .

no, some holy force. Yes, it had to be holy. There was not a scintilla of evil hanging about it. It filled him with a joy and purity such as he had not experienced in over a thousand years, when he had last held the Grail in his trembling hands and brought the sanctified liquid within to his lips, thereby blessing and cursing himself at one and the same time. And now the power it had over him was even greater, having become all the stronger in the intervening centuries.

Percival hadn't even been aware anymore that he was still walking, and suddenly he found himself in the middle of the amphitheater. He stopped, stood there wavering, feeling he was in the absolute midst of the power, as if it were reaching up to him and embracing him, even though there was nothing around him.

He heard soft cooing noises as from the throats of doves, but they were not remotely avian. Women were approaching him, and they were beautiful, and they were young, and they were smiling at him in ways that females had not done in years. It brought his mind, or what was left of his mind, to times of wild, orgiastic celebrations. Women would gyrate around him, moving toward him, their dark skin smooth and their bodies supple. Wild women, oftentimes Berbers, their thick lips drawn back in wolfish delight as their hands would play across the hardness of his body. They were nights that never seemed to end, that the dawns seemed to be stalled for many days so that the revels could continue beyond anything man thought possible. Musicians would be playing, and the smell of musk was everywhere. Once, once they had looked upon him and found him fair, those women, and he would regale them with tales of his adventures. And then he would leave Spain and return to Arthur out of a sense of duty, and in all the times that those women threw themselves upon him, he always resisted the ultimate temptation. Because he knew that he was meant for a destiny that required great control, great virtue, and great chastity. He could have avoided the women entirely, of course, but the sweet pain he endured from resisting their overtures stoked the fires of determination in his young heart, and told him that if he could withhold deploying his manhood despite the pleas of such as these, then he had the strength of character and self-control to accomplish anything. It was never an easy thing, for their caresses would set fire to his skin, and he could still taste on his mouth the salty passion of their kisses long after the coast of Spain was gone from sight.

Those memories swarmed over him now, and these women were not Berbers, or Moors, but some of them were dark-skinned, and some of them less so, and they were willing and filled with joy to see him. And standing here, in the middle of his place of power, the torture of his endless existence faded into nothingness. His guns were gone and forgotten, as was his machete. His past had returned to him and he embraced it, and for the first time in ages his future was of no interest to him whatsoever.

The women overwhelmed him, and the Percival who would have turned them away, who would have refused them, who would have prided himself on his self-control, was gone, long, long gone.

And he was healed.

SUNLIGHT FILTERING THROUGH high windows caused Percival to awaken.

He had the usual feeling of disorientation one experiences upon waking in a strange place. Still, Percival was too experienced the warrior to tip off anything, even the fact that he was awake. So just as he had the inclination to sit up, he promptly kept himself prone, lying there with his eyes narrowed to slits as he tried to take in as much as he could of his surroundings.

Staring straight up, he saw a mosaic upon the ceiling. It appeared to be a man and some sort of large animal, fighting a mammoth bull. But it was done in a very primitive style, and therefore hard for Percival to be absolutely certain.

Trying not to turn his head and thus betray his wakefulness, Percival glanced right and left as far as his peripheral vision would allow. The room had glistening marble walls and tiled floors, and vases upon pedestals that appeared to be centuries old. He felt as if he'd awoken in a museum; he fully expected that, at the far end of the room, there would be a hanging rope partitioning it off, allowing gawkers to pass by and stare in at him.

He listened carefully for any sign of movement, but there was nothing. He still wasn't entirely certain whether he was unobserved, but he had no intention of just lying there all day. That would hardly do him any good in any circumstance. Finally he rose to a seated position, looking around carefully to get a fuller appreciation of where he was. He glanced down to discover that he was wearing some sort of elaborate robes, made of what appeared to be silk. His guns were gone, as was his blade. He was defenseless, a situation of which he did not approve.

Percival rolled his mind back as he got to his feet, trying to retrace the events in his mind of the night before. Slowly it began to come back to him, and a flush of abashment crept across his face. What in the world had he done? What had he allowed to happen to him? How utterly humiliating; he could only pray that Arthur never found out about it, because most assuredly Percival would never, ever hear the end of it.

Suddenly he heard footsteps approaching him. He took a step back, glancing toward the window that opened up onto a bright, verdant yard. Percival considered bolting for the window, leaping through it, and escaping . . . but to what end? He had come here for a purpose; running away from that wasn't going to accomplish a damned thing. Better simply to remain right where he was and try to deal with whatever was being thrown at him, even though he was essentially weaponless.

The footsteps drew nearer. It seemed to be a single set, but the footfall was heavy. Whoever was coming was of some considerable build, and then a large figure filled the door. He was bronzed and bald, and quite serious of mien. Straps crisscrossed his sculpted chest, and he wore light armor covering his loins and stomach, as well as the outside of his arms. He was holding, of all things, a large spear. Yet despite the primitiveness of the weapon, Percival had little doubt that it could be employed in most lethal fashion, and further had no doubt that this behemoth was schooled in its use.

He said nothing for a time, and then gestured for Percival to follow him. Then he turned and walked away. Percival followed him, not saying a word since there didn't particularly seem to be anything for him *to* say.

Walking through the stately corridors of what he had now come to think of as a palace, Percival saw more statuary and pottery of the type that had been in his room, plus more frescos and such depicting heroic deeds from throughout the ages. Whoever was master of the palace was certainly schooled in derring-do from days gone by.

The hallways abruptly opened up in front of them, and Percival found himself entering what he knew instantly to be a great hall belonging to the master of the palace. From a stylistic point of view there was simply no mistaking it; Lord knew that Percival had been in enough places similar to it in his lengthy career . . . although more in the earlier days of that career than recently.

Sure enough, there was a throne. And seated upon the throne was one of the largest, most massive, most instantly dominant individuals Percival had ever met. In the days of Arthur, there had been any number of times when Percival had encountered brave warriors, warlords, soldiers of fortune, free lances, and the like. To engage in any of those professions, one had to be physically of a build and determination to be able to endure the rugged requirements of the endeavor. For the most part, they had been, and Percival had oftentimes been quite impressed by these invariably commanding examples of manhood.

But they were as nothing compared to the nearly naked personage facing him now. The individual on the throne sported what appeared to be a simple cotton kilt encircling his waist, trimmed with gold lace. Aside from the sandals on his feet and various glittering baubles and bangles around his arms, his neck, his legs . . . aside from those, he was unclad. He did not, however, seem the least bit self-conscious of his state of undress. He was probably rather proud of the unclothed body he possessed . . . and, truthfully, Percival could not entirely blame him.

The servant, or soldier, or whoever he was who had escorted Percival there, bowed deeply in response to a gesture from the man on the throne that Percival readily comprehended: a shooing "go away" gesture, dismissing the man from his presence. The servant/soldier then proceeded to back up, bowing and scraping, even as he vanished from the room.

Percival and the strange man in the chair were alone.

The man began speaking to him, but Percival didn't understand a damned thing he was saying. However, as the man spoke, he did so with a slightly tentative air, head cocked, and Percival quickly realized that the bronzed giant was trying out a tongue to see if Percival spoke it. Percival simply shrugged in response after a sentence or two. Without blinking an eye the man switched to another language, and then another. The latter had faint hints of familiarity, causing Percival to frown in concentration at first as he tried to pick up on where he might have heard it before. But it wasn't the language as a whole that he understood; just bits and pieces, a word or two here, a guttural sound there.

And then, to Percival's utter astonishment, the man began speaking to him in Arabic, asking him his name, where he came from . . . all the obvious questions one would ask, except that Percival had not been expecting to hear that language.

Consequently, Percival—trying to deal with the shock his mind was experiencing, and absorb the utter unreality of the situation—said nothing at all. The man on the throne frowned momentarily and then, obviously assuming that it was yet another language Percival did not speak, moved on to conversational Spanish. But it was very formalized, even archaic in many of its word choices.

Realizing what had happened, Percival quickly replied in Spanish, which seemed to please the throned man. Then, because his Spanish was rustier than his Arabic, Percival promptly switched back to Arabic, speaking quickly and confidently enough to convince this strange man of his veritas. The man on the throne was clearly confused, asking in Arabic, "Why did you not respond before?"

"Because you caught me by surprise," Percival responded. "Now if you'd like," he suddenly switched languages yet again, "I also know German . . . and English—"

"You know English!" said the man on the throne, looking most interested. "Are you fluent?"

"Very much so."

"Excellent," said the throned man in English, slapping his thighs briskly in a manner that indicated that the decision had been made, everything settled. "So . . . let us engage in a bit of deductive logic. You speak Arabic and Spanish. I should have known you earlier, simply from the look of you. You are, I take it, a Berber? Or a subset of that race known as—"

"Moors. Yes."

The throned man's eyes glittered with cold amusement. "The Moors. The Berbers who chose to try and 'civilize' themselves by invading France. That came a cropper for you rather badly, didn't it. So . . . you are centuries old, I take it."

Percival should have been taken aback by the effortless estimating of his exceedingly advanced age, and yet for some reason he wasn't. He didn't know why, but it seemed the most natural thing in the world that this charismatic individual would have been able to discern something of Percival's true nature. Nor did he make any effort to lie in response. Lying was not his strong suit, and besides, it would have seemed . . . insulting somehow. "You take it correctly, yes. But how——?"

The man waved dismissively. "One learns what to look for. When a man is unnaturally long-lived, he frequently develops a sadness in his eyes that is like none other. The sadness of one for whom loss is as routine an experience as breathing. One who has lost countless loved ones, or else deprives himself of love so that he need not endure loss. One who looks upon humanity for century piled upon century and sees the same mistakes, the same wars, the same foolishness, over and over, just cloaked in different guises and levels of sophistication. Yes, there are little signs, dark one, but to one experienced in reading them, they're as conspicuous as marked exits on a highway. Still, I am no mind reader, and need answers to the more elementary questions. In that spirit: What is your name, sir?"

"Percival. And you?"

"You," said the man on the throne, one eyebrow raised mockingly, "may simply address me as 'High King.' Or 'Highness,' if you are so inclined."

Percival draped his arms behind his back. He did not take his eyes off the High King for a moment. Something within him warned him that it would be most unwise to do so. Despite the High King's genial attitude, he nevertheless had an air of danger about him. "Very well, Highness. I notice that my clothes, and my possessions are gone——"

"You mean your weapons. Those are the possessions about which you are truly concerned, I take it?" He smiled thinly, and didn't wait for Percival to nod in response. "You will not need them. On this isle, weapons are not a necessity."

"The fellow who fetched me from my room seemed well-armed enough."

"Yes, well . . . guards will be guards. Although speak true, Percival . . . do I look as if I need a guard?" He rose then, seeming to uncoil from his throne, and Percival felt as if there was simply no end to the man. He tried not to appear daunted at the sight, but daunted he very much was. With slight impatience, the High King added, "That was not a rhetorical question, Percival."

"No. No, you do not look like you need a guard."

The High King smiled approvingly. There was a small mirror standing on a table nearby. The High King looked into it, checking his hair. *Vain son of a bitch,* Percival thought with no trace of amusement. "So . . . how did you find our little paradise?" asked the High King. "Did you come upon us by happenstance?"

Percival studied the High King carefully, looking for a sign of reaction as he said, "Actually . . . Joshua told me."

The High King's back was to him, but now he turned to Percival with a faintly sad air. "Joshua did that, did he?" He shook his head. "A pity. I knew that Joshua was unhappy here, but I foolishly took that as a simple phase that would pass. Obviously it did not. You encountered him, did you?" Upon Percival's nod, he continued, "And he told you where we were?"

"Not precisely. But he mentioned the Skeleton Keys . . . and Pus. Incomprehensible to me as clues at first, but I did some checking around, realized what he was talking about, and came here."

"I see. And did he mention anything else?" His voice was very cold, his expression one of great formality.

"Yes," said Percival, his gaze level. He knew he was potentially making things far worse for himself, but he wasn't about to back down. "He told me that people's souls were dying here. And he said what I now understand was, 'Beware High King.' "

"Which would be me," said the High King.

Percival nodded gamely. "Which would be you."

The High King slowly walked toward him, so that he was towering over the smaller Percival. "And are you, Percival of the Moors? Are you being wary? Of me?" When Percival didn't respond, the High King simply shrugged and said, "Well, if you aren't being wary of me . . . then that would be most foolish." But then he smiled broadly, extended his arms from side to side, and said, "Am I not magnificent, Percival of the Moors? Do you not think so? I certainly think I am magnificent. And you?"

Percival could scarcely believe the naked arrogance of the man. It was so ludicrous, so utterly over the top, that it was genuinely funny. Bowing politely, Percival said, "I doubt, Highness, that anyone could possibly think as highly of you as you do yourself."

The sarcasm in Percival's tone went right past the High King. Perhaps he simply agreed with the sentiment. "And the one you now serve . . . he is not remotely as magnificent, is he?"

The question brought Percival up short. His eyes narrowing suspiciously, Percival asked, "What makes you think I serve anyone?"

The High King's eyes grew colder still, even though the smile remained fixed in place. He had no weapons upon him, so theoretically he and Percival would be evenly matched, should something happen. But Percival wasn't kidding himself; he knew he could put up a fight, but in short order this High King would doubtlessly break him in half. "Do me the courtesy, Percival, of not playing word games with me. I know what I know. The one you serve . . . is he as magnificent as I?"

"No," said Percival, feeling that any further discussion along these lines would amount to nothing but foolishness.

Instantly the High King's face warmed up. "Well! It's settled, then!" He smacked his hands together briskly, with enough force that it sounded like a thunderclap in the room. "You will forget your foolish quest, and you will remain here and serve me instead! We will get along magnificently, you and I! You may join my hunting party, you may—"

"My quest?" Percival said, and then quickly amended, "Apologies, Highness, but . . . you assume I have a quest . . ."

The High King had returned to his throne, but he did

not sit. Instead he leaned against the high back and smiled in a matter-of-fact fashion. "The Grail. You seek it."

Percival said nothing.

"I am curious, though," continued the High King, ignoring the fact that Percival had not spoken. It was as if nothing that Percival could possibly have to say would be of any interest to him, because he had already considered everything Percival might respond with. "You are a Moor. A Muslim. Follower of Allah. So you should not accept the notion of the cup of Christ as being especially significant, for you would not see the spawn of Nazareth as a holy figure. Unless . . . are you a Morisco?"

Percival had to smile at that. This High King certainly knew his history. Granada had been the last Moorish kingdom, and it had been conquered by the Spanish in the late fifteenth century. Several years after its conquest, Ferdinand and Isabella of Spain had given the conquered Moors a choice: Convert to Christianity or leave the region altogether. Those who had remained, and converted, were known as Moriscos.

"No," Percival said softly. "But just because I do not believe in the origin of the Cup's properties . . . does not mean that I do not believe in the power of the Cup itself." He did not bother to add that his drinking from the Grail had been what had given him his own despised immortality.

"You are wise," said the High King. "For the power of the Grail predates the Christian Messiah by centuries."

"What?" Percival could scarcely believe what he was being told. "But . . . but how would you know this? How—?"

"I am the High King," he reminded him. "There is very little I do not know, and that which falls under that category is not really worth knowing to begin with."

Percival shook his head. "But . . . if you know the true origin of the Grail, then tell me . . ."

But the High King didn't seem particularly inclined to share his knowledge. In fact, he was beginning to look bored with the entire discussion. "Percival, I weary of this. I have been candid with you simply because I have no reason to fear the truth, for there is none who can gainsay me. The truth is this: Joshua was an interesting man, and we had many lively discussions. Had I known, though, that he would intend to leave, I would have taken steps to make certain he did not. That same option, however, remains a viable one for you. You wish to find the Grail. Need I make clear for you where it is?"

"No," Percival said slowly. "I know." And it was true, he did.

The High King stepped forward, and for a moment Percival thought the behemoth was going to reach over and try to snap his neck. Instead, he placed his hands on Percival's shoulders and said firmly, "Percival . . . you strike me as the sort who is a man of his word. I will give you the opportunity to prove that now. Renounce your previous master, swear undying fealty to me, and I will accept your promise as true. You will live here forever, and you will serve me, and live better than you could possibly have hoped to in the outer world. What say you? If you require time to consider it . . ."

"That will not be necessary, High King," Percival told him. "My loyalty is to another. I give you my word that I will not attempt to leave here with the Grail, even though I feel some proprietary interest, considering it literally vanished from my grasp ten centuries ago. But beyond that, I cannot guarantee."

"Vanished from your grasp?" The High King seemed most interested in this. "Tell me, if you would not mind . . . when was the last time you beheld it."

For a moment, Percival considered telling only part of the truth, or even saying that it was none of this person's damned business (which it wasn't, really). But then he decided that they'd very likely only wind up going around and around about it, plus he was too thoroughly in this person's home ground. Lack of candor was not only useless, but potentially deadly.

"As I told you: ten centuries ago it was. I had . . . obtained it for my liege," he said slowly. Despite the fact that fifty score years had passed, the events were as clear and fresh to him as if they had happened the previous day. "Its miraculous powers had cured him, and I had been told to replace it from whence I had obtained it . . . from the tree at the end of the world. I was told not to drink from it, under any circumstance." Even after all this time, the chagrin on his face was quite evident, the pounding embarrassment clear to any who might have observed him. "And I, like a fool . . . did. I wanted to see what it was like to drink from a vessel that had been sought by so many."

"And since you were not injured in any way," the High King said, smiling mirthlessly, "it granted you eternal life, did it?"

"Yes. First, however, it unleashed a burst of power that near to blinded me. When I recovered my senses . . . the Grail was gone. I never was in its presence again . . ."

"Until now?" inquired the High King.

Percival nodded. "Until now. Until I came to this island."

There was a long silence then, and Percival knew that a good deal was being weighed and considered in that absence of conversation. The High King's face was inscrutable. Percival found him a very difficult individual to comprehend. He seemed ruthlessly intelligent, even noble in his bearing. Yet the self absorption, his very manner, indicated the attitude of one who was little more than a bully. The High King sat back upon his throne and drummed his fingers for a time on the armrests. It was clear that he was not waiting for Percival to speak, but instead was considering the situation.

"So you will tell your liege lord of this place?" he asked finally. "Perhaps even endeavor to return?"

Percival shrugged helplessly. "You are asking me questions that I can't answer. That's hardly fair. I've tried to be honest with you, Highness, out of respect to your . . . well, to whatever position it is that you seem to hold here."

The High King stared at him, as if Percival had suddenly acquired a second head. Clearly he took Percival's words as some sort of challenge to his authority, which had not remotely been the former knight's intention. "My position? 'High King' is sufficiently clear, is it not?" He took a step forward, tilting his head and saying, "You really have no idea, do you? No idea who I truly am?"

Spreading wide his hands, Percival said, "Should I?"

And the High King started to laugh.

He laughed very loud, and very long, and it was one of the eeriest laughs that Percival had ever heard, for there was amusement and contempt and total self-confidence all mixed together in the one sound. "He asks if he should know me! He asks if he should!" the High King roared, as if it were the single funniest sentiment ever uttered by any human being, anywhere, in the history of the species.

Finally, finally, he managed to regain control of himself, wiping away the tears that his unbridled mirth had generated. "Moor," he said at last, "you have given me tremendous amusement. Truly, you have. And your honesty has been appreciated. Tell me, then . . . the name of your liege."

And there was some sort of severe warning in Percival's head then, something that assured him that the last thing he wanted to do was inform the High King of who held Percival's loyalties. "I . . . would prefer not, Highness," he said.

The High King cocked an eyebrow. "I do not recall," said the High King slowly, "asking your preference on the subject. Tell me."

Percival knew at that point that his instincts were solid. "There is no reason for me to divulge that information, Highness. Therefore I shall not."

He had a sense that the High King was going to snap his temper completely. The titan of a man was on his feet, and his body was trembling with barely contained fury. But then, like a dark cloud dissipated by an errant wind, he visibly pushed away the anger that was upon him. Several deep breaths steadied him, and then he shrugged. It seemed an odd gesture coming from one so massive, those corded shoulders rising and falling in feigned disinterest. "It does not matter," he said at last. "The point is . . . I knew you would be coming. It was foreseen. No matter what you say now . . . you will endeavor to leave this place with the Grail. It very likely does not matter, for even if you try to take the Grail, to harness its power, you will not succeed. The Grail is a harsh mistress. It is kept and maintained by force of will, as most harsh mistresses are, and you do not possess that sort of will in sufficient quantity. If you had, it never would have slipped through your fingers centuries ago. I have it now, and I will not chance that you could somehow result in my losing it. In order to avoid that, all I have to do . . . is make certain you do not leave. And you shall not. You will remain here, willingly or unwillingly, it is up to you."

"And if I do not do so willingly?" demanded Percival. "Then what? You shall kill me? Or try to?"

The High King shook his head sadly, looking disappointed that Percival would even say such a thing. "Percival . . . I've no need to kill you. I can simply throw you into a cell and keep you there. We have one ready for you. It is underground. It is quite secure. And you will be able to be there for eternity. That, Percival," and he actually sounded sad about it, "is where you will end your days . . . were they to actually end, which they will not."

Percival took several steps back, eyeing the High King cautiously. The High King, for his part, sat there and watched him, resting his head on his hands and obviously wondering what Percival was going to say or do next.

And Percival turned and bolted.

The move happened so quickly that it caught the High King off guard. Percival knew that in hand-to-hand combat he had no hope of defeating such a powerful-looking foe. The one thing he hoped he had going for him was pure speed. The High King looked too heavily muscled to be able to keep up with Percival when it came to sheer alacrity.

There was a window just across the room, and Percival was already halfway there with no guard in sight and the High King still by his throne, not even having taken a single step after him. His arms and legs pumping, Percival covered half the remaining distance, and then the High King shouted one word:

"*Enkidu!*"

The name struck a horrifying cord in Percival's head, and suddenly he knew who it was that truly faced him, and the impossibility of that barely had time to register when a blur of tawny gold streaked in from nowhere, claws making clacking noises on the floor, and there was a roar in his ears that threatened to blow his eardrums right out the side of his head, and then Percival went down and blackness befell him.

"*My name is Arnim Sandoval. All praise to our God in his glory.*

"*The American President, Arthur Penn, has masterminded yet another attempt to destroy me. I have not accommodated him. I still live, and will outlive him and all his supporters and his cronies. I will continue to fight him for as long as America endeavors to present itself as the world's lawkeeper. A country that claims to embrace diversity has shown itself, through president after president, to be intolerant of other peoples and their rights to conduct their own business as they see fit.*

"*As much as they may claim otherwise, America will only accept a world where the American way of doing things is permitted. Their culture infests all other cultures. Governments are afraid to stand against them.*

"*I strike from hiding. America, with its gunships and airplanes and missiles, call me coward because I hide, even though America's founders fought their oppressors from hiding. I do not have gunships and airplanes and missiles. However, I have my brain . . . and the knowledge that I am right.*

"*The American First Lady lies injured and will likely not recover. Those who believe her a tragic figure should consider her fortunate. She will not have to experience the continuing war of terror that will be conducted against her countrymen until such time that America agrees to total isolationism, to withdraw from the world stage, and to dissolve the imposed union upon the American states that bind it. Like any cancer, America must first be contained, and then made harmless.*

"*America rattles its sabers and calls for war. I am prepared. I have heard these calls before. I have outlasted all those who call for my head. I shall outlast this Arthur Penn, because God is great and God smiles upon me.*

"*God is great. There will be more attacks. You are warned.*"

CHAPTRE
THE SEVENTH

ARTHUR STORMED INTO the Oval Office, and it was everything he could do to resist drawing Excalibur and using it to cleave his desk in half.

He had taken to wearing the great sword again, strapped to his back. It gave him some measure of security . . . not for his physical well-being, but simply because it made him feel like a king again.

Ron Cordoba came in directly behind him, firmly closed the door, and turned to face his commander in chief. "Well, that went well," he said dourly.

At first Arthur paid him no mind whatsoever, instead stalking the Oval Office as if he thought the individual who had singlehandedly turned his life into a living nightmare was hiding there. "Give me a dragon," he snapped suddenly.

"What?" Cordoba clearly had no clue what he was talking about.

"A dragon!" railed Arthur. "Give me a nice, simple dragon tearing up the countryside. Give me an ogre, a Cyclops, any mythical beast. Give me a black knight, guarding a bridge and taking on all comers! Give me an army of foes, be they warriors or soldiers, of any caliber, any stripe. Then give me a horse to sit astride, Excalibur in my hand, and I will defeat them!" He slammed his fist repeatedly on the desk, emphasizing each word. *"I . . . will . . . defeat them!"*

"Mr. President," Ron started once more, trying to sound consoling.

"Two administrations, Ron!" he fairly bellowed. "Two previous administrations have been searching for this little bastard! Two previous administrations consider Sandoval the third rail of global security! They go after him, they don't find him, they look like fools, and they're voted out of office! You said it yourself during the campaign: Arnim Sandoval is where presidents go to die. Yet I took him on."

"You took him on, yes."

"Against your advice."

"Four square against it," Ron agreed. "The thing to remember—"

Arthur was standing at the desk, holding a perfectly sculpted glass globe that had been given to him as a gift by the President of France. And suddenly, seized with a fit of fury, his arm snapped back and he threw the globe with all the strength he could muster. It sailed across the room, smashed into the far wall, and shattered into a hundred pieces.

The sound brought the Secret Service in a heartbeat, pouring in through the door, three men reaching into their jackets in almost perfect unison as they went for their guns. But Arthur brought them up short with a sharp, "Everything is fine." When they hesitated, still unsure of the situation, Arthur raised his voice and ordered them out. They went.

"Shall I call maintenance, Mr. President?" asked Cordoba dryly.

Arthur had already forgotten about the globe, so caught up was he in his fury. "I had to sit there just now, Ron, and listen to the joint chiefs of staff and the heads of our top intelligence agencies tell me that with all their manpower, all their covert ops, all their spy satellites, all the means and ways at their disposal that twenty-first century technology has provided them, they have managed to pinpoint his location to *somewhere on the planet earth.*"

"We're reasonably certain he's not in the White House, sir, so that's one less place."

Arthur lanced him through with a glare. "Are you endeavoring to be amusing, Ron? Trust me, this is most definitely *not* the time."

"Yes, sir," was all Ron said. Then he took a step forward. "Sir, we're hardly at a dead end."

"The shooter, Ron," Arthur said levelly, "one John Smith, if you can believe that, was found dead. Suicide. He was a Sandoval acolyte, trained in his organization, but I was listening during the meeting. We've thus far run down ninety-seven leads on Mr. Smith, all of them taking us nowhere in pursuing Sandoval himself. And you're standing there with the temerity to tell me that we're not at a dead end." Shoving a finger against his temple, he leaned in toward Ron and snarled, *"One of his people put a bullet in my wife's brain, Ron, and you're standing here telling me we're not at a dead end! What sort of chief of staff are you, anyway?"*

And Arthur was taken aback as Ron shouted in return, *"I'm the one who's here!"* There was a fury in him such as Arthur had never seen, and Ron continued, "I'm here! I'm not an ages-old magician! I'm not a knight who drank from the cup of Christ! I'm not a reincarnation of royalty! I'm just a guy, okay? Just this guy, Ronald Cordoba, graduated Yale with a 3.9 GPA, with a doctorate in Political Theory, two ex-wives, a daughter I see *maybe* once a year, during which time I fight like hell to remain in some small way relevant to her life! And I've worked my ass off for you, and maybe I've never been a knight, and I've never slung a sword, but I know politics, I know this country, I know you, and I know that I deserve better than to be condescended to, shouted at, or treated like I'm mud that needs to be knocked off your shoes!" And then as an afterthought, he added, *"Sir."*

There was a deathly silence in the Oval Office then as Arthur regarded Cordoba for a long, thoughtful moment, and then very softly he said, "A doctorate, you say."

Ron looked confused for a moment, and then rallying, he said, "Yes."

"And you've never asked to be called 'Doctor Cordoba.' "

Letting out a long sigh, Cordoba stared at his president and said, "Always seemed a bit pretentious, Mr. President."

"Ron," Arthur began, feeling that there were things that needed to be said. But he was interrupted by a knock at the door, the brisk three-rap knock that always accompanied the diminutive Mrs. Jenkins as she stuck her head in. "Sir . . . the Vice President."

"What about him?" asked Arthur tiredly, rubbing the bridge of his nose.

"He's here, sir."

Arthur and Ron exchanged glances. "Now this is a rare event," noted Arthur. "Send him in, please."

Mrs. Jenkins stepped aside, and Terrance Stockwell entered. He strode forward, looked Arthur in the eye, and gripped his hand firmly. It had taken Arthur some time to become accustomed to such familiarities from people. He was far more used to people dropping to one knee, taking one hand reverently, and touching forehead to his knuckle. He had to say, he preferred that method of greeting quite a bit. Just one of the tragic losses from the old days.

"Good evening, Terrance," said Arthur.

"Evening, Mr. President," said Stockwell formally. Arthur gestured for Stockwell to sit, and he did so on one of the hard-backed chairs. It was dark blue; Gwen had picked out the upholstery. A minor, passing thought, but nevertheless it caused a slight jump in Arthur's heart as he recalled it.

"Thank you for the flowers, by the way," Arthur told him, stepping behind the great desk and sitting in the large chair. "I made certain they were placed quite near Gwen's bed, so that they'll be one of the first things she'll see when she awakens."

Stockwell shifted slightly, as if the chair was uncomfortable for him. "So . . . the doctor's prognosis is that she will be waking up, then? That her condition is . . . reversible? May I ask what her latest condition might be?"

"Terrance," Arthur said patiently, "I would think something is seriously wrong with you if you did not have that information already at your fingertips. When was the last time you received a complete update as to Mrs. Penn's condition?"

"Five minutes ago," admitted Stockwell.

Arthur nodded once. "I suspected as much," he said, leaning back and steepling his fingers. "It will very likely not surprise you to learn that her condition has not changed appreciably in the intervening five minutes. The fact is, Terrance, that although they were able to remove the bullet from her heart, the one in her brain is presently inoperable. There is probably brain damage as well. To all intents and purposes, my wife is very likely dead."

Arthur spoke with a surprisingly calm, even voice, so utterly devoid of upset that it prompted Stockwell to inquire, "Sir, if she's being kept alive purely by machines— as I believe to be the case—why not simply . . . ?"

"Pull the plug?" Arthur gave a brief, bitter smile. "Do not be deceived—either of you—by my relative calm. I am this way because I have to be. Inside I am screaming with fury, and the loudest of those screams tells me to maintain Gwen for as long as human ingenuity enables her to exist. I will not let her go, gentlemen, only to have a brilliant breakthrough in brain surgery be developed a month later, so that I can stand here in the office of the most powerful man in the world—which just so happens to be me—spread my hands wide, and say, 'Whoops.' "

"Very well," said Stockwell, and then his face went from tragic to extremely serious. "The question is . . . what are you going to do about it now?"

"The President has already been briefed, Mr. Vice President," Cordoba said firmly, "on all our military options."

"Then I suggest he take one or all of them," suggested Stockwell. "We cannot afford to respond in half-measures on this, sir—"

"No one is suggesting half-measures, Mr. Vice President," said Cordoba. "The President is prepared to do what needs to be done."

"I should hope so," Stockwell said firmly. "And the American people support what the President needs to do."

"Oh, is that a fact?" asked Arthur, unable to keep the sarcasm from his voice.

The tone seemed to rankle Stockwell somewhat. "Yes, sir, that is indeed a fact, and one that you should be very pleased to hear."

"Believe it or not, Terrance," Arthur shot back, his eyes cold. "Whether or not the people support something is not of particular moment to me. I do what I feel needs to be done, and I will not do what I do not feel needs to be done."

Cordoba started to reply, but Stockwell spoke right over him. He was staring with incredulity at Arthur. "With all respect, Mr. President, what the hell are you saying? That you're going to do nothing about this . . . this outrage! The American people are screaming for blood! They want—"

"War," Arthur said bitterly.

"Yes, sir," Cordoba stepped in, albeit reluctantly. "The Vice President is correct. Our polling numbers could not be more encouraging. Not only do you have a ninety percent job approval rating right now, but an astounding ninety-two percent supportive of the question as to whether we should go to war with Trans-Sabal over this incid—"

Arthur raised his pointer finger and said sharply, "The next man who refers to the attempted murder of my wife as an 'incident,' I will bisect him. Understood?"

Stockwell shrugged, but Cordoba was far too aware of the magic that kept Excalibur invisible and on the President's back. A bisection could happen at any time. Cheery notion.

"Sir," said Cordoba, "we're simply reiterating what the joint chiefs, all your own people, have said . . ."

Arthur rose from behind his desk, and the others started to imitate him reflexively. But he gestured for them to remain seated where they were as he paced slowly, his hands draped behind his back. "My own people. My people, you say. My people told me to drop bombs on Trans-Sabal. They assured me that only military targets would be affected. They said no civilians would be injured. They were wrong, weren't they? The military targets that we rendered inoperative were inoperative before we got there. Dummy targets. Sandoval still lives. The Trans-Sabal government now claims they have no idea where he is. They claim that perhaps he has moved to their neighbors, to the Pamanians, who have a long history of active terrorism of their own."

"He has to be given up," Stockwell said firmly, "that's all there is to it. Either Trans-Sabal does it, or Pamania does it. They have to be brought in line with our thinking."

"I see. And we're to bring them in line by obliterating them, that's the way of it?"

"Mr. President, the people are prepared for war . . ." said Stockwell.

"War?" Arthur sneered. "War? The American people know nothing of war. You call what you propose 'war'?" He leaned in close toward Stockwell. "You get your hands dirty in war. Hand to hand, face to face. You see your opponent, he sees you, and you have at each other. If you're a leader in a war, you stand there on the field of battle. You don't hide in buildings thousands of miles away, or in underground bunkers. You're shoulder to shoulder with your men, until you finally find yourself facing your enemy, and then it's either him or you. Every time I order some sort of strike from hiding or a safe distance, I feel like a coward."

"Mr. President, if I may, that is just absurd," Stockwell replied. "You seem to be laboring under some sort of woefully antiquated definition of what battle should be. You're the commander in chief of the most powerful country in the world, with a million troops at your disposal and enough weaponry to obliterate anyone who tries to stand against us. You need to embrace the modern realities of warfare!"

"It's not warfare," Arthur said quietly. "It's slaughter. And it's not honorable."

Cordoba was rolling his eyes. He naturally knew precisely the sort of mindset that generated Arthur's sentiments, but Stockwell was disbelieving. "Honorable? *Honorable?*" Now he was on his feet, pointing toward the window as if Sandoval were standing right outside. "Do you for one moment think that what Sandoval's people did was honorable? Do you think for one moment that a man who boasts that he's going to use terrorism to destroy America is honorable? What the *hell* is the *matter* with you? Are you going to do what needs to be done, or are you going to sit there and complain and hesitate and do nothing because this scenario doesn't fit some bizarre view of war you have that is shared by no one else?"

"That's enough," Arthur said sharply. He studied them for a long moment, and then turned his back and went to the window. He leaned against it, looking out, looking to the stars twinkling in the cloudless sky as if they would somehow give him the answer he needed.

"Mr. President," Stockwell said, trying to sound moderate, "the simple truth is, we're at war already. We have been for some time. Much of it has been fought through precision strikes, or secretly through intelligence circles. It's just a matter of committing our full might. The government of Trans-Sabal is making noises about setting aside the entire treaty. Our people are now saying that it might have been a stall all along. That they're trying to gather a coalition of other nations, with Sandoval as a figurehead. We have to be vigilant, sir. We don't need another Hitler being grown to fruition right in front of us."

Arthur turned to face him, and he caught his reflection in the mirror mounted across the wall. He felt that he looked much older than he had when the day began. He wondered what he'd look like by the end of the month. The end of the year.

Mrs. Jenkins once again appeared at the door. "Mr. President, the Russian President is calling . . ."

"Very well," said Arthur, feeling more relieved than anything. "All right, gentlemen, I . . . appreciate your time and your opinions. I will take it all under advisement. Thank you."

Stockwell and Cordoba headed for the door, but as Stockwell exited, Cordoba closed it and turned back to Arthur. Then he took a deep breath and said, "Mr. President . . . by striking at Gwen . . . Sandoval has made this extremely personal for you. And your instinct is to avoid involving anyone else in it. To go after him yourself, or to send a champion for him. I know that better than anyone else here because none of them know who and what you are. You're thinking of options that were available to you when you were Arthur, king of the Britons. But you don't have those options now. I'm sorry, you just don't. If you're not happy with who you are, you're going to have to reassess who you're going to be."

"I thank you for your diagnosis, Doctor," Arthur said.

"I mean it, Mr. President."

"So do I, Ron," said Arthur tiredly. "So do I."

NO CHANGE. NO change.

Every day he had been coming down there, and there was no change.

The descent into the lowest reaches of the White House had been disconcerting for Arthur at first; somewhat like getting a sneak preview of dropping down into hell. The elevator had seemed to go down forever, below a point where the indicators registered. The Secret Service men flanked him on either side, always silent, always vigilant, always doing their job. And they had, hadn't they? He was, after all, alive . . . even when matters had reached a point where he really had no interest in whether he lived or died.

The elevator slid smoothly to a stop, and the doors opened onto a hallway that seemed to absorb not only sound and light, but life itself. Arthur strode down the hall, his shoes clacking on the tiled floor, his reflection shimmering in the polished wall. Down one corridor, up another, to the side, and then through a door to the room.

The room.

She lay there in the bed, her head swathed in bandages, unmoving, her breathing assisted by machines. Her eyes remained closed. The only sound in the sterile room came from the devices that sustained her, monitored her.

When he had first seen her like this, it was hard for Arthur to believe that it was really her. Perhaps it was some sort of mannequin, or even a bizarre joke. Far closer to death than life, she really didn't seem recognizable as the glorious Gwen who had been so full of zest. The woman who, in her time with Arthur, had embraced existence with gusto, determined to wring every last bit of joy from the experience.

Nellie Porter was seated next to her. Although she had sworn to Arthur that she did indeed go home sometimes, he could not tell when that might be. Her dedication was stupendous. But Arthur couldn't help but notice that Nellie did not look particularly well. Her face had become drawn, her hair was disheveled. She'd stopped wearing makeup, had just let herself go. For a woman who valued her appearance as much as Nellie always had, it was a shocking transition to see. Arthur had tried to convince her that there were other things she could be doing, other duties in the White House that she could turn her attention to. But Nellie would have none of it. She had made her position very clear to the President: She was aide to the First Lady. And she would remain with her until her duty was discharged. When she had said as much to Arthur, it had been with a defiant tone that practically challenged him to relieve her of her responsibilities. Arthur wisely chose not to take the bait.

He had stopped asking her if there had been any change,

because they both knew that—if there had been—he would have been informed immediately. Instead he simply stood there, gesturing for Nellie to sit back down as she automatically started to rise out of respect to him.

"So how's it going, Mr. President?" she asked, but her voice came out a horrific croak . . . no doubt the result of crying, dehydration, and pure exhaustion. She put up a hand, excusing herself for a moment, picked up a bottle of water, and took a huge gulp from it. It was too huge, and she choked on it. It almost came back up through her nose, but she managed to gain control of herself. Letting out her breath in a slow, relaxed sigh, she repeated the question.

"It goes," he said neutrally. Then, with faint sadness, he said, "They want me to go to war against Trans-Sabal. Not half-measures. Full blown war, on Trans-Sabal and any other country rallying behind the banner and philosophies of Arnim Sandoval."

"Good," said Nellie. "Are you going to do it?"

For a long moment he was silent, the only sounds filling the room being the steady *beep beep* of the monitor and the enforced rising and falling of Gwen's chest.

"Well, that would seem the logical thing to do, would it not?" he asked finally. "Is that what you'd want to see?"

"Yes," Nellie said with such vehemence that Arthur was taken aback. She seemed to be radiating pure fury. "Yes, that's what I'd want to see. I'd want to see Sandoval stripped naked, marched down the street while being pelted with ripe fruit. Then they put him up on a podium and eviscerate him."

"You've been watching *Braveheart* again, haven't you?" he asked, hands behind his back, rocking slightly on his heels like a detective just having made a startling pronouncement.

"Yup," she replied, unabashed. "I have to say, when it comes to brutality, people from ancient times certainly knew their business."

To her obvious surprise, he spoke with a touching melancholy, as if he were recalling something that was irrevocably, irretrievably lost to him. "Yes . . . yes, I daresay that you're correct in that respect," he said, and there was such sadness in the voice that all it could elicit was a look of wonderment from Nellie.

He drew a chair over toward her from across the room and sat opposite her. Leaning forward, fingers interlaced, he said, "Tell me about the first day you met her."

"Oh, well," she laughed, "what do you think, sir? I was nervous as hell. The opportunity to be personal aide to the First Lady . . . it had the potential to be an incredible thrill, a huge challenge. When I went in for the interview, I was panic-stricken.

"I'll never forget, she was seated behind this huge desk." Nellie indicated the length with her hands. From her indications, it seemed to be twice as big as Nellie herself. "She was shuffling papers, moving them around, looking very, very important . . . or at least trying to. She said, 'Just a minute!' and continued to move things around, and I started to get the feeling—accurately, as it turned out—that she had no idea where she was putting anything yet. She just wanted to keep relocating things so she'd look busy and efficient."

"And did you tell her," he inquired, "that you were onto her?"

She was taken aback at the obviousness of the question. "No, of course not!" Then she smiled at the memory. "So anyway, when she was done being as businesslike as she could be, she leaned forward on the edge of her chair to start talking to me . . . and the thing, the chair, it was on wheels, and it just . . ." She slapped her hands together and then skidded one off the other. "Bam! It just spun right out from under her. And Gwen hit the ground like a box of rocks. I sat there and my jaw was somewhere in my lap, and then Gwen just bounced right back up again, grabbed the chair, sat, and pretended that it hadn't happened. But she was trying not to laugh, and I tried not to laugh, and we were trying so hard not to laugh that naturally we just completely broke up. And I came aboard almost immediately, and that was that."

"And that's what you wanted to do with your life?" asked Arthur. He had moved over to Gwen, and he had taken her hand in his. The warmth was still there, and he kept hoping, waiting for it to squeeze his in response, but there was nothing. He might as well have been holding a limp strand of spaghetti.

She looked thoughtful. "Well . . . not when I was younger. When I was younger, I wanted to be a poet. That's what I thought I'd be. But, you know, life hands you some funny twists and turns, doesn't it?"

"It does, yes."

"I remember, Mrs. Penn used to—"

Then she stopped, and her hands flew to her mouth, her moist eyes wide with chagrin and alarm. "Oh my God . . ."

"Nellie," Arthur started to say.

She might not even have heard him. "Oh my God . . . my God, I talked about her in the past tense . . . like she's not even here . . . like she's already . . ."

And then she started to cry, great wracking sobs so convulsive that it seemed as if her ribs were going to break. She cried and moaned like a lost soul, and although Arthur had not expected it to happen, he felt as if this were the final crack in his foundation of forced calm. All the national mourning at his wife's fate, all the dignitaries and notables who had spoken gravely to him over the phone or in person, clucked their sorrow, shared his grief . . . all that paled in comparison to this one woman crying her heart out.

Arthur reached over and gathered her into his arms, held her tight, and with effort kept his own chin steady and his eyes dry. "I'm sorry . . . I'm sorry," she kept moaning to him. "We . . . we were like mother and daughter, except we kept switching . . . some days she was the grown-up, sometimes I was, and why did this happen . . . ?"

The President said nothing, just simply continued to hold her, so that the only sound in the room was her crying and the steady beeping from the monitors. But within him, a roiling cloud of fury built and built, seeking release.

THUNDER ROARED OVERHEAD, splitting the skies and ripping free the huge cold raindrops that cascaded down. A change in temperature of a few degrees would have caused snow, but instead it was a rainstorm, the kind that fell with such ferocity that it couldn't possibly last long.

Arthur didn't care about the storm's duration, nor about the Secret Service men who were following him, or the crying woman he'd left behind. He cared only about the fury within fighting to be unleashed and he charged into the Rose Garden, uncaring whether word got around that the President had completely and utterly lost his mind.

He tore off his jacket, threw it upon the ground as the rain hammered at him, slicking down his hair, running down his face into his eyes and half blinding him. Yanking off his necktie and tossing that aside as well, he faced the statue of the person whom he had once called "teacher," and he howled in red-hot fury, "*Are you happy? Are you happy, demon spawn? Are you?*"

There was no reply, of course, from the statue, nor could there be, but that did not deter Arthur. He circled the statue, and bellowed, "You *never* liked her! Never! Not when I first met her, and she was a scared, frightened young thing, given me by her warlord father to cement a treaty! How much of her involvement with Lancelot was your doing, eh? For all I know, you arranged it! You wanted her out of the way, because you had your own plans for me, and she was a random factor! What did you really want of me, Merlin? Did you serve heaven, or did you serve the interests of the creature that spawned you? Was I to bring order, as you claimed, or chaos, as resulted? And now she came back to me! *Back to me!* A merciful God returned her, reincarnated her, and that made you even more insane with fury, because once again," and he stabbed a finger at the statue, "you had your plans for me! To put me on the world stage, to drive me forward, always forward! You know the difference between you and her? You never cared about what I wanted! You never even bloody asked! Everything that I accomplished, I did for you, Merlin, and when you were gone, then for her! She helped keep your dream alive, and even from beyond the grave, you still hated her! She even saved you from Morgan, but that didn't assuage your jealousy! And now she lies as one undead, and I can hear you laughing somewhere, Merlin! *Laughing, you demon-spawned bastard! At me! At her! At all of this! I have none to love me, none to guide me! Even Percival has deserted me!* Why in hell did you do this to me, Merlin!? Bring me to this time, this place, and abandon me, and let her be taken away from me as well! Damn you! Damn you to the hell I hope you're writhing in! Why couldn't you have let me die a thousand years ago? Why couldn't you have simply left me alone!"

And he was pounding on the statue, hitting it with all his fury. It was a futile endeavor, the statue neither noticing nor caring. Arthur raised his trembling hands, saw the blood pouring from the knuckles, being washed away by the pounding rain, and he gasped out a pitiful sob.

That was when he heard a low, mocking voice from behind him, saying, "Could you be *any* more melodramatic?"

He turned and saw her, separating from the long shadows. They stood there in the pouring rain, facing each other.

"How unworthy of you," she said. "Railing against your fate in the rain, pounding on dead magicians. Grow up, Arthur."

He looked at her levelly. "That," he said with a hint of warning, "is hardly the proper way to address one who holds your life in his hands."

She sighed in the manner of someone who was endeavoring to placate someone considered not really worth placating. "Hail, Arthur Pendragon, Utherson, former king of the Britons," she said formally, and bowed slightly at the waist.

Arthur inclined his head, and his voice raw from shouting, he replied, "Hail and well met Basiliskos, foremost of All Monsters, Scourge of All Living Things." And then Arthur reached behind his back, gripped a hilt invisible to all, and withdrew it. Excalibur gleamed in the darkness as he held it before him.

"You called me. I am come," said Miss Basil, eyeing the sword watchfully. "Have you brought me here to try and slay me?"

"No."

"Then," she said, "may we get out of the rain? Warm me, as my cold blood would prefer, and then we may talk of whatever you wish."

CHAPTRE
THE EIGHTH

I T IS ONE *month before the presidential election, and Arthur knows that something very serious, something very bad is going to happen. He is many things, but he is not stupid. He knows that it involves Merlin and Miss Basil, and he knows that it is going to happen soon.*

He is working until all hours in his office. Merlin is working as well, and he has been very quiet of late. He has resisted Arthur's questions, become even more taciturn than usual. There is a ticking of a clock nearby and it may be Arthur's imagination, but it seems as if it is getting louder and louder. There is a fearsome storm rolling in, a storm very similar in size and intensity to the one that will occur years later, when Arthur will face Miss Basil in the Rose Garden. Arthur does not know of that time to come, and yet he senses abruptly that something final is about to occur.

"Merlin," he says, half rising from his chair although he does not know why. Merlin looks up at him. He seems smaller, weaker than ever before, and there is a haunted look in his eyes. Is that fear? That cannot be fear. Not from Merlin Demonspawn. "Merlin?" he says again, and although he does not know why, he glances to the clock. The minute hand is nearly pointing at the number twelve. The hour hand is already there.

"Arthur," Merlin says, and it is the air of someone who is about to say something that he has been putting off for as long as he could. "Arthur . . . it is time."

"What?" Arthur does not understand.

"To pay the piper, Arthur," Merlin tells him. His black pants are neatly pressed, the line on his blue blazer immaculate. "The payment can be delayed for a week or an age or an eon, but sooner or later the bill comes due. It's due now."

"What are you talking about? What's happening?" Arthur raises his voice over the thunder, crackling like a boulder rolling over crumpled paper.

"Immortals can be restrained for a time, but not forever. I knew that when I restrained her." Merlin sighs, brushing a hank of hair from his face. "But the time is up. Do not interfere, Arthur. It is between her and me."

And still Arthur does not grasp it, but suddenly the lightning, which had been roiling through the sky, seems to leap right into the office. The impact knocks Arthur back, slamming him against the wall, momentarily stunning the once-king. He blinks furiously, trying to will away the blinding flash, and he hears Merlin's voice, but from within his head rather than without, saying, "Farewell, Wart. Remember you flew as a hawk. Time for you to fly alone."

There is a chiming, echoing, filling the office. It is the chiming of the clock, striking midnight, like a death knell.

"Merlin!" shouts Arthur, as the office recaptures its shape. There is no sign of the boy wizard, but the storm is a fearsome thing now.

He pulls Excalibur from its sheath and it glows in his hand, firm and warm, and he clutches the mighty blade with both hands and focuses on Merlin, Merlin, begging and pleading as a parched man would clutch a divining rod searching for water.

Ultimately he has no idea if the sword is actually attending to him, or if it is pure instinct that guides him, or some final last-minute change of mind and cry for help from Merlin, but something within him says, Up, up damn you, up, and Arthur is gone, out the door. As he runs past Miss Basil's desk he sees a depression in the chair, only just now rising, that would indicate someone had *been sitting there until recently, and that is when he suddenly comprehends. Not everything . . . but enough.*

He does not wait for the elevator, instead sprinting up the building's emergency stairs, and the thunder seems to be everywhere, even here in the stairwell. The stairwell ends at a doorway, on which there is a padlock. One swipe of Excalibur and the lock clatters away, as Arthur kicks the door open, accompanied by a thunderclap for dramatic effect. He bursts onto the rooftop just in time to hear a high-pitched male scream such as he has never heard before come from what can only be Merlin's throat, and there, revealed by a sheet of lightning across the sky, is Merlin as solid rock.

Not three feet away from him is a creature that seems to be blurring and shifting in shape, and it is Miss Basil who turns to face him. Her eyes are green, her throat scaled, her manner unhurried. "This is none of your affair, Utherson," she says, every "s" sibilant. "And it is over."

"No," Arthur growls. He clutches Excalibur, and there is a pounding behind his eyes, madness of loss steeling his heart and clearing his mind.

"My servitude to Merlin was at an end. He faced me in combat, as he knew would happen eventually." She makes no move, but her confidence is an awful thing to behold. "He looked into my eyes, saw all the wretchedness and evil that filled his soul, saw himself as he truly was without the rationale and justifications and little lies that all creatures of human skin tell themselves to get through each dreary day. All who meet my gaze beg for death rather than live with that knowledge, and I provide them with that which they ask for. For Merlin, well . . . it was different." She half smiles at that. "The stone in his heart, the stone in his soul, has overwhelmed him. He is on the outside as he was on the inside, and all is just. One side, Pendragon. Our business here is at an end."

Arthur does not move aside. Instead he advances, slowly, and although his body is trembling with fury to be unleashed, still is the great blade Excalibur not shaken in the least. The point targets the heart of Miss Basil, and she sees murder in his eyes. She does not retreat, but her confidence diminishes ever so slightly. "You cannot withstand my gaze any more than he could, Arthur," she warns. "I do not desire to kill you, for I do not kill kings lightly, but I shall not simply allow myself to be slaughtered."

He does not respond. He keeps coming, and Miss Basil tosses aside the final bits of her human imposture as one would dispense with a threadbare coat, and he keeps coming, and she is a terrible thing, a horror to behold, with those appalling green eyes that can burrow into the recesses of the soul and shred it, and the scaled skin, and fangs bared, her small but powerful wings unfurling, and from that mouth a hissing like a thousand broken radiators in a thousand tenement buildings, and a shriek like the factory whistles of old London sending dreary and hunched workers home to their lives of poverty and starvation . . .

And still he comes. The great blade Excalibur swings back and forth, a deadly scythe, and the Basilisk in full flower of her strength sends her mental power boring straight into the heart and mind of Arthur, and it makes no difference. For Arthur's anger is his shield, his virtue is his armor, and the fire in his soul burns away any doubts that the Basilisk could even hope to rise within him.

And for the first time in time out of mind, the Basilisk falls back, hissing and spitting and snapping, but Arthur will have none of it. She tries to flee, and Arthur slams forward with Excalibur, driving the great blade down and through the lower part of her great whipping tail, pinning her to the spot. She lets out a shriek that is drowned by the thunder, and then she is down, and he has one foot upon her long throat. He yanks Excalibur from her body, swings it up and is about to bring it down upon her throat, ready to cleave her head from her body.

And she cries out to him, "You do not want to do this, Pendragon!"

"Oh, do I not?" he snarls, but for the slightest moment the blade hesitates.

She speaks quickly, desperately, knowing that at any moment the mighty sword can come singing downward, and she will be done. "You must not destroy me! I am a work of art!"

The blade does not move. He is unimpressed.

And still she speaks, the torrent of words rushing from her. "When Sodom and Gomorrah were wiped clean by the wrath of

God, I, who was in the heart of the depravity, survived. Pursued have I been by heroes of all size, of all stripe, of all race, and still I have survived them all, because I am meant to! If you slay me, you slay a piece of living history. One of the great immortals. All that I have seen, all that I know, would die with me. You may think me evil, but I am truly one of God's masterpieces. To destroy me is to scorn his accomplishment. And more . . . the wheels of fate turn and turn for me as for others, and they are not done turning for me yet. I feel it!"

"What you shall feel is cold steel through your throat, and then oblivion reaching up to claim you." Overhead the thunder rumbles to punctuate this pronouncement, and rain begins to fall in large drops.

"On my honor, I know my time is not yet done, and I know that you need me!"

He spits upon her, full in her face. "A creature such as you has no honor, and I have no need of you, now or ever." The rain begins to soak him. He is in his shirtsleeves, the shirt already sticking to his chest.

"Wrong, and wrong again," she says, and now she speaks with some of the old confidence, although she remains wary. Her forked tongue flickers out her mouth for a moment and then withdraws. "I possess more honor than such as you can ever know, and you will need me. Think, Arthur . . . think with your mind, not your sword. Slay me now, and it will not bring Merlin back. He is done and gone. But allow me to live, and at a time of your choosing in the future, you may ask any boon of me it is within my power to grant."

"After you have taken revenge on those near and dear to me," he shoots back.

But she shakes her head. "No, Utherson. This I swear: No harm shall come to you or any within your sphere. I shall take my leave of you and our paths will ne'er cross again until you will it. And when you are ready to seek a boon of me, you need but summon me and I shall come to you."

"What could I possibly need you for?"

"You will know when it happens," she says, and there is some-

*thing in that voice, in those words, that suggests she knows more
than she is telling.*

*For a long moment, there is no sound but for the rain splattering.
Then, pressing the point of his sword against her throat just hard
enough to garner a gasp from her, he says, "What if I desire more?
What if I wish you to be in my power, my service, as you were for
Merlin."*

*She does not hesitate. "Then slay me now," she says, her green
eyes narrowing, "for I should rather be dead than a slave ever
again." Having had her say, she rests her head back and prepares
for the killing stroke.*

*Another moment then, longer than before, and he lets her wait
and wonder, but in his heart he already knows, and slowly he
withdraws the blade from her throat. She lifts herself up, never
taking her eyes from him. "You will not regret this, Utherson," she
tells him.*

*"I regret it already," he replies. He does not lower his sword or
his guard for an instant, despite her promises. Her vast, twining
serpent form looms above him, looking down at him. It remains odd
to hear a human voice emerging from such an ungodly form. He
continues, "If I have need of you, I shall summon you . . . how?
Through mystic incantation? A crystal ball of some kind you will
give me?"*

*She looks at him with disbelief. "Arthur . . . don't be an ass.
This is the twenty-first century," comes the voice of Miss Basil from
within the great monster, dripping with scorn. "I have a website:
www.basiliskos.com. Contact me in that manner."*

He should laugh. He doesn't.

*She shakes her large, diamond-shaped head. "You have yet to
fully accept what century you live in, Arthur. Have a care. It will
be the death of you."*

*There is a flash of lightning then, so bright that Arthur's arm
flies of its own accord to block his vision of it, and when the lightning is gone . . .*

. . . so is she.

*   *   *

"**T**EA?" MISS BASIL nodded, and Arthur lifted the tea-pot and carefully poured out a cup of hot water, which darkened moments later as the flavor from the leaves seeped through the tea strainer already in the cup.

"Gwen furnished this place herself," Arthur said, indicating the private room in the residence to which he and Miss Basil had retired. It was a sedate little chamber, done up in comforting pastels with a painting of John Adams hanging, and a single canopied bed against the far wall.

The Secret Service men had been dumbfounded, shaken, and profoundly disturbed when Arthur had emerged from the Rose Garden with Miss Basil at his side. She was wearing no identification tag as was standard-issue for the White House, and they could not begin to fathom how the hell she had gotten in there. They were extremely bothered by the notion—particularly during these times when security was at its highest level, and assassins seemed to lurk around every corner—that some woman could simply slip into the White House. Arthur made no effort to appease the Secret Service men's bewilderment, since he likely would have failed at it anyway. Instead he had said, with darkly furrowed brow, "Miss Basil is black bag covert ops, highest level. I decided to have her test security procedures. Her presence here indicates just how lacking they are. Work on that."

"That was very cruel, Utherson," she had commented in a low voice as they headed down the hallway, with Arthur's protectors keeping a respectful distance.

Arthur had merely shrugged. "So security around here will become even more stringent. Personally, I have no problem with that."

Now they were alone, an ancient king and an ancient monster, sipping tea in the White House. No words passed between them for a while. "Good tea," Miss Basil commented finally.

"Nothing but the best." He put his cup down carefully. "You did not," he said severely, "respond to my e-mail."

"I know, and for that I truly apologize," she said, bowing her head. "I did not have access to a computer for a time. By the time I did, I had already heard your little 'slip' on television. Very canny."

"Well, I am the President of the United States and the once and future king, so I'm not entirely a lackwit."

"Indeed." She sipped the tea again, and regarded him with her glittering green eyes over the rim of the cup. Her legs were daintily folded at the knee, and Arthur couldn't help but notice that—whereas he'd been dripping from the storm outside—she looked completely dry. Damnedest thing, that. "So, Arthur . . . a cowardly foe has struck at you from hiding."

"Not like the old days, is it?" Arthur sighed.

"You paint a bit more rosy of a picture than it was, Arthur," she said reprovingly. "Even in those days, there were still assassins, hired by men with little honor to strike in a dishonorable fashion. Still, I agree, there was far less rank cowardice then than now. Furthermore, do you know the main difference between now and then?" When he shook his head, she leaned forward as if she were warming to a subject. "Life was cheaper back in the day. Men stood ankle-deep in defecation, disease, and death every day of their lives. Women popped out children by the cartload since they knew that barely half of them would likely survive to adulthood. Men are less anxious to make themselves targets unnecessarily these days because they anticipate being around for much longer than we ever thought possible."

"We?" Arthur laughed self-mockingly at that. "I do not see how 'we' are qualified to speak of such things. I, a centuries-old king, and you, a creature who very likely has been around long enough to have suggested the wonders of apples to Eve in the Garden."

"Perhaps," she said noncommittally. "It might have been me. Or a relative. I don't think I shall say. A woman, after all, should be allowed a few mysteries at least, don't you think?"

Arthur said nothing; he merely stared down into the tea as if all life's answers could be found within the neat white cup with the White House emblem upon it.

"So," she said finally, "what would you of me, Pendragon?"

He took a deep breath and let it out slowly. "I want you to find the Holy Grail."

At that, Miss Basil laughed. "Oh, is that all?" she demanded, seeming tremendously amused by the prospect. "Now there is an intriguing notion: me, one of the greatest evils of humanity's history, on a quest to obtain the mythic relic considered the holiest of the holies. Do you find any irony in that, Utherson?"

"I care not for your concepts of intrigue or irony, Basiliskos," Arthur told her firmly. "What I care about is that the Holy Grail is her only chance. She resides in a twilight between life and death. No one should have to exist there. No one. The Grail may well cure her."

"It might," she allowed. "However, one would have thought that—if the Grail did exist—Percival in his wanderings would have located it. Do you not think so?"

Arthur, to his annoyance, could not meet her level gaze, although he held no fear of dying at her hands. "I do not know where Percival is. That does not entirely surprise me."

"It surprises me," said Miss Basil. "He is a knight, sworn to his liege lord, namely you. I would think that with his sense of duty, nothing could pry him from you."

Smiling slightly at the recollection, Arthur tapped the edge of the cup with his spoon. It gave out a tinny clinking noise. "Percival is by nature a questing knight. He was chafing remaining in one place, under my direct supervision."

"Really." She eyed him with skeptical curiosity, even challenge. "I seem to recall that before he reentered your service, Percival spent years as a washed-out drunk and homeless vagabond. Pray tell, for what was he questing during that time?"

"For himself. And for a reason not to be that way."

She promptly opened her mouth to reply, but then shut it again. "Very well," she admitted, "that is a valid enough response, I suppose."

"In any event, I gave Percival duties that would give him plenty of freedom. I fully anticipated the possibility that wanderlust might seize him, or he might find himself falling into some sort of quixotic excursion that fired his imagination. Oh, he swore that that would never happen," and he waved off the notion dismissively, "but I knew better."

"And have you given no consideration to the possibility," she suggested, "that Percival might be in some sort of trouble and requiring your assistance?"

"Percival survived just fine nearly half a millennia without my help," Arthur pointed out, regarding her skeptically. "It would be the height of condescension and insult to think that Percival is in a predicament from which he cannot extricate himself. I have utter faith in his resourcefulness, Miss Basil, even if you do not."

With a shrug of her slim shoulders, she said, "I have given virtually no thought whatever to Percival's resources, or lack thereof. I leave such speculations to the mind and imagination of a king, where such things rightly belong."

He rose from the chair, but did not move from it. Instead he leaned forward, his knuckles resting lightly on the tabletop. "Also," he continued, "I want you to find Arnim Sandoval. I want you to find him, and his cronies, and bring them down. I want an end to their threat."

Miss Basil cocked an eyebrow lazily at that, and leaned back in her chair. Steepling her fingers and peering over the fingertips, she inquired, "A one-woman black bag operation. Is that how you see me, Pendragon?"

"You are not a woman," Arthur reminded her. "At least not in the way that anyone could remotely understand it."

"Yes, thank you for that clarification." She tilted her head, making no attempt to disguise her quite obvious curiosity.

"So you would bypass a war? Take matters into your own hands in order to avoid it?"

"And why not?" demanded Arthur in return. He hesitated, looking both annoyed that he had to explain himself, and relieved that he was facing possibly the only being left to him in the world to whom he could speak his own mind—and she might well understand him. "I was a king. Ruler of a monarchy. It was not a democracy, nor did we hinge our decisions on such frail, nonsensical items as small dangling pieces of paper hanging from punch cards. My own hands is where I am accustomed to having matters. If there's been any one thing that I find suffocating about this position in which Merlin put me, it is having to politic, deal, and finesse my way through alliances with little pissant representatives who aren't fit to service my chamber pot, much less hold the awesome responsibilities that their elections have given them!"

His voice had been getting louder and louder in his ire, but he took several deep breaths after the initial outburst and managed to calm himself. He paused for a long time, and Miss Basil was more than content to wait patiently.

"Besides," he admitted finally, "it would be impossible to fight the sort of war that America is accustomed to—softening up the enemy with air assault—without hurting noncombatants and civilians. I can't ever . . ." He stopped, stared into the cup of tea he was holding as if the secrets of the world were within.

"Arthur . . . ?" Her voice sounded surprisingly gentle when one considered that she was an ages-old monster.

"There was one war," he suddenly said, "one centuries-ago battle I remember, against this petty warlord." He shook his head. "I look back on it now, and he was such a . . . a nothing. A pretender. But he was arrogant and self-assured, and made no effort to hide how much he despised me just because of who I was. His name was Malkon. I could have ignored him, could have let him just shout and bristle and make his noises, for he could not have harmed me. Not

really. But no. No, I had to let my . . ." Arthur drummed
his fingers on the tabletop. "My stupid, wretched pride get
the better of me. So I marched my soldiers to his stronghold,
and he had . . ." He gestured helplessly, as if trying to form
images with his hands since words were failing him. "He
had taken people . . . his own people, citizens, helpless people . . . and tied them to his weapons of war. To his catapults, to his war machines, to the very walls of the city, as
human shields. Spreadeagled, helpless, struggling against
their bonds."

Miss Basil made a clucking noise in the back of her throat.
"And they call me a monster," she said disdainfully.

"And he stood there, at the top of the parapets, and
taunted me, and challenged me to attack, certain that I
would not. He was testing me. I was a young king at the
time, you see, and everything was a test. Everything. My
every move was being scrutinized by hundreds of men, great
and small, all with their own ambitions." He turned to her
then, faced her, and spoke with an almost desperate energy,
as if he had to make her comprehend. "I was trying to forge
a nation of peace . . . but peace only comes from strength. I
could not let myself appear weak, for if I did, my allies
would have deserted me, and those who remained with me
would have done so only because they were waiting for their
moment to strike me down and take power from me."

Her eyes narrowed as, very quietly, she said, "You ordered
the attack."

"Yes."

"You attacked through the innocent people."

"Yes."

"You had a choice."

"One choice, Basiliskos, is no choice," Arthur told her. "I
told you why I could do nothing else."

"No, you've told me why your ego and your own fears
would not let you do anything else," she corrected him.
"Whether you could actually have done something else,
well . . . you did not choose to explore that option, did you?"

"No," he said, and his eyes were haunted. Visions of people strapped to walls, writhing as flaming arrows hit near them, or struck them square on . . . visions of people attached to war machines, screaming as great rocks descended upon them, hurled by Camelot catapults, crushing the machines, crushing the people . . . these and other horrors danced behind his eyes, and he could see them all, and saw himself sitting astride a great horse, watching it all, watching it all until finally he had to look away. "No . . . I did not choose that option. We were as careful as we could be under the circumstances . . . but we did not allow ourselves to be dissuaded from what needed to be done."

"And Malkon?"

"I beheaded him myself," Arthur said with grim satisfaction. "That, at least, I was able to attend to."

"So all in all . . . it was a good day for you, then."

Slowly Arthur turned and looked at her, pulling his gaze away from scenes centuries agone. "I thought so at the time," he said simply. Then he took in a deep breath and shook his head. "And then every night, for weeks thereafter, I dreamt of that scene, of those people. Of the horror of people writhing in the light of a burning city. I swore on that day that no civilians, no innocents or bystanders, would be hurt if I could humanly prevent it. That day, Miss Basil, was one of the cornerstones upon which chivalry and the Round Table were built. Might *for* right, and the protection of the helpless." He glanced through the window as if he could see with his unaided eye all the way to Trans-Sabal, all the way to Sandoval's lair. "Sandoval not only doesn't care about the innocent . . . he revels in their suffering, as does any bully. My refusal to do so is what differentiates me from him."

"That, and the fact that you're remarkably handsome," suggested Miss Basil.

"Yes, well . . . there's that, of course." He shrugged and even smiled slightly at the momentary leavening of the mood. But all too quickly, he became somber again. "Now you have some understanding, at least, why the notion of war is anathema to me."

"Then might I observe," she suggested, "that—considering you are 'commander in chief'—you might be in the wrong line of work."

"Your opinions are not really all that relevant," he said, sounding a bit stiff. He straightened his jacket then, squared his shoulders, made himself look that much more presidential. "Now then," he said briskly, "how long do you think it will take you to accomplish these things?"

"Accomplish them?" She sounded not only skeptical, but amused, as if Arthur was speaking in an alien tongue. "My dear Pendragon, it's not that simple."

"It isn't?" He seemed surprised.

She had been leaning so far back in the chair that she was almost supine, but now she came forward and it was almost as if her neck was elongating, her head snapping like a cobra's. For a moment Arthur was on guard, but she halted and simply smiled.

"What's in it for me?" she asked.

"For you?" He stared at her uncomprehendingly, and felt anger beginning to bubble within him. "Your integrity, for one thing! Your honor!"

Her arched eyebrow reached almost to her scalp. "You question my honor?"

"If you give me reason to, yes!" he said, raising his voice. "I spared your life, and in exchange, you promised that I could call upon you to do whatever I bade you to do!"

"My, my, my." She laughed, and there was something in her voice that chilled Arthur with its ageless confidence and disdain. "The tricks that memory plays on one. The certainty with which you speak, Pendragon. So much certainty for one so wrong."

"What are you talking about?" he asked dangerously. "You swore—"

"I swore," she overspoke him, "in very clear English. If

you could not comprehend it, that is hardly my problem. What I said was that you could ask any boon of me. 'Any' as in one. 'Boon' as in the singular. Do not speak of requests for multiple tasks, because they are not yours to ask, nor are they mine to give. Nor is even the one yours for the taking."

On the outside, he was absolutely immobile, like a lion waiting to pounce, but his insides were twisting with fury. "And why would that be?" He could barely get the words out in a calm voice.

"I said you could *ask* any boon of me. I *never* said I would *grant* it."

Arthur was across the room so quickly that even Miss Basil, with the reflexes of her serpent nature, was caught unprepared. His right hand swung, and had he been holding Excalibur, her shoulders would have been lonesome for her head. He was empty-handed, as it turned out, but he drove forward and his fist connected squarely with the side of her face. Miss Basil, who had been leaning back in the chair, was knocked clean off her perch. The chair clattered backward and she hit the floor with a thud.

Instantly the door flew open as Secret Service men started to enter, and Arthur whirled, his face purpling. *"Get out!"* he snarled. The agents looked at the President, looked at the woman lying on the ground rubbing her jaw, looked at one another, and silently withdrew from the room. Arthur wondered if word was going to be leaked that the President of the United States had taken up the hobby of battering women. At that point he didn't especially care. He turned to face her, reached his hand back to grasp the invisible hilt of Excalibur, the mighty sword strapped to his back.

If Miss Basil was perturbed over the prospect of suddenly finding herself at the mercy of an infuriated king and cold, enchanted steel, she did not let it show. She remained where she was, but her voice was hard-edged as she said, *"Now* who stands in danger of dirtying his precious honor? I spoke plainly last time we met. You know I did. You did not think to clarify it, nor did I volunteer the information. We had an arrangement. If you attack me now, it's simply because you have decided after the fact that you don't like it, and would rather annihilate the one with whom you made it than deal within the parameters you agreed to."

Between clenched teeth he spat out, "You are the very devil, Basiliskos."

"Eve said much the same," commented the Basilisk dryly. "And we all know what a deal with the devil is worth . . . and what it requires. You thought to get off cheaply."

"I should have killed you when I had the chance." His hand still hovered over the hilt. "I could kill you now."

Somehow the Basilisk sensed that if she made the slightest aggressive move, Arthur would give in to the impulses raging within him and carve her up. Cannily, she simply stayed where she was, maintaining her human form, looking up at him with affected wide-eyed innocence. "You very possibly could . . . and that is not an admission I make lightly, nor one that many who walked this world could claim. But if you slay me, then you will have neither your Grail nor your vengeance against Sandoval . . . whichever you opt to pursue."

Slowly, very slowly, he lowered his hand. He did not, however, extend it to her to help her up. Instead he simply glowered at her, and Miss Basil hauled herself to her feet, dusting herself off. "That was an enchanting encounter," she said.

"So am I to understand," he said, "that you are asking me to choose between the healing of my wife . . . and the destruction of he who assaulted her?"

"Yes," she said reasonably. She picked up the fallen chair, placed it upright, and sat in it once more. All the time she did so, she did not take her eyes off him, perhaps concerned that he would suddenly change his mind and decide that the world would be better off without the Basilisk in it. "And I can see the predicament you face." Her voice sounded almost sympathetic to his plight, but he knew that truly she was mocking him. "On the one hand, you have the pros-

pect of bringing back your beloved wife from—as you say—
the twilight within which she presently dwells. However,
in doing so, you will be accomplishing an action that will
largely benefit two people and two people only: you and
your wife. On the other hand, if I destroy Sandoval and his
cronies—"

"Can you? And will you?" His eyes were hard. "Spell it
out for me."

"Yes," she said with no hint of prevarication. "I can, and
will, put an end to him, and to his organization. And I can,
and will, do so in a way that the world knows Sandoval is
no longer a threat. And should I do that, why . . . think of
all the future terrorist acts that will not occur thanks to
you . . . and me, of course," she added, almost as an afterthought. "Of course, in that event, you will not have the
Grail in hand, and Gwendolyn may never recover. A tragic
choice." Her lips twitched. "I'm pleased I don't have to make
it."

A silence hung over them then, for there was something
else remaining, and they both knew it.

"What do you want?" he asked finally. "You said that the
boon was not simply mine for the taking. You want something in exchange, I presume." She nodded almost imper-
ceptibly. "Well? Out with it. What do you want, devil? My
soul?"

Miss Basil laughed lightly at that. "Arthur, Arthur . . .
how quaint. Not your soul literally. And what I want, really,
is a very little thing in the grand scheme of the world, and
what you will get in return—either the end of a formidable
foe, or the return of your beloved mate. No, no . . . I don't
want your soul." Then she stopped laughing, and Arthur
was sure a chill swept through the room as she said,
"Not . . . your whole soul. Just a piece of it."

"Name your price," he said stiffly.

She told him.

Giving it to her was easier than he expected. In retrospect,
he would have thought that agreeing to it should have been
harder than it was. But it wasn't. Indeed, the choice of which

boon to request was harder than the meeting of the Basilisk's price . . . but he made that choice as well, even though it sickened him to the portion of his soul that he had remaining.

"I'm sorry," he whispered when the agreement was made, and the Basilisk was gone, but it was impossible for him to be sure just to whom he was apologizing.

CHAPTRE
THE NINTH

†

 THE DARKNESS SLOWLY lifted from around Percival, to be replaced by another darkness altogether.

It had been quite a long time since Percival had been knocked unconscious. It had been back during the Depression era, when there had been a riot in Birmingham, Alabama, that erupted from the sense of frustration overwhelming the city. A police officer's truncheon had knocked him cold. When he'd come to, his brain having sloshed around in the brainpan like a loose omelet, he'd endeavored to obtain medical assistance. No hospital would admit him. "We're full," they'd told him before admitting white patients who came in behind him. Eventually he'd healed on his own; the enchantment of the Grail that still flowed through his veins even after all these centuries had attended to that. Still in all . . . it had not been a happy time for him, and the sensation of that club smashing him in the head was as vivid now as it was for him then.

But this was a new assault, with a feeling all its own, and there had been no club involved. Instead there had been a creature, a creature that walked like a man and, if the legends were accurate, spoke like one as well. A creature of bestial strength. Its breath had been hot and overwhelming, and the deep-throated roar had seemed more appropriate to the wilds of the Congo than the interior of an immaculate, polished building of marble and ivory.

As Percival slowly came to full consciousness, he fought off the nausea that threatened to wash over him in waves. Instead he took in a deep breath through his nose, smelled the dankness in the air, heard the steady dripping of water from nearby. All of this told him, even before he managed to open his eyes and fully view his surroundings, that he was in some sort of dungeon.

He'd hoped it would be decorative or innovative in some way, but he was disappointed to see it was just a plain old dungeon. Heavy walls of brick and mortar, and at the far end a door of metal . . . or, at the very least, a metal sheet attached to heavy wood that would be impenetrable to anything short of a jackhammer. There was a very, very narrow window at the top of one wall through which Percival might have been able to escape if he'd possessed the ability to transform into a squirrel. Unfortunately that was not a power in his repertoire, thus limiting his options all the more.

Hay was strewn around the floor, which was of the same sturdy surface as were the walls. The situation did not look especially promising. His fatigues were lying in a heap.

Percival took a step toward the door to examine it, and then staggered. The room wavered around him, and this time the nausea overwhelmed him. He sagged to his knees and dry-heaved violently, bracing himself with his hands flat on the floor. It seemed an eternity before he finally managed to compose himself. He had a feeling that if he weren't who he was, with the restorative and recuperative powers he possessed, he'd probably be suffering from a concussion. Slowly Percival stood again, and this time, although there was slight dizziness, it wasn't anything he couldn't handle.

It was a damned heavy door, all right. There was a large keyhole that doubtlessly accommodated some sort of very old-style key. Above it sat a massive iron ring, welded to the door so thoroughly that nothing short of a rampaging elephant tied to the opposite end of a chain could possibly pull it off. So obviously there was some sort of latch operated via a key outside, and the door was pulled open and closed via the ring (which doubtless had a mate on the other side). He glanced over with only mild hope before he verified for himself that the hinges were, of course, on the outside. Well, no one said this was going to be easy.

Percival's strength was considerable, certainly above the norm, and had only grown since he had cleaned himself up and left his days of alcoholic haze far behind. But he was not a superman. He couldn't simply reach out, seize the door with one hand, and yank the thing free of its frame. This knowledge didn't stop him from trying, however. He gave several experimental pulls, but was rewarded with nothing in return.

"All right," he said softly to himself.

He heard footsteps just outside the door then, and a very small window—narrow enough to reveal a pair of eyes and no more—slid open at eye-level. It was at that moment that Percival also noted a slot at the bottom of the door, which would be large enough to accommodate a plate of food being slid in . . . or, he noted as he spotted a small chamber pot at the other end of the room, a container with waste material being slid out. How cheerful. He'd been in prison a number of times during his life, usually because he'd been in the wrong place in the wrong time or on the wrong side. Prison food could oftentimes be indistinguishable from waste matter. He wasn't especially anxious to test the cuisine of his latest dwelling.

Although he could see only the eyes looking in at him, he knew instantly who was on the other side of the door.

"They said you were awake," came the voice of the High King. "I trust my faithful brother in war did not hurt you too much?"

"How comforting that you have taken an interest in my

welfare," and then he paused and, hurling the name like a spear, added, *"Gilgamesh."*

The eyes on the other side crinkled slightly in amusement. "It certainly took you long enough," he commented. "What gave me away? The greatness of my being? The majesty of my personality?"

"No, the presence of the one whom you addressed in front of me as Enkidu." Percival took several steps back from the door, and there was rough humor in his eyes and disdain in his voice. "Posturing lords of the land are a dime a dozen. I've seen them in all shapes, in all forms, my entire life. But one in the company of a great beast such as that," and he shook his head. "That would make you either Gilgamesh, or possibly Tarzan of the Apes."

Gilgamesh laughed loudly at that . . . the sort of laugh one has when one is totally and completely in control, and knows it. "A good jest," he said, "a very good jest. I know this jungle lord. We may be out of the way here, but we do acquire works of fiction, usually from the occasional new arrival. But you do me a disservice, Grail Knight. A posturing, dime-a-dozen lord? I am the first hero of all history, Percival. I was king of Uruk in Babylonia . . . I was, and am, two-thirds god, one-third man . . ."

"I don't care if you're two-thirds orange juice and one-third vodka," shot back Percival. "I'm aware of your background, aware of everything that's attributed to you, aware of your place in history. But this isn't history. This is here and now, and to me you're just a jailer, no matter how many thousands of years back you hail from. Now if you want to prove your magnificence to me, then act in a way that's more suited to your self-esteem and let me out of here."

Gilgamesh actually seemed to consider the request for a moment, which was a moment longer than Percival had thought he would consider it. He took a step closer, his eyes seeming to bore right through the back of Percival's head, but when he spoke it was with a tone that came across as remarkably reasonable. "You know now that the term 'high king' is not simply an affectation," said Gilgamesh. "I am truly a king . . . the first one of literature. The first one of acclaim. There are none who are more worthy of the title of High King than I."

His mind racing, Percival was able to sense the considerable arrogance that seemed to permeate Gilgamesh's tone. It was certainly something that he could use to his advantage. "You make a strong argument in that regard," he admitted. "You are legendary, Gilgamesh."

"This man you work for," asked Gilgamesh with disdain, "would any say that he is legendary?"

More than you would think, mused Percival. "I would say so, yes."

"But not as legendary as me."

Percival said nothing. He just stood there, pulling on the large ring attached to the door.

"No . . . no, he couldn't be," Gilgamesh said with obvious, eminent satisfaction. Lord, the man was insufferable. Then again, he'd had plenty of time to become so. "Do you know what I think, Percival? I think I shall give you another chance. My opinion of you has not altered from before."

"It hasn't."

"No, it hasn't. I still think that you are an honorable man, Percival. And I believe that if you tell me that you will remain here . . . forsake your liege, come into my service . . . that your word can be taken. And if that should happen, why then," and he thumped his meaty hands together so loudly that it echoed off the walls, "just like that, you will be released. Released, and welcomed here, to act in my service and enjoy life here on Pus Island." ·

Percival had to laugh out loud when the name was spoken. Far from being put off, Gilgamesh shared the amusement. "The name of our little paradise strikes you as amusing, does it?"

"It shouldn't," Percival said. "But yes, it does."

"I did not give it that name, Percival," Gilgamesh informed him. "It bore that unlikely moniker when I first came here, long centuries ago. An island of lepers, it was. Pathetic, destroyed creatures. Lepers, and plague sufferers. Poor creatures, barely recognizable as human, making their way here. So many died in that futile pursuit. Do you know why they sought to come here?"

"Because they heard," said Percival knowingly. "They heard that you were here."

Gilgamesh shook his head. "They heard something was here. They had nothing to lose. They came in huge numbers, died in huge numbers, and only a few—call them hardy, call them lucky, whatever you desire—only those precious few made it here. Here, to 'Pus Island,' the home of infection and pain and suffering. No one but the most pathetic of humanity's dregs would brave the journey. Why should they? Who in the name of Nineveh would want to come to someplace called 'Pus Island?' " Without waiting for an answer, he responded to his own question. "About as many people as would desire to brave Iceland, and would instead seek the warmer climes of Greenland. Of course, they'd arrive in Greenland, find a brutal and intemperate place, and reason that either they should stay and die . . . or else leave and let someone else make the same foolish mistake." He smiled at the recollection. "Ah, the joy of outwitting one's intellectual inferiors."

"What pleasure is there in that?" Percival inquired, genuinely curious. "True joy only comes from outthinking an equal or superior, not one who is hopelessly behind."

"I'll defer to your opinion on that, Percival, what with you being my guest and all."

"Guest?" He looked around. "The accommodations leave something to be desired."

"That, I'm afraid, is your choice. Really, Percival," and he was sounding a bit impatient, "I think I'm being somewhat ill-used here."

"*You're* being ill-used?" said Percival incredulously. "That's rather amusing considering which side of the cell door you're standing on."

"Here am I," continued Gilgamesh as if Percival hadn't spoken, "prepared to release you, taking you at your word. *Your word*. The amount of trust that indicates is truly overwhelming. But instead you simply stand there, gawking at me, refusing to acknowledge my generosity and pledging your fealty to me. I don't know what else I'm supposed to do."

"Let me go."

Gilgamesh's voice dropped, and sounded very dangerous and very ugly. "That is not going to happen. Do not tempt my generosity, Percival, for you will most certainly not enjoy the consequences. Now will you pledge your loyalty to me?"

For a long, long moment Percival studied him as comprehension slowly dawned upon him. "You," he said at last, "are afraid of me."

Gilgamesh responded exactly as Percival thought he would: so loudly, so over the top, that the very urgency of the reply said far more than anything Gilgamesh actually articulated. "That is absurd! I am Gilgamesh! Two-thirds god, one-third man!"

"Doesn't make no never mind to me how big you are, how tough you are, how wonderful you think you are. To me you're just a quivering little craven, afraid of a future that is as unforeseen to you as it is to anyone else."

"That's where you're wrong!" Gilgamesh shot back. "I'll have you know that . . . !"

And then he stopped, catching himself. Percival was intrigued; obviously Gilgamesh had been about to let slip something of great significance, and who knew what impact it might have on Percival's current or future situation. But instead of continuing in that vein, Gilgamesh simply smiled lopsidedly. "That was good, Percival. That was very good. I think we shall have a very interesting association, you and I. You have a very quick mind. Mine is far more learned, of course, but even so . . . yes. Yes, a very interesting association. I think I will find your time with us most stimulating, even if you do not. You will be attended to, and I will visit regularly, and you will provide intriguing conversation and the occasional battle of wits over many topics. For you see, Percival," he said, sounding a bit sad, "I am somewhat isolated here. I have very little word on what has been going on in the outside world. Not that I've been all that interested, but still . . . there's no harm in a man being informed, now, is there?"

Percival stepped back from the door and briefly allowed anger to seize him as he lashed out with a furious kick. The pain of impact shot up through his leg, all the way to his hip, but the door didn't seem particularly impressed. Nor was Gilgamesh.

"That didn't do you any good," he observed.

"I will get out of here," Percival warned him. "And you know I will. That's the reason you're afraid of me. That's the reason you won't even try to kill me. Because if you do, you'll know for all time that you're a coward."

Gilgamesh threw his head back and laughed. "Your words mean nothing to me, Moor. I do not have to prove my bravery to such as you."

"Yeah," Percival replied. "Yeah, you do."

For a moment, Gilgamesh's eyes were burning coals in the darkness, and then, without another word, he turned and walked away. From behind him Percival called, "I know you for what you are, Gilgamesh! I know you now! And you know too! I will get out of here! I will escape! And you know it! *You know it!*"

His voice echoed down the corridor, but no response came from Gilgamesh. Finally Percival sagged against the door and stared at the dank wall opposite him.

"Shite," he muttered.

And then he turned, gripped the massive ring with both hands, and began to pull.

And pull.

And pull.

CHAPTRE
THE TENTH

✝

FRED BAUMANN FLASHED his press ID for what seemed the hundredth time in the course of the evening, and then stood with arms extended while the security guards checked him over.

He had to believe that he didn't exactly fit the profile of the standard terrorists against whom the Capitol dome was being guarded. Baumann was a heavy-set, very Caucasian, very unthreatening-looking man pushing his sixties. His blond hair had long since turned white and gotten thin, and annoyingly he seemed to be acquiring hair every place he didn't want to have it: His eyebrows were getting bushy; there was hair coming out his ears. He would look at his face in the morning, with a swelling nose courtesy of too many late-deadline-prompted beer orgies, and the bags under his eyes, and he'd wonder, *Jesus, Fred, when did you turn into an old man?*

Young reporters in the press briefings would try to push him aside to find favored seats, but Baumann didn't care. He could just as easily get attention from the back of the room, and it made it that much easier for him to get out of the room when the briefings were over.

The Capitol building was alive with activity this night, and Baumann felt as if he was reliving the State of the Union. Hopefully, that wouldn't be the case. He hadn't been outside to see when the First Lady had been gunned down, but God almighty, what a zoo it had been that night. It had been hard for him to concentrate, because he'd come to like Gwendolyn Penn, having gotten to know her as a person before she acquired the iconic position of First Lady.

And now the President was going to address Congress and the nation once again. The reason was obvious to most of the press corps: He was going to rally the spirit of the American people, still in shock and in mourning over the fate of the First Lady. He was going to let them know that he was broken, but unbowed. He was going to show them who was in charge. At least, that's what everyone else was saying.

Baumann, as he took his seat in the press galley overlooking the busy hive of activity on the floor of the House below, wasn't so sure.

WHY IS IT *always raining at times like these?*
Arthur stared at the window of the limo as rain cascaded through the night skies. It sounded heavier than usual to him as it fell upon the roof in staccato fashion. He wondered if there was some hail mixed in with it. His senses felt heightened, as if he were highly attuned to everything that was happening around him.

When he had first come to Washington, he had been surprised by how much it reminded him of the days of old. He had arrived as part of a general tour given to mayors of major cities, and he'd been struck by how much the White House seemed like a castle. They all did, really, all the major buildings. Great structures that housed and protected the lords of the land, so that they could conduct the business of the nation and affect the fates of millions of people. Instinctively, he'd felt very much at home here.

Now it all seemed alien to him. He was merely a stranger, a charlatan, someone masquerading as that which he was not. He felt separate and alone, and he wanted to blame Merlin for pulling him into this madness instead of leaving him to the mists of legend where he belonged. Or he wanted—as irrational as it seemed—to blame Gwen, because so much of it he had done for her. He could, of course, blame Sandoval, for it was his actions that had brought Arthur to this pass.

Ultimately, though, he realized that all such thoughts were unworthy of him. He had made the decisions, he had cooperated, he had done what he felt needed to be done. And if it had not worked out the way that he had planned it, well . . . it certainly wasn't the first time.

A loud clearing of a throat, perhaps half combined with a cough, caught Arthur's attention, and he realized that he'd been sitting there wrapped in his thoughts and ignoring Ron Cordoba and Bob Kellerman, both of whom were seated opposite him. Kellerman fidgeted with his hands as he usually did when he wasn't seated in front of a computer working up a draft of a speech for the President. Kellerman was a lean, balding man who had only stopped performing hideously obvious comb-overs because Arthur threatened to whack him personally with a baseball bat if he didn't cease doing so. It was Cordoba who had made the noise in his throat, and Arthur looked at him expectantly "Yes, Ron?" he inquired.

Cordoba seemed surprised to be addressed. "Yes, what, sir?"

"You made a noise."

"When?"

"Just now. I thought you were trying to get my attention."

"No, Mr. President," said Cordoba, pulling in slight discomfort at his shirt collar. "If I were trying to get your attention, I'd probably just say, 'Mr. President.' That usually does the trick."

"Ah," Arthur said.

Now that the long silence had been broken, though, Kellerman leaned forward and there was a look of true perplexity on his face. "Mr. President, I admit I was just wondering . . . are you satisfied with the speech?"

"Of course I am," said Arthur, clearly a bit surprised. "I said it was your best speech ever, Bob. I'm using your first draft."

"Yes, sir, I know. That's . . . with all respect, that's what I find puzzling."

One eyebrow cocked, Arthur asked, "How so?"

"You've never used a first draft of mine. Ever."

"I know."

"Not ever."

"Yes, I know, Bob," Arthur acknowledged with a touch of impatience. "It was perfection. I said to you, 'Write me a speech that I can deliver to a special joint session of Congress, because all anyone remembers of the State of the Union is what happened afterward, and I need to cleanse that from the collective American memory. Write me a speech that will say what I need to say to the nation about terrorists in general and Sandoval in particular.' I saw no reason to change a word of it because it suited my purposes to the proverbial tee. So I don't quite understand what point you're trying to make."

Bob's mouth moved, but no words came out. "It's nothing, Mr. President," he finally said.

But Ron had been watching the exchange, his eyes narrowing, and when Kellerman declined to pursue the matter further, Cordoba said softly, "I think what Bob here is wondering . . . is whether you accepted the first draft because you truly thought it was ideal . . . or because it didn't matter what he wrote, because you're planning to say something completely different and this text is simply a decoy."

"Is that it?" Arthur asked. Bob met his gaze for a moment and then looked down. "Well, well. It seems the little jest I made prior to the State of the Union had a longer-ranging effect. You remember: where I said that I was just going to 'wing it' instead of going with the prepared text?"

"Yes, I know, Mr. President, I remember," said Ron, and there was a hardness in his eyes, but also a sadness, as if somehow . . . he knew. "However, I also seem to recall that you're a man who prides himself on speaking the truth. And I noticed that you're not actually denying what I just said."

"Ron," Arthur began.

Kellerman was looking in confusion from one to the other, but Ron's gaze never left Arthur's. "Mr. President . . . what's going on? Don't you think I deserve to know?"

Cook, the Secret Service agent who was seated in the front section of the limo, half turned and called behind him, "Mr. President, we're here." Indeed, the long black car was slowing, the Capitol building looming in front of them.

Arthur drew in a deep breath and then let it out very slowly. Then he said, "You will find, Ron, if you live long enough, that very little of what happens in life has anything to do with what one deserves. The innocent, the good, the pure of heart die horrible deaths. Those whom we term evil live long, healthy lives in want of nothing. And mankind clings to quaint notions of God and an afterlife in order to gain some solace that the hideous unfairness that is our daily existence will somehow be sorted out."

"Quaint notions?" said Ron, his face barely discernible in the darkness. To Arthur, the shadows felt almost alive, as if extending icy black tendrils about him. "I seem to recall your believing in the Holy Grail. Nothing 'quaint' about that."

"Perhaps. Perhaps," Arthur said with a rueful smile. He suddenly felt every one of his thousand-plus years of age. "But if there is a God, Ron . . . what has he done for me lately?"

Before Ron could answer, the back limo door was opened by a Secret Service man who was holding an umbrella overhead to shield Arthur from the rain. "Mr. President," Ron began, and it was clear from his face that he suddenly felt as if things were slipping away from him.

"Showtime," was all Arthur said as he clambered out of the limo.

Kellerman looked with concern at Ron. "What just happened here? What's going on?"

Ron just shook his head. "You heard the man. It's show-time."

"MR. SPEAKER . . . THE *President of the United States!*" Everyone was on their feet, warmly applauding, as Arthur made his way down the aisle toward the Senate floor. The place was absolutely packed, a sea of dark suits and familiar faces. So many of them had stood in opposition to him on so many things, that Arthur couldn't help but feel as if a goodly chunk of them were damned hypocrites for pretending to be happy to see him. Then again, perhaps some of them had changed their feelings toward him. He had, after all, been subjected to a great personal tragedy in front of millions upon millions of Americans. News stations and newspapers had been filled with editorials and articles about "getting behind the President" at this time of national crisis. He should have regarded such a swelling of support as uplifting. Instead, he couldn't help but feel as if the entire country was pitying him.

He'd known that feeling before, all too well. Back when Guinevere's duplicity, her adultery with Lancelot, had become public knowledge. He had felt the eyes of his knights upon him, regarding him with pity or, even worse, contempt. Perhaps these men were seeing him the same way. Perhaps they were thinking: *How can you possibly defend the United States? You couldn't even protect your own wife.*

He tried to tell himself that he was imagining it all, but the uncertainty burrowed its way into his heart, into his soul, and he became more convinced than ever that his course was the correct one.

Arthur wasn't even aware that he had reached the floor of the Senate until he was turning to face his audience, which was still applauding. He raised his hands, indicating that enough was enough, that they should take their seats so he could get on with the purpose of his having come there. Just to show their independence, Congress remained on its feet another few moments before finally settling down into its seats.

The TelePrompTer had Kellerman's speech displayed on it, as opposed to the State of the Union, which he had committed to memory. In the galley seats above, the press core waited for Arthur to speak the words that had already been released to them in the preprinted speech. It was as if he were an actor, taking the stage, whose only job was to—as Hamlet implored—speak the speech trippingly and on the tongue.

Arthur gripped the sides of the podium, and once again breathed deeply in order to relax, like a sprinter about to embark on the most difficult race of his life. He had no reason to feel nervous, he knew. He had never been one to be nervous about anything once he'd made his mind up about it, and he most definitely had done that in this case. So there was nothing to do but get on with it.

"Mr. Speaker," he said, "esteemed members of Congress . . . members of the press . . . and my fellow Americans. I thank you for allowing me to come to speak before you this evening."

Then he stopped.

It was not simply a dramatic pause. It was of sufficient length that it began to be uncomfortable. Congressmen were looking at one another, as if trying to affirm to one another that something seemed off. The words glowed on the TelePrompTer, moving slightly up and down, trying to reset to the proper place in the speech, the operators concerned that Arthur had lost his place in the text.

"So!" Arthur abruptly said with such force that some people jumped slightly in their seats. "Here we are again. It seems just yesterday that I stood before you in much the same circumstances, speaking of our successes . . . speaking of the greatness that is this country, and the inevitability of our success against terrorists. Then I step out of here, and the next thing I know, terrorism nearly claimed the life of the First Lady . . . of Gwen, my wife."

The reporters were looking in confusion from the prepared text back to Arthur. They were realizing that what he was saying wasn't reflected in what they had in front of them. Still, it might be chalked up to simple ad-libbing, but they nevertheless appeared a bit disconcerted. Only Fred Baumann, whom Arthur spotted toward the front of the galley, didn't seem perplexed. Instead he appeared almost anticipatory, not even bothering to glance at the copy as if he knew that it was about to be rendered moot.

Arthur caught a glimpse of Cordoba and Kellerman toward the back. Kellerman looked perplexed. Cordoba didn't seem the least bit surprised.

"So . . . I must have looked like a bloody fool to many of you," Arthur continued. "Overconfident. Smug. Preening. And yet, I have experienced nothing but an outpouring of sympathy from all of you, and from the American people. The cards, the letters . . . we've received enough flowers at the White House to reforest the Amazon rain forest. We've received enough offers of blood donation to provide sufficient plasma for a hundred thousand first ladies. It has all been very, very appreciated. I don't . . ." He drummed softly for a moment on the podium. "I don't think I truly comprehended the nature of this country's character until the support that I've seen from its people in this time of my very personal crisis.

"And I have also been told, uncategorically, that Americans are firmly behind anything that I do in retaliation. The general consensus seems to be that I should order a nuclear strike against Trans-Sabal. That's the simplest answer, you see. Nuke them. Drop a bomb on them, be done with them, because of course that will solve everything. At the very least, declare a full-scale war upon them in response to what's been done.

"I am here to tell you . . . what I'm going to do."

Again he took a deep breath, and he was certain that he was the only one breathing in the room at that moment.

"I'm going to get the bastard."

Immediately there was a roar of applause, and everyone was on their feet, banging their hands together like so many trained seals. Arthur tried to gesture for silence, but they would not be denied. And why shouldn't they react in that manner? He'd said exactly what they'd wanted to hear. Like a hero in an action movie, he'd drawn a line in the sand and effectively told the bad guys that they were going to pay for having stepped over it. It was a quintessentially American response to the situation.

They weren't stopping. If anything, the applause seemed to be feeding upon itself, growing and growing with each passing moment, and finally Arthur shouted the words that would be prominently featured in stories in every newspaper the following morning, the words that would be showing up on computer news services in less than twenty minutes:

"I am . . . but you're not."

That stopped them dead.

Never had Congress looked quite as collectively stupid as it did at that moment. Many of them were frozen with their hands in mid-clap, unsure that they had heard what they thought they just heard.

"Sit down," Arthur said very softly.

They sat.

He felt sorry for them. It was as if he had just slapped them in the face. They looked confused, even betrayed. Well, let the betrayals continue.

"Do not think for a moment that the decision I have made is one that I make lightly . . . or even willingly. But I have studied the Constitution . . . and I believe I know not only what is in my own heart, but was in the hearts of those wise men who drew it up." His throat was suddenly feeling constricted, and he cleared it forcibly. "When I think of what happened to my wife . . . when I think of her lying there, unmoving, unspeaking . . . not experiencing a life but instead a simple existence . . . such anger floods through me that clouds my brain, chokes my reason." His voice grew louder and louder. "My heart cries out for vengeance, and I hear the cries of revenge coming from my people, urging me on, egging me on. Nuke them all! Annihilate them all! Destroy them all!" With each of those three sentences, he slammed his fist on his podium forcefully for additional emphasis. Then he flattened his hand on the top of the podium as if bracing both it and himself, and continued, "And it is one thing for the average citizen, secure in his living room, pontificating from his easy chair, to talk of such things. But I am a president. I am an individual who can make such things happen, who can destroy all that lies before me! I can reduce countries to rubble, people to ashes. With every fiber of my being, I want to do this thing.

"I cannot trust myself."

He paused once more, and there was confused murmuring from the Senate floor. People were shaking their heads, still not fully comprehending what he was saying. Some were beginning to tumble to it, though, and noise was starting to flow from the press galley as cell phones were being pulled out, stories being dictated even as events were unfolding.

"I have given it a great deal of thought . . . looked long and hard into myself . . . and I feel that my judgment in this matter cannot be unclouded. Because of the personal turn that recent events have taken, I do not believe that I can make the sort of dispassionate decisions that this country requires. If a possibility for compromise presents itself, my anger might very well propel me away from such a circumstance, and instead down a path that will lead to the deaths of American servicemen simply to sate my own quest for vengeance. Thirst for retribution fills my throat like bile . . . and the American people deserve better than that. They deserve someone with a clear head, uncontaminated judgment.

"Therefore, it is my considered opinion that I am not fit to carry out the duties of the office to which I have been elected."

Never had there been such a thunderous uprising of shouts, confusion, chatter as there was at that moment. Bafflement reigned among the politicians, and above all the clamor, Arthur's voice soared. "Therefore," he continued, "pursuant to Article Two, Section One of the Constitution, and Section Three of the Twenty-fifth Amendment," and reaching into his jacket pocket he produced a document that he turned and handed to the stunned Speaker of the House, "I am presenting my official resignation as President of the United States of America. I intend to devote my remaining years to my wife's bedside, and to settling old scores in a manner that need not drag an entire country down the road to war. Thank you and good evening."

No one applauded because everyone was talking at once. All sense of decorum and tradition had evaporated. In a perverse way, it was one of the most exciting moments of Arthur's life. The place resembled more the floor of the stock market during the height of trading frenzy than the floor of the legislature.

As if he were above it all, Arthur stepped down from the podium and started for the far exit. People were converging upon him, words colliding with one another and shattering into incoherence. He made no endeavor to respond to anyone, but he did not lower his gaze. Instead he was looking everyone in the eye, nodding in acknowledgment. He did not want to seem the least bit ashamed, did not want anyone to think—even for a moment—that he felt as if he had done something wrong. The Secret Service escort formed a wedge around him, plowing through the throng that was amassing in front of him. No one was attacking him, certainly, but it was as if everyone was pressing forward demanding some sort of further explanation, or utter their condolences, or shout their rage, or voice their disapproval-but-understanding. The words remained indistinguishable, but the wild variety of sentiments flowing over him were certainly comprehensible enough.

I'm doing the right thing . . . I'm doing the right thing . . .

"**Y**OU'D BE DOING *the right thing."*

She smiles at him, Miss Basil does, in a most satisfied manner. It may be that she is simply relieved that Arthur has not reacted with pure rage to the mere suggestion.

"Resign," *he says incredulously. He had not expected it, and yet now he wonders why he is at all surprised.* "You want me to resign the presidency."

She moves around him with inhuman smoothness and grace, like a dancer whose body is lighter than air. It's hard to tell if she's even touching the floor. "The truth is, Arthur, that you want to resign the presidency. You do. I am simply giving you the opportunity . . . in exchange for a glorious vengeance upon your enemy."

"Why," *he asks,* "do you think I would possibly want to resign? I have never walked away from a challenge in my life."

"Of course not," *she replies. She speaks with assured confidence, as if she already knows what the answer is going to be, and everything preceding it is just the merest game.* "But then . . . you've never done anything in your life for yourself, have you? First you did things at the order of your adopted father and brother. Then all that you did, you did for Merlin. Then for Guinevere, and for Lancelot, and for Camelot, and then for Guinevere and Lancelot and Camelot all together. And here you are, a thousand years later, and the first thing that happens is that you're back to doing what the little wizard wants you to do. Truth be told: You have no real interest in leadership anymore. Every day, as you sat in that cave, wondering when the call would come, you dreaded it. If you could have remained hermited in that cave forever, you would gladly have done so."

"You think you know me so very well," *he says, trying to sound full of contempt. But he doesn't manage it nearly as well as she does. She exhales scorn the way others do carbon dioxide.*

"I know you well enough to be aware of the fact that you've yet to tell me I'm wrong," she points out.

He says nothing. Instead he simply stares into space.

"The simple fact, Arthur," she continues, "is that you have never, in your life, truly been in control of it. As a king, as a president, you have commanded millions of souls, and yet never commanded your own. I dispatched Merlin, and part of you despises me for it, but another part is relieved, and do not bother to turn upon me and express fury that I would say such a thing. You will simply make yourself look foolish, and I will not believe you in any event. I am a monster, Arthur, masquerading as a woman. You would have me seek out and destroy a man masquerading as a monster. Yes, he does that, you know. He masquerades. For he quivers in fear of his own mortality, just as most men do." Her voice grew softer, more wheedling. "I will dispatch him for you. Him . . . and his entire operation. Think of all the American lives that will be spared. Think of all the women who will not have to mourn their sons as their bodies are shipped back, in pieces. Think of all the good that those brave young soldiers will be able to do as they are allowed to grow up, grow old.

"You will have doubts, Arthur, of that I am most sure. Any man would have doubts, and you are certainly not just any man. There will be some who will not understand. They will speak harshly to you, say that you have turned your back on your country. But you and I, we know the truth. This is not your country. These are not your people. Your people are long dead. The creatures who walk this continent . . . they are merely Merlin's means to your end. The only one who truly mattered to you is Gwen, and in the final analysis, you were not able to protect her. But you can avenge her, through me . . . by ridding yourself of the office that you never truly would have sought if it had been left up to you. The simple fact, Arthur, is that there really isn't a downside here. It's all benefit for you. All of it.

"Take time to think about it, if you wish . . ."

And what astounds Arthur, then and now, is how he ultimately needed no time at all. Everything she says is true. Everything. He was and is a man out of his own era, and he has spent much of *his time here living the dream of others. He lived Merlin's dream. He lived Gwen's dream. He did it for them. But Merlin is gone, and Gwen is not quite gone . . . but she is not there, either.*

Only Arthur is there.

And he does not wish to be there anymore.

"Sandoval's death must be incontrovertible. Everyone must know of it," *he says to her.*

She smiles, and for just a moment her eyes seem to flash with yellow and slits. "So we have a bargain, then."

He nods.

She stretches out her hand, extends one long finger, and draws it across her outstretched palm, leaving a thin ribbon of blood across it. Arthur hesitates only a moment, then withdraws Excalibur from its scabbard. The sword sings as it is pulled, and usually the song it makes is a tune of joy as it anticipates battle. But this time it is a mournful song, funereal, like a dirge. It knows. Arthur slides his palm along the blade ever so carefully, ever so gently. Too hard and it will slice through his hand, sending the upper portion splattering to the floor. A moment later, he too has a line of blood upon his palm.

She extends hers upright, and he presses his against hers. "Let the gods see that freely, and of my own will, by this agreement I am bound. I am bound. I am bound," *she says.*

Staring into her eyes, which now look normal and human again, Arthur likewise intones, "Let the gods see that freely, and of my own will, by this agreement I am bound. I am bound. I am bound." *And then, almost as an afterthought, he adds,* "May the gods have mercy on us all."

She laughs at that then, laughs loud and long. Arthur would like to know what is so funny, but does not ask, nor does she volunteer the information. He suspects that he most likely would not want to know.

CHAPTRE
THE ELEVENTH

✟

THE ENTIRE STAFF of the White House looked as if they'd been in a head-on collision with a truck. As Arthur walked briskly through the corridors, those who would have once called out, "Good evening, Mr. President," mumbled or nodded or in some other way indicated that they knew he was there, but sullenness and solemnity was the order of the day.

Surprisingly, the hardest to deal with was Mrs. Jenkins. She looked up at Arthur from her desk, her eyes red. He wondered how long she'd been crying, and how recently she'd stopped. He tried to think of what to say, and "Be strong" came out of his mouth. But it sounded insincere and foolish, and he regretted it the moment the words were out. Nevertheless, she smiled and nodded as if this was the best advice in the world, and he mused over the fact that sometimes it didn't matter what one said as long as one said something.

He was not remotely surprised to find the Vice President waiting for him in the Oval Office. Stockwell rose to meet him, and without preamble, said, "Take it back."

Arthur blinked at him in polite confusion. "You know, Terrance, of all the things I thought you'd say first, somehow that wasn't among them."

"Take it back, Mr. President. The resignation. Take it back."

"I think simply 'Arthur' will do, don't you?" asked Arthur, circling around to his desk. He was about to sit down, and then stopped and looked at the vacant chair. He stepped around it, his hands resting on the back. "I think this is yours now. Probably wouldn't be appropriate for me to be sitting here. I believe a swearing-in ceremony is already being scheduled for you, so you'd best clear your immediate calendar."

"Sir," Stockwell said, and his fists were trembling as if he was trying greatly to maintain control. "You've been through a great deal recently. People will understand."

"The people."

"Yes."

"They will understand."

"Yes, sir, they will," said Stockwell firmly, nodding his head.

"Terrance, I interrupted their favorite television shows to inform them of my decision," Arthur said patiently. "The only thing that made that event palatable to them was that they witnessed history. If I recant, they'll *never* forgive me."

His face tight, Stockwell said, "You seem to think this is funny, sir."

The rain was coming down harder, and Arthur was certain there was some definite sleet in there. Well, it was certainly the season for it. If he'd been an overly fanciful individual, or extremely full of himself, he would have thought that the gods were weeping over this day's events. Then again, it was far more likely that—if they were indeed sobbing—it was because some child had just starved to death in an impoverished nation without having the slightest chance to make his or her mark upon the world. The decisions of well-fed, well-off adults . . . why should these things be of the slightest interest to whatever divine beings there might be?

"Terrance," said Arthur, his voice very soft and tinged with sadness. "The first thing they teach you in leadership school—be you president of a country, monarch of a realm, or captain of a garrison—is that the quality of the decision you make is of far less importance than the fact that you make it and stick to it. Better to hold to a decision that might be bad than vacillate over whether the contrary notion might be good."

It was as if Stockwell had only heard the part he wanted to hear. Pointing a finger like a hunting dog discerning where a shot duck had fallen, Stockwell said, "Then you admit it might be a bad decision."

"It might be," allowed Arthur. "Time . . . and my successor . . . will tell."

Stockwell was shaking his head vehemently, moving about the Oval Office as if he had misplaced his car keys and was scolding himself while trying to locate them. "If you resign, I'll resign."

"Terrance, don't be absurd," Arthur told him, feeling a flash of impatience. "We both know that you've always believed yourself more fit for this office than I ever was. Who knows? Perhaps you'll prove to be right."

He turned to face Arthur. "I make no bones about wanting the office, sir. But this isn't how I wanted it."

It was all Arthur could do to suppress a laugh, and he wasn't entirely successful. "What, you only wanted it over my dead body? If I throw myself off the top of the White House, will that satisfy your sense of decorum?"

"That's not the . . ." He gestured out the rain-splattered windows as if indicating the whole of the American population. "They will never accept me in the capacity of commander in chief. They'll believe I acquired the office through questionable means . . ."

"Balderdash," Arthur said firmly, slapping his open palms on the desktop. "There's no confusion here, Terrance. No misread ballots, no court decisions, no split between the popular and electoral vote. The Constitution could not be more clear. A president resigns, the vice president takes over."

"But they will see me as the man who—"

"No!" Arthur cut him off, even more forcefully than before. "See, that's where you're going wrong, Terrance. It's not about the man. It's about the office. The man leaving this office may be leaving with a smear on his escutcheon, if that is how some choose to perceive it. But the office itself remains intact and pure and undiminished. So stop complaining about it or acting as if you can't appreciate it because it's being 'handed' to you or somesuch. Besides," and he smiled wanly, "the people of this country have memories like sieves. It'll take them no time at all to judge you not by how you came into the office, but what you did with it once you had it. And I have every confidence that you will do right by it . . . even if you have trouble believing that yourself."

For a long moment, Stockwell said nothing. Then he drew himself up, looked Arthur in the eye . . . and saluted.

"I disagree with every fiber of my being with the decision you've made, sir," Stockwell told him, sounding very formal. "But I shall defend your right to make that decision, and—until such time as the people speak with their voice in a future election—I shall see myself as the caretaker of the presidency you began."

"I don't see how I could leave it in better hands."

Stockwell extended his hand, and Arthur took it and shook it firmly. It was the first moment of genuine warmth that had passed between the two men in all their political history.

"I certainly hope you're not expecting me to hug you, sir," said Stockwell stiffly.

"It didn't cross my mind, Terrance."

"Because some would consider this an overly emotional moment, but I have not, nor shall I ever be, a hugger."

"You needn't concern yourself," Arthur assured him.

"Good. And know this, Mr. Presi—sir—that if there is ever anything I can do to accommodate you . . . anything at all that's within my power . . . you need but ask, and it's yours."

It was a promise that Stockwell would have great reason to regret before the year was out, but at the time he intended it sincerely, and Arthur smiled and took the promise in the spirit that it was meant.

"Well . . . Terrance . . . I just have a few things I'd like to attend to here, if you don't mind," said Arthur.

"Not at all. There's just one other thing, sir. I suspect it's something I'm going to be getting a considerable number of questions about."

"Yes?" Arthur's eyebrow was cocked questioningly, but he had a suspicion that he knew what Stockwell was going to ask. It turned out he was correct.

"You said . . . you were going to 'get the bastard.' In reference to Sandoval . . ."

"Yes, I remember."

"You didn't say how."

"Yes, I know." He gave it a moment's thought. "And it's your belief that you're going to be asked about this?"

"Knowing the press corps as I do, I would say it's a certainty."

"Well then . . . I think an old army man such as yourself should be able to appreciate what I'm about to say . . ."

But Stockwell was ahead of him. "Don't ask, don't tell?"

Arthur nodded.

Pondering this, Stockwell said—as if testing the words to see if they carried credibility—"You were speaking from a sense of anger and rhetoric more than any specific plan of attack. My belief is that it's your hope, eventually, to act in some sort of diplomatic capacity, speaking against the evils of terrorism, and in that way bring down the Sandovals of this world."

Arthur patted Stockwell on the shoulder. "I have a feeling you're going to do just fine in the job, Terrance. Just fine."

*   *   *

FRED BAUMANN STOOD on the street in front of the White House, staring at it through the fence that ringed the perimeter. He saw the lights burning long into the night, drew his coat more tightly around himself against the inclement weather that pounded upon him.

His deadline was half an hour away, but he was confident he was going to be able to file his story in time. It was almost entirely written in his head. But he wanted one long moment of atmosphere that he could add to it. One long moment of simply looking at that great sanctuary that had housed president after president for years.

And would now house one less.

At which point, Baumann knew exactly what his lead sentence was going to be.

"The bad guys won one tonight," he said, trying to determine how that sounded as a lead, and deciding that it was pretty darned good. He took one more look at the White House, and just for a moment fancied that he could actually see Arthur in one of the windows. *Idiot,* he thought, and headed off to write his story.

RON CORDOBA COULDN'T remember when he'd started drinking that evening. Now that he was deep into an alcoholic haze, he wasn't sure when, if ever, he was going to stop. At that point it was his intention to drink until he couldn't remember anything at all.

The rain from earlier had tapered off, and he wandered out into the Rose Garden. The grass was slippery, and Ron was barely capable of supporting himself, and yet somehow he managed to stagger over to the statue of Merlin until he was a foot away, glaring at it balefully. He was in his shirt-sleeves, the wind cutting through him, but he didn't feel it.

"It's all your fault, you little shit," he said, although his words were slurred and it came out more, "Sallerfall, yalil-shid." The thing was, he wasn't sure why it was Merlin's fault . . . but something just told him that it was. His resentment toward the mute statue grew and grew, and he wanted to speak, but the rage was so great that it rendered him inarticulate. So instead he aimed a great kick at the statue, lashed out, missed clean, and wound up flat on his back, staring up at the night sky.

And there he lay until a female voice said, "Oh, my God. Oh, Jesus. Ron! Ron, what the hell are you doing out here?"

He forced his eyes open and looked up. Nellie Porter was staring down at him, her eyes wide, utter confusion in her face.

"Stretching m'legs," he managed to say.

"Oh, Jesus," she said again, and reached down to grip his arm. She stood uncertainly on her heels, trying to haul Ron up, but it was like trying to lift a bag of bricks, and in short order the inevitable happened: Her feet went out from under her and she wound up flat on her ass on the wet lawn. As she clambered back to standing, the commotion was enough to prompt several members of the Secret Service to come out to the Rose Garden and see what was going on. They looked extremely puzzled. She couldn't blame them; she was in the middle of this mess and didn't understand it any more than they did.

"All his fault . . . all his fault," Ron kept saying as she hauled him up. Then he focused his bleary vision on Nellie, smiled lopsidedly, and said, "Y'know . . . I always thought you were damned attractive. Wanted to go out with you. Or stay in. Or . . . anything."

She didn't know whether to laugh or cry. "Is that a fact," she said, pausing where she was and shifting Ron as his body sagged against hers.

He nodded vehemently. "Yeah. Y'know why I didn't? Job. Damned job. Working day and night." He coughed deeply, wiped his arm in an unglamorous fashion under his nose, and then once again said roughly, "All his fault. All . . . his fault." Nellie simply figured that he was referring to Arthur, and Ron's effectively being out of a job. And this was what she kept thinking as the statue of Merlin stared unblinkingly after them when they were escorted into warmer climes.

ARTHUR WAS SEATED at Gwen's bedside, listening to the steady beeping of the monitors, when he heard someone behind him. He'd always had a gift for recognizing footfalls behind him; indeed, it was a knack that had saved his life on one or two occasions. This time was not life threatening. Without turning, he said, "Good evening, Nellie."

There was no response, and for a moment he wondered if he wasn't losing his touch. He turned and, no, sure enough, there was Nellie. She looked rather bedraggled. "You look like you were wrestling a wet cocker spaniel," he observed.

Still she said nothing, just stared at him unblinkingly.

"Yes?" he finally prompted.

"I just . . ." She let out an unsteady breath.

"You just what?"

Instead of continuing the sentence, she pointed at Gwen and said, "I hope she never wakes up."

The words were harsh, the tone angry, and Arthur was taken aback by the vehemence of both. "Nellie, you don't mean that . . ."

"Oh, the hell I don't," she said fiercely, and she approached Arthur, looking for all the world as if she wanted to hit him. "The last thing she would have wanted you to do was quit. And when you mentioned her name, it was like . . . like you were doing it because of her."

"Partly, I am . . ."

"*Don't you say that,*" snarled Nellie. "I know her!"

"As do I, what with my being her husband and all—"

"So what? I spent more time with her in the past few years than you ever have." Nellie's voice choked; she was fighting back tears. Arthur instinctively reached out to her, but just as instinctively she stepped back, distancing herself. "I know her likes and dislikes, I know the woman who's lying there, and I'm telling you that she'd hate you forever for doing what you did and blaming her for it."

"I didn't *blame* her, Nellie. There's no fault involved . . ."

"Bullshit! You left this country knowing beyond any question that if Gwen hadn't been shot, you'd still be president! You're walking out on us because of what happened to her! You're blaming her, and if you say otherwise, then you're just being a chickenshit asshole!"

The anger had exploded out of her, and it left her breathless and aching, and Arthur just sat there, staring at her sadly.

"I'm sorry," he whispered finally.

"Yeah, well," and she wiped those damned tears from her face, "save it for being sorry for yourself. You'll have more than enough time to do it."

She turned and started to walk away, but stopped when Arthur called after her, "I'll need someone to continue handling Gwen's affairs. She still gets tons of letters, and probably will for the foreseeable future. It's a bit outside your job parameters, but I was wondering if you'd care to stay on with her . . . with us . . . in a sort of caretaker capacity."

Nellie turned, looked back at him as if he were crazy, and said, "I hope to hell you didn't think I was going to have it any other way."

"Of course not," Arthur said immediately.

She walked away then, and Arthur again called after her, "How did the back of your clothes get soaked?"

"Go to hell," she called back, and moments later Arthur was once again alone with the unmoving, comatose Gwen.

He sighed, crossed his legs, and asked, "So . . . how was *your* day?"

No answer was immediately forthcoming.

CHAPTRE
THE TWELFTH

WASHINGTON HAD A crisp feeling in the morning air as Fred Baumann headed for the press room, tossing back the mandatory third cup of coffee that morning. He had his morning rhythms down so perfectly that the slightest variation could throw him off for an entire day. He'd have that third cup, then he'd pick up the morning edition of the *Daily News*, which would be on his desk waiting for him, then he'd have his morning sit-down on the can, after which he'd head off to the morning press briefing. Most days of the year, those were pretty routine affairs. This morning, however, was certainly not going to be one of those days. It excited him in a way, but also saddened him greatly. He couldn't help but feel that, not only did Arthur deserve better, but the whole damned country deserved better.

He approached his desk, where the glowing computer screen awaited him. Even after all this time, he still hated the things. Baumann had come up through the ranks as a typewriter jockey. To him a newsroom was the clattering of keys and the dinging of teletype every time something major happened. It would have been dinging like a squad of ice cream trucks last night in city rooms throughout the country if it was still done that way. But no, not anymore. File rooms were referred to as "morgues," but that could easily have applied to city rooms these days, considering how quiet they now seemed compared to Fred's heyday.

At first Baumann had strenuously resisted the advent of computers, but eventually even he had to give in to the inevitable, and had forced himself to master—albeit reluctantly—the ins and outs of writing stories on computer. Now he tapped a key at random (that day when he had, in confusion, scoured the newly alien keyboard for the "Any key" so he could press it and continue—and the snickers he'd gotten from other reporters when he'd asked for assistance—still rankled after all this time) and his boringly old screen saver of flying toasters vanished. He saw that he had e-mail waiting for him. He scanned the incoming names. Some assorted people in government, his editor, his ex-wife, one from . . . ah, he recognized that next one, all right. "LuvUMadly" was the sender, and there was an attachment. He'd been warned about it: one of those umpty-ump computer viruses going around. Download it and kiss your hard drive good-bye. Well, he'd delete that one without reading it, and that would take care of it, and the rest could wait a few minutes until he completed his morning sit-down.

He picked up the *Daily News*, seeing on the front page what he knew would be there: Arthur addressing Congress, with the words "I QUIT" blazoned across the top. Baumann hadn't been a headline writer in years, but even he had known a mile off what the headline would say this time around. As he started to head for the bathroom, nodding "Good morning" to other reporters already at their work stations, he turned to page three to read his story.

His lead sentence was gone.

Much of his story was gone, in fact. And what there was of it had been heavily rewritten.

He slowed in his steps, his brow furrowing in confusion. "What the hell . . . ?" he muttered under his breath, and automatically his gaze flicked to his byline. It was still there . . . but there was another name next to it. David Jackson. And Jackson's name was first.

He knew Jackson. Jackson was a new guy, sent up by the *News* a few weeks ago to aid Baumann in covering the Hill. But Baumann was the main man, the go-to guy. Hell, Jackson hadn't even been at the speech! *"What the hell?!"* he said again, this time loudly enough to attract the attention and curiosity of the other reporters nearby . . . not that it took a great deal to attract the curiosity of a reporter in any event.

The needs of his bowels suddenly forgotten, Baumann spun and headed back to his desk. He sped through the e-mail messages waiting for him and stopped on the one from his boss, Hugh Weaver on the national desk.

He punched it up, still standing, and he felt the blood draining from his face as he read it. Someone from nearby called, "Fred? You okay?" and he realized that he must have looked as if he were having a heart attack or something similarly calamitous. Nevertheless, he didn't reply. Instead he sank into his chair and dialed a phone number from memory.

It was picked up on the second ring, a tired voice saying, "Yeah?"

"You son of a bitch," Baumann growled.

"Oh . . . hi, Fred," said Weaver with a significant lack of enthusiasm. It was possible that Baumann was getting him out of bed and he was trying to shake off the cobwebs even as he spoke. "Look . . ."

"No, you look! You can't be serious about this! After all this time, after—"

But Weaver's voice cut through. "Look, Fred, I can't cover for you anymore, okay?"

Baumann stopped talking, confused, even a bit frightened. "Cover? What the hell do you mean, 'cover'?"

" 'The bad guys won one'? " Weaver said with incredulity. "How the hell could you possibly have thought that was any kind of good writing, much less news writing?"

"*You're letting me go because you didn't like my lead?*" His voice had carried more than he would have liked, and now eyes from all over were upon him. He ignored them. He couldn't stand the thought of looking in their faces, seeing contempt or—even worse—pity. "Hugh, for God's sake—!"

"It's not just that. We're cutting back, Fred. You must've known that. Circ is down, profits are down, CNN and AOL and all of them are killing us. We have to trim back."

"And seniority doesn't mean a goddamn thing, does it?"

"Yes, it means you're highly paid and therefore a target."

Fred was clutching the phone so tightly to the side of his face that it was leaving an imprint against his ear. "If you think my shit salary somehow qualifies as 'highly paid' . . ."

"You're being offered a great retirement package, Fred. I suggest you take it."

"Retire and do what? Sit around and wait to die? This is nuts!" Fred was shaking his head in denial. "And what's supposed to happen? There's a press conference, for chrissakes! Who's gonna cover it? Jackson?"

There was a pause. And that's when Fred really, truly understood. His voice a whisper, he said, "This was already in the pipeline, wasn't it? That's why you sent him here. I show him around, then get shoved aside, he steps in. Right? And you didn't warn me."

"Fred, I'm your friend," said Weaver sadly. "How would you suggest that I have told you . . . ?"

"Oh, I dunno. How about, 'Fred, heads up, we're planning to screw you over.' " Hugh started to talk, but Fred overspoke him. "This is about ageism, pure and simple. I get old, you shove me out to pasture. I'm a sixty-two-year-old reporter. Who the hell is going to hire me?"

"Fred, rest assured, you can come to me for a referral if it will—"

"*Fuck you and your referral, and fuck you for thinking you're my friend!*" And with that he slammed the phone down.

His heart was pounding in his chest, his temples throbbing, and he became aware of someone standing behind him. He knew without even turning. "Hello, David," he grunted.

Sure enough, Jackson's voice came from behind him. "Fred . . . I . . ."

"Save it. Fact is, I was a young punk once. They probably shoved some old guy aside for me." His fists tightened on the edge of the desk. "This is just payback, that's all. Goes around, comes around. You know the drill." He turned and looked at Jackson, so young, so eager. "Give me five minutes to finish off some e-mail and I'll get out of your way."

"Fred, you're . . . you're taking this rather well. Do you . . . do you need help getting your stuff together . . . ?"

Baumann was already seated at the computer going through the e-mail. He snorted disdainfully. "If you think I'm gonna be so pathetic to walk outta here with a cardboard box filled with possessions, you can forget it. Got some notebooks in the drawer there. Pull 'em out for me, would ya? Thanks."

He shot through the e-mail while Jackson gathered the notebooks he had requested. He got a large padded envelope, slid the notebooks in, and placed them on the edge of the desk.

"File is downloaded," the computer voice said, and Baumann rolled back from the desk and looked up at Jackson, smiling thinly. He stood, took the envelope, and tucked it under his arm. Then he held up the newspaper.

"Taking the copy. Last one. For a souvenir," he said.

"You're . . . you're handling this like a pro, Fred," said Jackson with as much sincerity as he could muster, and he stuck out a hand. Baumann shook it firmly. "I learned a hell of a lot from you in our short time together."

"And the lessons will just keep coming," said Baumann as he turned and walked out, ignoring the outstretched hands or words of consolation from other reporters.

Jackson didn't understand what he meant by that remark until a few minutes later when he tried to reboot the computer with his own password . . . only to discover the image of huge, kissing lips appearing on the monitor, and the words "LuvUMadly" running across the top.

Then he realized.

"Son of a bitch!" he shouted as the virus ate the entire hard drive.

CHAPTRE
THE THIRTEENTH

IT TOOK A while for Arnim Sandoval to realize that the missiles had stopped dropping. He had been in a drunken haze for a time, only partly paying attention to the world around him. It was understandable. The world around him had consisted of cave walls for, it seemed, as long as he could remember. He felt like some vampiric creature of myth, or perhaps a science fictional mole person, confined to subterranean haunts lest the rays of sunlight sear the skin from his skeleton and leave him nothing but bleached bones toasting in the noonday sun.

The cessation of the barrage, however, slowly penetrated his consciousness, and he began to sober up slowly, by degrees. His lieutenants had stayed away from him during his latest binge, because they had known that there was simply no talking to him or reasoning with him when he was in this condition. But they were most pleased to see the turnaround in his deportment and demeanor.

Bit by bit, Arnim Sandoval climbed out of the bottle that had been his home away from home for what seemed like days. With the halting of the bombardment, his people were able to restore electricity and running water to the intricate network of caves that constituted his organization's hideout. Sandoval was able to bathe for the first time in days, and it was a gloriously refreshing feeling.

And once he was bathed, and dressed in clothes that did not reek of liquor, his lieutenants sat him down and told him the news.

Sandoval's eyes, still a bit bloodshot, widened as he took in what they were telling him. Four of his top men were with him, but the one who had told him the developments in the United States was Muelle, a strong-featured, dark-skinned man who had been Sandoval's friend and confidant since they were children. Muelle, even at a young age, had borne the twin attributes of being well-muscled and stubborn, and Sandoval had nicknamed him "the Mule," a moniker that had followed him even into adulthood. The Mule had never minded. He was entirely loyal to Sandoval, and if it was something that amused his good and great friend, then that was enough for him.

"When . . . did this happen?" Sandoval asked, running his fingers through his tangle of unruly hair.

"Two weeks ago."

"Two . . . *weeks*?" Sandoval could scarcely believe it. He was seated at his desk in the barely functional cavern that served as his office, and now he rose so quickly that he nearly banged his skull on the low overhead. He caught himself at the last moment and only grazed his scalp. "And you only thought to tell me *now*?"

The lieutenants looked at one another sheepishly, and again it was the Mule who was the spokesman. "No, Arnim," he said gently. "We told you when it happened. And several times thereafter. You were not capable of . . . retaining the knowledge."

Sandoval stared at the Mule with open incredulity, and then to the others for confirmation. They nodded almost in unison. Sandoval glanced over at a half-filled bottle of wine that was situated on the far end of his desk. He reached across, picked it up, and then upended it. The contents splattered onto the floor and he held the bottle rigidly as the liquid glug-glugged its way to freedom. Within moments it was empty.

"I appreciate the symbolism," the Mule commented straight-faced, "but I would have appreciated the offer of the liquor much more, if you weren't going to have it."

Sandoval laughed at that. He couldn't remember the last time he'd laughed. It felt good. "Two weeks, you say." He shook his head in wonderment.

"We have it on tape," said one of the lieutenants, a dyspeptic older man named Gregor.

Sandoval could barely retain his excitement upon hearing that. "Where?" he said eagerly. "Show me. *Show me!*"

This in turn caused much laughter among his lieutenants, who thought his almost childlike enthusiasm to be most amusing and certainly not at all in keeping with the image of the terrorizing Arnim Sandoval that the rest of the world knew. In short order, they had set up the videotape machine, and Sandoval was front and center as they watched the departure of President Arthur Penn from the White House.

A helicopter was situated on the great lawn in the back of the White House, and the place was wall-to-wall bodies . . . press, presumably, although there were clearly White House staffers in evidence. The Vice President was nowhere to be seen, which was certainly standard operating procedure. Sandoval couldn't help but think what cowards the Americans were, that the two most powerful men in the country were never allowed to make any sort of public appearance together lest they fall prey to terrorist attack. Here the Americans told themselves that they were carrying on with business as usual, and yet even the most heavily guarded people in the entire country allowed Sandoval and others like him to dictate where they went and what they did. It filled him with a swelling sense of pride and accomplishment. It made him feel powerful. It made him want to have sex. He glanced for a moment at the urn across the way and put such thoughts out of his head.

The sky above the White House was charcoal gray, and a few snowflakes were falling lightly. "Tell me he crashed in a blizzard," Sandoval commented.

The Mule shook his head. "One must not ask for too much, my friend, or God will become most ungenerous."

"True. True," agreed Sandoval, and kept watching.

There came the wife on some sort of large rolling bed device. She was held completely immobilized within a metal structure, and Sandoval could see tubes and whatnot attached that were serving to keep her alive. Her eyes were closed as one dead. For a moment Sandoval couldn't help but wonder if she truly was already dead, and this was all some great show to try and convince the American people that she was still alive. It was certainly possible. Americans believed just about any damned thing that their leaders or their beloved Madison Avenue commercial agencies told them.

He was surprised to hear Gregor say, quite softly, "She . . . was a beautiful thing, wasn't she?"

Sandoval turned and stared at Gregor. "You are not sympathetic for these people, are you?" There was no hint of warning or threat in his tone. He simply seemed a bit surprised.

"I have as much for them as they have for us," replied Gregor, watching as the immobilized Gwendolyn Penn was hoisted up into the bowels of the waiting helicopter. "It is simply an observation."

Sandoval nodded slowly and turned back to watch. And then a broad smile broke across his face. Because there he was on the screen, the ex-president himself. Arthur Penn, wearing a long black coat that whipped around in the wind. His shoulders were squared, but his head was down, and Sandoval couldn't tell for sure if it was in shame or if he was simply lowering his head and soldiering on against a brisk wind. The crowd was pressed in on their side, although

Secret Service men were clearly in evidence, taking nothing for granted as they provided a human shield between themselves and their former chieftain. And as Penn walked the long path between the back of the White House and the helicopter that would take him on his way, the people he passed—one by one—saluted. He did not seem to acknowledge them. Sandoval wondered if Penn was fully aware of where he was or what was happening. He wondered if Penn had spent *his* last days getting drunk. *We all have our own caves*, Sandoval thought bleakly. For perhaps a microsecond he actually felt a smattering of sympathy for Penn. How inappropriate. He was almost embarrassed to feel that way.

Penn kept going, and the people along the way held their salutes. When he had gotten all the way to the stairs of the helicopter, he turned with one foot upon the bottommost stair and faced the people who had come out to see him off. He brought his right hand up and snapped off a brisk and efficient salute in response to those who were facing him. Then he smiled, but he looked pallid and world-weary. *Now you know how I feel, you bastard. Now you know how I feel.*

"Remarkable, isn't it?" the Mule said as Arthur took the final, long walk up the stairs to the helicopter.

"Remarkable . . . what?" asked Sandoval.

Mule shifted in his chair. "Here we are . . . we with our network, our organization, we 'little men,' as someone once called us. And we have caused an American president to step down. We," and he thumped his chest with obvious self-satisfaction, "have unveiled, for all the world to see, the fundamental weakness of the so-called leader of the free world. No one will ever look at such a man again without having doubts as to his courage or his spiritual endurance."

"Yes . . . yes, you're right!" Sandoval said with growing excitement. On the TV screen, the helicopter was preparing to lift off the pad, but Sandoval already wasn't paying any attention to it. "And that's going to be the point of our next tape!" He was on his feet, pacing in that way he had when seized with some sort of new enthusiasm. "We're going to drive home to them that American leaders are so weak, so unable to stand up to us, that they depart when terrorism strikes home."

"And not only that," the Mule spoke up, "but we can say that the American leaders obviously don't care when other citizens are killed. You never saw Penn offering up his resignation when strangers were blown up. Clearly he didn't give a damn about them. Only his precious wife."

"I don't know, that might be pushing the point," Gregor said doubtfully.

But Sandoval was shaking his head. "No. No, that's not pushing it at all. That's exactly on target."

As was always the case when Sandoval's organization was preparing another media assault, there was much eager discussion about exactly what to say and how to say it. It was a given that nothing would be written down. Without exception, Sandoval never worked off any prepared text. He wanted his comments to look spontaneous and unrehearsed, in order to distinguish himself from the meticulously prepared, painfully affected manner in which so many other heads of state chose to present themselves to the world.

They talked for an hour, covering the general parameters of what Sandoval would say. Once the tape was completed, one of their people would bring it to the standard news drop. It was a regular drop-off spot that had been arranged between Sandoval's people and a reporter for CNN. Sandoval found it endlessly amusing that a major news organization would willingly act as a shill for the supposedly hated and feared terrorists. It made him realize that, for all their rhetoric and great discussion of the immense evil that Sandoval supposedly represented, the world nevertheless found him incredibly fascinating and couldn't wait to see what he had to say next.

Once fully satisfied with all that he had to say on their next presentation, Sandoval placed himself in front of the video camera while the Mule adjusted it as best he could, considering the dim lighting conditions within which they had to work. "This is the longest that I can recall that we weren't being shelled by someone or other," commented the Mule. "It certainly makes it easier to concentrate."

"Perhaps they've realized the futility of it," replied Sandoval. "Their intelligence information is so piss-poor, they haven't even come close to hitting us." Then Sandoval noticed that Gregor was sullenly going about connecting the lights to provide as much illumination as possible. "Gregor . . . you have something to say?"

Gregor merely shrugged. "I am . . . suspicious, that's all. Suspicious of any 'gift' to us, even if it's something as simple as quiet for a time."

"What are you saying?"

"Nothing. I'm saying—"

But Sandoval walked toward him, feeling a faint buzz of warning in the back of his head. "Are you suggesting that they've stopped shelling because some other form of attack is about to be made?"

Again Gregor shrugged. "I could not say."

The Mule waved dismissively. "The Americans have not yet committed to any sort of ground attack, and every other regional army knows better than to try and engage us in these caves. We have three hundred men at strategic locations, unassailable themselves, and easily able to pick off any intruders. We need not worry about anything."

Sandoval nodded, realizing that everything the Mule was saying was the truth, and he had been foolish to consider even for a moment that any sort of danger could possibly be at hand.

The simple fact was that they had won a great victory. Sandoval wondered if he hadn't lost the ability to appreciate such a thing. Perhaps in some ways he had become too battered down in his ongoing struggle for . . .

For what?

He stared at his own image in the monitor and pondered, not for the first time, what was the purpose of it all. His people remained scattered throughout four different countries, repressed and without rights in all of them, and a homeland had yet to be offered by any country. He knew that his cause was a just one. The scriptures of the prophets had been clear on his destiny. Oh, yes, there had been spirited discussion as to whether he was indeed the Favored One, he who had been selected by God to lead his people to a place of security, of safety. But he did not doubt it, not for a moment. The signs were all clear, the details of his birth meshed with what was known of the Favored One. His destiny was assured, his reason for being indisputable. There was no question at all that he would, in time, win. The "how" of it might be in dispute, but the result was immutable.

Still . . . in this place where day and night blended together, the passing of the sun in the sky meaningless as they dwelt in darkness . . . sometimes he would wonder and would doubt. And then, as quickly as he could, he would shove those doubts aside, for they benefited no one.

The lights abruptly flickered. They looked around in confusion, and then they straightened themselves out. "Are we ready?" demanded Sandoval, beginning to feel not only a bit impatient, but sorry that he'd dramatically poured out the wine.

The Mule gave him a confident nod, and his other lieutenants stood around with their arms folded, watching and smiling. They always loved when he did this. He cleared his throat and said, with utter calm, "The American President has fled from the scene of battle like the coward that he is. But I am still here. And the terrorism will continue—"

"Perhaps. But not with you."

The unexpected voice startled them so completely that Sandoval—whose full concentration had been upon the camera lens—jumped half out of his chair, banging his knees on the underside of the desk. The others in the cavern whirled to face the newcomer, and were collectively dumbfounded to see a raven-tressed, gray-clad woman with piercing green eyes staring at them.

Sandoval wasn't sure why, but the temperature in the cave suddenly seemed to drop. The Mule was so distracted that he neglected to turn off the video camera.

"Who are you?" demanded Sandoval.

She smiled, and it seemed even colder. "I am for you, Arnim Sandoval. For you and your associates." She moved with an almost casual sinuousness. "I am the one who comes in the night and slinks in the day. I am the one who knows, and laughs at that awareness. I am the one with gaze of stone and blood of ice, and none speak of my heart, for I've none to speak of."

They had no idea what she was talking about, but they didn't have to comprehend her to have their sidearms out and pointed at her. She took in the weapons with one sweeping glance and seemed more amused by them than anything.

"How did you get in here?" Sandoval said. He was still standing behind his desk, and for no reason that he could articulate, felt some degree of comfort in the fact that he had a large, obstructive object between them.

"I go where I wish."

"I have men guarding all the entrances."

She shook her head, the black hair framing her face. "Not anymore."

The temperature dropped further still, and Sandoval felt chilled to the bone. He suddenly had an urge to relieve his bladder, and it was all he could do to hold it. When he spoke again, it was with less vehemence than he'd used before. "What do you mean?"

"I killed them." She approached them with long, leisurely strides, and the men backed up but kept their guns leveled upon her. "One by one, or sometimes two or even three at a time. Very quiet. Shhhh," and she brought her finger to her lips. "Wouldn't have wanted to disturb anyone."

Gregor was looking at the total absence of weapons upon her. The gray shirt and pants she wore were so tight that they almost appeared to be a second skin. Clearly she was hiding nothing. "Oh, really," he said skeptically. "You killed three hundred men."

"I don't know. I lost count."

"I see. And how, exactly, did you kill them?"

"Like this."

She seemed to make a very slight move with her right arm. It should have meant nothing; she was still a good four feet away from them. At most, there appeared to be a quick blur in the air, nothing more.

And Gregor staggered back, blood fountaining down the front of his shirt. His mouth moved powerlessly, but no words came out. Instead it was nothing but short, stunted gasps that no one would have been able to hear unless they were standing right there.

Before anyone could react, the woman took a quick step forward, bringing her within striking distance of two other men. Her arms blurred once more, and still it seemed as if her targets were too far away to fall victim to her, and yet down they went. They dropped their weapons, clutching at their throats, their faces going dead white as their lives drained down the front of their chests and onto the floor. They had called themselves Brothers in Blood, and never had it been so accurate as now, with their blood freely flowing into one another, the floor becoming thick and dark crimson.

The Mule took a step back and opened fire on the woman. His gun spat out bullets in rapid succession, and almost every one of them hit home. She staggered slightly from the impact of each one, but the smile never left her face. "Is this how you treat a guest?" she asked, sounding slightly put out.

Horrified, uncomprehending, the Mule backed up and banged into the video camera as he did so, knocking the entire tripod mount to the ground. The camera spun as it went down and landed at an angle. Both the Mule and the advancing woman were now within range of its lens.

Sandoval, paralyzed, glanced at the monitor. What he saw

there caused him to scream for the first time in several years. And that time, it had been a scream of pure mourning. This was pure terror.

He heard a ripping sound, the sound of flesh being torn away and something liquid spurting like a faucet knocked off a sink, and he looked back just in time to see the Mule's head *thump thump thump* across the floor, an expression of permanent surprise etched on his features. Flecks of blood had spattered onto the woman's face and her tongue darted across it. He looked back at the monitor, convinced that he was losing his mind. On the monitor the tongue was forked, the face nothing human, but the eyes were still that poisonous green.

She caught where his glance was going. "You like to watch television," she said with what sounded like dawning comprehension. "So much violence these days. Let's see what else is on." She shoved the camera over, and it slid up against the Mule's arm, outstretched from his fallen body. The upper half of Sandoval's body was clearly visible.

"What . . . what . . ." The words came out barely a whisper, his voice choked by the constricting vocal cords. He still had his gun in his hand, but had forgotten it was there.

"What am I?" she said helpfully. "Well, at least you're asking better questions now. 'What' rather than 'who.' But the question that's more important at the moment, Arnim Sandoval, is . . . what are you?" She smiled mirthlessly. "Would you care to find out?"

He tried to shake his head, but was paralyzed by her green-eyed gaze, and then something seemed to thrust into his very being, to bisect his brain, to devour his soul, and he saw everything that he was and would never be. A warm, yellowish stain seeped over the front of his pants, his bladder finally giving way. He didn't even notice. He could barely stand up, his legs were trembling so violently.

"You think you know terror?" she asked him. "You can't even begin to comprehend the word. Let me show you," and she stabbed forward, her body elongating, and Sandoval threw his hands over his head and screamed, but there were none left to hear him.

*T*HE VIDEO CREATES *a sensation. There is huge dispute as to its factual content, for the images that appear upon it are simply too insane to be believed. Some sort of gargantuan snake—an anaconda, some speculate—swallowing Arnim Sandoval whole. This is, of course, preposterous. There are no snakes of any size whatsoever in all of Trans-Sabal or any of the surrounding regions, much less something that grotesquely huge. Yet there it is, for all to see, on video released on CNN with commentary from clearly astounded newscasters who obviously can't believe what they're witnessing.*

Not since Abraham Zapruder decided to film a home movie of John F. Kennedy's motorcade through Dealey Plaza is any visual record so subject to intense scrutiny. The original video is made available to the most sophisticated digitizing labs in the country, who study it over and over and over again. The reason they keep studying it is because they keep coming up with the same, impossible results every time they do so: What is being displayed on the tape is absolutely authentic. The great dictum of Sherlock Holmes is bandied about almost routinely on evening news shows, namely that once the impossible has been eliminated, whatever remains—however improbable—must be the truth. And the truth is that every expert on digital analysis is ready to swear on a stack of Bibles that the tape is genuine, and furthermore each expert is perfectly capable of producing reams of laboratory studies to back that up.

Further backup is obtained when ground forces sweep into an array of caves that is believed a possible hiding place of Sandoval's people, only to find the place filled with bodies. Bodies literally by the carload, and blood everywhere. The place reeks of decaying corpses, and when word of this state of affairs spreads, that is all that is needed to begin a massive, global hailing to whatever divine providence has delivered Americans—and every other democratic people—from the terrorist grip of Arnim Sandoval.

Is Sandoval's the only terrorist organization that presented a threat to the world? Naturally not. But it is the largest, and the best organized, and Sandoval had certainly been one of the most charismatic leaders of them all. Furthermore, although there is no way to prove it, the nature of Sandoval's obvious demise gives pause to even the most rabid of terrorist leaders. This is not simply a man being shot, or crushed by bombs from overhead, or dying in any sort of remotely normal situation. No, this is a man who is consumed by a great beast of a creature. It has the spark of divine intercession about it. The political pundits even suggest that Satan himself, represented as in days of old by the great serpent, has materialized on earth to claim Sandoval for one of his own.

Arthur Penn considers it a mildly entertaining notion, and watches the spread of this theory on religious talk shows. And he nods in silent approval as talk of war dissipates like sugar in hot water. With the most prominent enemy dead—with spiritual restitution taken out of the hide of Arnim Sandoval—there is no point.

Of every being who walks and crawls and breathes on the face of the Earth, only Arthur Penn knows the truth. He tells no one. Who is there to tell? Ron? Best he not know the unholy deal to which Arthur agreed for the sake of his wife. Nellie? She still remains oblivious of Arthur's true background, and there's no reason to change that state of affairs. Merlin? He's solid rock. Percival . . . ?

Arthur sits and stares at the unmoving body of his wife. He listens to the steady beep of the monitors. Sunlight that she will likely never see again filters through the window, dancing upon her upturned face, and garnering no reaction.

"Percival," he says out loud, wondering where in the world his last and greatest knight could possibly have gotten off to.

But he does not dwell on it. He sees no point in doing so.

He sees no point in much of anything anymore.

Gwen's breathing remains regular and regulated, and Arthur finds himself wishing that all the years of immortality could catch up with him in one, great burst of chronological impossibility. That the years would wash over him like a mighty tidal wave, and once *they surge away from him, there is nothing left except foam and air.*

It does not happen.

Time stretches. People's attention spans remain, as always, short. Days turn into weeks, weeks into months, and while Terrance Stockwell does an excellent job as President, the public does what it does best.

It forgets.

PARTE THE SECOND:

𝔖words

❧

CHAPTRE
THE FOURTEENTH

✝

IN TIMES PAST, when Percival had been imprisoned for various offenses, he had kept a running, crude calendar charting the length of his incarceration. He had not been inspired to do so this time, however. He wasn't entirely sure why he had foregone this slightly sour tradition. He could only think that it was because—on some level—he didn't want to dwell on the length of an incarceration that might be permanent.

So instead he passed his days in occasional conversation with Gilgamesh, eating, sleeping, relieving himself, and pulling.

The discourse with the High King invariably ended in exactly the same manner, even though the conversations themselves would range over an array of topics. Sooner or later, Gilgamesh would demand undying fealty from Percival, Percival would tell him where to shove it, and that would be that for the rest of the day. Sometimes a week or more would pass, depending upon how anatomically insulting Percival had been, before Gilgamesh would show up again for another talk.

The food they gave him was minimal in its quality. It didn't matter to him all that much. He was effectively immortal, after all. So his body only needed the most meager of rations in order to survive, and the remarkable healing ability provided him by the holy waters of the Grail centuries ago did the rest. Still, an occasional filet mignon might have been nice, but he wasn't expecting such a treat to be forthcoming.

And the rest of the time, he pulled on the great ring attached to the door, which never seemed to give any indication of noticing any of his efforts. That did not deter him, though. He was a knight of the Round Table, and though Camelot might be long gone and the table smashed to splinters, he possessed an admirable single-mindedness that had served him well in the past and—ideally—would continue to do so in the future.

Because time had lost meaning to him, Percival was unaware of the fact that it was precisely the eighth minute of the eighth hour of the eighth day of the eighth month of his captivity when the great welded ring, and the door to which it was attached, began to give way. The numerology of the moment wouldn't have meant a damn thing to him even if he had known. All he cared about was results.

He'd been yanking on the ring in the exact same manner that he'd always been, and so couldn't believe it for a moment when this time—as opposed to the futility that had greeted his earlier efforts—the door suddenly began to buckle. It happened with no warning at all, but Percival instantly capitalized on the unexpected boon. His foot braced against the wall, a sudden surge of energy and strength vaulting through his limbs, Percival gritted his teeth and pulled harder, ever harder, his heart racing with anticipation.

From down the hall he suddenly heard a guard's voice call, "Hey! What's going on in there?" in response to the creaking of the door, and Percival felt a brief rush of panic.

If his constant pressure on the door all these months had actually brought it to the brink of collapse, and he was caught out, they'd simply tie him down or chain him up while they replaced it . . . and he would be right back where he started.

But the panic, rather than shattering his concentration, instead focused it like a laser, and Percival put every last remaining dram of strength into his actions. All his frustration, all his anger, all the fury that he felt at the ages-old High King for keeping him imprisoned in this manner, all of it telescoped down for him and converged upon this one single obstruction.

And with the shocking suddenness of a heart attack, the great iron ring and the locking mechanism to which it was attached gave way, ripping free of the door like a cannon shot. The door was almost half bent inward as Percival grabbed the newly made, gaping hole and yanked the door open as hard as he could.

The beefy guard was standing there. Had he been sporting a machine gun, it might have been problematic, but instead he was standing there with a sword slung on his hip, still safely in its sheath. He obviously hadn't realized the severity of the problem he was about to face; he'd just been checking out what sounded like excess noise in Percival's cell. His jaw dropped even as he took a step back and grabbed for the hilt of his sword.

The sword, apparently not as well-oiled as it should have been, stuck for a moment in the scabbard. Truthfully, it wouldn't have mattered in the end if it had come clear when he'd first pulled on it, because Percival was simply too fast. With one quick movement he closed the distance between the two of them and brought his fist up in a blur. It connected squarely with the guard's throat, temporarily paralyzing his vocal cords so he could not cry out. The guard should have considered himself lucky. If Percival had struck harder, he could have crushed his windpipe and doomed the guard to suffocation within minutes.

As it was, the guard staggered, grabbing reflexively at his throat and still trying to cry out. Percival moved with the practiced ease of one for whom combat is not a hurried endeavor, but instead something that is won through maintaining one's center of calm. He took two steps forward, deftly turned sideways as a desperate punch from the disoriented guard glanced past his chest, and backhanded the guard in the face. The impact sent him staggering back and he slammed his head against the wall of the corridor. Consciousness slid away from him even as he slid to the floor.

Percival unbuckled the guard's sword belt and strapped it around his own waist. He yanked out the sword then, swept it back and forth. He smiled approvingly. The balance on the weapon was certainly respectable, and the edge of the blade seemed quite keen. He hoped he wouldn't have to use it, though. He'd had more than enough trouble during his unexpected stay.

Nevertheless, he gripped the sword firmly as he started cautiously down the corridor. It was illuminated with faintly flickering torches. It was hard for Percival to believe that he was in the twenty-first century, considering everything around him seemed transported from an earlier age. He moved with impressive silence, his feet padding along the floor. Out of his cell, he became aware of the stink that was radiating from his body, and he felt as if he was going to pass out from his own stench. He wondered whether that alone would be enough to raise some sort of alarm.

He turned a corner.

Gilgamesh was right in front of him.

Both of them froze for an instant, each equally surprised to see the other, but it was Percival who recovered faster. His action was instinctive and, therefore, impossible to foresee.

Percival swung his right foot up with as much strength as he could muster and delivered a powerful kick directly to the private parts of the High King.

Immortal or not, warrior or not, legend or not . . . a kick

in the balls remains the great leveler of all men.

Gilgamesh went down, gasping, his eyes widening in shock. For a heartbeat Percival considered bringing his sword around and down and trying to behead Gilgamesh on the spot. But he sensed, correctly, that anything he did to prolong the encounter would work in Gilgamesh's favor, would give him time to recover. Gilgamesh was powerful enough that, even in his agony, he would be able to block a sword thrust with his bare hands, and as Percival continued to try and assail him, Gilgamesh would slowly work through his pain until the knight eventually found himself facing a fully recuperated and wildly infuriated High King.

All of this became quite clear to Percival even as he realized that the best place for him to be at that moment was anyplace but where he was.

Percival vaulted forward, landing squarely on Gilgamesh's back, which was not a difficult chore since Gilgamesh was bent over at that moment. The impact shoved the High King flat onto his stomach, a stunned "Bastard!" shoved out from him, but Percival kept going. And as he ran, he heard Gilgamesh gather what little air he was able to get into his lungs and gasp out, *"Enkidu!"*

That was exactly the name that Percival did not wish to hear escape the High King's lips, but he had no time to dwell on it. Instead, he ran.

Gods, he had forgotten what that was like. Cooped up for over half a year, he had exercised constantly in his cell because he'd really had nothing much else to do. He had kept his muscles honed and stretched, so they would not become lax from lack of use, but this was the first opportunity he'd had to really cut loose. And he seized the opportunity with both hands . . . and, even more accurately, both legs.

He sprinted through the corridors. There was a door at the far end standing in his way. He had no idea what was on the opposite side: Enkidu, an opposing army, or freedom. It didn't matter, nor did he slow. He hit the door at a dead run and it splintered and burst open from the impact.

Full daylight struck his eyes, and he felt as if the sun was going to sear his eyeballs from the sockets. For the briefest of moments he paused, shielding his face, squinting against the brightness. There were no clouds overhead, and he inhaled deeply the invigorating air of freedom.

He had emerged onto a flat but verdant plateau, and there was thick tree coverage less than a hundred yards away. He glanced briefly behind him, saw a simple building that looked like a jail of old, and then thought no more of it. He was far more concerned with what was ahead of him than what was behind him, liberty as opposed to more captivity.

And he would not be captured again. He'd sooner die first . . . presuming death was truly willing to take one such as he.

He sprinted for the forest, and that was when he heard the ground beginning to shake beneath him. Something was coming, and it was large and making no endeavor at all to hide its arrival.

Behind him, at the opposite end of the clearing, was more of the forest; apparently it ringed the area. He heard the crashing of limbs from that area behind it. Whatever was coming was already hard on his trail, and he wasn't going to have much time. Taking a deep breath, Percival ran. He tried to tell himself that, once he gained the woods, he would be safe. He knew that he was kidding himself, but it helped him to believe that pleasant notion rather than the truth . . . the truth being that the creature pursuing him could probably track him through forest, across desert, and even into hell and back.

He reached the woods, practically threw himself into them, and kept going. There was no easily demarcated trail for him to follow, but fortunately things were not incredibly overgrown. If he'd needed to hack his way through, he wouldn't have had a prayer. Not that his chances were very promising as things stood.

He heard a cessation of branches crashing behind him.

His pursuer had reached the open land, and would be back after him within seconds. Unfortunately, Percival had absolutely no idea where he was going. He reasoned that, since he was on an island, he couldn't go terribly wrong if he just headed in one direction. Sooner or later he would get to the edge of it. He just couldn't be sure whether that was a good thing or a bad thing.

There was a distant roar, and once again the noise of pursuit reached his ears. The ground was angling upward, the slick ground beneath his feet not providing much in the way of traction. He tried to tell himself that if the angle of the terrain was slowing him down, it would have the same effect on his pursuer. And right after he told himself that, he further told himself that Santa Claus would likely swoop down with his magic sleigh and whisk him away to safety.

Branches whipped into his face and he shoved them aside, running blindly. He wasn't feeling any exertion, which was good. What was bad was that he was positive his pursuer was gaining. It was becoming obvious what he was going to have to do. He was going to have to pull out his sword and take a stand against whatever the creature stalking him was. He wasn't looking forward to it. Legends of Enkidu's prowess had been handed down for century upon century, and Percival might be an immortal man and a powerful man, but a man he remained. He had encountered Enkidu only briefly those long months ago, and granted, yes, he'd been taken by surprise, but even so the speed, strength, and power of the creature was so overwhelming that Percival did not count his chances as being particularly good.

And suddenly he was out in the open.

For a heartbeat he thought he had gone in a circle, but no. No, the ground was continuing to rise, and he ran across the open area as fast as he could, his arms pumping . . .

And then skidded to a halt.

He was at the edge of a huge cliff. Obviously Pus Island was not entirely flat. It had some serious elevation to it. He looked down. It had to be at least a two-hundred-foot drop,

and there was the ocean slamming into the bottom of the
cliff, and he was reasonably sure there were some jagged
rocks there, too. There were some darker areas of blue as
well indicating that there was some depth, but if he hit the
wrong area, he would wind up a battered and broken shell.
Perhaps it would be a devastating enough injury to kill even
him. Or he might recover from it. Or, worst case scenario,
he would remain immortal and trapped within a meat sack
of a body that was human in name only.

The prospects were not promising.

He turned, briefly considering the option of heading back
into the forest at a different angle, perhaps evading his pursuer long enough to find his way around to another point
with less altitude. Instead he froze in his place as Enkidu
emerged from the woods, looking not the least out of breath
after having chased Percival all this time.

The distance between them was not more than about
twenty yards, and yet Percival felt as if they were staring at
each other over a span of centuries. Percival retreated, and
Enkidu remained precisely where he was.

It was the first time that Percival had seen the creature
out in the fullness of the sun and standing still. If it weren't
for the fact that Enkidu was chasing him down in order to
drag Percival back into the darkness, he would have found
much to admire about the great beast-man.

Enkidu was naked in the sense that he was devoid of
clothing. But he had need of none. His entire body was
covered with thick, glistening, tawny fur, with an extremely
liberal amount of darker brown, manelike hair in the area
of his loins. It matched the mane of hair that surrounded
his face, and he had an extended snout that was—at the
moment—pulled back in a sort of grimace. His teeth were
bared, his nostrils twitching, and he looked as if he were
fighting to rein himself in. Despite the thick pelt, Percival
could see incredible, rippling sinews in his arms, his shoulders, his legs. He was not, however, as massively built as

Gilgamesh was. But the power was there nevertheless, sleek and potentially devastating in the attack.

His posture was definitely human, as was much of his basic musculature. His hands did not end in pads, but extended with elegant, tapered fingers and opposable thumb . . . albeit with long, hard nails that bore not a little resemblance to claws. His eyes, though, were the most human thing about him. They were large and brown and, despite all the raging power that the beast clearly contained, appeared to look upon the world with infinite sadness. The color was different, but in every other way those bottomless eyes reminded Percival of Arthur's.

For a long moment nothing further occurred after Percival's minimal retreat, each of them waiting for the other to make some sort of move. Percival realized that he wasn't more than a foot from the edge of the cliff, and obviously Enkidu was aware of that as well.

Percival's lips and throat were suddenly very dry. He licked them with what small moisture he could manage, and then said, "Can you speak?"

Enkidu didn't reply at first, and then he made a sort of bodily motion, which Percival realized was close to a shrug. Enkidu's mouth opened and the voice that emerged was surprisingly light, gentle, reflecting that same sadness borne in the eyes. "What is there to say?" he asked, in very carefully enunciated English, with an accent that Percival couldn't place.

"Well," Percival said, trying to sound reasonable, "you could say you were going to let me go."

"I can't." He shook his head. It was the slightest of movements, but on him everything seemed huge.

"Yes, you can. You can simply walk away . . ." When Enkidu once again shook his maned head, Percival continued, "So you're not saying you can't. What you're saying is you won't."

Again that shrug. Then he tilted his head slightly and

asked, with obvious curiosity and even a touch of hope, "Are you to fight me?"

Gods, I hope not, thought Percival. "I'd as soon avoid it, if I could," he replied.

"Oh." Enkidu looked a touch disappointed upon hearing that. "It has been too long . . . since I have fought."

"Well, I'm sorry to disappoint you," Percival said. He remained at the ready, poised on the balls of his feet, not allowing his concentration to stray from Enkidu for so much as a second. "In this instance, I'd just as soon go for avoiding a conflict altogether."

Enkidu frowned at that, and shook his head more vehemently, as if trying to shrug off a tormentor. It was a far more animal-looking reaction than any so far. When he focused on Percival once more, he spoke with a rumble from deep in his chest. "Too many words. Come here."

"I'm afraid that wouldn't exactly be in my best interests to—"

"Come here!" This time it sounded far more like a roar, and suddenly Enkidu was tired of waiting. He did not even require a running start. His legs simply coiled and then unwound like released springs, and Enkidu vaulted the distance between the two of them, landing squarely on the spot on which Percival was standing.

Except that Percival was no longer standing there. What he did might have been seen as insane or foolhardy or wildly brave, but as far as Percival was concerned, it was simply a matter of having no choice whatsoever. The instant that Enkidu was airborne, Percival pivoted, bolted for the edge of the cliff, and leaped.

Enkidu let out a roar of frustration, skidding to a halt and barely stopping his forward slide by digging his talons into the ground. As it was he tore up a good chunk of ground before arresting his headlong skew. Anchored, he threw himself forward as far as his powerful body would allow himself to extend and swiped at the empty air as Percival's legs cleared the assault by barely a centimeter.

Percival arced through the air as far as the hurried thrust of his legs would carry him. The rolling waters far below him seemed to tilt at an odd angle, and then he threw his arms forward in proper diving form and plunged. Behind him was the frustrated roar of Enkidu; below him was the beckoning roar of the ocean. What flashed through his mind was the knowledge that nothing was definite when it came to the Holy Grail, and this might actually prove to be the end of him. On one level, that didn't seem such a horrible thing. On another, it very much did, particularly because he was utterly convinced—for no reason he could really determine—that it was imperative he tell his liege lord what he had discovered upon this bizarre island.

Don't let me die . . . I have too much I still need to do, he pleaded, wondering who it was he was pleading to, and there were the rocks right below him and he wasn't going to clear them, he just knew it, and suddenly the rocks were gone because he was falling at an angle, and a watery grave yawned upward toward him as he hit the water far more cleanly than he would have thought possible. But the impact stunned him nevertheless, his mind going numb, the world swirling black around him, and the cold enveloped him and carried him away.

CHAPTRE
THE FIFTEENTH

ELLIE PORTER COULDN'T shake the feeling that she was being watched.

The streetlights had come on, casting a glow that should have been comforting but only seemed eerie to her. The small one-bedroom house in which she lived was half a block away, yet might as well have been a mile off for all the comfort she derived from its proximity. It was a crisp, unseasonably cool September night. A brisk ocean breeze was blowing in, as was not unusual for this time of year in Avalon, New Jersey.

She couldn't comprehend what it was that Arthur saw in the place. Avalon was a perfectly decent resort town, considered by some to be the best in New Jersey. Situated in Cape May County, the main thing the town had to offer—until the arrival of a former president, that was—was excellent family-oriented shore facilities. The population was just under two thousand, which made the Secret Service men happy. Agent Cook had once told Nellie that they easily had enough bullets on them to blow away the entire citizenry in the off-chance that the whole of the population should arise en masse against Mr. Penn. Oddly enough, she had not taken tremendous comfort in this piece of information.

In truth, Nellie wouldn't have minded simply living full-time at the modest domicile that housed Arthur, Gwen, and the other staff people who occasionally came in and out. But Arthur had insisted that Nellie have a place of her own. "You're a young woman, Nellie, and should have a life outside of this half-life that Gwen and I live," he had told her firmly, and had arranged for her little home out of his own pocket. It was nothing extraordinary: a modest A-frame, creamy white with red shutters and a fireplace that would suit her nicely during the winter months. She didn't much see the point: The entirety of Nellie's existence focused around the Penns, attending to as much of their daily business as she was capable of, taking care of Gwen, monitoring her fluid intake, and endlessly looking for some sign of higher life functions, even though she knew none would be forthcoming.

She had realized months earlier that she was literally in a dead-end job. She did not, however, care. Her devotion to Gwen was absolutely unassailable.

There.

A clicking of heels on the sidewalk behind her.

Instantly, taking a breath and steeling herself for whatever she might see, Nellie spun to face whoever it was that was pursuing her.

The street was empty. There, illuminated not only by the streetlamps but also the full moon hanging in the cloudless sky, Nellie could see that she was the only one around.

She let out a deep, unsteady breath and quickly walked the rest of the way to her front door. She pulled her keys out of her coat pocket, but her hand was still shaking a bit from the near-incident manufactured by her own imagination, and so she dropped the keys. They clattered to the ground and she started to kneel to get them.

A gloved hand reached out and scooped them up before

she got to them, and a rough voice said, "I got 'em."

She jumped back, letting out a startled shriek, her hand clutched to her bosom to still the racing of her heart. Her eyes were wide as she saw a familiar, square-jawed face grinning at her. "Dammit, Baumann!" she snapped out. "What the hell are . . . ?"

Nellie looked hurriedly right and left to make sure they were unobserved. Then, with an angry grunt, she snatched the keys out of his open palm. Fred Baumann was grinning at her nervousness. "What, you worried Eyewitness News is gonna come roaring up?" he asked.

"Shut up," she said tersely, turning the keys in the lock. "Go away."

"Just wanted to talk."

"*Go away!*"

"Thanks for the invite," he said, and as she opened the door, he stepped right in behind her, bracing it with one hand so she wouldn't be able to slam it in his face. At first she tried to push it shut against him, but then with a low, frustrated groan she stepped away and allowed him to enter behind her, giving one last look to make certain they were unobserved.

The moment the door was closed behind them, she turned to face him, her hands on her hips. "Okay, Baumann, what the hell do you want?"

He looked aggrieved at her tone. "Is that any way to treat your bestest friend in the whole wide world?" He sauntered across the room, hands in the pockets of his battered overcoat. Nellie glared at him in a manner that she hoped would flay the skin from his bones. Unfortunately he didn't appear to notice and remained distinctly unflayed. At least he didn't remove his coat, which gave her a modicum of hope that this would not be an extended visit.

"You going to offer me anything to drink?" he asked. He glanced around. "Dark in here. Trying to save money on electricity?"

"I don't want to put on the lights because I want to lessen

the chances of anyone seeing you here. And what the hell are you doing here?" Mail was scattered on the floor, having been pushed through the mail slot at the bottom of the door and now kicked around because of the hurried way in which she'd entered the front hallway. With an angry hiss of air between her teeth, Nellie knelt down and started gathering up the mail. "You called me a month ago and I told you nothing was happening. What part of 'nothing' was unclear?"

"You're not trying."

She stood, grasping the mail and putting it on a small table near the front door. In the darkness of the room, she gaped at his indistinct outline. "*Not trying!* Look, Baumann," and she strode toward him while shaking a finger in his face, "what the hell do you want from me? I can't manufacture an inside story for you. I can't pull something newsworthy out of my ass. The simple fact is that today was like the day before, and the day before that, and the chances are spectacular that tomorrow's going to be just like today. All that's going to happen is that Arthur sits around, talks to Gwen while she lies there and doesn't hear him, answers a few letters, and that's the day. He doesn't go out. He doesn't do lectures. He. Just. Sits." She let out a deep breath and then shook her head in disgust. "You ask me, it's a waste of material. There's a lot more he can be doing about so many things. But it's like he's . . . he's lost the will to do anything about it."

"What are you saying?" Baumann asked, his voice rising in eagerness. He'd pulled a notepad from his inside jacket pocket and clicked out a pen to scribble. "That he's suicidal? Is that it?"

"*No!*" she said in frustration. She stepped forward and batted the notepad out of his hands, sending it to the floor. Baumann glowered up at her as he leaned down to get it. "God, for a minute I forgot who I was talking to. Would you just get out, please?"

And suddenly Baumann had walked right up to her, and

he wasn't grabbing her or making any physical contact, but there was almost no room between them, and Nellie backed up, bumping into the table as she did so. There was anger, and also a bit of fear, in his voice. "Okay, look, Nellie," he said, and although the phrasing sounded friendly, there was definite threat in his tone. "I got my own problems, okay? I'm a goddamn freelancer, peddling my papers wherever I can, and the *only* thing I got going for me is you being able to give me a heads up on anything Penn might be up to. But for months now you've been giving me nothing."

"*There's nothing to give!* There's no stories of any interest having to do with Arthur Penn or his wife!"

For a long, uneasy moment, Baumann said nothing. And then, very quietly, he said, "Ohhhh yes there is. And we both know it."

She took another step back, knocking over the small table completely. Back onto the floor fell the letters, but at that moment she didn't care at all. "No," she said. When he nodded, her voice fell to a hoarse whisper. "Look . . . I've done everything you've ever asked, cooperated, done you favors . . ."

"Let's make something clear, kiddo," Baumann said sharply. "*I'm* the one who did *you* a favor. You and Arthur and Gwen. I've known about this story since before Penn became mayor, and I could've blown it wide open then. And in defiance of every good journalistic ethic in existence, I didn't do it. Do you know why?"

"Because for a brief moment, you had a conscience?" said Nellie, her eyes momentarily flashing in defiance. "Or because you figured that if you kept it under wraps, you could use it to land bigger fish down the line?"

"No. Because I liked the guy, and I liked her, and I wanted them to win, so I sat on it. Never even told my editor."

"You're a prince," she said sarcastically. "Prince of darkness."

He smiled lopsidedly at that, but then his face darkened

once more. "I'll go with the story if I have to. I still have the photographs."

"We had a deal!"

"All deals come with expiration dates, and I have my own problems."

Nellie had never been a violent woman, and she had no idea from where the impulse came. Nevertheless her arm suddenly swung as if on its own, and she punched Baumann in the face. She'd been aiming at his nose, but she was hardly any sort of accomplished pugilist, and all she managed to do was have her knuckles glance off his cheekbone. It barely staggered him, but her intent was clear, and Baumann rubbed his face in irritation. "I should go with the story right now just because of that," he snarled. "Luckily for you . . . I'm a nice guy. I need some decent material, Porter. Give me something useful, within the month, or I'll go with what I have."

She opened her mouth to respond, but nothing came out. Without another word, he turned, opened the door, and strode out, not even bothering to close the door behind himself. She kicked the door closed, and then tried not to cry out with the anguish she was feeling for fear that he might hear her, and she had no desire to give him that satisfaction.

CHAPTRE
THE SIXTEENTH

---

†

THE SQUALL HAD come in unexpectedly. It wasn't much earlier that Arthur had been gazing out upon the Atlantic Ocean and seeing a body of water that was as calm as its sister ocean on the other side of the continent. But then dark clouds had rolled in through the night sky, and far off there were flashes of lightning, and the ocean was roiling up as if a great hand had reached in and started stirring it about.

The temperature had dropped considerably as well, but despite the chill of the night air, Arthur sat on the back porch and wasn't the least bit discomfited by it. The screen around the porch protected him from the rain that was sweeping through as well, but even if the moisture had been soaking him to the skin, he wouldn't have given it a second thought. He had, after all, grown up in the harsh climes of Britain, and it took a considerable amount of ill weather even to get his attention, much less make him feel uncomfortable.

As he watched the storm out at sea, and wondered if it was going to move closer to land, Arthur leaned back in his recliner and speculated about what was going on in the world. What new crisis was presenting itself in the Oval Office? What new dictator was rising up from the ashes of his predecessors to wreak destruction and havoc? What country was experiencing drought or famine or war? Somewhere out there, there was want and need and deprivation, and none of it was his concern anymore.

Except he couldn't help but feel that it *was* his concern. It was just that he was no longer capable of doing anything about it.

"Don't dwell on it," he said to himself, sinking his hands into the pockets of his cardigan. He slouched a bit, looking as if he was withdrawing into himself.

"Don't dwell on what?"

He instantly chided himself for being so inattentive that he had actually permitted someone to approach him unawares. What a ghastly error for one who had once prided himself on being a warrior king . . . particularly since the new arrival was making no attempt whatsoever at stealth. The fact that anyone at all was present was hardly cause for alarm, because any new arrival would have had to be cleared through the Secret Service agents who were permanently assigned to the former President. And the voice, even the footstep of the new arrival was instantly identifiable to Arthur. Still, he had let himself become unaccountably sloppy. He had to watch that.

He slid easily up out of the recliner and extended his hand to welcome Ron Cordoba, not allowing the slightest hint of his personal annoyance at his own ineptness to be reflected on his face. "Ron," he said genially. "The chief of staff takes time out of his busy schedule to meet with a former boss? I'm flattered."

"The storm shut down Newark Airport, so I'm stranded for a bit. Plus, I'm only chief of staff, I suspect, through your good graces," Ron said evenly.

Arthur made a dismissive sound. "You tendered your resignation in good faith and took your chances. President

Stockwell's choosing to keep you on was his decision, fair and square. Can I get you something to drink?"

"No thanks, I'm good."

He studied Ron closely, not immediately releasing his grasp on the man's hand. Ron was impeccably dressed in a crisp navy blue, double-breasted suit, with a heavy black coat over it. He had grown a pencil-thin mustache, which Arthur had to admit he wasn't particularly impressed by.

No, what struck him was Cordoba's overall appearance. Cordoba apparently noticed the way that Arthur was looking at him, because he said warily, "Everything all right, sir?"

Arthur let his hand go then and gestured for him to sit in a chair identical to his situated nearby. As Cordoba sat, Arthur assured him, "Everything's fine, Ron. It's just . . . well, you look a bit more haggard than I remember. The demands of the office wearing you down a bit?"

Cordoba laughed. "Sir, they were already wearing me down back when you were running the show. It's just that you didn't notice because you were right there beside me, getting worn out along with me."

"Yes . . . yes, that's true," Arthur allowed. "And how do I look now?"

"Refreshed. Relaxed." He paused and then added, "Regretful . . ."

"No," said Arthur firmly, shaking his head as he gazed out at the ocean. He interlaced his fingers on his lap and, as if working on convincing himself, he said again, "No. No regrets, Ron. That way lies madness. I did what I had to do."

"I know you believe that . . ."

Arthur fired a look at him. "Are you patronizing me, Ron?"

"No, sir."

"Well, good."

A long moment passed in uneasy silence then, and Arthur was suddenly feeling confined, even useless in his recliner.

He rose from his chair smoothly, uncoiling like a great cat, and the movement made him realize just how much he'd been sitting around lately. It was as if old muscles, long unused, were just begging to be pressed back into service. "Why are you here, Ron? Yes, I know, you said the airport was closed, but still . . . certainly there are more important things you could be directing your time towards than hanging about the residence of a former president." Try as he might—and admittedly, he wasn't trying all that hard—he was unable to keep the bitterness from his voice.

"There's no ulterior motive here, sir," Cordoba assured him. "I just wanted to see you and her, and see how you're doing. I . . ." He laughed softly. "I feel like . . ."

He was clearly having trouble articulating it, and Arthur glanced over his shoulder at him. "Feel like what?"

"I feel like your story's not done."

Arthur made a low, annoyed growl in his throat. "You've read too many fantasy tales, Ron. I'm no storybook hero . . ."

"But you are," Ron insisted, and he got up from his chair with considerably less grace than Arthur had displayed. "I know. When I was a kid, I read the storybooks, and there you were in them."

"It wasn't me," Arthur replied softly. "It was this . . . construct that storytellers cobbled together. Bits and pieces of legends, strewn through history, endlessly interwoven and reinterpreted for new generations. I was young or old, wise or witless, knowledgeable or just damned lucky, depending upon the needs of the narrators. Who I really was, what I truly hoped to accomplish, my own wants and desires . . . none of them truly knew."

"Did you?"

Arthur didn't answer immediately, and then, finally, all he did was shrug. "I think I did once. But it was a very long time ago . . . and for some reason, it seems to matter very little to me now."

"So you've given up."

He took in a breath and let it out slowly. "I do not think," he said to Cordoba, "that I appreciate the direction this conversation is going, Ron."

"Well, I'm sorry about that, but—"

"No, I don't think you are."

"Fine, I'm not!" Ron said impatiently. Arthur glared at him, but the forceful gaze of an ancient king simply wasn't what it used to be, in the twenty-first century. "Dammit, Arthur, you were . . . you were on a quest! A quest to do great things! And you walked away from it!"

"We had this all out at the time, Ron."

"Perhaps you did, sir. Me, I was pretty stinking drunk, and so don't remember much of it."

"Yes. Yes, you were," Arthur admitted. "I was a bit embarrassed for you, frankly. But none of that changes anything—"

"Arthur—"

"Ron," he interrupted him before he could continue, "take a look at the world." He made a wide, encompassing gesture. "It goes on just fine without me. It goes on whether I'm there or not."

"Just as Gwen would have."

His face darkened at that. "Leave her out of it . . ."

"I wish I could." He looked down, staring at the tops of his shoes. "I stopped in her room a minute ago before coming out here. She just lies there, withering away. Except she's doing it on the outside, and I think you're doing it on the inside."

"Don't presume to know me, Ron."

"Well, you said it yourself, didn't you? You hardly know yourself anymore, so why shouldn't others take a whack at trying to figure you out."

Arthur turned toward him, suddenly seeming a good deal taller than he had before. In the distance, the thunder rumbled, mirroring his own mood. "What would you have me do, Ron, eh? Take back my position? Tour the world as some sort of ambassador of goodwill? Or perhaps I should hunt down a dragon or two to slay, eh? Rescue a few damsels in distress? I could try to go out and catch a unicorn by the tail."

"Arthur—"

"I don't know what you want of me, Ron!" he exclaimed, pacing furiously. The confines of the screened-in porch suddenly seemed far too small for him. "I don't know what any of you want from me. All the storytellers, all the fantasists . . . and even the realists such as yourself, who can't help pinning heroic aspirations upon me because of tales they read in their impressionable youth. I'm just a man, Ron. A man who did the best he could with what was given him. A man who didn't have his priorities in order, and once he realized what they were, it was too bloody late."

And to Arthur's surprise, Ron's response was heated. "I think you still have no idea what your priorities are, sir."

"Oh, really. And what, young man, do you think my priorities should be."

Ron took a deep breath, as if he were about to jump off a cliff, and then said, "I think you should be out on a quest."

Arthur stared at him, his eyebrows arched so high that they nearly came to the top of his scalp, and then he laughed. It was not a hostile laugh, but rather one of pure, almost joyous amusement. Ron looked suspicious, clearly unsure of how to gauge the former President's reaction. He almost took a step back when Arthur's hand came around, but he simply clapped it on Ron's shoulder and smiled. "How very charming," he said.

"Charming, sir?" asked Ron.

"I keep forgetting that I'm a legendary sort of fellow," said Arthur. He leaned against his chair, gazing out at the ocean without really seeing it. "Most American presidents aren't legendary. Formidable, yes. Famous or infamous, as circumstances may dictate. There have even been some who have bordered on bigger-than-life. And certainly those unfortunate few who were martyred, felled by assassins, come close to the legendary. But I am the true stuff of legend. Before me, you more or less have to go back to Thomas

Jefferson. And because I am legendary, you naturally seek out a legendary means of finding a pastime for me."

"It's not simply a pastime, sir," Ron assured him. "You need something to focus on. Some great crusade that's part of something bigger and greater than you could ever hope to be. Sir, I've read the medical reports. We both know that Gwen could stay like . . . like that," and he pointed in the general direction of her room, "indefinitely."

"No." Arthur shook his head sadly. "No. Hardly indefinitely. I know a bit about such things."

"She'll age. She'll die. And so will you. And you'll never accomplish another thing in your life."

"So?" said Arthur with a shrug. "Haven't I accomplished enough? Isn't being a legend sufficient?"

And in an unexpectedly harsh voice, Ron replied, "A legend is what others have made you into. What you've made yourself into is a quitter."

Ron never saw Arthur's hand move, but he certainly felt it as it cracked sharply against his jaw. The next thing he knew he was airborne, and then he crashed against the far side of the porch.

There was the sound of running footsteps, and two Secret Service men were standing there, looking around in confusion, their hands in their jackets to pull out their guns. They stared at Arthur, who did not appear the least perturbed, and then at Ron on the floor, who was trying to pull himself together and having only marginal success.

"Do either of you gentlemen have a handkerchief?" Arthur asked coolly.

The Secret Service men exchanged looks and then one of them reached into his lapel pocket and produced a small white cloth. Arthur took it from him, and then nodded and said, "Thank you. As you were." Without a word, they pulled their hands out of their jackets and stepped away from the doors.

Arthur tossed the handkerchief down to Ron. "Your nose is bleeding. You may want to staunch that."

Ron glared up at Arthur as he did so. "Your concern for my welfare is touching," he said, his voice understandably congested.

"It's certainly greater than your own concern for your welfare, if you're foolish enough to say such things to me," retorted Arthur. "Honestly, Ron, how did you *think* I was going to react when you said that?"

"I wasn't thinking that far ahead."

"That much is obvious," he said with an annoyed sniff. "I may not be what once I was, Ron, but that does not make me nothing, nor will you address me as if I were. I trust we understand each other?"

Ron looked as if he were going to say something else unwise, but then obviously thought better of it and simply nodded, standing carefully as he did so.

"Good." Arthur shook his head sadly and said, "When you've been around for as long as I have, Ron, you learn not to toss around such terms as 'quest' lightly. A quest is a . . . it's not just a search for something. Not just a walkabout where half a dozen jolly friends with swords are seeking out some glittering treasure somewhere. A quest is something that comes from the soul and defines a man. It's not arbitrary or capricious. You don't just stumble upon it. I can't simply walk down to the nearest convenience store and order a quest from the counterman like a taco, or go down to the beach and discover that a quest has rolled up onto the shore . . ."

"What the hell . . . ?"

Arthur didn't understand for a moment why Ron had reacted in that manner, but then he realized that Cordoba wasn't looking at him at all. Instead his attention had been drawn to something at the water's edge. He turned and followed Ron's gaze.

A man was lurching out of the surf. He was not dressed in any sort of bathing gear; instead he was wearing what appeared to be some sort of fatigues. Looking like the proverbial drowned rat, he staggered forward a few steps, and looked in the general direction of Arthur's house, tossing off a cheery wave before collapsing to the sand.

The name was out of Arthur's mouth before his brain had even fully processed it: *"Percival!"* He was out the back door of the porch, sprinting across the beach, with Ron desperately trying to catch up with him.

Arthur almost stumbled once as the sand shifted under his feet, but quickly he righted himself and got to the missing knight just as Percival rolled over onto his back and stared up at the night sky with wonderment. His chest started shaking; he actually appeared to be laughing. Arthur ran up to his side and stared down in incredulity at the Moor, his own chest heaving from the sudden exertion of the run. "Stars and blazes, it *is* you! Percival!"

"So . . . so it is," gasped out Percival, showing no inclination to sit up. He coughed deeply several times, clearing sea water from his lungs. "Good . . . to see you, Highness. Ah. And Ronald," he continued as Cordoba skidded to a halt at Arthur's side. "Here as well?"

"Where the hell have you been!" demanded Arthur. He didn't know whether to feel relieved or angry, and compromised by being both at once. "You disappeared, Percival! Bloody disappeared! Without the slightest . . . *why are you laughing again?"*

"Because," Percival managed to get out, "I'm seeing myself . . . in my mind's eye . . . a whale on the beach . . . a great black whale . . . Moby Black . . ."

"Stand up," said Arthur, and there was no trace of amusement in his voice.

Percival heard that tone and his response was immediate. His legs were wavering a bit, but that did not deter him from sitting up, situating his legs under himself, and then pushing himself to a fully standing position. He put his arms out to either side to balance himself as if he were upon a tightrope, and once he was fully confident that he was not going to topple over from what was clearly exhaustion, he bowed slightly at the waist to acknowledge his liege.

Arthur very briefly embraced him then, relief flooding over him at the sight of his only remaining knight after a year's absence. Then he took a step back and said, with as much of a scolding tone as he could muster, "You scared the hell out of me, you know. Disappearing like that."

"It was not exactly my option," Percival told him.

He was starting to shiver, his teeth chattering slightly. Arthur promptly removed his own jacket and draped it around the Moor's shoulders. "Come. Let us get you inside, before the storm rolls in . . ."

"It's not going to. It's going south to north, not east to west."

"How do you know?"

"Because I was in the middle of it," said Percival. They started toward the house, and Percival's words came out in an almost frenzied rush. "When I escaped, I swam and swam and was picked up by a tramp steamer bound for Singapore, and while aboard that I learned of what had happened to Mrs. Penn, so I jumped ship and caught passage on a tuna boat bound for the States, and then learned that you'd relocated to your house here in Avalon, so when we passed the Jersey shore I absconded with a lifeboat and made my way here, except the storm sank my boat, so I swam the rest of the way . . ."

"You can't be serious," Ron finally managed to squeeze in.

"Have you ever known me not to be serious?"

"Gods above, Percival, what an escapade!" said a wondering Arthur. "But . . . I don't understand. Escaped from where? Where were you?"

And Percival stopped in his tracks, turned to face his liege, and—forcing his voice to stay calm and even—said, "I found the Grail. It's on an island. It's *of* an island. And the residents of the island don't age and don't die. I think . . . I think if you bring Gwen there . . . she can be healed."

Arthur and Ron gaped at him.

"Is there anything around here to eat that's not fish related?" inquired Percival.

T HE HIGH KING *burns with a deepening fury.*
He is barely able to look at his beloved Enkidu. Enkidu has not groveled before him. Enkidu has too much pride, too much of the wild about him, to prostrate himself before even the glory of the being who is two-thirds god, one-third man. "You have failed me," he says to Enkidu, and the lion-man does not dispute it or apologize for it or grovel over it or even offer his life in penance.
Instead he simply says, "Yes."
Gilgamesh supposes that he should be grateful, even appreciative for that. It is not within Enkidu, as it is within others, to serve up excuses. It is clear that, as far as Enkidu is concerned, he has done his best. If his best is not good enough for Gilgamesh, then clearly that is the High King's concern rather than Enkidu's.
And yet, Gilgamesh cannot help but find this complacent attitude all the more annoying.
He considers taking his mighty sword and hacking at Enkidu, but he knows this will be a waste of time. So instead he storms away from his great friend, moving through his palatial estate like a thundercloud, rumbling and fulminating in that unique way he has. All know to steer clear of him when such a mood seizes him.
He endeavors to summon the Aged One, but no one seems to know where he is. This infuriates Gilgamesh all the more. Despite his great age, he can and occasionally does act like an overgrown brat, and this is one of those times. He resolves to close himself in his room and remain there with neither food nor water, without human company, without anything except a resolve to punish people by his absence. So taken with his own fabulousness is he, that it does not occur to him that one person's punishment is another's blessing.
He goes to his room and does indeed shut himself in. The doors slam with a thundering thoooom *and he remains in the fairly dramatic pose, leaning forward against the doors with his palms flat against them. His jaw is set and his breath comes in ragged gasps even though he has not especially exerted himself.*

"Alone at last," says a voice from behind him.

He whirls, caught flat-footed. It is a slightly exciting experience, to be so off guard. It has not happened to him for many, many a year.

The woman is standing several feet away from him. She looks human. She smiles like a human. Her eyes glitter green, and he is Gilgamesh, two-thirds god and one-third man, and he knows in a heartbeat that she is very far from human.

"What manner of creature are you?" he demands.

She appears impressed, her head tilted inquisitively to one side, like a cocker spaniel. "You see me, not perhaps for what I am, but at least for what I am not. You have learned much, High King."

"Since when?" he says suspiciously.

"Since I first came to you millennia ago, when you were king of Uruk in Babylonia, and it amused me to pose as a serving girl. You were in your later years at the time. Older. Not the handsome specimen which you have become." She moves toward him, and does not seem to walk so much as she undulates. She runs her fingers over a faint white line that crosses his chest, almost invisible to the naked eye beneath the deep tan that adorns his vast expanse of muscled flesh. "I gave you this. Do you remember?"

His eyes go wide. "Of course I do," he says, his body tensing in preparation for a possible offensive maneuver on the woman's part. "The meat was hanging off my body in a great slab. Some thought I would die from such a mortal wound."

"Some, yes. But not you. Never you. You never doubted," and she runs her tongue across the tops of her lower teeth, "did you? Not for a moment."

Slowly he shook his head. "No. I never doubted. It was . . . simply another challenge. The High King likes a challenge."

"I was young . . . and new to the world."

He tries to disengage her, but does so halfheartedly. After a moment he ceases doing so, and instead looks down at her firmly. His thoughts fly back to a time when he was in a jungle several centuries ago, searching for large game, and he discovered a great snake wrapped around a ferocious leopard and slowly, methodically, squeezing the life from it. "How young and new to the world could *you have been, if I had my way with you?" he asks.*

"I never knew you to shrink from even the youngest of girls, High King, but I was not young in that sense. Tell me, High King . . . tell me the story of the Plant of Life."

He pauses, now completely disengaging himself from her. He stares at her suspiciously, and part of him wishes to remain silent. But he is being asked to discuss an aspect of his legendary adventures, recorded by Sumerians in clay tablets two thousand years before the man known as Jesus of Nazareth walked the earth. The High King is incapable of ignoring such invitations.

"I . . . traveled to speak with he known as Ziusura. It was said that he knew how to defy death, to live forever." *He watches her eyes carefully, searching for some reaction to his words, although he doesn't know precisely what it is that he seeks.* "Finally, I found him. He explained to me that the gods had rewarded him with immortality, for he had served them well and helped the world's animals survive the Great Flood. Obviously his peculiar situation was of no use to me. But before I left, his wife told me of a magical plant that could at least restore me to my youth. At great risk, I obtained the plant, which grew at the bottom of a great sea. On my way home, however, while I was bathing, a passing serpent snapped up the plant. The last I saw of it, it was slithering away and shedding its skin . . ."

He pauses then, and looks into those eyes, and he has a glimmering of comprehension. She smiles in a grim and yet amused manner.

"You begin to comprehend," *she tells him,* "the debt I owe you. For I was that serpent, High King. An ordinary, ground-crawling serpent." *He stands immobile, staring down at her, and once more she insinuates her arms around him. He does not at all resist this time, although he is not entirely sure why he does not.* "When I ate that plant, however, it had a much greater and more catastrophic effect upon me than it would have upon the humans for whom it was intended. It made me, High King, into who I am today. A creature of human and serpent qualities. The first of my kind, although I have spawned others since."

The High King trembles with suppressed rage. "You . . . are a monster. I am a slayer of monsters."

"Indeed. But all things must even out, High King. If a stroke of your sword destroys, then fate decrees that you must in some manner create as well. That is the way of the world."

"And the way of Gilgamesh is to hunt down and slay prey . . . which is all that you are," he tells her. He even tries to reach for his sword, but is surprised to discover that—although he envisions his hand motioning toward his weapon—it is, in fact, not budging.

"Why slay, or at least attempt to slay, that which poses no threat to you. Indeed, that which has come to warn you."

Her hand wanders across the hard flatness of his belly and is continuing in a southerly direction. He feels as if he should be repulsed by this . . . this creature in the shape of a woman. Yet his attraction to her is palpable, like a thing alive. He feels as if it is another aspect of his personality altogether, previously unknown to him. "Warn me?" he says roughly, and feels as if there is too much blood in his throat, making it difficult to speak.

"Yes. Warn you of impending disaster. I am able to follow the threads of fate, High King, and see to where they lead. I am she who perceives the turning of the wheels of fate. I know things even before those who are most affected by them could possibly perceive them. I am drawn to disaster, not unlike a tornado drawn to a trailer park."

He stares at her blankly. The edges of her mouth crease, as if she finds his inability to comprehend her comments to be delightfully enchanting. He sees the amusement in her expression, and his face hardens. Clearly he is not enamored of even the slightest possibility that he is an object of fun. "I have warnings already," he says, adding archly, "from one even older than you. I have interpretations of my dreams. I am not concerned over facing Calad Bolg."

At that her eyes narrow. She is not someone accustomed to having disassociated new names thrown at her. "What is Calad Bolg?" she asks, albeit with reluctance, for one as old as she does not like to admit to ignorance of anything.

Quickly he speaks to her of the sword of hard lightning. She listens, and nods, and then she says, "I know this sword. No one can stand against it."

"I am not no one. I am Gilgamesh, the High King of Uruk, builder of walls, he who was born two-thirds god and one-third man and defies death even to this day."

He pushes her away for a moment, although it is with effort, and then he strides across the room to an ornate trunk. There is no lock upon the trunk. It is not necessary. The cover is so heavy that none but the High King could lift it. It opens with a resounding creak, and then Gilgamesh reaches in and down and withdraws a great sword. He holds it flat across his two powerful hands, displaying it so she can see it. The serpent woman recognizes the type immediately. It is a scimitar, the blade curved and fearsome. Its handle is ornately carved, bearing the head of a lion with—curiously—the ears of a donkey set upon it.

"The blade of life and death," says Gilgamesh with satisfaction. "Taken from the hand of Nergal himself, lord of the underworld. The blade of hard lightning cannot stand against it, should it come to that."

"It might well," the woman tells him, "but I admit that it is a marvelous thing, this blade. The way the light reflects from it warms my cold blood. Do not underestimate his power."

"Whose power? Who is the individual who will oppose me?"

She smiles. "Arthur Pendragon. Arthur, son of Uther."

The High King appears surprised by this news. He steps back away from her, no longer looking at her, but instead appearing to be staring inward. "I have heard of him," he admits.

"You sound surprised."

"I am. More often than not, I forget the names of those I meet since they are not of sufficient greatness to warrant my attention. But Pendragon, I know. I have seen him."

Now it is her turn to be surprised. "Have you?"

He does not seem inclined to continue the conversation in that direction. Instead he refocuses his attention upon her. His lips thin into a curled sneer. "And what, I wonder, shall I do with you?"

"With me?" She is slightly taken aback by the flat way in which he speaks, and her own pride rises. "None do anything 'with

me' that I do not desire to have done." She circles him, never removing her gaze from him. He likes the way she regards him. To
be the total focus of her attention is equal parts exhilaration and
fear, and since the High King knows no fear, there is a disproportion
of satisfaction for him. *"You speak so proudly of your royalty. Of
all that you are. Yet you began life with a father who was a king
elevated to divinity, and a mother who was a goddess to begin with.
I was a mere serpent. Yet look at all that I have accomplished.
Immortality is mine, as is the most feared reputation of all monsters.
I have crawled beneath humans and walked alongside them, but
have always truly been above them. I am the Basilisk. Treat me
dismissively at your own great peril."*

"Very well," says Gilgamesh grimly, and he grips her by the
shoulders as a feral smile pulls at his lips. He bares his teeth, and
the scarcely contained animal passions that have always fired him
from within are visible in his mien. *"Then what would you have
me do . . . with you."*

She pauses only a moment, and then her head strikes forward
snake-quick. But it is not the head of a monster that moves toward
the face of the High King, nor the mouth of a monster that presses
itself with cruel fierceness against the High King's lips. It is instead
that of a woman, albeit a woman who is merely a monster cloaked
as a woman.

And the High King, who is something of a monster in his own
right, meets her aggression with some of his own. His scimitar slips
from his fingers and clangs to the floor. Neither of them notices.

CHAPTRE
THE SEVENTEENTH

✝

ELLIE PORTER WAS dumbfounded the next morning when—upon reporting for duty just as she had done so many times in the past—she approached the room in which Gwen was being kept only to be stopped at the door by two towering Secret Service men. She recognized them from when she had worked in the White House, but neither of them gave the slightest inclination of knowing her. They were all business.

"I'm sorry, ma'am," one of them said, putting a hand out to halt her where she stood. "You can't go in right now."

"What's wrong?" demanded Nellie, at first tentatively and then more forcefully. "Has something happened to Gwen?"

"We're not at liberty to say, ma'am."

"Stop calling me 'ma'am'! I'm too young to be a ma'am." She felt disoriented and annoyed. She didn't need Secret Service bullshit first thing in the morning, particularly before she'd had the first of her five cups of coffee for the day. "My job is to attend to Mrs. Penn. I can't do that if you won't even let me in the damned room."

"Ma'am, please step away from the door," said the slightly shorter agent in a monotone that made him sound more like a robot than a human being.

"I will not step away!" Nellie told him indignantly, and folded her arms resolutely to indicate her complete defiance of the edict issued by the insensitive brute.

The larger of the guards didn't seem in the least put off by her defiance. Instead he stepped forward, gripped her by either elbow, and lifted her off the ground as if she were weightless. She gasped, her body stiffening, which only made his job easier. He placed her down moments later, a good ten feet away from the door, and then turned on his heel without a word and returned to his position outside the door.

Nellie was feeling well and truly steamed by that point, but before she could give them a severe piece of her mind— which she realized even before she opened her mouth would have very little impact on the situation—the door opened and Ron Cordoba and Arthur Penn emerged from the room, deep in conversation. "Sir!" she said with as much indignance as her wounded pride could muster. "Would you mind telling me what's going on here?"

Arthur looked at her as if truly seeing her for the first time. Then he blinked owlishly a couple times before saying, "Actually, Nellie . . . something has come up, and I won't be needing your services for several weeks. Possibly longer. Possibly . . ." He paused, and then started again. He strode forward, putting a hand on her arm. "Perhaps it'd be best if we discussed this in private . . ."

Nellie's eyes widened even as she allowed herself to be led down the hallway by Arthur's gentle but firm hand. Ron followed a step or two behind him. No words passed between them as they walked into Arthur's private study. As soon as they were inside, it suddenly seemed to Nellie as if a silhouette was separating itself from the other shadows in the room. Just as quickly, she recognized it to be the man who'd been introduced to her (a lifetime ago, it felt like) as

"Percival." His relationship to Arthur had, for quite some time, been somewhat confusing to Nellie. She had initially come to the conclusion that he was some sort of "black ops" person, although that was not intended as any sort of pun on his skin color. He had vanished for quite some time, and yet the fact that he was here, now, was not entirely surprising to her. He simply seemed like the sort of person who would be capable of disappearing and then reappearing at curious intervals.

"Sit down, Nellie, please," said Arthur, gesturing toward a chair facing his large oaken desk. He did not sit behind the desk himself, but instead leaned against the side. Nellie smoothed the skirt of her simple white outfit and then brought her arms to her side in a vaguely military bearing. "Gentlemen, I believe you can wait outside. Percival, shut the door behind you, if you'd be so—"

"I don't think we need to be alone if you're planning to fire me, sir," Nellie said stiffly.

"Ah," was all Arthur said for a moment. Then he nodded. "That's what I've always liked about you, Nellie. Straight and to the point. You see—"

"No, I don't see," she said, cutting him off a bit more abruptly than she had intended, but feeling that she'd gone too far to back off her aggressive attitude. Anger and hurt and frustration were raging within her far more intensely than she'd have thought possible. "You've said nothing to me about any fall off in the quality of my work, either in attending to Mrs. Penn's needs or answering mail or handling queries . . ."

"There's been no fall off," Arthur said mildly. "Why should I comment to you about something that does not exist?"

"Oh." That threw her, and then something new occurred to her and she instantly became contrite. "Oh! Oh . . . my God . . ."

"What is it?" asked Arthur with some concern.

"She's dying."

"She is?" Arthur began to look rather agitated. "Why do you say that?"

"Well . . . I mean . . ." She gestured toward herself. "I just . . . figured you were getting rid of me because you didn't need me, and you wouldn't need me because . . ."

"Oh! Oh, no, no, my dear," Arthur said, relief visibly sweeping through him as he sagged against the desk. "No, it's nothing like that. It's just . . . well . . ."

"The need for your services may well be drawing to an end," Ron Cordoba spoke up. "But the details are . . . sketchy at the moment."

"The reason we were in Gwen's room," Arthur said, "was because there's a secured line in there directly to the White House."

"Instead of in here?"

"No, in addition to. Sort of a backup. However, when I made this particular call I just, well," and he smiled slightly, "I wanted to be with Gwen. Ron and I were, well . . ."

"Laying some groundwork," Ron said, "with the President. I needed one or two things and was prevailing upon him to provide them."

"What sort of things?" she asked.

"I . . . don't believe we need go into that," Arthur assured her. "Trust me when I say, they aren't really going to impact on you. Ron has also been making some calls in regard to you. And you have my personal guarantee that you will have your selection of several very exciting jobs in the government, along with my highest recommenda—"

"I don't want your recommendation. I want to know what's going on."

Percival stepped forward with such an economy of movement that it was hard to believe that he'd moved at all. "I believe Mr. Penn is saying it's not possible to accommodate your wishes at this time."

She didn't even look at him, her gaze upon Arthur never wavering. "This is about Mrs. Penn, isn't it? Something's happened with her condition. I'm right, aren't I? Is she going to be all right?" she continued without pause. "'That's all I want to know."

"I believe she will, yes," Arthur said, and he took a few steps forward, gesturing toward the doors of the study. "And that's all I can really tell you. Nellie, believe me, I don't mean to be rude to you, because truly you've done so much for us. But we're on something of a timetable here, and there's a great deal to—"

She stepped away from him, turning to face him straight on, her chin slightly arched in a defiant manner. "This has something to do with you being King Arthur, doesn't it?"

It was as if an anvil had been dropped into the middle of the room, and the men were waiting for the reverberations of the *thud* to cease before they responded. It was Arthur who spoke first, clearing his throat and obviously endeavoring to laugh it off. "Nellie," he began, "that entire 'Camelot' business during my mayoral race in New York . . . you have to understand how the media can exaggerate—"

"Please," said Nellie in a flat, no-nonsense voice, putting up a hand in a fashion that was so preemptory that it was startling. She was continuing to stand, although she did rest the fingers of her other hand lightly on the desktop. "Please don't patronize me, or think that I'm stupid. I know everything. I know about Merlin the miniature wizard, frozen in stone by a Basilisk. I know about how Mrs. Penn is the reincarnation of Guinevere. About the invisible sword you keep with you at all times, sir. About the cave you lived in for a thousand years until you returned because you were needed. About Morgan Le Fey. About Percival," and she nodded in his direction, "and how he drank from the Holy Grail. About all of it."

Arthur visibly paled. "How . . . how did . . . ?"

"Mrs. Penn," Percival said slowly. "It had to be . . . no offense, sire, but expecting a woman, even a first lady, to be circumspect . . ."

Nellie vigorously shook her head. "No. It wasn't her."

"Then who?" Ron demanded, looking well and truly

pissed off. His arms folded, he faced her angrily and continued, "Because it's obvious that we have some sort of major security leak, Ms. Porter, and if you have any pretense to being faithful to the concerns of Mrs. Penn or the former President, then you'll be forthcoming in—"

"It was you, you idiot," said Nellie.

All gazes went to Ron. He stared at her in confusion, shaking his head. "That's . . . that's ridicu—"

"It was on the night Mr. Penn resigned. You got stinking drunk and tried to beat the crap out of what I thought was a simple statue." She seemed to be relishing the recollection. Ron, for his part, appeared to be getting visibly sick. "And while you were busy being completely blasted, you told me the whole thing."

"Well done, Ron," Arthur said sarcastically. "Oh, bloody well done. You didn't happen to tell her the launch codes for our nuclear missiles while you were at it, did you?"

"I don't know those offhand," Ron replied, his voice thick.

"Well, that's a damned good thing, now, isn't it?" Arthur said. His gaze swiveled back to Nellie. "Frankly, Miss Porter, I'm surprised that you would so willingly believe such an elaborate concoction, particularly considering Ron's somewhat inebriated state."

For the first time Nellie did sit, daintily crossing her legs at the knees. She displayed the air of a woman who is, as a general rule, exceptionally proud of herself when she has taken firm control of a situation. "You'd think I *would* dismiss it out of hand, wouldn't you? But here's the truth of it, sir. There are times when one's life is filled with all sorts of things that are strange. Damned strange. Looked at individually, they don't mean anything. Take them as a pattern of occurrences, however, and they leave you with a lot of questions. And when an answer presents itself, even when it's an answer that seems ludicrous . . . you find yourself thinking, 'Yes, but . . . that makes so much sense.' "

"And that's how it was for you in this instance, was it?"

asked Arthur. She nodded. At that, Arthur sighed and then shrugged in a most expressive manner. "Are you planning to tell anyone?"

"No, sir," she said firmly. "But . . . I'd like you to do something for me."

One of his eyebrows shot up. "Blackmail, Miss Porter?"

"A request, Mr. President." She looked from the chagrined Ron over to Percival and then back to Arthur, and for the first time she looked uncertain of her emotional and political footing. She decided the best way to deal with the situation was simply to plunge right into it. "I'd like to be a part of whatever's developed with Mrs. Penn. I've been with her a good long time. I've . . . come to think of her as a friend, in addition to being one of the greatest women I've ever met. I don't know that I'd say I have a *right* to know, but—"

To her surprise, Arthur interrupted her with a firm, "I would say that. You do have a right to know. However, Nellie, understand," and he raised a cautioning index finger, "once you know these things . . . once you fully acknowledge and realize that the circumstances that spawned us are incalculable in their power, merciless in their vengeance, and arbitrary in their victims . . . once you realize all that, that would be the point where you *should* know."

She looked at the grim faces surrounding her, then back to Arthur. "With all due respect, sir . . . what are you *talking* about?"

A flummoxed Arthur looked as if he were about to start over again, and then he simply lowered his head and sighed. "Percival, Ron . . ." he said, his voice trailing off.

Percival turned to face her. He spoke with a touch of pride, the mark of someone who had experienced a significant hardship and lived to tell of it. "I assume you've heard of the Holy Grail."

"Of course. The old story about . . ." And then she stopped, her mind racing, and she intuited exactly where the conversation was going. She could barely speak above a whisper, so suddenly taken with the notion of hope where there had been no hope before. "You've found it? Is that where you're going with this? You've found the Holy Grail, and you can use it to help Mrs. Penn?"

Percival looked somewhat disappointed. "You certainly don't allow a fellow to build up any sense of drama."

"This is the twenty-first century. We have no sense of drama," she informed him.

In deference to Nellie's obvious desire to cut straight to the heart of the matter, Percival outlined for her in quick, clear summary all that had transpired, beginning with his encounter with the rapidly aging man in South America. She listened raptly, not interrupting even once. Percival was clearly pleased about that and warmed to his tale, giving Nellie the impression that his narrative had constantly been halted by Arthur earlier on in the first go-around. The most she offered was nodding and an occasional "Hunh!" or "Wow!" She was embarrassed to discover that she was actually holding her breath during the part where Percival faced off against Enkidu. When he finally got to the point where he staggered ashore in New Jersey, she felt genuine relief, as if she'd forgotten that he'd obviously survived since he was sitting opposite her.

When Percival finished, there was a long moment of silence. Finally Nellie asked, a bit nervously, "So . . . so what happens now?"

"Well, that was what we had been in the process of discussing," Ron said evenly. He was still looking a bit sheepish over the fact that Nellie was being brought into the loop because of his indiscretion. "When we were in Mrs. Penn's room just now, I was speaking to President Stockwell about arranging transport to Pus Island."

Nellie made a face at that. "Uhm . . . could we call it something else? Because that's, y'know . . . pretty disgusting."

"Fine. 'Grail Island,' then. How's that?" When she gave a nod of acquiescence, he continued, "So . . . we spoke with the President, and he displayed some hesitation at first. I made it clear, though, that I felt the need to take some time off as chief of staff, and I was hoping that he'd be willing to accommodate me on this matter."

"Time off?" She looked perplexed. "Are you allowed to do that?"

"It's not outside the realm of the possible," Ron said dryly. "You see," and he cast an amused glance in Arthur's direction, "I've decided that I need to make my life a bit more exciting by going on a quest. And I can't think of a better person to have accompanying me."

Nellie could barely contain her excitement. She was on her feet, her eyes alight with newly resurging hope that she wouldn't have thought possible. "I'm coming along."

"Nellie," Arthur began.

But she didn't want to hear it. "You don't get it," she said with growing urgency as she paced the room. She seemed to be talking as much to herself as she was to any of the men in the room. "Day after day of seeing Mrs. Penn just lying there, withering away. No hope . . . I thought she had no hope. I had no hope for her. And suddenly this . . . this whole thing is presenting itself, and I've got to be a part of it. You can't tell me I can't be a part of it. I need to. I need to be there for her . . ."

"Nellie, your loyalty is touching . . ." Arthur tried to interrupt.

Ron was looking at her suspiciously. She didn't like the look in his eyes, although obviously he couldn't quite put his finger on anything. She locked gazes briefly with him for a moment, then turned back to Arthur. "Sir," she said, sounding as formal as she could, "you don't understand. I can't begin to post a résumé like yours with quests and great feats and . . . and all that stuff. I'm not a 'great feats' person. I'm more a 'feats of clay' person. But my time with your wife . . . it's as if I've been part of a great adventure. And now that adventure is taking a bizarre and exciting turn, and . . ." Her voice faltered for a moment and then she rallied. "And I have to be there for it. That's all. I just . . . I have to be there. I have to see how it all comes out. I can't be on the outside looking in. I just know I'll never have an opportunity like this again, to be . . . to be part of something truly 'great' in every sense of the word. To be legendary even. Don't shut me out. Not from this. Not now. Please."

"I'm sorry, Nellie," Ron said as gently as he could. "But I'm afraid that—"

"She can come," said Arthur.

Ron blanched, turned to Arthur with what was clearly every intention of arguing. Then he saw the amused but firm look in the face of the once and future king, and simply sighed and said, "But I'm afraid that I cannot guarantee you a window seat on the plane when we go to Pus Isl—I'm sorry, Grail Island."

Excitement bubbled within her, but she didn't even try to say thank you, since she was concerned that, once she started saying it, she wouldn't be able to stop. That she'd just be babbling like an idiot. That was hardly the way to underscore the notion that she would be of value to the expedition.

So instead she confined her concerns to more immediate issues. "When do we leave?" she said. "From where do we leave?"

"At dawn," Arthur said. "That's always a good time for such things. There's a newness in the air that makes just about anything seem possible, no matter how ludicrous. A transport helicopter will arrive to bring us to a private airfield, and a small craft will be meeting us there to transport us to Grail Island." He smiled. "I like the sound of that. 'Grail Island.' It sounds very . . ."

"Arthurian?" offered Percival.

"Yes. I was just going to say that. You know, I never thought it would happen, but I'm finding I rather like being an entire genre."

*   *   *

"**P**US ISLAND?"

Baumann's voice sounded puzzled over the phone. Even though she was in her own home, Nellie realized that she was looking around as if convinced that someone was watching her, spying on her, preparing to rat her out for ratting Arthur out.

"Yes. That's right. Have you heard of it?"

"Yeah, I think so. It's part of the Skeleton Keys, a small group of islands off South America." He paused and then laughed to himself. "Jeez, the crap you pick up from a lifetime of reporting." She could hear scribbling over the phone; he was jotting it down, making notes to himself. All business, he continued, "So Arthur's heading up a little excursion there? For some sort of faith healing thing for the former first lady?"

"Something like that. Maybe even more than that. It could be huge, Baumann. It could be really huge."

"How huge?" He sounded skeptical, even pitying. "I'm telling you right now, Porter, I've seen people with terminal family members break themselves to bits trying to find cures, and it's always a washout and it's always pathetic. It'd be a pity to see a former president go down that same route."

"You're saying you wouldn't report the story?"

He snorted over the phone and she made a face at the noise. It was like chatting with a hog. "Of course I would. Make a hell of a piece. I have a favor or two I can pull in and get myself over there. I'll wait a day or so before I do, just to give you guys time to settle in and get involved with . . . with whatever you're getting involved in."

"It's big."

"I doubt it."

"Okay, but . . ." She knew she was sounding increasingly desperate, but she didn't care. "But if it is big . . . you have to promise me . . . we're done. No more holding anything over me. This is *the* story, this squares us, okay?"

"I dunno . . . it'd have to be pretty big . . ."

"It is. I swear to God and on my mother's life, it is."

"Just your mother?"

Her mouth twitched in annoyance. "Well, I never liked my father much."

He uttered a short, seal-like laugh on the other end. "If it's that big, fine, fine. But we're talking pretty damned big. What's on this island, anyway?"

"As near as I can tell . . . God."

"Fine. Tell God to say 'Cheese' when I show up."

T HE WATER SPEEDS *past him below. The former king of the Britons watches it with a sort of distant appreciation, finding the entire thing something of a wonderment. He does not glance around the interior of the vehicle at his companions. If he did, he would shudder inwardly, for it is a very ragtag and disparate group he is bringing with him.*

Madness. It is madness. It should have just been him and Percival. The only two who truly know and appreciate what's going on. What's happened to him? Has he totally lost the ability to make an intelligent decision? No matter that the additional people in the group have a vested emotional interest in the endeavor. It means nothing in the situation that they're going into. He should have left them behind.

Madness.

There is someone moving over toward him as the powerful rotors overhead drive the vehicle forward. He does not have to shift his gaze from the window. He knows who it is by his tread. Upon the distant horizon, he sees that the sun is beginning to creep upward. The first gentle rays are seeping over the ocean. The sky appears red. That is never a good sign. It's even part of a saying. Something about a sailor taking warning of such a condition.

Ron Cordoba eases himself into the chair next to the former king. He glances around at the passengers, and because he does so, Arthur does as well. There is Percival, strapped into a seat in the decidedly non-luxurious body of the vessel, but he does not look the least bit perturbed over what may be a coming battle. Despite the fact that he is being flown into the very island that he labored so long to escape from, there is not the slightest fragment of concern evident within him. He could not be more relaxed. His head leans back against the wall, and his breathing is regular. His eyes are closed. He is asleep . . . although Arthur suspects that if a danger suddenly presented itself, Percival would be the first one up and with a weapon in his hand.

Nellie is no longer looking out a window. She had been earlier. Apparently it made her sick, since she is making such a pointed effort to avoid making the same mistake. She appears decidedly paler. If there had been any question in Arthur's mind that bringing her was a bad idea, this simply confirms it. But hindsight, as always, remains twenty-twenty, and it is simply too late to do anything about it now. Nellie manages to pull herself out of her motion-sickness-induced discomfort long enough to check on Gwen's vitals.

Gwen.

It tears him up to see her like this. Strapped into a bed, monitors all attached, tubes sticking out of her every which way. Had there been any concern on Arthur's part that he was doing the wrong thing, all such fears become allayed when he contemplates her current condition.

Ron, however, does not appear to have lost his fears or allowed them to become allayed. No, they're quite, quite unallayed. He strikes a delicate balance, trying to speak loudly enough to get above the vehicle's rotors, but not so loudly that all concerned can hear every syllable of what should be, ideally, a private conversation.

"So . . . who do you think he is, really?" he asks.

Arthur stares at him blankly, not comprehending. "What 'he' would that be, Ron?"

"This lunatic that Percival was talking about. This guy who says he's Gilgamesh. Who do you think he really is?"

"Ah. I've been giving that some long and hard thought," Arthur says, stroking his beard in a manner that suggests serious *pondering is going on.* "I believe I have it solved."

"Really?"

"Yes. I think he's Gilgamesh."

Now it is Ron's turn to stare. "How can you say that?"

"It is not difficult. The words form rather easily between tongue and teeth . . ."

"No! I mean . . ." Ron blinks furiously, obviously endeavoring to keep his temper in check since he believes that Arthur Penn is not taking the situation seriously. "How can you believe this lunatic is truly Gilgamesh."

"You would ask that?" Arthur tells him with a tone of gentle rebuke. "You, who know me for who and what I am?"

"That's different, though."

"How? Because I am only ten centuries old, while he is more than four times that? Are you saying, Ron, that your suspension of disbelief will stretch only so far and no further? What is the maximum that you will allow for skepticism? Eleven centuries? Twelve?"

Ron is unable to keep the annoyance from his voice. "All right, all right, I get it. But how did he survive all this time?"

"I don't know. But it's going to be interesting finding out, isn't it?" He sees Ron's dour expression and chucks him on the upper arm. "Come now, young sir. You spoke so zealously of quests. Embrace that which you've wished for."

"Don't they always say, 'Be careful of what you wish for'?" Ron shakes his head. "At least we have some Secret Service men with us. They'll provide some protection." He glances around. "Where are they?"

"Back at the airstrip," Arthur says coolly.

Ron obviously can't quite believe what he is hearing. He shakes his head as if trying to remove water from between his ears. "What?"

"They are back at the airstrip," Arthur repeats very carefully, as if stepping over eggshells. "Percival made sure they were off the vehicle before we took off. Don't worry, Ronald. I'm sure he was quite gentle about it."

"Gentle about it?" His voice is louder than he had anticipated, causing confused glances from the others in the cabin. He fights to lower it at Arthur's cautioning gesture, and is only partly successful. "How can you be so . . . so . . ."

"Calm?" Arthur shrugs. "Matters will play out as they will, Ron. I am not interested in going in as a military force. I've no desire to challenge this Gilgamesh in a show of prowess. And if I can take anything that Percival says as a guide, it would do us no good at all to try and muscle our way onto his island. Do you not understand, Ron? I may be legend . . . but Gilgamesh is the stuff of legend. It would be insulting to walk in with armed guards."

"Insulting to Gilgamesh?"

"No. To me. It would seem to him as if I were afraid to fend for myself. Besides, the Secret Service has no idea of my true background. I would just as soon keep it that way. No, Ron . . . this is a situation that calls for subtlety and delicacy. Neither of those will be accommodated with gunmen at my side. I am entering Gilgamesh's terrain and seeking his help. Threats and shows of force are not appropriate to the situation."

"Really?" says Ron, feeling as if his bowels have suddenly turned to cold cheese. "And what would you say is appropriate, then?"

Arthur smiled. "Charm."

"HE COMES."

Miss Basil, lightly clad in a green robe that flutters in the steady breeze, looks to the evening sky. Gilgamesh walks up and drapes an arm lightly on her bare shoulder. The cold of it strikes him, not for the first time. When they make love, he feels the warmth in her then. But he suspects that, in point of fact, the warmth is drawn from he himself. That she is incapable of producing it without him. That would not surprise him, since he knows who and what she is. Still, it is a thought that fills him with unease.

It is Miss Basil who has spoken now. She studies the skies, her eyes unblinking. She seems to be staring with very great intensity *in a particular direction, but there is nothing there that Gilgamesh can discern. Yet with a certainty she repeats, "He comes."*

"He. Pendragon, you mean?" She nods in response to his question, not shifting her gaze from the nothingness in the dark. "He is coming? How know you that he is coming?"

Her nostrils flare slightly, savoring the air. Night is reaching its nadir, and within a couple of hours will cede its control of the sky to the sun, slinking off into nothingness until its time of dominion returns some hours hence. "I smell him. And it."

"It?"

"Magic in the air. The wheels turning once more. You should be able to sense it as well, High King."

"I regret to inform you that I do not."

She seems most puzzled to hear that, and she tears her gaze away from the nothing-particularly-substantial and instead focuses her gaze upon her lover. Her long, tapering right hand rests upon his muscled forearm. "I do not understand that," she says flatly. "You have lived as long as I. Beings such as we . . . we become attuned to our surroundings as no mortal can. When one resides upon the earth for such a length of time, we become as one with the rhythms of the life upon it. Certainly you must have felt it. You can feel it in you now, can you not?"

The High King closes his eyes, reaches deep within himself. He searches for the connection that the monster tells him must be there. She watches him with an unblinking, hypnotic stare. The silence seems interminable. When he opens his eyes once more, there is no sadness or confusion or anything within.

"Nothing," he says.

"That cannot be."

"A man who has lived for millennia and a Basilisk cannot be, either," he replies reasonably, "and yet we are. I tell you, woman, that I feel nothing. Occasionally dreams are visited upon me, visions of the future, but they never make sense to me. I depend upon another to interpret them for me. The connection you speak of . . ." He shakes his head. "I am alone. It has always been this way, and it always shall be. I surround myself with worshipers. Enkidu, my brother in battle, would do whatever I requested of him. But ultimately, I

am alone. The world may be calling to me, but I do not hear it, and would not know it if I did."

"You sound self-pitying."

He gives a slight shrug. "It is not my intent. I am who I am. I do not, cannot, regret that. I am two-thirds god, one-third man, and that is far more than any man that you ever can hope to meet."

"But if you—"

"I do not wish to discuss this matter any further."

That does not sit well with the woman, but when she opens her mouth to speak, he places a single finger on her lips, shushing her before she can utter another syllable. "The High King has expressed his desires on this matter," he informs her, "and I will have no one gainsay me. Not even you. Is that clear?"

She obviously wishes to respond, to say more, to pick a fight, to refuse to back down. But it seems hardly worth the effort, and in the final analysis, he really is a rather pretty thing. She shrugs as he did earlier, but the gesture by her shapely shoulders looks far more attractive on her than it did on him.

Once more the High King looks to the sky. "He comes, you say?"

She nods.

"Why then," the High King says, "we must make ready."

PARTE THE THIRD:
We Three Kings

❦

CHAPTRE
THE EIGHTEENTH

🗡

THE AGED ONE had a regular routine down. When one has been around for about as long as humanity was actually capable of stringing together complete sentences and expressing opinions in a manner other than simian in nature, one tends to fall into ruts. That did not bother the Aged One, though. What advantage was there to being the oldest man on earth if one could not indulge one's little rituals?

Every morning he would awaken, sit up in bed, and sniff the air to see if the End Times were coming. Once he was satisfied that such was not the case, he would rise from his place of slumber. Then would come a series of morning ablutions, followed by reading, meditation, lunch, a nap, a stroll around the island, and free time that could be used for a variety of purposes. Then would come the evening, prayers, and to bed. For someone who was essentially spending his days waiting to see if anything was going to change, it was a fairly pleasant way in which to occupy one's time.

He had become so accustomed to the routine that, this

particular morning, he almost missed it. He did not, at first, recognize the scent for what it was. Indeed, he had begun to swing his scrawny legs off the side of the bed when he froze in mid-motion, his brain only just then processing what his olfactory senses had tried to tell him. He blinked several times, and then—just to make sure—he hauled himself back onto his bed, lay down, stared up at the ceiling for a long moment, and then proceeded to sit up all over again and inhale deeply. The thought was that he might encounter a different sensation this time.

He was wrong.

The thing was, in all the time that he'd been scenting the air for it, he had never actually known what it would smell like. He had just been aware that—like art one knows when one sees it—he would recognize the smell when he encountered it. And sure enough, there it was, the indefinable essence that spoke of only one thing.

"The End Times," he whispered.

He was not afraid. He had lived too long to fear anything. There was no threat to his life; no such threat existed. That was both his blessing and his curse. Nevertheless, just speaking the words, even in the soft, tentative manner that he just had, jolted him to the bottom of the soul that he had forgotten he had in the first place.

Afterward, the Aged One would not even recall throwing on his robes and dressing. His morning ablutions were forgotten for the first time in . . . well, for as long as he could remember, and that was a fairly far piece. All he knew was that he was outside, and looking to the sky, and was so fixed on doing so that he nearly bumped into the High King before he caught himself at the last moment.

Gilgamesh gazed down at him in amused confusion. The High King looked quite at ease, so much so that it made the Aged One aware of just how disconcerted he had allowed himself to become. It took him more effort than he would have thought possible to reclaim his customary look of dispassion and vague contempt.

Still, nothing slipped past Gilgamesh. His gaze never wavering, he said slowly, "You seem rather . . . anxious, Ziusura."

The Aged One's face darkened. He did not like the casual use of his name, and the High King knew it perfectly well. The fact that he was doing so regardless of the Aged One's preferences spoke volumes to Ziusura. "Do not presume to judge my frame of mind, Gilgamesh."

"I presume nothing," said Gilgamesh mildly. "I simply made an observation. Voiced an opinion. Agree with it or not at your discretion."

And before Ziusura could reply, Enkidu was standing right in front of him. The great man-creature's abrupt appearance startled the Aged One. He had not heard him at all. Compared to the stealth with which Enkidu moved, even the greatest of jungle predators sounded like a train wreck in their approaches.

"We are to have visitors today, Aged One," Gilgamesh said blithely. He sounded unconcerned. It was difficult for Ziusura to determine whether the lack of concern was genuine or feigned. Without bidding, images of the dream Gilgamesh had described to him all those months ago came roaring back to him. The dreams of Arthur Pendragon (for such did Ziusura know him to be) with his great sword in hand, and that infinity sign, or perhaps the number eight.

"Eight months," said Ziusura slowly.

"Yes." Gilgamesh was nodding. He was by no means a fool, the High King. The thought had occurred to him as well. "Dream imagery. Infinity? Eight? We do not know. We may never know. But all of that pales in comparison to that which we do know, specifically . . ."

"That Gilgamesh will triumph," said Enkidu. As always, he chose his words carefully. He also sounded out of breath, as if the mere pronouncing of words exhausted him.

"Yes, my brother," Gilgamesh said with confidence. He placed a hand on Enkidu's shoulder and looked at him affectionately. "As always."

Ziusura glanced around and, making no endeavor to keep the distaste from his voice, asked, "Where is your woman?"

"She is not my woman."

"That much is true," said the Aged One. "She is not any sort of true woman. Nevertheless, you . . . associate with her. I was curious."

"She is attending to other matters," Gilgamesh said. There was something in his voice that told Ziusura the High King was being less than forthcoming. But there really wasn't much point in pursuing the matter any further. The High King always liked his little secrets and games, and in the insulated environment of Pus Island, he didn't have the opportunity to practice them nearly enough.

So the Aged One simply bobbed his head slightly in acknowledgment. Then he realized that Enkidu was looking at him. It was rare that the creature did so, which normally suited Ziusura just fine. There was something so unnatural about Enkidu that the Aged One always felt better when the walking beast's attention was elsewhere. Such was obviously not the case now, however, and so Ziusura looked him full in his furry face and said, "Do you have something on your mind, Beast Man?"

"You will not speak so to him," Gilgamesh said sternly.

"And you will not speak so to me," replied the Aged One. He turned to leave, and then stopped short when Enkidu spoke up in that soft, deep growl that passed as his voice.

"You know."

That was all Enkidu said, but it was enough to fully latch the Aged One's attention upon him. For a long moment they regarded each other, as if truly seeing each other for the first time. Finally Ziusura replied, "Yes. Yes . . . I do."

Gilgamesh looked in puzzlement from one to the other. "What are you referring to? What do you know? What do the both of you know? Do I know it?"

"You know it, too, yes," Ziusura told him reassuringly.

But then he added, "You simply do not know that you know it."

The High King's forehead creased in a frown, but before he could pursue the conversation further, Enkidu—who had been crouching until that point, like a great lion poised in the high weeds—suddenly came to full attention. His ears were quivering, all his attention focused on one point in the sky. "He comes. I hear him."

"I hear nothing," said Gilgamesh, and seemed a bit annoyed with himself over that. Nor did Ziusura detect anything. He did not, however, doubt Enkidu's word on that. First, he didn't think the creature was truly capable of lying, and even if he were, he certainly would never lie to Gilgamesh, to whom he was so dedicated.

"How can you not?" Enkidu did not sound challenging in the statement, but instead almost disappointed that his friend and liege could be so deaf and blind to the world around him. "The very air currents bend to him." It was a long sentence for him, and did not come without effort.

Gilgamesh was about to reply, and suddenly he sensed it, or saw it, as well. It was a speck on the horizon, coming in from the north, but it was moving quickly. Closer it drew, and still closer, and the details were still difficult to discern, but the High King was not waiting. Instead he drew himself up to his full height, and when he spoke it was posed as a question but, really, there was no degree of uncertainty in his voice. "It is he, isn't it? Percival's liege lord." Neither person on either side confirmed it for him. Neither needed to. "Well then," he continued, "we must arrange a greeting for him in keeping with his status. Come then. Let us attend to it."

The Aged One wasn't paying attention to them as they walked away, Enkidu listening to the plans that Gilgamesh was unfurling. Instead his attention was focused on the rapidly nearing object in the sky.

He felt some degree of frustration, but such concerns were

quickly set aside. The simple fact was that the gods detested stagnation. They sought to shake things up occasionally, just to keep themselves interested, and bewailing one's lot in life in that regard was not only a waste of time, but was probably the exact sort of sniveling self-pity that caused the gods such amusement. No, it was far better to simply acknowledge the gods' superiority and make preparations for whatever insanity they might be preparing to inflict.

Ziusura was most definitely ready. If there was one thing eternal life had taught him, it was to be prepared for anything the gods might try to throw at him. And this object heading straight for the island was most definitely a mighty large object that the gods were lobbing in his direction.

So Ziusura went to the place where he had made his preparations for just such an eventuality, and checked them over to make certain everything was still just as he'd left it. Finally, satisfying himself that all was well, he returned to the main section where all was being made ready for the arrival of Percival's liege lord, the noble Arthur Pendragon, late of the Britons.

F ROM HER PLACE *in the trees, Miss Basil watches with her unblinking green eyes.*

She is very aware of her function, of what needs to be done. So much so, in fact, that she has not even felt the need to check with Gilgamesh to make certain that her actions are what the High King desires. She knows him all too well.

Indeed, the truth of that amuses her somewhat. The High King fancies himself a great thinker, a great man of depth and complexity. Two-thirds god, one-third man. But the lesser part of him is so much lesser that it tends to overwhelm the greater, is her opinion. The truth is, there is about as much depth to Gilgamesh as in the average tuna salad. Nevertheless, she does owe him for her very existence, and for that alone if no other reason, she allows the wheels of fate to bring her to this point.

And she owes Arthur as well. Owes him greatly. And Basiliskos always repays her debts in full . . .

I T WASN'T DIFFICULT for Ziusura to find the location. There was enough racket and hullabaloo that if Ziusura had been deaf, dumb, and blind he still would have been able to make his way to the anticipated arrival point. There he discovered that Gilgamesh and Enkidu had acted very quickly in rounding up many of the inhabitants of Pus Island . . . particularly a significant assortment of the attractive female ones. Scanty outfits and tanned, bare skin were both in copious supply among the greeters who had gathered with a mixture of fear and anticipation.

Such gorgeous women, such a bounty of youth and beauty. And it had been so long.

For the first time in quite a while, Ziusura thought about his wife. He did not do it very often, because doing so saddened him beyond his ability to articulate, and why should he subject himself to that? But for just a moment, the look and scent and smile of her came flooding back to him in such a way that it nearly overwhelmed him, and then Ziusura thrust the recollection away with effort. Now was not the time for such things, although he wasn't really sure there ever *would* be a time.

Closer still drew the flying object, and Gilgamesh was staring at it with perplexity. He was wearing his large crown with the powerful curved horns adorning either side. His bloodred cloak, which he sported on only the most important of occasions, hung draped around his shoulders. His kilt was decorated with the images of lightning bolts, and his sandals were laced up to just under his knees. His sword was sheathed and hanging upon his back, but the Aged One knew of Gilgamesh's speed, and was aware that the sword could be in his hand in a literal instant.

"What . . . is that?" asked Gilgamesh slowly, as the flying

vehicle that appeared both ungainly and yet graceful cut through the air.

"It's an Osprey," the Aged One promptly replied.

"That is no bird . . ."

"A Bell Boeing V-22 Osprey," Ziusura continued. "It's a model of VTOL . . . a Vertical Takeoff and Landing vehicle."

Gilgamesh turned and stared at the Aged One with amazement bordering on reverence. "You know of such things?"

"Of course. Why don't you?"

"That is not the point. How can you know of it? Do the gods visit dreams upon you? Do you study augeries? Do you upon occasion wander the earth seeking knowledge that you can—"

"I have an Internet connection, you great lummox. How else?"

Gilgamesh and Enkidu exchanged looks of surprise. "A what?"

The Aged One blew air impatiently out between his lips. "Gilgamesh, reside in as primitive a style as it suits you to. Be a living monument to a time long past. Some of us, however, prefer to exist in the current century rather than one millennia agone. I know I do. Oh, your green-eyed girl-friend does as well. I found her website. Very twisted material, that one."

Gilgamesh's response was drowned out by the roar of the rotors as the Osprey had drawn right overhead. The residents of Pus Island were falling back. Some of the men and women were clutching at their exotic scraps of clothing to prevent them from blowing away. Others were just standing there with smiles, not caring what sort of disarray their ensembles were left in from the wind kicked up by the rotors.

As the VTOL lowered, even the hardiest of the Pus Island residents stepped back, shielding their eyes so as not to let any of the flying dust land in them. Nearby trees were bent backward by the power of the blades. The vehicle hovered a moment more, as if trying to decide whether landing was really such a good idea, and then the air vessel touched down. This simple act brought a smattering of applause from the onlookers, which amused Ziusura.

There were two rotors upon the Osprey, one on either wing, both of them now shutting off. The Aged One could see that the ends of the wings swiveled, capable of having the propellers facing forward like an airplane for long-distance flight or—as was the case now—shifted into an upright position at a ninety-degree angle to the wings, making the Osprey evocative of a helicopter.

"Amazing," Gilgamesh said. The truth was, the Aged One was impressed as well, but he wasn't about to admit to it.

Long after the noise of the engines had ceased, the blades were still whirring. Now all was silent upon Pus Island, and the Aged One suddenly remembered that the Osprey was equipped with such goodies as multi-barrel rotary machine guns. If Arthur Pendragon had come in looking for war, he could just start opening fire on everyone who was standing around the Osprey, hoping to litter the landing pad with corpses. He would, of course, get something of a surprise should he go that route, but there would be a good deal of blood and screaming and noise, and it did not sound to Ziusura remotely like a fun time.

Happily, such was not the case. Instead, after some moments, the large cargo door on the side unlatched with a noise that sounded like a cannon shot. Then it slid open and standing in the doorway was a large black man whom the Aged One recognized instantly.

So, too, did Gilgamesh. He waved and hailed him as if greeting an old friend and ally. "Well met, Percival!" he called out. "You raised quite a ruckus the last time you walked our humble shores and then escaped them."

"No thanks to you," said Percival evenly. He had braced himself within the door, hands holding on to either side of the frame.

"No thanks to me," Gilgamesh acknowledged without the slightest indication of shame. "But I do not resent you your . . . antics. Nor does Enkidu. Do you, my warrior brother?"

Enkidu shook his head briefly, but he never took his gaze from Percival. It was hard for Ziusura to get a real feeling just how Enkidu felt about Percival's having eluded him during their chase through the forest. Enkidu prided his hunting skills above all else, and his having failed to capture Percival very likely rankled him, no matter what sort of cheery face Gilgamesh was trying to put upon it.

The Aged One watched in silence as the passengers of the Osprey stepped off. Percival hopped down, then turned and helped a young woman off the vehicle, swinging her lightly to the ground. She let out a surprised little gasp of air. A man quickly followed, taller and a bit more careworn than the woman. Both of them seemed very mundane, and were of little interest to Ziusura. The woman looked around in perplexity, and then cried out involuntarily when her gaze fell upon Enkidu. Reflexively she grabbed the man by the arm, clutching it tightly. He saw where she was looking, and his face went slack as if all the blood had evaporated from it in one great rush, but at least he managed to contain himself and not cry out. Whether Enkidu had noticed either of their reactions was difficult for the Aged One to say. He simply stood there with his feline inscrutability. Such a contrast he was from Gilgamesh: The High King restrained his passions with effort, while Enkidu had to struggle inwardly just to display even the mildest of reactions.

And then Arthur emerged.

Even if Ziusura had never set eyes upon an image of the former president of the United States before, he would have known this man for what he was. He stood straight and tall in the door. Whereas the men who had just emerged were perspiring in the heat, their shirts already sticking to their chests, Arthur was the picture of mental and physical cool. He was dressed simply in a dark suit, a rust-colored shirt open at the neck, and his suit jacket draped casually over one arm. He radiated confidence and charisma.

Until that moment, the residents of Pus Island who had come to serve as greeters had seemed almost amused by the whole thing. It was in some ways a grand joke to them. But with the appearance of Pendragon, the very air seemed to change, to crackle with an energy that had not been there before. The people shifted in their place, glanced at one another, silently affirming whether each of them was getting the same impression from this new arrival.

Gilgamesh remained blasé. Without taking his eyes from Pendragon, he said in a voice just low enough to be heard by Enkidu and the Aged One, "This is a warrior king? He does not seem particularly impressive, this one."

Ziusura couldn't quite believe what he had just heard the High King say. He stared at Gilgamesh, managing to keep his astonishment from his expression. Gilgamesh actually appeared bored, even disappointed by Arthur's appearance. *How can he not see? How can he not realize?* It was almost enough to cause the Aged One to doubt himself. Almost. But not quite. *It's true. He doesn't realize. How very tragic.*

"Ah, well," Gilgamesh murmured, "even if he is not as I pictured him, he is still a king and therefore entitled to certain courtesies." At which point Gilgamesh raised his voice and began to chant. The song had an eerie quality to it, and the words were of a language that had not been widely spoken since a time when the gods themselves were young. Arthur had stepped down from the vehicle and now he merely stood, listening very attentively to the chant. Ziusura was struck by the intensity that Arthur displayed, taking in every syllable as if he understood when, obviously, he could not possibly have done so.

The song went on for several minutes. It was the only sound that could be heard on the island. Even the waves of the ocean, normally heard lapping on the distant shores, seemed to silence themselves, and the caws of birds and sounds of other animals upon the island ceased as well. It was as if the entire world had halted to attend to the chanting of the High King.

Finally Gilgamesh ended his song, the last notes still hovering in the air, and Arthur bowed deeply. Gilgamesh did not return the gesture, but instead simply inclined his head in acknowledgment.

"In greeting for me, I take it?" Arthur inquired.

"Just so," replied Gilgamesh. "You are Arthur Pendragon?"

"Nee Pendragon, 'Penn' of late. 'Sir' is always preferable, but between us two," he said, his voice both light and yet with an undercurrent of subtle expectation for respect, "I would think 'Arthur' would suffice. And you, I take it, are Gilgamesh?"

"Just so," he said again. He squared his shoulders and seemed to add another five inches in height. Arthur angled his head slightly to keep his eyes upon the High King's, but if the additional build of the High King at all disconcerted Arthur, he gave no indication of such. "And you," continued Gilgamesh, "have come to my island uninvited. But not, I daresay, unheralded." He nodded in Percival's direction.

"You know my name," Arthur observed, "and yet I was led to understand that my man, Percival, was not forthcoming with that information."

"Indeed he was not. Did you doubt his word?"

"Never. I was simply curious as to how you knew."

"I am a king, Pendragon. I have my sources." And he smiled enigmatically.

"Very well." Folding his arms across his chest, Arthur said evenly, nodding toward the beast-man to one side, "And this would be Enkidu, I take it? Yes, of course it would. And . . . you?" He looked blankly at Ziusura.

"This is the Aged One," Gilgamesh said. "Also known as Ziusura, and also Ut-Napisti."

Arthur stared at Ziusura, obviously trying to pull up a recollection, and then it clearly came to him. "Ut-Napisti? I . . . know that name. According to legend, you saved animals from a great flood, much like Noah."

Ziusura shook his head. "No," he corrected politely. "Noah was much like me."

"And the gods rewarded you with eternal life."

With a shrug, Ziusura said, "I wouldn't say for sure just how much of a 'reward' it was, but yes. That is correct."

The young woman standing near was apparently thunderstruck by what she was hearing, and the man with her was just shaking his head. They didn't believe, or were having trouble believing. That was of little consequence to Ziusura. How did it possibly matter to him whether they accepted or not? His existence, his world, was not predicated on their acceptance.

"Well, this is an honor," Arthur said, and bowed to Ziusura. The Aged One found, much to his annoyance, that he liked the younger king. It seemed odd that he should develop a liking for one who would very likely bring his world crashing down upon him, but Ziusura supposed that if one is going to be destroyed by someone, better that it be someone one likes rather than someone one detests.

"And these," Arthur continued with a slight flourish, "are my associates, Ronald Cordoba and Nellie Porter. Come forward, my friends. Greet the foundation of all legends."

"Uhm . . . good to meet you," said the one introduced as Cordoba. He extended a hand. Gilgamesh eyed it for a moment, and then enveloped it in his. Cordoba blanched slightly upon seeing his hand vanish into that of the High King. Perhaps he was concerned he would not be getting it back anytime soon. But Gilgamesh simply shook it slightly, as was the custom, and then released it.

The one called Porter, perhaps stuck for something to say,

stared up at the impressive-looking headgear atop Gilgamesh's skull. "Those are . . . very large horns," she observed.

"Thank you," rumbled the High King. "It's an interesting story, actually. You see, the goddess Inana desired me for a lover, but I spurned her. To retaliate, she unleashed the Bull of Heaven upon my people. But Enkidu and I killed it. And these are its horns."

Percival eyed the horns and said solemnly, "That was a lot of bull."

"Yes," said Gilgamesh, who then appeared perplexed when there were titters of laughter from people standing nearby. They were quickly silenced by his look, and then he continued, "You have come a long way, Pendragon. Tell me why."

"I believe you know why. And I feel the need to tell you, Gilgamesh, that I do not appreciate the manner in which my man, Percival, was treated by you."

Gilgamesh bristled slightly, and it was the Aged One who promptly stepped in. "I daresay, Mr. Ex-President, that an uninvited trespasser in the White House would have been treated as ungently as your Percival was treated here."

"A trespasser in the White House would have been subjected to the laws of the United States, not the whim of one individual."

"Laws made by men," Gilgamesh said disdainfully.

"With rights that come from God."

"And I am two-thirds god and one-third man," countered Gilgamesh, "giving my laws far more weight than anything conceived by mere mortal. For that matter, whatever ill treatment Percival may have received at my hands was solely because of his refusal to cooperate. Had he sworn fealty to me, as every other resident of this island has done, he would have been freed and given the same rights accorded any other. He chose his path, Pendragon. You cannot fault me for forcing him to walk it."

Percival stepped forward, in between Gilgamesh and Arthur, and turned to face his liege. "I beg you, sir, do not protest on my behalf. We are here for a purpose, and that purpose is dependent upon this man's good graces," and he indicated Gilgamesh.

"The Moor speaks wisely," said Gilgamesh. "You would be well-advised to heed him."

Arthur's gaze hardened for a moment, and then Nellie Porter said, "Sir, with all due respect . . . if the purpose of this was to help your wife, raging testosterone challenges aren't going to help things."

Ziusura was taken aback by the woman's words. It seemed to him an inappropriate manner for anyone, much less a woman, to address a king. But Arthur smiled slightly, and said, "Indeed. Very well. If Percival holds no resentment," and when the Moor nodded, Arthur continued, "then I would be straightforward with you, High King. It is my understanding that this island we stand upon is the holiest of holy grounds. Is that true?"

Gilgamesh laughed softly. With his hands clasped behind his back, he walked in a small circle around the group. "And what do you think makes it holy, eh?"

"It belonged to our lord," said Arthur.

"Your lord. *Your* lord. Do you hear them, Aged One? Do you hear their words, my beast brother? Their lord. How little you know or understand of such things. Tell me, Arthur Pendragon . . . has it never occurred to you that, rather than the cup you seek deriving its power from your lord . . . your lord, in fact . . . *derived his power from the cup?*"

Arthur made no immediate reply. He looked stunned at the notion. So did the others.

Gilgamesh, however, was looking at Percival. He smiled and pointed and said, "This one knew. Or at least he sensed it, did you not?"

Instead of answering, Percival shot back, "You know what my liege wants. I know you do. You and I both know we stand upon the Grail. That it has different forms, and the land is one of them. So will you grant him aid? Yea or nay?"

"Such petulance for one who is asking a favor," said Gilgamesh.

And then Enkidu spoke, in a voice filled with more human pity and sadness than possessed by many humans that Ziusura had encountered. He turned to Gilgamesh and said in a voice that was both firm and pleading, "Help them."

The High King was clearly surprised. But then he shrugged his mountainous shoulders and said, "If it pleases you, beast brother." He looked back at Arthur and asked, "The woman is on the vehicle?" When Arthur nodded, he continued, "Very well. But for a wound as severe as I know your woman to have, it will take the Grail land time to work. And I do not like having that . . . thing," he gestured to the Osprey, "upon my land any longer than is necessary. Once you have brought your woman upon the land, it must depart immediately."

"Now wait just a minute . . ." Cordoba spoke up.

"This is not a negotiation," Gilgamesh said firmly. "It will be as I say, or you may all climb back upon the vehicle and depart straightaway."

The newcomers exchanged looks, and Arthur said, "Ron . . . Nellie . . . perhaps it would be best if you returned to the—"

"No," Nellie said firmly. "I came this far. I'll see it through. You can do what you want, Ron."

"Thanks for the permission," said Ron. "I came, I saw, and . . . well, I haven't exactly conquered, but I'm not bailing at this point either."

The Aged One felt a flash of admiration for the two of them. These were not trained warriors or ageless beings. These were clearly two utterly ordinary people, trying to deal the best they could with extraordinary circumstances. Then the admiration was quickly replaced by pity. *Poor bastards have no idea what they've let themselves in for.*

It was the work of but a few minutes to offload Pendragon's mate from the waiting vehicle. She was strapped to a wheeled bed, with all manner of tubes protruding from her. She looked pale and barely alive. The Aged One knew all the details, of course; unlike Gilgamesh, he had remained aggressively part of the real world. He knew only of Gwendolyn Penn, however, through what he had seen of her on on-line news items and feeds. He knew enough to know that what one presents to the world via the media oftentimes bears little resemblance to reality. So he had no true idea of what Mrs. Penn was like in real life. He could only think that she must be quite a remarkable woman for a man to have gone to all this trouble over her. Ziusura had not met many women of that caliber, and he'd been around quite some time.

He was extremely puzzled, however, at the second thing that was lowered—not without effort—from the Osprey. It was a statue of what appeared to be a young man, standing there with a rather pained expression on its face. Gilgamesh looked as confused as anyone else, although Enkidu naturally maintained his customary deadpan expression. Pendragon's concern, however, was quite evident, and amidst cries of "Careful! Careful with him!" he did not relax until the statue was safely upon the ground. The ship's pilot, a young and handsome fellow with a square jaw and confident manner, crouched in the doorway as Arthur spoke to him, clearly giving him instructions. The pilot, who was wearing a small name tag that said "Roderick," was obviously not enthused about what he was being told to do. He even began to offer some meager protest. But Arthur was quite firm, and some minutes later the hatch door had been closed tight and the Osprey was lifting off. It stayed low to the water as it angled away and soon disappeared behind a grove of trees.

Gilgamesh sauntered over to the bedridden woman, barely casting a glance at the statue. Arthur stood nearby, watching the woman with obvious concern. "So . . . what happens now?" inquired Arthur.

Without a word, Gilgamesh knocked Gwen, gurney and all, to the ground.

Arthur's reaction was immediate as he lunged toward Gilgamesh, uttering a curse, and he started to reach behind his back as if to pull something from it. But Enkidu was faster, interposing himself between the two of them, and Percival was now gripping Arthur from behind, saying urgently, "No, my lord! Wait!"

"You bastard!" snapped out Arthur. "*How dare you!* A helpless woman! A—"

"Arthur?"

The voice floated up to Pendragon, and he stopped in his tracks, eyes wide, body rigid. Gilgamesh had a confident smirk on his face, and Enkidu relaxed his tense posture as the immediate danger obviously subsided.

Gwen was lying on the overturned gurney, staring up at Arthur and blinking in confusion against the brightness of the morning sun. As dissipated as her body seemed, her eyes were filled with life and light and considerable bewilderment. "Arthur?" she said again. "Darling . . . would you mind telling me why I'm tied up? I mean, yeah, I know I had this kinky birthday wish that one time, but . . ." Then her gaze fell upon Nellie Porter, who was staring at her with unmasked astonishment, and she said in a mortified voice, "Okay, uhm . . . you didn't hear that . . ."

ℜ ODERICK IS NOT *pleased with the current situation.*
Even as he propels the Osprey across the water, his mind is racing as he is confronted with the reality of what he has to face. He must now return to base and inform his superiors that he has dropped off a former president of the United States in the middle of fricking nowhere. He must explain that Arthur Penn gave him a direct order to depart for twenty-four hours and then return. But a good deal can happen in twenty-four hours. He is even less happy over the certainty that he will be taken to task and held personally responsible for this growing debacle, particularly considering that

he is now aware that the Secret Service men whom he had assumed were with the ex-president are, in fact, nowhere to be seen.

He should have refused to leave. He tried to do so. Technically Arthur Penn had no say over him since he was no longer the commander-in-chief. But Penn had been forceful and confident and even though every scrap of common sense in Roderick's mind told him to stay put, here he is flying away from Pus Island and mentally flagellating himself.

Well, he is going to return, and in considerably less time than twenty-four hours. He is going to return to base and tell command personnel there exactly what happened, and he's going to come flying back in short order with more bona fide army men than anyone knows what to do with. And that bronzed giant who was standing there like he was God Almighty, and that other guy next to him wearing the weirdo Halloween outfit that made him look like some sort of whack-ass lion . . . well, let's just see how large and in charge they feel when they're looking down the business end of an AK-47.

"Yup," he says out loud, as much to convince himself of the rightness of his intended actions as anything else. "Yup. I'm coming back and we're gonna show those local yokels just who's in charge."

And suddenly the headset he is wearing is ripped from him, and a female voice whispers in his ear with honeyed sweetness, "They already know."

He turns in his seat, and he just barely has time to see a flash of green eyes, and they are driving deep into him, into his soul, and he sees himself for the pathetic, wretched, posturing fool that he is, and he cries out in horror at the miserable creature he now knows himself to be even as he drives the Osprey down, down to the water, sending the Osprey into a coffin roll. It plummets four thousand feet at just over a hundred miles an hour, and when it hits the water, it crushes in on itself, metal creaking and rupturing in one huge, ear-splitting shriek. Roderick, divorced father of two, is mashed into unrecognizable pulp. The possessor of the green eyes, whose name means Little King, is already gone through means known only to herself.

She is not a big fan of the water. Oh, she can swim well enough, and the slithering return to Pus Island will not overtax her. Nevertheless, she mildly resents the inconvenience to which she has gone, but decides to consider it simply another case of noblesse oblige.

CHAPTRE
THE NINETEENTH

✟

ARTHUR HAD IMAGINED all the ways that Gwen would react to her return to the land of the conscious. He had played it over so many times in his head that it had reached the point where it hurt just to contemplate it, for it seemed so impossible a goal.

But now the goal had been achieved. A hell of a feat, even for one who had already racked up so many accomplishments. Somehow, though, in all those imagined scenarios involving Gwen's unlikely resuscitation, the notion of her being absolutely furious with him never crossed his mind.

The events immediately following Gwen's miraculous recovery—which had occurred within seconds of her physically coming into contact with the hallowed ground that was Pus Island, or Grail Island, or whatever one wanted to call it—were something of a blur to Arthur. He remembered the stunned look on Ron Cordoba's face, and that Nellie Porter was crying, openly and unashamed. Gwen continued to look perplexed even as he hastened to release her from the straps that had kept her bound to the gurney. She yelped as tubes were pulled out from her, and she seemed completely disoriented.

Through it all, Gilgamesh had looked on with a satisfied air. On the surface he seemed quite happy for the good fortune of Arthur and his wife, but there was just enough reserve, just enough distance in his attitude that it sounded faint warning bells in Arthur's head. But they were very faint indeed, and when Gilgamesh offered to provide them with accommodations in his own vast residence, Arthur was only too glad to take him up on it.

Only Percival seemed detached from the controlled pandemonium that followed Gwen's return to life. He seemed far more interested in fixing his attention upon Gilgamesh and Enkidu, particularly the latter. Arthur could guess the resentment that was likely filtering through Percival's mind. He had, after all, once held the Holy Grail in his hand. It had disappeared, and it was evident that Gilgamesh had been the one who had absconded with it. Or . . . could such a thing really be considered any one person's property? Did it not, in many ways, belong to the ages? Perhaps it was presumptuous for any one person to say that it was his. Of course, by that train of logic, Gilgamesh was no more entitled to "own" the Grail, in any of its forms, than Percival was. Arthur suspected, however, that it was unlikely that the High King would willingly relinquish possession of it.

Well . . . why should he? He was living peacefully here on this island of miracles with his followers, harming no one and presenting a bona fide miracle to Arthur and his wife. Who were they to say that he was acting inappropriately or unfairly?

The chambers that Arthur and Gwen had been brought to were elaborately furnished with rich tapestries upon the wall and intricately carved furniture that would have fetched thousands of dollars were they on sale back in the United States. Arthur marveled at the craftsmanship even as Gwen sat there, trying to pull her scattered thoughts together and develop a chronological comprehension of what had occurred.

It was when she finally managed to do so that the trouble began.

She was sitting in a chair that was much too large for her, her feet dangling several inches above the ground. She was attired in clothes given her by Gilgamesh, a simple one-piece white garment that looked vaguely similar to a toga. She looked lovely in it, although she would have looked lovely in anything. Her color and vitality were already returning to her, and her face was looking cheery and pink, which would have pleased Arthur no end had he not realized that she was in fact becoming flushed with mounting anger.

"You . . . quit?"

She was barely able to form the two words, and what was most disturbing was that Arthur had told her that five minutes earlier. He was already long past that part of the narrative, having moved on to describing Percival's first encounter with Gilgamesh and the events that had led to their arrival upon the island. Yet she was only just now processing the information that Arthur had resigned his office.

Still, there was nothing for it but to deal with the situation in as straightforward a manner as he could. And so, gamely, he nodded and said, "Yes, Gwen. I quit. But you see, it isn't as bad as all th—"

"You quit?"

He blinked, a bit concerned over her inability to grasp such simple concepts. "Yes."

"The office of the presidency?"

"That's right."

"They . . ." She seemed barely capable of framing the words. "They didn't force you to go? Tell you to get out or anything? You just . . . left on your own?"

"That's right, Gwen. Under the circumstances, I didn't see how I could—"

"*You asshole!*"

Arthur was utterly taken aback at her fury. "Gwen! I . . . I really don't think it's appropriate for you to—"

"*Appropriate?!*" She had jumped down out of the chair

and wasn't just approaching him, she was stalking him. Reflexively he backed up, even though she posed no physical threat. Or it could be that he was overconfident, considering Gwen looked ready to tear him limb from limb with her bare hands. Indeed, not only ready, but capable. "Appropriate? My God . . . I don't believe it! He'll kill me! He's going to kill me!"

Taking her stated concerns as the literal truth, Arthur immediately tensed and felt completely on his guard, wondering where this new menace to Gwen's welfare was going to emerge from. "Who's going to kill you, Gwen?" he demanded briskly, reaching to take her by the shoulders.

But she pushed him away, shrugging him off. "Merlin!"

"What?" he asked in bewilderment, and then he understood. "Oh," he said, much more softly.

"You bet your ass 'oh'!" Gwen said heatedly. She ran her fingers through her strawberry blonde hair as if she were going to rip it out in her consternation. "It was just what he was always afraid of! That somehow I was going to wind up interfering in your great destiny! And I did! I so completely did! Because of me, you—"

This time he did grip her by the upper arms, and even though she struggled to pull away, he didn't let her go. He managed to keep the anger and hurt and frustration from his voice, but it was a Herculean effort. For if he had been certain of one thing, it was that Gwen would always understand and support the decisions he made in his life and career. Maybe not always agree with them, but understand and support. But now . . . now she seemed baffled by the actions that he had taken, even though he had been so certain that they were the correct ones at the time.

"*Listen to me!*" he ordered her, so sharply that it commanded her attention. "You were not responsible! Do you understand that? Sandoval's people were responsible for shooting you. It was they who put your life in peril, they who brought you to the edge of death. It was nothing you did. And it was my decision to devote the fullness of my attention to you—"

"The country needed you, Arthur!"

"*The country stands, Gwen!* Don't you see?" He choked on the emotion he was feeling for a moment before continuing, "When Camelot lost me, it came apart. The United States . . . it needs its president, in all likelihood. Needs its government and people to run it. But they never needed me specifically. Just someone with vision to fill the office, because the office is far greater than any one man, even me. And you have no idea how difficult and even galling it was for me to accept it. But it's true. But you, Gwen . . . you truly needed me."

"*I was in a goddamn coma!* In what way did I need you?"

"You needed me," he pointed out, "to bring you here."

"No, I needed Percival to bring me here. You were just along for the ride."

The moment she had spoken the words, she would have given anything to be able to retrieve them. She stepped back and Arthur made no effort to hold on to her. Instead he simply fixed his hurt but level gaze upon her, and she tried to stammer out an apology, but Arthur simply nodded and said, "You are right. Never apologize for being right."

"But Arthur, I . . ."

"Never." He let out a slow, steady breath. "Gwen . . . we had one president who pardoned another, and it was a wildly unpopular move, but he did it because he felt the country had been through enough. If nothing else—removing this entire issue from concerns regarding you—I felt the country had once again been through enough. An opportunity was being handed to me to rid the world of Arnim Sandoval. I took that opportunity. I had to."

"Oh yes," she said with ill-disguised bitterness. "My great and glorious supporter, Miss Basil, stepping in out of the goodness of her heart."

"She did the job."

"I don't trust her, Arthur."

"She's the Basilisk. There's no reason that you should."

"And I don't trust you."

If she had hauled off and slapped him across the face with a brick, he could not have been any more staggered. "How can you say that?" he was barely able to whisper.

"How can I not? Arthur . . ." She looked ready to cry, and it was only through force of will that she kept tears from rolling down her face. "Arthur . . . after everything you went through, everything you achieved . . . to just . . . just throw it all away . . ."

"I got something back for it. I got Sandoval . . ."

"*He was one man!* Don't you see . . ." Her hands flailed about. "The presidency . . . it's more than one man. It's an office. It's greatness. It's bigger than any one person, bigger even than you. And when you left it behind, you let down the office . . . and Merlin, and me . . ."

"Stop it," he snapped at her fiercely. "You don't understand . . ."

"You got that right."

"Gwen . . ." His frustration was mounting. This was so completely off the direction that he had thought this reunion would take. "Don't you see? I've spent my entire life doing what was expected of me. Doing things for Merlin, for the people, for you. But with you gone, with Merlin gone . . . I was left in a position of asking, What am I doing for myself? I ask you: When does it happen? When am I entitled to attend to my own desires, to what I want to do for myself?"

And with such sadness as he had never seen in any human face, Gwen told him, "You don't."

"What?"

She took in a deep breath and let it out slowly. "You said it yourself, Arthur. I'll never forget. You said, 'We are creatures of destiny, you and I.' That's what you told me. Do you remember?"

He nodded. He couldn't find the words, even a word as simple as "Yes."

"You can tell yourself that you left office because you wanted to rid the people of Arnim Sandoval. But in doing that, you elevated his importance above your own, and the truth is that you just wanted revenge on him. Quick, clean, easy. And you got it. But look at what it cost you in return. Just look."

"Has it cost me you?" asked Arthur, not certain he could cope with the answer.

She looked down and said the three words that were even worse than "Yes, it has," or "No, it hasn't."

"I don't know."

And Arthur wanted to scream at her. To grab her, shake her, make her realize everything that he had done, howl in fury over her inability to comprehend that which had been so clear to him.

"You hate me, don't you?" Gwen said, her voice choking in her throat. Arthur made no reply. His thoughts, his passions were so completely scattered that he didn't know what to think or what to say, and in such cases it was always better to say nothing at all. "Well," she continued, "I hate me, too. I hate me for what I caused you to do . . . and even if it was your decision, I was still responsible for it, and I . . ."

She couldn't speak. Instead she turned and fled the room, and every impulse that Arthur possessed told him to run after her, to hold her, to try and make it right again.

He stayed where he was.

A S THEY WALKED along the shore, Ron Cordoba couldn't help but notice that Nellie Porter's attention seemed focused on the sky. "The Osprey isn't due back until tomorrow," said Ron.

"Oh. I know," she said quickly, almost guiltily.

Cordoba had shucked his jacket and also his socks and shoes. Nellie was likewise barefoot, her shoes resting with Cordoba's property on a rock a short distance back. Ron crouched and picked up a fistful of the warm sand, allowing it to trickle between his fingers. "Hard to believe, isn't it?"

"Which hard-to-believe thing are you referring to?" she ask wryly.

"This. Look at it. Looks like normal sand. Hard to believe," he said, shaking his head, "that this is some sort of . . . of Holy Grail territory. That just standing on this island somehow cures all your ills. It's true, though. I can feel it."

"You can?"

He paused and then said to her, "Do you know what tinnitus is?"

She was a bit surprised and confused by the change in topic. "Ringing in the ears, isn't it?"

"Yeah. Well . . . I have it."

"Really? I had no idea . . ."

He shrugged. "It's not something I like to advertise. Some days it's better, some worse, but I've learned to live with it. Well, I was here for two hours and suddenly realized it was gone. Just like that."

Nellie shook her head, obviously scarcely able to credit what she was hearing. "You're sure you're not imagining it?"

"I think I know the difference between reality and imagination."

And Nellie let out a laugh that was filled with confusion and bitterness. "Well, I'm sure glad you do! Because me and reality, we haven't been on speaking terms for a while now."

"What do you—"

"*Ron, for God's sake, look at us!*" she shouted, her agitation painful to see. "We're rational people! Or at least we're supposed to be! Have you completely lost sight of how insane all of this is?"

"You mean with Gilgamesh—"

"I mean with all of it!" She was walking in a small circle in the sand, gesticulating broadly. "Look what's being handed to us! I mean, I could barely wrap myself around the whole Arthur and Guinevere thing! And now you're asking me to accept Gilgamesh, and gods, and Noah . . . *Noah*, for crying out loud, and a great flood, and gods making people immortal, and it's all just . . . just nuts! I am a twenty-first-century woman, Ron!"

"And I am a twenty-first-century man."

It was not Ron who had spoken. It was Gilgamesh, standing directly behind Nellie, who jumped several feet in the air because she was so startled. She came down with her feet tangled and staggered back, falling against Ron, who caught her and prevented her from hitting the ground. She clutched at her bosom as if afraid that her heart was going to explode through her chest.

"Well . . . more like a twenty-seventh-century man, actually," continued Gilgamesh quite casually. "It's just that my century is B.C., whereas yours is A.D. But that shouldn't pose too much of a problem, should it?"

"Where did you come from?" Nellie gasped out.

"Uruk, in Babylonia," he replied. "In the territory that you would now call Iraq."

"No, I mean . . ."

"I know what you mean. I can be most stealthy if I am so inclined," he said.

Ron was not ecstatic with the way Gilgamesh was looking at Nellie, as if she were some worshiping slave girl that he could just snap up as a between-meal snack at any point he was so inclined. But he said nothing, and instead simply steadied Nellie so she was able to stand on her own two feet.

Gilgamesh sighed in a sad, almost pitying manner. "It seems too much for you, doesn't it? Yet your leader accepts me, accepts the things that I have told him. Why can't you?"

There was no hesitation in Nellie's response. "Because at least he's mortal," she said. "He's never claimed to be anything else. A normal man who has incredible things happen to him . . . okay, it's a stretch, but it's a stretch I can handle. But you! You say you're . . ."

"Two-thirds god, one-third man." He nodded. "My

mother was the goddess Ninsun. My father was Lugalbanda, born mortal man but later deified."

"Okay, see, that's what's getting to me. Gods and bulls from heaven . . ."

"Oh, the bull of heaven was nothing in comparison to true challenges, such as Huwawa," Gilgamesh said casually. "Guardian of the Cedar Forest, protected by seven deadly radiances, slain by Enkidu and me—"

"That's another thing! Enkidu! He's like an animal on two legs! Creatures like that, they . . . they don't exist!"

"According to whom?" asked Gilgamesh, genuinely interested.

"To rational minds! It's stuff from the Bible or fairy tales—"

"There are those who believe that the Bible is literal truth," Gilgamesh reminded her.

Ron snorted in grim acknowledgment of that. "Tell me about it. The people who gave us grief about teaching evolution, even in this day and age, you wouldn't believe . . ."

"This day and age." Gilgamesh said the words with remarkable sadness, as if speaking of someone long dead and still sorely missed. "This day and age, my friends, is vastly overrated. You have no idea, no . . ."

His voice trailed off for a long moment, and Ron found himself fascinated by the great man before him. If he truly was what he claimed he was, he was indeed the foundation for all legends, all heroes who had come after him. He wasn't just "living history." He *transcended* history.

Gilgamesh slowly walked away from them. He stared out at the water lapping upon the shore, looked with attentiveness to a flock of birds angling overhead. "You don't understand," he sighed.

"Then explain it," said Ron.

He didn't even look back at them. It was as if he were staring into a world they could never hope to see.

"The world is far more subjective than you realize," he said. "Perception shapes reality."

."Oh, well, I could have told you that," said Ron. "I'm in politics. It's never more true than there."

"It's more than that," Gilgamesh said. "Reality . . . the world . . . is far more fluid than you can even begin to comprehend. Once upon a time . . . in a world that to you is purely the stuff of myth . . . people knew very little about what you would term the 'reality' of the world. And so they filled in the gaps with their collective consciousness. They believed those things you would attribute to science—lightning and thunder, earthquakes, eclipses—they believed them to be the work of gods. And so they were. Even earlier than that, on a primal level, when man was huddling around fires and yellow eyes gleamed at him from the forest, man imagined those eyes to belong to monsters beyond describing. And so . . . they were." Now he turned toward them, and his face was alight with an excitement that had been absent before. "There were giants in those days, my friends. Giants and magic and gods who stalked heaven and earth amidst the worship of those who trembled before them. And their presence was a very real thing, and their wrath was real, because the mind of humanity *made* them real. The love, the adoration, the fear, and the worship made them real . . ."

"And you?"

Nellie had posed the question, and his eyes narrowed. "What do you mean?"

"You're two thirds god, one-third man, or so you say. Does belief help make you real?"

He did not answer, save for a slight and even sad smile. "It was a more interesting time," he finally said. "A time when anything was possible. When the world was not circumscribed by science. Ignorance is not necessarily bliss, but it is oftentimes preferable to the reality that is created by a little knowledge . . . which, as I recall, is said to be a dangerous thing."

"And are we supposed to believe that reality is just that elastic?" asked Nellie.

"It still occurs," Gilgamesh said. "For instance: A man is accused of a crime. More often than not, he is believed to be guilty, for it is far easier to believe the worst of people than the best. In short order, the actuality of whether he committed the crime is beside the point. He is treated by society as a criminal. Even those who are friends, or loved ones, look at him differently. In the eyes and belief of the world around him, he is guilty. The perception of him creates his new reality, a reality in which he is guilty of a crime. Tragic for him, I suppose. But I'll have you know that it's a mere vestige of what the world was once like, before so many people thought they knew so much. It was a far more interesting place than what we have now. I miss it. Miss it terribly. And I have had plenty of time to compare it and consider it. I've wandered the earth for so long . . . so long. So many names I've acquired in that time. Methusaleh, some named me. Later I was Ahasuerus. Heracles was another popular name . . ."

"Heracl . . . you mean Hercules?" asked Nellie in surprise.

"A being of great strength and godlike descent. The legends grew and grew. And who am I to say no to a legend?"

A gentle breeze wafted across them, an invigorating scent filling Ron's nostrils. The world smelled new just from Gilgamesh's recounting of what it once had been. "How are you here?" he asked at last. "How are you still alive? Is it because of the Grail?"

Slowly he nodded. "Yes. My birthright gave me extended life. Life beyond anything that any mortal has known. But even that life was not an eternity, for that the gods denied me. When I happened upon the Grail, my existence was nearing its end. But with the Grail in my possession, everything became different and anything became possible." His voice rose, almost musical in its sense of triumph as he continued, "My beast brother was able to return to me as I braved the gates of the underworld itself. Magic, old and powerful magic such as was almost crushed from the world by those who would not believe. But the legend of the Grail is too strong, even for modern man, who 'knows' so much. And from that legend and that belief comes strength, and none here will ever die, and I will be strong and young forever . . ."

"And what about us?" Nellie asked the question that had occurred to Ron, but he was a bit too apprehensive to ask it.

Gilgamesh looked at her, his face unreadable, and Ron felt a chill because there was something in the way that he did not immediately respond that warned Ron they were potentially in over their heads.

And that was when they heard Gwen scream.

CHAPTRE
THE TWENTIETH

G WEN WASN'T REALLY paying attention where she
was going when she bolted from the room she'd been
sharing with Arthur. Her mind was whirling and confused,
and she was beginning to feel just like that time when she
had first been pulled into Arthur's world. Here she was,
having fully adjusted to such things as trans-dimensional
castles and youthful wizards, even taking them for granted.
And now she was right back with that feeling of disorientation that her initial exposure to the unreal reality of Arthur
instilled within her.

The sun was drawing low on the horizon as she ran from
the building. She dashed past residents of the island, all of
them looking so young and relaxed and filled with contentment. *God, it's like the beach in Malibu, only a hundred times
worse*, she thought.

There was a clearing ringed with towering, sculpted rocks
that reminded her of Stonehenge. No one was around, and so
she made for it, just wanting someplace where she could sit
and think and perhaps clear her head, except her head had a
bullet in it, and wasn't that all wonderful, and how was she

ever going to pass through a metal detector again . . . ?

Insane, it's all insane. Maybe that's what this is: a deranged dream. Maybe I'm actually lying in a coma on a hospital bed somewhere and all of this is something I'm just concocting in my subconscious. Yes, I like that. I like that a lot more than the notion that I was responsible for Arthur walking away from everything that was real and important . . .

She leaned against one of the stone columns and then, feeling overwhelmed by sheer spiritual exhaustion, she sank to the ground, trying not to cry. And suddenly she let out a startled gasp, her head flying back and causing her to crack the back of her skull rather nastily.

Merlin was standing at the far end of the clearing. At least, the statue of him was. It bore that same, somewhat frustrated look it always had. She hadn't realized he was there at first because he sort of blended in with the other stone objects.

"Hey, Merlin!" she said, her voice giddy, waggling her fingers. "Good to see a familiar face! And you'll be thrilled to know, you were right! You were right," and her voice choked slightly as she said it. "And I didn't even have to do anything actively to screw things up for Arthur. All I had to do was get myself shot and lie around like an oversized doorstop, and his guilty conscience did the rest."

She started to sob uncontrollably, and felt all the more foolish for coming unglued in this manner. *Damn you! After everything you've gone through, after everything you've faced, this is how you react? By turning into a weeping mess? You faced down Morgan Le Fey in her lair! Nothing should throw you after that!* But her mental chiding did nothing to rein her in, and she continued to cry and feel nothing but rising anger at herself, and the anger fed into the mourning, one building atop the other. And she found herself saying "I'm sorry, I'm sorry" over and over, although she had no clear idea to whom she was apologizing.

"Calm down, dear, you're making a spectacle of yourself."

Gwen rubbed her eyes with her fists, trying to clear them, to see who was addressing her. Her eyes widened as she saw a familiar face, with an expression as mocking as the tone of voice.

"M-Miss Basil!"

Miss Basil bowed slightly. She was dressed all in green, in a leotard so form-fitting that it almost looked like her skin. In fact, Gwen wasn't entirely certain it wasn't.

She didn't reply beyond the physical acknowledgment of Gwen's presence, prompting Gwen to force herself to continue rather than let a silence build. "What . . . are you doing here?"

"Why, I'm talking to you, little queen," Miss Basil said. She appeared genuinely delighted to see Gwen, which naturally put Gwen all the more on her guard. "There should be no harm in that, should there? You do still talk? You remember how to do that?" Gwen, with effort, nodded. "You seem quite concerned, little queen. Are you not happy to see me? No, you don't seem so. You seem distressed. How unfortunate. After all, did I not provide you valuable service in that business with Morganna? Your actions in that affair won you the undying loyalty of Arthur, did it not? So I'd think on that basis alone, you'd welcome your old ally with open arms."

Gwen took in a deep breath and let it out slowly to calm herself. She only partly succeeded in steadying her nerves. "Yes, you'd think that. On the other hand, since that time, you turned Merlin into . . . into that." And she pointed at the statue.

"He turned himself into that." Miss Basil sniffed. "I simply provided him the opportunity and motive. The action was all his. Still, Gwen . . . it's something of a pity that you'd hold that against me. It's the nature of things, you know. It's physics. For all actions, there is an equal and opposite reaction. On the one hand, I helped you . . . on the other hand," and she shrugged, "I destroyed Merlin. These things all balance out."

"What are you implying, that Merlin turning into that is because of me? That some sort of karmic scale had to be evened out because you helped me?"

"I'm not implying that, no, but . . . if it will serve to give you sleepless nights, then believe it. I won't be bothered."

Gwen's anger was beginning to overcome her fear and even her common sense. Now on her feet, she approached Miss Basil, her clenched fist trembling as if she were planning to punch the taller woman in the face. "Why are you like this? Why do you insist on trying to make people miserable when you have it in your power to help them?"

"I do help them," Miss Basil said casually. "Or hadn't you heard: I was responsible for putting an end to the person who engineered the attack that put a bullet in your head."

"Yes, I heard," Gwen responded in a heated voice. "But the condition for it was blackmailing Arthur into giving up the presidency."

"Is that the way the story was told to you?"

"Do you deny it?"

Miss Basil laughed. "Deny it? Darling, I revel in it. But the truth was that Arthur's heart really wasn't in it anymore. I did him a favor. I gave him an excuse to lay down his burden."

"You exploited him when he was at his lowest, is what you did."

"Same thing," she said carelessly. Then she smiled, the light of her eyes dancing as if in contemplation of something so greatly mischievous she could hardly contain her delight. "Does it bother you so much? That I removed Sandoval from this world in exchange for your husband's resignation."

"Yeah. Yeah, it bothers the hell out of me."

"Well." She clapped her hands with pleasure. "If that's the case, I have a surprise for you. I'd actually been saving it for Arthur, but I suspect you will appreciate it even more."

And then Miss Basil began to open her mouth, wider and wider. In seconds her jaw had distended beyond anything that any human being could possibly duplicate. It was as if her head had split in two. Her neck began to stretch, to undulate, and her entire body was lengthening, twisting around and back. Her clothing did not tear from the stretching, making even more suspect the notion that it was any sort of fabric at all.

The air was filled with a low hum, as if some sort of power were building up, and Gwen might have been imagining it, but it seemed that the ground was beginning to vibrate beneath her feet.

Miss Basil was no longer recognizable as anything human. Gwen shielded her face, looking askance so as not to stare straight on at the creature before her. She had no clue what, if anything, would happen to her if she did look full upon Miss Basil, but she had no desire to find out.

There were hideous sounds then, although she had no idea whether her refusal to look directly at the source made the sounds better or worse than they would have been. There was a deep coughing, and the sounds of liquids being spat up and hitting the ground, and she could resist the impulse no longer as she looked squarely at Miss Basil, or more accurately, the winged serpent that she had become. Gwen gaped in confusion, unable to comprehend what she was seeing.

For a heartbeat, she flashed back to an awful, awful moment when her parents had taken her, as a child, to a zoo. She had stared at a hamster-shaped bulge in the middle of one of the snakes and inquired of her father what that bulge was doing there. Her father's unadorned, straightforward answer was met with shrieks of hysteria and a hasty and premature departure from the zoo.

What she was seeing now was evocative of that bulge, but there were two differences. The first was that Gwen was not screaming, for her throat had completely closed up so that she could barely draw in sufficient air to breathe, much less shriek. And second, it was not in the shape of a hamster, but rather in the shape of a man.

The Basilisk thrust upward, her muscles contracting with

effort, her mouth exceedingly wide. And then, in what could only be described as a grotesque perversion of the birth process, the top of a head became visible in the creature's open mouth. It was impossible to tell what color the hair had been, or even if it had at one point possessed any hair. The Basilisk convulsed once more, and then a third time, and then with a rush of liquid and a splattering and spattering that would haunt Gwen to her dying day—however imminent that might be—Arnim Sandoval was vomited up from the belly of the beast.

He flopped onto the ground eight months after having been consumed, and he was still alive.

The digestive juices had worked very, very slowly upon him. His clothes were mostly eaten away, as was some of his skin on his back and arms. His flesh looked as if it were starting to curdle like milk, and the stench of him washed over Gwen so violently that she dry-heaved, slumping back against one of the stone columns for support. He was shaking, like a man who was freezing, or perhaps seized with a horrific case of Parkinson's disease. He stared up at her without truly focusing upon her, without having the slightest clue where he was, and then he started to reach for her and murmur something that did not sound at all human but instead came out more like a vile gurgling noise.

That was when Gwen screamed, and screamed, and kept screaming, and somewhere in the distance of the moment, Miss Basil was laughing loudly, but Gwen did not hear a thing.

GILGAMESH, RON, AND Nellie were a distance away when they heard the scream, and immediately started in the direction from which it had originated.

Elsewhere, Percival, who had been fighting a feeling of unease about the Osprey but could not determine exactly why, also heard, and he started running from the other direction. Seconds later, he was passed by a fleet-footed Enkidu, moving so quickly that Percival felt as if he'd been standing still. So much so, in fact, that he briefly did stand still just to give himself some basis for contrast.

None of them got to the scene first, however. That honor belonged to Arthur, who was not only the closest to begin with, but had finally gotten up off his metaphorical ass and gone after Gwen because, really, dammit, what else was he supposed to do?

So barely had the first sounds of Gwen's initial shrieks faded when Arthur appeared over the rise, running as fast as he could. Even as he sprinted, he stared in confusion at the liquid mess of a human who was lying on the ground five paces from Gwen, and then the human lurched to his feet and Gwen screamed even louder, and that was when Arthur recognized who and what it was that was menacing his wife.

"Oh my God, no," he whispered, but the shock didn't cause him to break stride. Nothing short of getting his legs cut off could accomplish that.

Remarkably, he did not notice the twenty-foot-long (or longer) serpent with the small wings that was lurching about the area. The serpent with the voice of a woman that was laughing loudly at what it had wrought. It was a measure of Arthur's focus that his sole concern was Gwen and the monstrosity that was facing her. So it was that when he pulled out Excalibur from its place upon his back, preparing himself to wield the glowing weapon, his attention was upon his wife and her threat, rather than the greater jeopardy posed by the Basilisk.

The Basilisk, for her part, was overlooking absolutely nothing. The defeat she'd known at Arthur's hands, the bargaining for her existence, all still rankled her. Yes, she had accomplished some small measure of vengeance, but it was insufficient as far as she was concerned. More was required, and more she was prepared to deal out. So it was at the moment Arthur drew within distance, the fearsome tail of the Basilisk whipped around and caught Arthur on the side of the head just as he was closing on Sandoval.

The intensity of the blow knocked Arthur flat. The fact that he was able to hold on to Excalibur was nothing short of miraculous, but Miss Basil was not prepared to let that thrice-damned sword stand in her way. Arthur lay on the ground, clearly disoriented, but still a dangerous foe.

Miss Basil's impulse was to strike quickly. It was, after all, in her nature. She feared, however, the precipitous action lest she rush headlong into a situation that was not going to be to her liking.

A quick movement to her right caught her attention and her head snapped around, her forked tongue lancing out with a threatening hiss. Gwen had been advancing on her, carrying no weapons, offering no real threat of any kind, but still trying because she felt like she had to do something. She froze in place the moment that the Basilisk saw her.

"Gwen! Don't look at her!" Arthur shouted, staggering to his feet. He drove forward, swinging Excalibur, but the Basilisk saw it coming and, quick as lightning, ducked under it, slamming her body around and trying to knock Arthur's feet out from under him. He vaulted lightly over the coils as Gwen tried to shield her eyes, and suddenly there was an animalistic screech and Sandoval plowed into Arthur. How in God's name the wretched thing that had been a terrorist leader was functioning enough to do so, Gwen would never be able to figure out, but Sandoval accomplished it. Perhaps he was just that driven by hatred, or perhaps all that was transpiring was little more than a dream to him and he was simply reacting within that context. But the fact remained that Sandoval saw a person whom he obviously hated above all others, and he was responding with pure gut instinct. Under ordinary circumstances, Arthur could easily have brushed him aside, but he was distracted by both Gwen and the Basilisk, and so it was understandable that Sandoval was able to blindside him. They went down in a tumble of arms and legs.

Gwen automatically moved to help him, and the creature

with the eyes of oblivion and the voice of a human woman intercepted her. Again Gwen froze, and the soft voice of Miss Basil emerged from the serpent's mouth, hissing, "Ssssweet little queen, you never truly appreciated my generosity in the past. But since you're deprived of it in the present, perhaps you'll appreciate it more, for the time that's left to you . . ."

And suddenly there was another rumbling, but this came from another source, from above and around. A shadow fell upon them and Gwen barely had time to look up before she saw that one of the great stone pillars that had been embedded in the ground surrounding them was now floating horizontally overhead. It sailed past Gwen, hovered for a fraction of a second above the Basilisk, and then—as if an invisible hand had been supporting it—was suddenly released.

"Oh, shit," the Basilisk barely had time to say before the pillar crashed down upon her. The pillar did not shatter. The Basilisk, pinned under the weight of it, was not quite so lucky as Gwen heard something break within the creature. Her head was still partly visible, but pinned beneath the column, and most of her body was likewise immobilized. The only thing moving was the end of her tail, whipping back and forth in frustration but not accomplishing much otherwise.

The sound of the impact distracted the still-confused Sandoval, and Arthur brought the pommel of Excalibur up and around and slammed Sandoval in the side of the head. The terrorist fell over, more from the violence of the contact than any actual pain. It was entirely possible that he wasn't capable of feeling pain at that moment; his mind was likely not yet functioning to that high a degree. Having been shoved off Arthur, he lay on his back and—his thoughts wandering—started to make incoherent noises.

Gwen knew that she was supposed to be angry with Arthur, to be resenting like hell his decision to leave office, but at that moment all she cared about was his safety as she ran to him, dropping to her knees and throwing her arms around him in a fierce, protective embrace. But he did not respond, and she pulled back and looked at his face, and saw that he was staring elsewhere with amazement. She turned and looked where he was looking, and her jaw sagged in disbelief.

Merlin was standing there, distinctly not paralyzed and most certainly not dead. He was brushing some dirt off his sleeves in a very particular manner, and without even glancing in Arthur and Gwen's direction, he said dismissively, "Please, don't say anything, because it will likely be cliched drivel amounting to perplexed questions that I'll answer when I'm damned good and ready, or relief that I'm alive, which is expected and predictable, or thanks for my dropping that oversized paperweight on top of Miss Basil, which, if you weren't so bloody out of practice, Wart, I wouldn't have had to do. And don't think it wasn't a strain considering I broke out of paralysis about forty-five seconds ago. And please, if you were planning to make any coy comments about no longer being 'statuesque' or some such, save those as well."

There was a long silence, and then Gwen looked at her husband and said, "*Why* did we miss him again?"

CHAPTRE
THE TWENTY-FIRST

✝

ARTHUR WAS STUNNED, unable to say a single word as, ignoring Gwen's somewhat snide comment, Merlin strode toward the pinned creature and said cheerily, "Hello, Miss Basil. It's been a while."

"*You little bastard,*" she managed to spit out.

"Right on all counts," replied Merlin with no diminishment of his good spirits.

"*I killed you!*"

"You overpowered me. Be proud; that alone is an impressive feat. As for failing to kill me, well . . . a great many people have failed, so at least take further pride that you're in good company. Ah! Well, hello, you're a lusty chap, aren't you."

Enkidu had arrived on the scene. He surveyed it with dispassionate curiosity. Arthur noticed his nostrils were flaring, apparently as he caught Merlin's scent. "You were the statue," he rumbled.

"Yes."

"Now you're not."

"Right again."

Enkidu considered that a moment, and then moved toward the pillar, clearly preparing to lift the thing off her. Merlin stepped forward, putting up a cautioning hand. "I wouldn't."

"I would," replied Enkidu, and Arthur didn't see how it would be remotely possible for anything of flesh and blood—even this bizarre creature who stood before him looking like an upright lion—to even come close to budging it. But Enkidu braced himself, one clawed foot on either side of the Basilisk's head, and getting a firm grip on the stone column, he grunted and started to shove. The muscles in his arms, in his neck, stood out like sinewy cords, and it seemed as if there was just no way it was going to move. And then, just like that, he thrust with one arm and one leg and the pillar rolled to one side.

He looked down at the broken coils of the Basilisk and said simply, "You'll heal." Arthur was extremely skeptical at the pronouncement, but it turned out the beast-man was right. Within moments Ron, Nellie, and Gilgamesh had arrived on the scene, and Miss Basil had already left behind her serpent form. She stood there as a normal woman, glaring at Merlin but doing so with such an affectedly sweet manner that it was all the more frightening.

"All right. What's happened here?" demanded Gilgamesh, looking around at the fallen pillar. He stared at Merlin. "Weren't you made out of rock?"

"Yes."

"And why is that pillar down?"

"It was atop her," Enkidu said, indicating the pillar and Miss Basil in turn.

"Why would that be?" Gilgamesh seemed to be striving to maintain his patience in the face of a most confusing state of affairs.

"I levitated it and dropped it on her," said Merlin.

"Did you? I see. You assaulted her, in contravention to the law of this island." His voice had become low and dangerous.

But Merlin didn't seem particularly perturbed by it. "First, I didn't know the bloody law of your bloody island. Second, she was doing the assaulting. And third, who are you supposed to be in that ridiculous Babylonian-style ensemble, anyway? Gilgamesh?"

"Yes," he growled.

Merlin blinked several times, and actually seemed impressed, which in turn impressed the hell out of Gwen. "Ah. All right, then. None of that changes the fact that she was the one who launched the assault . . ."

"Did you?" demanded Gilgamesh of Miss Basil.

"We were simply having a fairly intense discussion," said Miss Basil, primping her hair slightly and batting her eyes.

"Oh, this is asinine," Arthur said impatiently, and he approached Gilgamesh while gesturing broadly. He was still holding Excalibur as he did so. "You can't listen to her, she's—"

And Gilgamesh's sword was in his hand before Arthur drew any closer, and he fully extended it, catching Excalibur by the flat of the blade. The scimitar in Gilgamesh's hand glittered in the twilight, and Arthur was taken aback, because when the two swords came together, they emitted an eerie noise. It was almost like a chant of recognition, as if the swords were two halves of a soul, bifurcated at some distant point in the past and only now rejoined. And then that abstract tone turned dark, even angry, as if the two halves of the soul abruptly remembered that they weren't terribly fond of each other and fully intended to do something about that hostility.

Arthur felt a tremble, a shiver go up his arm, and he quickly stepped back, pulling the sword away. The sound immediately ceased. Gilgamesh remained utterly stoic, his sword still in a defensive position. "I wasn't attacking you," Arthur said.

"A king approaches with his sword drawn. What else am I to assume?"

Arthur almost said "My apologies," but something

warned him that displaying anything even slightly akin to weakness in the presence of Gilgamesh could wind up having some very negative backlash. So he simply slid Excalibur smoothly into its sheath, and the versatile blade promptly turned invisible as its ensorcellment enabled it to do.

"Sir, are you all right?" asked Ron of Arthur, but he was staring at Merlin even as he did so. Nellie was likewise gaping at the young/old wizard, and Arthur suppressed a smile with some difficulty.

"I'm fine, Ron."

"Yes, he's just fine, Ron," said Miss Basil. "Isn't that good to hear?"

"Oh . . . my God," said Nellie, for she saw the liquid and slime-covered mass of humanity lying a few feet away, still burbling occasional inarticulate sounds. "Is that . . . Sandoval?"

"Yes," Arthur told her, firing a look at Miss Basil. "Courtesy of our serpentine friend here."

"What can I say?" inquired Miss Basil. "I had him over for lunch and he just wouldn't leave."

"You do nothing without reason, woman," Merlin snapped at her. "What's your game now?"

"I am but living life, Merlin. And life is a great and glorious game, is it not?" Her quiet hatred for the mage was obvious to Arthur, but she was controlling it with impressive effort.

"There is great hostility here," said Gilgamesh.

"Oh, y'think?" asked Ron.

Gilgamesh ignored the sarcasm. "It would be best if we retired to my court, to work out a harmonious means of coexistence."

"With all respect . . . one king to the other," said Arthur, "I'm not entirely certain I see the need."

And suddenly Enkidu stiffened, looking off into the distance. His ears were twitching like mad, and again his nostrils were flaring. Arthur saw his reaction, although he had no idea what it was he might be reacting to. Gilgamesh, always attuned to the needs and desires of his beast brother, said quickly, "What say you, Enkidu?"

"Another flying vessel."

"The same as before?" Gilgamesh exchanged what was clearly a puzzled look with Miss Basil. Arthur didn't know precisely why Gilgamesh would react in that way to the announcement of a coming airship. He did have, however, the beginnings of a dark suspicion, and it was not one that he considered particularly heartening.

"No," Enkidu said firmly. "Smaller."

Island folk were now coming up over the rise, pointing and shouting out to Gilgamesh in confusion. None of them had the faintest idea what was happening, and they were going to Gilgamesh for the answers. In a way, it had a certain charm to it. Arthur found himself envying Gilgamesh the moment. In Arthur's case, particularly as President, people who approached him always seemed to do so with the conviction that they already had all the answers and simply needed to convince Arthur of the rightness of their viewpoints, thereby ensuring that everything would fall into place. It must be refreshing to have subjects who are very open about the fact that they are utterly clueless and are looking to you for explanations and assurances that everything is going to be all right.

And right in the middle of them was Percival. He did not look confused or frightened, but instead quite grim. He outdistanced the island folk rather easily and drew up alongside Arthur just in time to say, "We've got a problem, sire."

And then the chopper was approaching. It was small and maneuverable, painted blue and white. A man and a woman were inside, visible through the wide windshields. The woman was the pilot, wearing a leather jacket and sunglasses and operating the vehicle with practiced expertise. And the man next to her had a camera, and he was—

"Baumann!" It was Nellie who had cried out, and Arthur would realize later that she had done so almost involuntarily.

At the moment, all Arthur could think of was that Nellie was obviously right: It was Fred Baumann, the newspaper reporter, and he had somehow tracked them there. Nellie was waving frantically in a wide gesture that indicated that he should get the hell out of there.

"*And what is that?*" demanded Gilgamesh, looking extremely put out.

"It's an AS350BA Astar," Percival said. "Effective little chopper when you're trying to take pictures in low-lying areas and over water."

"You know your helicopters, Percival," Arthur noted.

Percival shrugged. "When you're immortal, you'd be amazed the hobbies you take up."

"True. And you're also right that we have a problem," said Arthur. He glanced at Gwen. "He's got pictures of you, dear. Of both of us. Of all this. We'll have to deal with it."

"I fully agree," said Gilgamesh, and before Arthur could move—before anyone could make the slightest motion to stop him—Gilgamesh drew his mighty right arm back and forward, and then the scimitar was hurtling up through the air, itself moving like a lethal propeller. It seemed to pick up speed with every revolution, as if it had a life of its own, and then the scimitar carved right through the helicopter's engine without so much as slowing down.

"*No!*" shouted Arthur, a cry echoed by Gwen, but it was far too late. A plume of flame erupted from the top of the Astar, and there was the briefest of moments where Baumann realized just exactly what had happened, and what was about to happen. His mouth was open and he was clearly screaming, but he couldn't be heard, and in all likelihood what he was shouting was simply a string of profanities.

And then the Astar exploded. Arthur instantly threw himself atop Gwen, bearing her to the ground, shielding her as heat sizzled the air, and there were screams from all around him. Flaming pieces of metal tumbled around them, and it seemed a miracle that they weren't struck by any of them. Then something squishy landed near them, and Arthur realized it was the lower part of a leg, scorched almost beyond recognition. He batted it away before Gwen could see it.

The shrieks and cries of confusion were still coming from all around, and then Arthur was on his feet and advancing on Gilgamesh, rage boiling over within him. He was so infuriated he didn't even think about Excalibur strapped to his back. Instead he shouted, *"You didn't have to do that! You just killed two people!"*

Gilgamesh, towering over him, studied him as if he were a flea. "I killed two spies. They behaved with discourtesy. And I would have a care how you address me, were I you."

"You barbaric animal——!"

And then Enkidu was between the two of them, his lips drawn back emphasizing his fearsome teeth, and he gave a low, warning growl, which froze Arthur but did nothing to dissipate his ire.

Very slowly, very dangerously, Gilgamesh repeated, "I would have a care . . . how you address me . . . were I you."

There was the hiss of metal departing scabbard, and Percival had his sword in his hand. He was several steps away from Enkidu on the right, and there was determination burning in the Moor's eyes. "It's a little late to start preaching about caution, High King."

Astoundingly, it was Miss Basil who came forward as the calming voice of peace. "Gilgamesh," she said in her customary sultry tone, "perhaps it would be best if we retired to your court. There everything can be sorted out . . . can't it, Miss Porter."

The fact that she addressed her remark to Nellie caught Arthur off guard, and indeed, Nellie herself paled when she heard her name spoken by the creature calling itself Miss Basil. But Basil's gaze was fixedly upon Nellie, and Nellie looked as if she wanted to be anywhere else doing anything else, which was enough to make Arthur wonder just what was going on. It was not sufficient, however, to make him lose sight of what had just occurred.

Gilgamesh, in the meantime, seemed to have lost interest in Arthur altogether. Instead he was staring fixedly at the trembling form of Sandoval in much the same way that a child becomes fascinated by an insect once the wings have been torn away. "Would this be," he inquired as casually as if asking about the weather, "the man responsible for the assault upon your wife?"

"Yes," said Arthur tightly. It was all he could do not to use Excalibur to chop Sandoval to bits.

"Well then," Gilgamesh said in a very cheery voice, "we shall bring him along and add him to the Determination."

The others looked around in confusion. "The what?" asked Percival.

"A Determination!" The island people were chanting the word, and it spread from one to the other as more and more showed up, saying again and again, "Determination! Determination!"

Arthur heard Gwen mutter to Nellie in a low voice, "Ever read *The Lottery* by Shirley Jackson?"

"Oh God, yes, I was thinking the exact same thing," replied Nellie.

Arthur had no idea what they were talking about, but he knew what a single-minded mob sounded like, and he certainly wasn't liking the sound of this one. They kept chanting that same damned word over and over, "Determination," and furthermore he saw the way they were looking at Gilgamesh. They were dancing around him, their arms waving about like stalks of grain, their bodies undulating, and he realized at that point that he was surrounded by worshipers and fanatics. None of this was going particularly well, and he was wishing more and more that he'd had the good sense to leave Ron and Nellie behind. They weren't part of this.

Except . . . the way that Nellie was looking around, and staring at the shattered pieces of the helicopter, led Arthur to believe that maybe she was more a part of it than he'd originally thought.

Merlin. Merlin would know.

For long, long months Arthur had felt as if he were wandering in darkness, deprived of his greatest and most assured advisor. But now, miraculously, Merlin had been returned to him, obviously restored through the potent magiks of the Holy Grail. It must have taken a much longer time to overcome the dark sorcery responsible for his paralysis, but overcome the sorcery had been. And now, finally, after all this time, he could turn to Merlin for advice and counsel, and everything would be vastly improved.

He turned toward Merlin.

Merlin was gone.

ZIUSURA WAS BUSY in his quarters, which were both large and cramped: large due to the pure space involved, and cramped thanks to the many, many books that occupied every available bit of space. And not just books: parchments, scrolls, stone tablets, just about anything that maintained the written word upon it. And his computer, as well. Ziusura was particularly proud of that one, and he'd just about finished packing it up when he heard a noise at the door to his study. He turned, surprised, confused, and just a little annoyed, to see a young man standing there. The young man had a faintly amused look and an attitude of age beyond his years.

Ziusura did not recognize him, and yet felt as if he'd known him for centuries. He paused for only the briefest of moments, and then said, "Aging backward?"

"Pretty much," said the young man. He stepped forward, extending a hand. "Merlin Demonspawn."

"Ziusura," replied the old man, shaking the hand firmly.

Merlin cocked an eyebrow. "Ut-Napishti. Of course. I should have known. Where he would go, you would go."

"Hardly," said Ziusura with a disdainful cough.

"Then why are you here?"

"Everyone has to be someplace."

"That's no answer."

"Heh." There were crates and cartons all over. He continued to pack objects into them in no seeming order. "You will find, my reverse aging friend, that there are really only three answers to all questions in the world: Everyone has to be someplace; God told me to; and—"

"It seemed like a good idea at the time?"

Ziusura looked surprised. "You know that one?"

"Everyone knows that one."

"Ah."

Ziusura studied him for a moment. "Weren't you a statue?"

"Yes. But I got better."

"I see. And without the power of the Grail . . . would you get worse?"

The wizard shook his head. "My condition was based in magic. Once it was disposed of, it cannot return."

"That may come in handy."

"Yes."

Merlin watched silently for a time as Ziusura went about his business. Ziusura was not in any particular mood to chat, and at first Merlin made his life rather easy by keeping his mouth shut. Eventually, though, he asked, "So . . . what's all the packing for?"

"What do you think?"

He gave it a moment's more thought, and then said, "I think you're thinking that this is all going to end badly."

"Oh, yes."

"And you want to be prepared when it does go bad."

"Oh, yes. Expect nothing, anticipate everything, that's my motto."

"A good motto," said Merlin. "And have you anticipated just precisely what you're going to do if it does end badly?"

"Oh, yes."

"Not to sound indelicate, but . . . you're referring to a means of escape from a situation that is becoming increasingly tenuous, bordering on unfortunate."

"That is correct."

"And you are preparing this because . . ." When Ziusura did not immediately respond, Merlin finished, ". . . it seems like a good idea?"

"At this time? Most definitely." He eyed Merlin thoughtfully. "They're all quite mad here, you know. All of them."

"Yes, I know."

"And you were quite mad to join them. You and your friends. They *are* your friends, are they not?"

"Well, 'friends' might be too generous a term. But it's not as if they had much choice."

That comment caught Ziusura's interest, and he paused a moment and stood fully, staring down at the young man. "What do you mean?"

Merlin smiled enigmatically. "The wheels of fate, Ut-Napishti. They turn, as they always do. But there are some who, even though they may appear paralyzed and helpless, are capable of greasing those wheels to their advantage."

Ziusura gave a laugh that sounded like it was filled with phlegm. "You are quite something, young man. You claim you manipulated the strands of fate in order to put all this into motion? Is anyone walking the earth that devious? That diabolical? That utterly amoral?"

"And if there is . . . ?" asked Merlin neutrally.

"Then he should help me pack."

Merlin grabbed a carton.

CHAPTRE
THE TWENTY-SECOND

✝

THE HIGH KING *looks out upon his people. They are gath-ered unto him, here in his great court, and they are calling his name and are upon bended knee, swaying back and forth and chanting in a most harmonious manner.*

It has been far, far too long since a Determination has been held. The people love when he does this. When he listens to various com-plaints and decides the future path that will be taken. They want to be led. They want to love and be loved. And he is fully prepared to give them all they desire. For he is their High King, their alpha and omega, their beginning and end. It is his right and obligation to provide all they need and more.

Admittedly . . . it wearies him occasionally. He sees their raw need, their hunger for his attention and love, and he begins to feel his ageless age.

But . . . on the other hand . . .

. . . he is not dead.

And that is what it all comes down to, really. He still lives and breathes. His heart pumps blood through his system, air is still drawn into his lungs. He knows what it is like to be dead, for he has walked the byways of death, and is certain that such places are not for him.

For the High King, it is not enough that his legend will never
die. He must never die as well. Never.
It's just that . . . every so often . . .
. . . he forgets why not.

ＯNCE IN A while, when Arthur closed his eyes, he
could still recall the sensations of sitting in his great
hall in Camelot and holding court. The brisk winds that
would blast through the castle in the winter, the remarkable
heat that would hang heavily in the summer. The rustling
of pennants upon the wall, the clanking as armored feet
would march in upon official business, or the soft padding
of leather or barely held together cloth serving as footwear
for the peasants. From the highest born to the lowest, the
richest to the poorest, they all came before Arthur with their
problems, their arguments, their life-and-death situations.
He would always sort through them and endeavor to pro-
duce some sort of compassionate and reasoned decision,
much of the time feeling like a total fraud who might be
caught out at any time because he was just guessing. But
people would nod their heads and smile and the wisdom of
King Arthur would be hailed by all. And his beloved queen
would beam at his side, and Merlin would make some cutting remarks, but always afterward and always in private,
and that was the way of things.

He sorely missed those days . . . and the insanity that
presently represented his life made him all the more nostalgic.

The great hall of Gilgamesh was in some ways evocative
of the long-gone Camelot. It was, however, decorated far
more ostentatiously, particularly considering that it was re-
plete with statues and busts that were clearly all supposed
to be representative of Gilgamesh himself. The hall itself
was packed with island residents, all of that same uniform,
glowing health so abundant that it was starting to get on
Arthur's nerves.

Nor were they simply there to watch. They were there to worship. That was the most disconcerting thing of all. Arthur may have been king, there may have been those who foolishly believed that the hand of God had reached down, tapped him on the shoulder, and said, "You there, with the confused expression and the slightly irregular features . . . you're in charge now. That's all right then, isn't it?" But for the most part, everyone coming to Camelot knew that they were coming to witness the judgments of a simple, mortal man. Divinely inspired, perhaps. Wise . . . well, that was subject to debate. A man, though, in the final analysis.

Here, though, reigned a being who was—by his own incessant proclaiming—two-thirds god and one-third man. They had come to bask in his presence. They had come to bow down to him and adore him. That bothered the hell out of Arthur. He disliked the notion of something being worshiped while it was walking the earth.

Percival, Nellie, Ron, and Gwen had arranged themselves around Arthur, forming a sort of protective semicircle, which he had to admit he found somewhat sweet. The people of the island were back to swaying and chanting, and during all of that, Arthur was relieved to see a very annoyed-looking Merlin push his way through and approach Arthur, shaking his head in irritation. "May we all be saved from fanatics," Merlin muttered when he drew within range, and Arthur could not have agreed more.

A roar went up, which was more than enough to alert Arthur that Gilgamesh had made his entrance. He came in from the side, and the people threw themselves upon the ground.

"Look at them," Nellie muttered, "prostating themselves."

"Prostrating," corrected Ron.

"What?"

"Prostrating. It's prostrating, not prostating. Prostrate is to throw yourself flat in supplication. The prostate's a gland in men that enables us to ejaculate. When we're in our late forties, we have to start getting it checked via a rectal exam."

Nellie stared at him and then informed him, "You've no idea how happy I would have been not to learn that."

Despite the seriousness of the situation, Arthur suppressed a smile. He finally understood why Ron and Nellie were along: comic relief.

Gilgamesh was followed by Miss Basil, looking tall and cool and serenely elegant in a flowing green gown. And behind her was Arnim Sandoval. Arthur hadn't known what to expect of a man who had just been regurgitated by a giant snake after spending eight months residing within. All things considered, he'd actually cleaned up fairly well. He had bathed, and he was wearing simple white slacks and a shirt, although Arthur couldn't guess where Gilgamesh might have acquired something that relatively contemporary. His hair was clean and combed, his beard neatly trimmed, and there was no longer any delirious confusion in his eyes. Instead there was just glowering hatred, and he leveled his gaze upon Arthur with such intensity that it might well have plowed straight out the back of Arthur's skull if given half a chance.

There was a movement at Arthur's side, and then Gwen's hand had slid into his own, her fingers intertwining. He turned and looked at her with a questioning eyebrow.

"I think it was a damned fool thing to do," she said softly, but there was no anger in her eyes. "But you've lived your life doing what you thought was right, and I don't see how I can fault you for doing that now, however much I might disagree with it. So . . . we're good. You and me, I mean. There's, you know . . . no resentment or anything on my part."

"Oh, good," said Arthur, smiling.

"And thank you for going to all this trouble in the hope of reviving me."

"Not a problem."

"I just hope it doesn't get us all killed."

"Same here."

There was a loud, reverberating, rhythmic thumping, and Arthur quickly realized that Enkidu was standing to one side, holding a long and powerful-looking wooden staff. He thudded it repeatedly on the floor, the sounds catching everyone's attention and letting them know that all attention was to be paid to Gilgamesh. The chanting, the praying and swaying, all of it promptly tapered off. People were ringing the outer edge of the court, while Arthur and the others stood toward the center of the room, about ten paces away from the High King. As for Gilgamesh, he stood next to his throne. The kilt he wore was elaborately decorated with gold trim that seemed to be made of genuine gold. A fur-lined cape was draped over his shoulders. He was not wearing his horned helmet, and his hair was hanging in interwoven strands that ran down to his shoulders. He was the most naturally regal-looking individual that Arthur had ever seen, and considering the number of kings and assorted rulers that Arthur had encountered in his time, that was saying quite a lot.

Slowly he lowered himself into his chair. Gwen had once told Arthur she always imagined the effect a well-placed whoopie cushion would have on the solemnity of such moments. The recollection gave him a small smile, and he reflexively squeezed Gwen's hand a bit more tightly as if to affirm to himself that she was genuinely there.

"Very affectionate," Merlin said in a low voice. His face was carefully neutral. "I'm touched."

"In the head, I'd wager," shot back Arthur in the same subdued tone. "There's a good deal of things to be said between us, Merlin, but right now the only pertinent one would be an inquiry as to just how much power you have at your command."

"Remember when I dropped the pillar on Miss Basil?"

"Yes."

"That was it."

Arthur looked at him askance. "All right," he said slowly. "It's not much, but . . . dropping pillars on people could be effective if used correctly . . . this could still be a plus . . ."

"You don't understand, Arthur," Merlin corrected him. "When I say 'That was it,' I mean, that was *it*."

"What . . . you mean . . . *it?*"

"Have you become hearing impaired in my absence?" Merlin asked testily, his voice raising slightly before he brought it back down again. "I've been out of commission for quite some time. Managing to sustain myself in that . . . imprisonment . . . took a great deal out of me. The fact that I was able to accomplish anything against Basil was nothing short of miraculous. But it's going to be a time before my empowerment is back up to its previous levels."

"All right. Fine," said Arthur. "That will just make it all the more interesting."

Gilgamesh surveyed the waiting throng. "Well," he said finally. "It seems we have some situations here that must be dealt with. Let us attend first to the individual who was truly responsible for the events that have led to this matter. Sandoval, I believe your name is?"

Sandoval glowered at Gilgamesh. And to Arthur's utter surprise, Miss Basil cuffed him on the side of the head as if he were a recalcitrant child. Sandoval glanced at her once, and then genuflected, going to one knee in front of the High King. As he did so, he reached up to just below his jawline and scratched rather vigorously. Arthur's eyes narrowed. It might have been his imagination, but he thought he saw a few flecks of green skin there.

"Respectful. Good to see," said Gilgamesh. "Stand. Good. Now speak to me. Did you attempt to have this man murdered and, as a consequence, cause his mate grievous bodily harm?"

"No," said Sandoval flatly.

"Of course he says no," said Arthur. "Of course he would deny it."

"I deny what is untrue. You overestimate your importance in the world, Penn. Had I wanted you dead, you would have been dead. I wasn't trying to kill you. I was trying to kill her."

Every muscle in Arthur's body clenched. Gwen's hand rested gently on his forearm, which was the only thing restraining him from launching himself across the room. In his mind's eye he could already see Excalibur sweeping through the air and reducing Sandoval's height by a head. So seized with rage was he that he could not even get a word out.

Gilgamesh, for his part, was quite serene. "And why did you do that?"

"Because he killed my wife. And my children."

"*That's a damnable lie!*" Arthur shouted.

Sandoval's voice was flat and oddly absent of the anger one would have expected in such a situation, although contempt seeped out of every syllable. "No. It's not. And it wasn't even in my country. It was during one of your 'measured responses' in the Middle East, dropping bombs on so-called military targets. And you missed. Oh, at first you pretended you didn't. First you claimed that a block of apartments was actually a terrorist training ground. And finally you apologized. How nice for you. How nice for my wife, who was visiting her sister, and my children playing with their cousins." Slowly he advanced on Arthur, his body beginning to tremble with suppressed rage. "Tell me, Mr. President . . . do you think they had any idea before the bomb hit that they were about to die? Eh? Was the high-pitched whistling of the falling missile a warning? Or were they so busy singing childish songs and playing childish games that they had no clue whatsoever? I keep telling myself that's the case, so I don't have to put myself into their heads and imagine their last moments as being filled with terror."

Arthur's jaw twitched for a moment as Sandoval halted several feet away. There was deathly silence in the hall. "If what you say is true . . . it is regrettable. And I sympathize with your loss. But it does not excuse your retaliation. I remember that Middle East strike, and it was in turn retaliatory because one of our embassies had been blown up. Your anger should have been directed at those responsible for our assault—"

"A fine way to dismiss your culpability," sneered Sandoval.

"And furthermore," Arthur said, raising his voice, "accidental deaths are not remotely comparable to the painstaking and carefully planned attempted assassination of an innocent woman—"

And the anger which Sandoval had been containing until that time finally kicked over the edge. *"There are no innocent women! No innocent men! No innocent American people! The sooner you understand that, the sooner you'll comprehend the world you're faced with!"*

"Of all the—"

Gilgamesh raised a finger. "Let him speak."

Arthur did not want to let him speak. Arthur wanted to carve him into kibble. This business of allowing Gilgamesh to run things was rapidly wearing thin upon him, but still he restrained himself. The weight of Excalibur upon his back was of great comfort to him.

Sandoval's arms were relaxed at his sides as he stared at Arthur and the others, but the tension in his voice belied the ease of his posture. "There are no innocent Americans . . . because to be an American means that you are part of the problem. It means you support the government that believes it can do whatever it wants, wherever and whenever it wants. A government that pretends to operate on behalf of the American people but is actually wholly catering to the interests of the same major corporations that are trying to worm their way into every part of the globe. A government so hypocritical that it pretends there is a separation of church and state, but is the only government to put declarations of religious fealty on its money. Do you have any concept of the sanctimony involved to put 'In God We Trust' on your currency . . . as if that automatically makes you morally superior to every other civilized nation?"

"Civilized nations," growled Percival, "do not oppress their citizens."

"No," shot back Sandoval, "they just slaughter the indigenous people and take their land. They import people from a foreign land and sell them into slavery. They imprison thousands of their citizens on racial grounds after one of their harbors is bombed." He shook his head. "Don't you comprehend that that's why so many countries hate you? Because you live and breathe hypocrisy? Because in your arrogance you strut around as if the American way is *the* way, and every other inferior race on the planet is either with you or against you. You are hated because your citizens expect everyone else to speak English, or expect to find fast food franchises in any country they visit. You are hated because your brands and business interests are slowly cleansing nations of their individuality, exerting influence over every aspect of day to day life. You are hated because poor people see the fat, rich American way of life flaunted in your movies and television programs and it sickens them because you continue to want more and more and more, and are never satisfied, while they have nothing and are expected to endure. You are hated because you sit in judgment of other countries as if you yourself don't have racism, or executions, or poverty. You are hated because you are no better than the least country in the world . . . but act as if you are the greatest. And as long as that incredible arrogance seeps from every pore of the skin of every American, you will be hated and targeted and destroyed."

The words rang out and then hung there for a long moment.

And then, very slowly, Arthur smiled. "You forgot one."

Gilgamesh, who had seemed fascinated by Sandoval's words, looked to Arthur in surprise. "One what?" .

"One more reason America is so hated. That's all right, though . . . he's not the only one. Two hundred years ago, it was such a given, such a taken for granted thing, that they clean forgot to put it into the U.S. Constitution until it was pointed out that there might be others who *don't* take it for granted. So they put it in as an amendment, although they made it the first one out of deference to its importance.

"You forgot, Sandoval, how much America is hated for the very thing that you just did: the right to talk about all the things you hate about America. In America, you can talk about such things in newspapers, or in pamphlets, or on street corners, or on television, or shout it from the highest rooftops. And you can do so with impunity. You don't have to worry that the government is going to fine you or imprison you or cut your tongue out and execute you.

"Because when people are able to speak out without fear of repression, that's where ideas come from and change comes from. Yes, the indigenous people were slaughtered . . . but not anymore. Yes, people were enslaved . . . but not anymore. Yes, Asian citizens were imprisoned . . . but not anymore. Practices and actions taken by the government and the people it represents are constantly changing, developing, growing as new thoughts and new ideas are presented. Sometimes they change in positive ways, sometimes negative, but they change. And change is good. Except it's not good to repressive governments. They fear change because change potentially means loss of control, and if they cannot control their people, then they fear the people will turn against them. So they hate and fear the United States because we represent the notion that change and free thought are positives, and they teach their people to hate and fear the United States because God forbid the people should get it into their heads that they should be able to think for themselves. Because if they did, they might start thinking about how their governments could be working to better the people instead of keeping them buried in fear and vicious traditions going back centuries.

"They hate and fear the United States because the United States was built upon ideas and a desire for freedom, and those are anathema to repressive societies. But ideas are not so easily extinguished. The people will find them and root them out, and to such governments, they believe they have to destroy the United States of America because they know they're on the clock. They know the longer our country exists, the greater the likelihood that their people will demand the right to determine their own destinies. And that's what they fear most of all."

In a low voice, Ron said, "Could you say all that again, but slower? I'd like to write some of it down for the President's next speech." Arthur suppressed a smile.

Gilgamesh, however, was not smiling. "I find arguments over self-determination amusing . . . coming from one who was once a monarch."

Arthur shrugged. "As I said . . . things change."

"Not all things. Self-determination can be overrated." He paused for a heartbeat, and Arthur sensed in that pause a world of danger, but then he simply shrugged and said, "However, that is not the question before us at the moment, is it? Sandoval . . . the reasons for your actions are intriguing . . . but they remain simply reasons, rather than excuses. Pendragon . . . ask your mate to step forward."

"I . . . believe her to be capable of doing so without my requesting it," Arthur said. He was not ecstatic; who knew what Gilgamesh was planning? Nevertheless, Gwen stepped forward.

Gilgamesh smiled once his attention was focused upon her. "You are a toothsome little thing. So tell me, wo man . . . what would *you* have me do with this individual? You are the one sinned against. You are the one he assaulted. Vengeance is yours."

"Is it?" she asked. She did not sound especially pleased about it.

Miss Basil moved away from Gilgamesh's side, toward Gwen, not seeming to walk so much as slither as much as a human being—or someone shaped like a human being— could manage. "Do not downplay the joys of vengeance, my dear. Your husband understands it quite well. I gave him

PETER DAVID

the choice of either having you restored to health or having vengeance upon his wife's assailant. He chose vengeance. He chose to rid the world of a terrorist rather than to bring you back to life. His priorities are quite interesting, don't you think?"

Arthur's blood ran cold, and he saw that Gwen was staring at him, her eyes unreadable. "You never said she offered a choice. Is that true?" she asked, knowing that he would answer honestly.

"Yes." He didn't endeavor to make excuses for his reasoning. He simply responded in the affirmative.

She took that in a moment, considered it, and then nodded. "Good," she said.

Miss Basil looked as if she'd sunk her teeth into rancid meat. *"Good?"*

"Yes, good." Her face filled with affection for Arthur. "Here I'd been so upset with Arthur for resigning because of me. I thought it was selfish. But placing the needs of the world above my needs by trying to have Sandoval disposed of . . . that's the unselfish man that I've known and loved. If he didn't place what he saw as the requirements of the people above his own needs, I doubt I'd have been able to recognize him anymore." And as relief flooded through Arthur, she continued, "However . . . there's a time and place for everything. There are people in various countries who are at war because someone's great-great-great-great grandfather killed a cow belonging to someone else's great-great-great-great grandfather, and they still haven't gotten over it. People expend so much energy figuring out so many innovative ways to kill each other, punish each other, hurt each other . . . but not to forgive each other. Even religion, which should be *only* about that, gets distorted into providing excuses for creative punishment, and if you're not of the 'right' religion, forgiveness can't be yours no matter what you do. So . . . Arnim Sandoval," she said, her voice steady, her chin upraised, "I forgive you."

Sandoval's face paled.

Steadily, one delicate step at a time, Gwen approached him as she said, "I forgive you your assault on me. It's over. It's done." And she extended a hand. "I grieve for your loss. But now it ends."

"Yes. Yes . . . you are right," said Arnim Sandoval . . .

. . . and leaped at Gwen's throat.

Arthur moved toward them, as did Percival, but quicker still was Enkidu, and he was upon Sandoval and grabbed him by the back, and twisted so quickly that even before Arthur had taken two steps, Sandoval was now across the room, having slammed into the far wall and sunk to the ground with a dazed expression. "Ow," he said in a distant manner.

"That," Gilgamesh said to Sandoval with an air of disappointment, "was wholly unnecessary."

"Or wholly appropriate," Miss Basil countered. She walked over to Sandoval and helped him to his feet. Her solicitousness for the terrorist struck Arthur as extraordinarily odd. It wasn't as with one lover for another. More . . . maternal, in its perverse way. "Arnim, at least, has not lost sight of the fact that this woman is responsible for the violation of our privacy and threat to our security. Specifically, the helicopter that came in overhead and began snapping photographs of us."

"That is a serious problem," acknowledged Gilgamesh, his face clouding over. "Do we know for certain that she is the cause?"

"Gwen is here because her husband brought her here. But the helicopter," and Miss Basil's eyes glittered, "was because *she* brought them here." And she pointed straight at Nellie Porter.

Arthur, befuddled, looked from Miss Basil to Nellie. "What is she going on about, Nellie?"

Nellie tried to shake her head, but her gaze was locked with Miss Basil's. "No-nothing. She's . . . I dunno what she's talking about . . ."

"Oh, really," replied Miss Basil, and—taking her hand

off Sandoval, who had managed to steady himself—she began to approach Nellie. "I think you do. I think you know
what I'm talking about and much, much more." Her gaze
seemed to bore right into Nellie, carving her up.

"Get away from her," Merlin said angrily, "or—"

"Or what? You'll make obscene gestures? You're not exactly at full strength, Merlin, but the same can't be said of
me. Besides, all I'm interested in is the truth. I thought
that's all any of you seekers of goodness and light were interested in." She continued to advance. "You have no idea,
Nellie Porter, what I'm capable of. No idea how completely
and thoroughly I can burrow into every innermost recess of
your soul. You can speak now of your own volition, or what's
left of you can speak when I've forced it from you."

"That's enough!" shouted Arthur, starting to reach for his
sword.

"Enkidu!" Gilgamesh called out, and the beast-man was
upon Arthur with that same inhuman speed, but Arthur
managed to twist down and away, sliding from the creature's
grasp before he could fully get a hold upon him, and then
Excalibur was clear and shining and its song sliced through
the air with the same purity as its blade. Enkidu froze where
he was, watching warily, his eyes flashing with caution but
also controlled excitement.

And that was when Nellie Porter, legs trembling so
violently that she could barely stand, suddenly began to
sob. Gwen went to her, holding her, and she said, "It's all
right . . . you don't have to listen to any of—"

"He came because of me! He's dead because of me!"

The admission stunned everyone present, with the exception of Miss Basil, who simply smiled in such a display of
self-satisfaction that Arthur had never so desperately wanted
to cave in the face of a female in his life. But his attention
was split between that desire and the need to hear just what
it was that Nellie was talking about.

Gwen was looking at her, trying to comprehend.
"Nellie . . . I don't understand . . . how . . . why was—"

Nellie couldn't face her. She stared down and away from her, trying not to tremble. "I was feeding him stories from time to time. Okay? Nothing threatening national security or anything like that . . . hell, I probably didn't even *know* anything that threatened national security. And I told him about this whole thing. *I didn't think it would work.*" Now she did look up at Gwen, desperate pleading in her voice. "I mean, they told me about the whole Grail thing, but I didn't really, *really* believe it, y'know? I just . . . I figured it was like some faith healing thing, like terminal patients going to South America where some faker pulls chicken guts out of their stomachs. So I . . . I told Baumann where we were going, the destination. And he must have rented a copter or called in a favor or something, and . . . and . . ."

"But . . ." Gwen clearly couldn't comprehend. "But why?"

"He was blackmailing me, okay? Can't we leave it at that?"

"No, Nellie, we cannot," Arthur said, moving toward her, his voice stern. "This is a gargantuan breach of trust you're informing us of. What could he have known that was so terrible?"

"Sir, please . . ."

"*Tell me!*" Arthur said heatedly.

It was Ron who intervened. "Arthur, leave it be."

"Ron, this is none of—"

"*Leave it be.*"

Arthur was taken aback. There was something in Ron's expression, something that indicated . . . Arthur didn't know what it indicated. There was an unspoken warning there, and even though he was certain Ron didn't know any more than he did about what was going on, there was nevertheless something there that said, *Don't ask. You don't want to know. You really, truly don't want to know.*

He weighed the possibilities, the impulse to keep pushing until he knew exactly what was going on. He looked to Merlin, inscrutable, and Gwen, who was still having trouble coping with the loss of trust in a woman whom she had trusted implicitly. And his own inner voice said, *This is not the time.*

"All right," he said finally.

"Pendragon," said a chiding, surprised Gilgamesh, leaning back in his throne and looking for all the world like a Roman Caesar enjoying a ripping good day watching gladiators have a go at one another. "You don't intend to simply leave it there, do you?"

"Yes, I intend to do just that," said Arthur. "Furthermore, I . . ."

He paused and noticed for the first time that the people of the island were watching him. That was interesting, because initially their gazes were completely fixated upon Gilgamesh. It hadn't mattered who was talking at any given moment; Gilgamesh remained their focus. But Arthur began to realize that slowly, person by person, attention had been drifting away from Gilgamesh over to Arthur. He didn't know why that would be, but he had some suspicions. He also suspected, judging by Gilgamesh's gradual change in manner, that Gilgamesh was noticing it as well, and the High King did not seem particularly pleased about it.

"Furthermore," Arthur continued, keeping his voice carefully subdued, "while fingers are being pointed this way and that, I think we should not lose sight of the fact that you, High King, killed two people without so much as a second thought."

"What of it?"

"*What of it?* It was a helicopter pilot and a reporter. They were not attacking you. They were simply two people doing their job—"

"As I, too, did my job, and you would be well advised to watch your tone. I could not simply allow them to fly away from here, knowing what is on this island."

"Isn't it a bit late to be worrying about that?" asked Percival. "What about the VTOL that dropped us off here. The pilot of that vehicle knows. He's going to be coming back for us in . . ."

And then his voice trailed off.

Gilgamesh was slowly shaking his head.

A chill gripped Arthur's spine.

"What is it?" said Gwen. "What's wrong? What's . . . ?"

Merlin looked toward Miss Basil. "You did it, didn't you? You killed the pilot. Crashed the vehicle."

"He crashed it himself. I merely went along for the ride down," she said.

"Oh, my God," whispered Ron, who looked as if the world was lurching about him. "Oh, my God . . ."

"You bitch," Arthur snarled. He had not resheathed Excalibur, and the blade hovered threateningly up and down. "How dare you . . ."

"*How dare* she?" demanded Gilgamesh, and now he was on his feet and his voice filled the room like thunder. "What she did, she did at my instruction, Pendragon, and how dare you judge her or, by extension, me. I am High King here, the king of ancient legend. Basiliskos is the Little King, as the Greeks called her, the king of legendary creatures. And you are Arthur Pendragon, king of modern legend. We three kings are not to be judged by the laws and rules of others! We are above such considerations! We are laws unto ourselves!"

"Careful what you say, Arthur," murmured Merlin.

"You're insane!" Arthur told Gilgamesh.

Merlin rolled his eyes. "Good, well played, you handled that perfectly."

*T*HE HIGH KING *slowly descends from his throne. He walks down the small set of stairs that lead from the raised platform to the floor, and he does not seem to get any shorter as he descends them.*

He pulls his scimitar from his sheath. It makes a glorious noise as it emerges.

"For centuries," he says as he stares at his reflection in the curved, gleaming blade, "I wandered the earth. I saw cities that I built with my own hands crumble to dust. Saw every individual I loved taken from me. I, who once feared death more than any other creature on the face of the earth, discovered the heritage that aged me so slowly that I was virtually immortal, and grew to curse it, and myself. Older I became, and older still, bent and weaker, but still did not die, and then . . . I came upon the Grail. It was in its incarnation as the land, but I knew it for what it was, and I took it and cherished it and drank from it, and because of my divine nature, it made me young and whole again. And then I mastered it and convinced it to transform itself into its incarnation as a sword. With it, I descended into the underworld, and I fought past the gidim, the spirits of the dead, and I fought past the demons, the offspring of Arali, and I confronted Ereskigal and Nergal, the queen and king of the underworld, and I took this sword from him as well, this very sword, and with blades in either hand I demanded that he restore Enkidu to me, for I could bear to be alone no longer. And Enkidu, who was unfairly and untimely ripped from me by the gods An, Enki, and Utu, was restored to me. I keep Nergal's sword to this day, to prove to all my mastery of death. And then I came here, found this island, transformed the Grail into the land, and followers came, in small numbers, selectively, but they came, and I rule over them all. And with all that I have experienced, all that I have accomplished, you think that your pathetic labels of sanity and insanity apply to me? If I am insane . . . then the gods are insane."

And the upstart who calls himself Arthur Pendragon looks defiantly at Gilgamesh and says, "That is not an unlikely possibility."

Gilgamesh hears this and laughs bitterly, although the truth of it pricks at him. Then he extends his sword, and calls out, "A Determination has been made!"

No one responds.

This confuses him. Usually the people immediately chant "Determination!" with such a pronouncement. Instead, this time there is dead silence, and even a few looks of confusion and even regret.

"A Determination!" he shouts once more, and this time they pick up their cue and begin to chant, "Determination," although it sounds to him a bit halfhearted.

"Arthur Pendragon," Gilgamesh says loudly, "you are too well known to the outside world. I see that now. Your disappearance will raise too many questions, and others may endeavor to seek you out. You and the man and woman with you called Nellie and Ron must leave. A small craft will be provided you, and you will depart."

Percival says with great vehemence, "It is unlikely they would survive such a trip in an open vessel, High King. That I did was nothing short of miraculous, and due only to my nigh-immortal nature . . ."

"Give me time," Merlin assures Gilgamesh, "a week . . . two . . . and I will be recovered enough to transport us away."

"It must be done immediately," Gilgamesh tells them. "As for the one called Gwen . . . she may remain."

Gwen laughs in amazement at that. She has a lovely laugh. Gilgamesh will like this one once he has made her his. "But . . . Arthur is my husband. I don't want to be without him. If he leaves, so do I."

"Then you will collapse and very likely die."

This information stuns them. He likes the look of shock on their faces.

"What?" Arthur says.

"She will collapse and she will die," he repeats. "She cannot depart this land."

"Of course," says Percival, the truth of the matter dawning upon him. "Unlike drinking from the Grail, its restorative powers as the land only exist while one stands upon it. Should one depart the land . . . the restoration dissipates, as it did with Joshua."

"Leave her behind, Pendragon. She will live forever here. What greater gift can you give her than that?"

Pendragon steps forward. Gilgamesh watches the point of the sword. Arthur Pendragon is not wielding it in a threatening manner, at least not yet, but the blade is almost hypnotic in its beauty.

Gilgamesh finds himself desirous of that sword as well, but one thing at a time.

"You say this is your island. You say that you are in charge of it. You have asked me to leave. You speak as one who believes he is very much in control of the situation . . . of the people . . . of me."

"I am," the High King tells him confidently.

Slowly Arthur shakes his head. "That may be what you say. But Excalibur knows differently. And because it does . . . I know differently. It knows the fear that eats at you like a cancer. The terror of death, which has so consumed you that you have isolated yourself, put yourself into this prison of an island, surrounded yourself with worshipers, pretended that you are more than what you are."

"I have no need to be more than I am to deal with you," the High King says in an airy voice, "since I am already far more than you."

"No. You are far less. Because I do not depend upon worship to survive. You do. If you cannot live without pretension, you cannot live at all, but you are afraid to face the alternative. You have lost sight, Gilgamesh, of what a hero should be . . . provided you ever knew that to begin with."

Arnim Sandoval, listening and taking it all in, appears less than impressed. "What would you know of it? You, sitting safely in your White House, ordering bombers to drop explosives upon your enemies thousands of miles away. Do you think that requires the actions of a hero?"

"Does blowing up innocent people?" *Percival counters.*

"There are no inno—"

"Yes, we've been through that," *Arthur interrupts. He smiles ruefully.* "Perhaps, in the final analysis, Gilgamesh, heroism isn't about what we are . . . so much as about what we aren't. Like the sculptor who looks at the great block of marble and chips away everything that does not look the way the finished product appears in his head. So, too, are heroes. We chip away all that is venal or selfish or self-absorbed in the human condition, like fat sliced off a fine cut of meat. And that which remains . . . is truly choice."

Gilgamesh laughs loudly at that, because the sentiment expressed is so absurd, so pretentious, so pathetic. Then he is startled to realize that the people are not laughing with him. He finds this most disturbing as he glances at the assembled residents of his island. The people appear to be listening to Arthur. The world as they see it should be filtered through the perceptions of Gilgamesh. If he approves, they approve; if he finds something lacking, so, too, should they. But in this instance . . . that is not happening. They appear to be thinking . . . independently.

A worm of momentary fear slides into his belly, and he quickly pushes it away. "You seem to be under the impression, Pendragon, that this land is similar to your beloved democracy. That endless discussion is required over every decision, no matter how significant or insignificant. Well, let me disabuse you of that belief. What I say is the final word. Certainly you, as a one-time king, should appreciate it."

"Oh, yes," *replies Arthur.* "Once upon a time, I even would have envied you for it. The ability to get Congress to do what I wanted, when I wanted. It has a certain allure to it. But we live in a more complex world now, Gilgamesh."

"I don't."

"You do. You simply have chosen to ignore it."

And the rage begins to bubble out of him, unchecked but not unexpected. "I will not be lectured by you!"

"Too late," *mutters Merlin, apparently not taken with the direction of the conversation.*

He feels control beginning to slip away, and his body trembling, he says, "Only one object on this island can bring true and final death, and I hold it in my hand. The decision is made, Pendragon. The woman remains here, and you will leave. It is the price for her life and all of yours. This is your last chance!"

"No," *replies Arthur very, very quietly, and the sword seems to be humming in the air.* "It's yours."

CHAPTRE
THE TWENTY-THIRD

✝

THE WAY IN which Gilgamesh had looked at Gwen had frightened her. It had been brief, ever so brief, but Gwen had become all too accustomed to men's gazes upon her. When she was young, single, on her own, men hadn't given her a second thought. But since she had entered the public eye, she had developed a knack for sensing the way that different men looked at her. It was an instinct, but invariably borne out by comments the men subsequently made (which she usually heard about secondhand from staffers who were always ready to pass along the sentiments expressed about her when she wasn't around).

So now, when Gilgamesh had been conducting this . . . this peculiar trial that was unlike anything she'd ever encountered . . . he had locked eyes with her briefly, and a knowing smile had appeared on his face. But she'd barely registered the smile, because it was the eyes on which she had focused, the eyes that had so disconcerted her. She felt as if there were some primal force within him that was assessing her, even threatening to devour her. She knew that he wasn't seeing her as a person, or even a human being.

The capricious whims of the "High King" had been struck by this woman, and she sensed immediately where his mind had gone.

To the High King, Gwen—the wife of the man who had been King Arthur—was the closest to a genuine queen that he was going to come upon in this isolated sphere. The notion had obviously caught his fancy, as had she. She was not vain enough to think that Gilgamesh had maneuvered all of them into this situation simply because he desired her. He was far too mercurial a personality for that. He had just noticed her, that was all. Had just arbitrarily decided that he was going to take a fancy to her, and that made his decisions and pronouncements all the easier . . . not that they were difficult to begin with.

And now it had come to this: Arthur and Gilgamesh in a war of words, facing each other down, all because of her. And if Arthur died at Gilgamesh's hands, which was entirely possible because, God, Gilgamesh was the size of a Sherman tank and Arthur, well, she loved Arthur dearly, and he was a stout-hearted and valiant warrior, but this was ridiculous . . .

"No," Arthur said, "it's yours."

There was a gasp from the people surrounding them, no doubt at the sheer audacity it took to say such a thing to the being who purported to be two-thirds god and one-third man. Gilgamesh's eyes, those beacons of barely controlled fury, darkened even more, and suddenly Gwen blurted out, "Arthur . . . go. I'll stay here."

Arthur turned, looked at her in bewilderment, as did the others. "What?"

"You go. I'll be fine."

"Excellent," said Merlin briskly. "That all worked out. Right then, off we go . . ."

"She doesn't mean it, sir!" called out Nellie Porter, ignoring the young wizard who was heading for the door. "She's just trying to be self-sacrificing for you!"

"Yes, Nellie, I'm quite aware of that," Arthur said patiently. "Gwen, I'm not leaving you."

"You'd ignore her wishes, then?" There was challenge in Gilgamesh's tone. "After all that you'd criticize me for thrusting my desires upon others, you now ignore the stated preferences of your own wife?"

"If I thought for a moment that they were genuine, I would act upon them," said Arthur. He turned back to Gwen and looked at her with those piercing blue eyes that had first caught her attention at what seemed an eternity ago.

She desperately wanted to lie to him. Gwen even opened her mouth, endeavoring to form the words. But they stubbornly refused to emerge. She didn't shake her head, but her muteness spoke more eloquently than her words possibly could have.

He nodded, as if an opinion had been affirmed. Then, since his back was to Gilgamesh, he turned his head slightly toward Percival and, in a very low voice, said, "You were the Grail's master before Gilgamesh. Can you regain control of it?"

Percival indicated no with a very slight shake of his head. "I don't know that the Grail can have a 'master.' But his control over it is far more thorough than ever was mine, thanks to the many years that it has been in his possession."

"How now, Pendragon?" called Gilgamesh testily. "Your answer."

Arthur regarded the High King with a mix of contempt and pity and said, "Is this what it comes down to, then? A great man rendered so small that he must use the power of life and death as a club on people in need just to keep them in line? The greatness of Gilgamesh is mythic . . . but is it also myth?"

For a long moment, Gilgamesh was silent. All manner of emotion seemed to be at war in his face. "And what would you have?" he suddenly asked.

It was, to Arthur, a surprisingly passive response, but he

did not hesitate. "I would that you gave the people of your realm a choice. Transform this . . . this land back into the Grail. Let each and every creature here drink of the Grail individually, so that they can experience its salutary effects for themselves."

"There is no guarantee that, in so doing, they would acquire virtually immortal life," replied Gilgamesh warily.

"In the real world, Gilgamesh—the world from which you have so carefully shielded yourself—no one receives any guarantee of a life span," Merlin pointed out. He strode forward, walking with that customary swagger that Gwen remembered so well. He cast a glance at her . . . and actually winked, which surprised her. It was as if he were regarding the whole encounter as some sort of great game. The thought did not fill her with a warm feeling.

"Arthur has put forward an excellent idea," Merlin continued. "You would be giving these people freedom of choice. Are you averse to that notion? Freedom of choice? Or is that, along with dying, something else that you are afraid of?"

Gwen wasn't ecstatic with the way he'd phrased that. It sounded entirely too challenging. And it was obvious to her that Gilgamesh had caught the tone and wasn't any more enthused about it than she was.

"Do you," he asked with an edge of danger in his voice, "seek to challenge me?"

"We seek to end this peaceably!" countered Arthur.

And Merlin sounded very sad as he said, "But that's not going to be possible, is it?"

"Merlin! For Uther's sake—"

"I wasn't talking to you, Arthur," said Merlin, still sounding rather melancholy, even weary. "I was talking to you, Gilgamesh. This will not end well, will it? Your insufferable ego won't permit it. Your need to be loved, to be in control . . . it's going to overwhelm everything else, won't it? Every good instinct you ever possessed, every heroic impulse that might have brightened and ennobled your soul . . . none of it matters, does it?"

"Merlin!" Arthur sounded to Gwen as if he was utterly mortified.

Merlin didn't react to him. Instead he walked slowly toward Gilgamesh, and continued, "And the truly tragic thing is, you believe you're unique. That there are none who understand what you are going through. How little you know. All you have here, Gilgamesh, is a cult of celebrity. You're no different, really, than any major movie star or fool who measures his own self-worth by how others view him. You've become so lost in the need for adulation—or so mired in self-pity—that you forgot what you truly are."

Arthur blinked at that, and looked at the mage with a raised eyebrow. "Merlin, was that partly directed at me?"

"Partly," admitted Merlin, sounding a bit sad.

"So you claim," Gilgamesh said, "that Pendragon and I are much alike."

Percival spoke up. "No. You're not."

"And why do you say that?"

"Because Arthur simply forgot, for a time, what he truly is . . . no offense, Highness. But you, Gilgamesh—after all those months speaking with you, I'm not sure you ever knew who you truly are to begin with. And please——" he raised a hand—"don't tell me 'Two-thirds god, one-third man.' That describes your parts . . . but not the sum of who you are. Look long and deep into yourself, Gilgamesh."

And Miss Basil made an angry, dismissive noise. She came around and stood between Gilgamesh and the others. Facing the High King, she said, "I cannot believe that you are listening to this nonsense. A miniature wizard, a musty king of a long-lost kingdom, his wife with a bullet in her brain, and a Moor are telling you what to do and who you are. And you're listening to them?"

"We're here, too," Ron spoke up.

"Yes, but you don't count."

Despite the seriousness of the situation, Gwen suppressed

a laugh as Ron Cordoba bristled at that. Then Nellie put a restraining hand on his arm and muttered, "Ron, for God's sake, shut up. The last thing you want to do is attract her attention."

There was wisdom in what she was saying, but very briefly, Gwen made eye contact with her, and then looked away. She still could not get over, or even comprehend, Nellie's actions. What in the world had happened? What could Nellie possibly have done to leave herself open to such a blackmail threat? It was completely insane. There had to be some sort of explanation for her actions. Unfortunately, now was neither the time nor place. The problem was, she wasn't sure whether the time or place would ever have the opportunity to present itself.

"You cannot let them persuade you to act against what you know is best for your people," Miss Basil was saying.

"As if you know what is best for anyone except yourself," snapped Merlin.

Her head whipped around. "Stay out of this, Merlin."

"You keep away from him, creature," Arthur said warningly, and he brought Excalibur up meaningfully.

"Be careful waving that about, you might hurt yourself," said Miss Basil before refocusing her energies on Gilgamesh. "High King, listen to me . . ."

"So she can steer you off the proper track."

"No one asked you, Merlin."

"Then I'm telling you. Gilgamesh, listen to me—"

"Gilgamesh . . ."

"High King, this is absurd. You . . ."

THE HIGH KING *is losing his patience.*
Pendragon is babbling at him. The short wizard is babbling at him, and the Moor, and now the Little King, the snake who slithers like a woman, is babbling at him as well. They speak in rapid succession, each trying to convince him to do what they want, each demanding that he look into himself, examine himself,

question himself, when the truth is that each of them just wants something for themselves, *and no one save Enkidu truly gives a damn about the High King. No one has in centuries. In millennia. No one ever truly has.* The High King knows the truth of the world: that everyone simply wants something for themselves, and believes that the High King should hand it to them out of generosity or heroism or some other pretense.

And the Little King keeps raving at him, and now Pendragon is speaking, and the mage is trying to talk over both of them. The High King can almost see the words themselves as physical entities, colliding in the air and blasting apart, letters scattering to the four winds. And there is the one called Gwen, the queen, looking concerned, and thankfully not filling the air with more verbiage. It makes him appreciate her all the more, desire her all the more.

All of them, hammering at the High King, trying to pull him in a dozen directions at once, and he can sense the eyes of all his people upon him, and Enkidu as well, and he has never, ever, felt this disconcerted, this frustrated.

This must end. It has to end now, this instant, and it must be done in a way that all know without a doubt just who is the High King, who is in charge, who is two-thirds god, one-third man. There is no longer time for pensive consideration or bargaining or compromise.

He feels his hold beginning to slip away . . . not only his hold upon his people, but his hold upon himself. Even if they all rise up against him, they still cannot harm him, not really, for he is the High King and greatness unto himself, but still, *this must end* for the sake of his sanity, for his self-esteem.

"End it now," screams the voice in his head, "now, put an end to it now, now!"

T HE CLANG WAS deafening, the vibrations so mind-numbing that Gwen actually sank to one knee, clutching her hands to her ears. Nellie fell over completely, and Ron nearly collapsed on top of her. Even Arthur and Percival were staggered.

Merlin just stood there, looking put out. *Figures*, she thought.

There were moans and cries from the assembled populace, who were similarly affected. The origin of the ear-shattering noise was quite evident.

Gilgamesh had taken the sword upon his back and swung it with all the force that his two-thirds divine parentage afforded him. It had struck the tiles beneath his feet and set up the resounding noise that had practically deafened everyone looking on. There was now a large crack in the floor, busted up tile scattered about.

"Enough!" bellowed Gilgamesh. "The Determination has been made! The Destiny is set! Pendragon and his companions will leave now! The woman stays!" His eyes narrowed. "And the sword stays as well. Fitting punishment for daring to trade words with the High King."

A grim smile played upon Arthur's lips that Gwen knew only too well. When it came to Gwen's fate, there were matters of self-determination at issue. But no one was ever going to pry Excalibur from his hands while Arthur lived. She knew that beyond question. And she also had the feeling that Gilgamesh knew that as well.

He said nothing. He didn't have to. He merely tightened his grip upon his sword and held it at a battle-ready position, and that was all that was required.

And there was Percival at his side, and he had his own sword out. It was not remotely as striking as Excalibur, of course, but it was a fearsome-looking thing . . . a formidable war sword with a gleaming point and razor-sharp edges, effective for both jabbing and slashing. The two bold warriors with their weapons at the ready, facing a rippling, bronzed, godlike man who had his own blade prepared.

Although Gwen appreciated the otherworldly, times-past feel to the moment, she realized she would have liked it even better if Arthur or Percival were wielding something a bit more twenty-first century . . . like a machine gun, or even a bazooka.

Gilgamesh studied them a moment, and Gwen couldn't tell whether he was anticipating the conflict to come . . . or regretful. Then his features hardened, and whatever doubt there might have been was clearly gone. "Enkidu," he said stridently, "attend to the Moor. I have no desire to deal with fleas while I am busy disposing of the dog itself."

There was a smile of triumph on Miss Basil's face. Next to her, Sandoval was watching with equal pleasure and anticipation, and he glanced briefly at Gwen in a manner that seemed to say, *You're next.* Gwen wished she had the ability to wipe those smug expressions off their faces. She had never felt more helpless in her life.

And then . . .

. . . nothing happened.

The fact that Enkidu had not leaped through the air, roaring with fury, claws outstretched or teeth bared or whatever it was he was going to do, did not immediately sink in on Gwen, or anyone there, for that matter. But the widening gap of time between Gilgamesh's order and Enkidu's failure to carry it out quickly became very pronounced. Momentarily flummoxed, the High King looked to Enkidu, his right-hand man (or whatever).

The great beast was simply standing there, unmoving. One would have thought him carved from stone, as if he'd gone three rounds with the Basilisk and lost. Only the slight twitching of his ears indicated that he possessed any ability to move.

"**E**NKIDU," GILGAMESH SAYS *again, not sounding cross so much as puzzled. It does not appear terribly likely that Enkidu has not heard him. Enkidu could hear the feathers falling off a bird from twenty feet high.* "Enkidu . . . the Moor . . . attend to the—"

Enkidu slowly moves his great head and stares fixedly at his lord and master, his friend, his companion.

And suddenly Gilgamesh has never felt more alone.

*   *   *

ERCIVAL WAS POISED, ready. Every muscle in his body was an odd combination of tense and relaxed. Frankly, he did not like his odds. Percival had fought many a human foe, but Enkidu was not that. The creature was standing not twenty feet away, and Percival knew that the beast-man could cover the distance with one quick thrust of his legs. Which meant that Percival would have exactly one chance to react to Enkidu's onslaught, and if he miscalculated the timing of his swing, or didn't manage to kill the beast on his first try, he was going to have a problem.

He was reasonably sure that Enkidu couldn't kill him. Not only did the power of the Grail flow in Percival's veins, but none who stood upon the island could die. On the other hand, if Enkidu lifted him over his head so that he was technically "off" the island and proceeded to tear him to shreds, Percival wasn't entirely certain what his chances would be. Nor did he have the slightest desire to find out.

And still Enkidu remained frozen, as one paralyzed. Percival gazed at him, assessing him as he had done so many foes back in his days as a knight, and he saw in the mighty beast-man no hesitation, no uncertainty. He was not frozen by indecision. He just wasn't moving.

"Beast brother," Gilgamesh said slowly. "How now?"

For a fraction of an instant, Percival saw misery on the creature's face as he had never seen on the countenance of anything on God's earth that walked upon two legs. He suspected that Enkidu had no tear ducts, for if he had, he might well have dissolved into sobs.

"I cannot," he said.

Gilgamesh took a step toward him, eyeing him carefully as one would an exceptionally intriguing bug. "Cannot . . . or will not."

"Both, if it pleases."

"It does not please, beast brother." The danger in the voice of the High King was escalating. "For all that I love you, Enkidu, do not think that I would hesitate to express extreme displeasure with you. This man. . . . this 'Grail knight' . . . he escaped you once. You have unfinished business with him. Attend to it. Now."

And once again: "I cannot." And then, as an afterthought, ". . . or will not."

Percival saw Gilgamesh stand there, every emotion imaginable playing across his broad face.

"You're not . . . actually in agreement with these . . . persons? You do not actually think they are . . . right?" an appalled Gilgamesh asked.

When Enkidu spoke, it was not without effort. Percival had not heard him utter more than a few words at a time. "Right and wrong . . . means nothing. They are . . . fictions of men's minds."

"Nonsense," snapped Gilgamesh.

"Is a female killing and devouring her mate . . . wrong?"

"Of course it is!" Gilgamesh sounded horrified at the notion.

In a soft voice, Enkidu asked, "And if the female . . . is a black widow spider?"

Gilgamesh opened his mouth, then closed it. Percival was amused; it was the first time he'd seen the pompous High King stuck for an answer.

Again, Enkidu said, "There is no right. There is no wrong. There is just . . . what nature intends. And what you do here . . . is unnatural."

"Unnatural!"

"All creatures . . . should be free. All creatures . . . should die, sooner or later. In both respects, you defy nature and the gods. No one does such a thing forever, my brother," he said sadly. "Not even you."

Gilgamesh began to shake with barely contained fury. "You would say this to me?" he demanded. *"To me? After what I did for you! Damn you, Enkidu . . . I went into the afterlife and brought you back to the land of the living!"*

The beast-man served as stark contrast to Gilgamesh, the

former becoming calmer as the latter got more agitated. "I did not ask you . . . to do so."

"You preferred that dreary, bleak land of shadows and nonexistence to this?" He grabbed Enkidu's hand, clasping it firmly. "Feel the blood pounding through you! Feel the air in your lungs! Inhale and draw a thousand different scents through your nostrils! What possible advantage can dwelling amongst the dead have to offer?"

"None . . . save that it is the natural order of things."

"The gods murdered you!"

Enkidu shook his head. "No. I died of a broken heart. I died . . . because of you."

*H*E LIES. THE *High King knows he lies. This is too much. Too much.*

And he is not aware that another voice is whispering within his head. "Kill them," it tells him. "Kill them all. They seek to undermine you. To unman you. You must not tolerate it. You must do what needs be done."

*A*RTHUR SAW GILGAMESH reel back, as if gut-stabbed. He seemed stunned, even short of breath. Arthur could sympathize. It was how he felt the night that Gwen was bleeding upon him in the back of the limo.

"What?" Gilgamesh was barely able to get the word out. "You . . . blame me . . . ?"

It all came out of Enkidu then, like a sigh long contained, unburdened at last. "No. I blame . . . my own weakness. I saw . . . how far you had fallen. I saw you consumed . . . with selfishness. With impurity. With impiety. I was ashamed. I could not . . . stand to see you . . . in that way. My heart . . . could not go on. It ceased its beating. Perhaps . . . through willpower . . . I could have maintained it. But I did not. In a way . . . I myself was selfish."

Gilgamesh was shaking his head in disbelief. "And in all

this time . . . you never told me of any of this? Why did you not?"

And looking as if he knew the next words would hurt most of all, Enkidu said, "You never . . . inquired of me. You never cared . . . enough to ask."

The High King just gaped at him. He seemed to have forgotten that he was holding his sword. The world was spiraling away from him, as if something within him had broken. Finally he found his voice. "And . . . what would you have of me . . . ?"

"Release the land," Enkidu said. "Release the people. Be of the world . . . instead of simply in the world. And let nature . . . take its course."

He's listening . . . gods . . . he's listening, thought Arthur. *Look at his face . . . his entire manner . . . he's actually going to attend to Enkidu's words . . . I can't believe it's going to be that easy . . .*

A heartbeat later, it wasn't that easy at all.

"**K**ILL THEM!" COMES *the voice in his head, louder, more strident, more insistent, refusing to accept any alternative. "You have the sword of the underworld! You can destroy them. Kill them, I say! Kill them all!"*

IT WAS GWEN who spotted it. Gwen who saw Miss Basil's mouth forming the words just before Gilgamesh shouted, "Kill them all!"

"*She's doing it!*" shouted Gwen. "She's making him say it! She's doing something to him!"

Miss Basil's head snapped around to face Gwen, and her mouth drew back in a twisted expression of fury as a hiss escaped her lips, and Gwen felt Miss Basil's gaze starting to bore into her, and she tried to look away but could not avert her eyes. And suddenly a bust of Gilgamesh slammed into Miss Basil's head, thrown with unerring accuracy by Nellie

Porter. Miss Basil let out a startled shriek and went down, blood welling up from a vicious wound on her forehead.

Gilgamesh staggered, putting his hands to his temples, trying to regain his footing and then finding it. He pivoted and faced Miss Basil, who was on the ground, momentarily disoriented. "Was that you, just now? In my head? Telling me to kill them?"

"Yes," she said without hesitation, cold fury in her eyes.

"Do you see your true enemies now, Gilgamesh?" Arthur called, his voice ringing out amongst the assemblage. "Do you see the way of things, the way they should truly be? Do you see that those who care about you want only the best for you?"

Gwen didn't want the best for him. The bastard had killed Baumann. She had not forgotten that, and although she resented the hell out of him for whatever hold it was he had over Nellie, he certainly hadn't deserved to die that way. But she restrained herself with effort. This entire insanity, after all, had occurred because of her. If appealing to Gilgamesh's nobler side—presuming there was one—was going to get them all out of this intact, who was she to protest? Because obviously Gilgamesh, faced with evidence of the manipulation of his mind, was going to do the right thing. That had to be what was about to happen.

𝕿HE HIGH KING bridles upon the realization that his demonic lover has insinuated herself within his mind. She had made him want to strike down Pendragon, to take the woman, to take the sword, to act purely on behalf of his selfish wants and desires.

Now she is gone from his head, distracted, unable to reestablish her influence.

Now he is free to think for himself.

And the first thought that occurs to him is that he wants to strike down Pendragon.

The second is that he wants to take Pendragon's woman. The

*third is that he wants the sword, and his selfish wants and desires
are the wants and desires of a being who is two-thirds god, one-
third man, and how dare anyone, be they king, queen, or beast
brother, tell him what he can and cannot, should and should not,
do.*

*Yes, the Basilisk influenced his mind. But that was just her
enjoying her machinations, playing her games, making certain that
all went as she wanted. The truth is that her priorities and his
are already very close. That is why they get along so well. That is
why, of the three kings in this room—the King of the Britons, the
King of Babylonia, and the Little King—only the latter two matter.*

*He grips his scimitar firmly. It has come to this. Fine. He will
do what needs be done. May the gods have mercy on all their souls,
for he most certainly will not.*

RON CORDOBA KNEW people.

He had succeeded as much as he had, gotten as far
as he had, because he was able to read them instantly. Faster
even than such reliable judges of character as Arthur, Ron
had an infallible sense of what people were going to do
before they did it. It benefited him tremendously, allowed
him to anticipate moves before others even knew they would
be making the moves, and adjust accordingly.

Within the course of a minute, as matters progressed, he
knew the following:

He knew Enkidu was not going to attack before Enkidu
actually spelled it out.

He knew that Miss Basil was somehow screwing with
Gilgamesh's mind. Gwen had shouted a warning barely a
second before Ron was going to sound a similar alert.

He knew that, freed of Miss Basil's influence, Gilgamesh
was nevertheless going to swing that terrifying blade of his
and start hacking at whatever was within range.

He knew that Arnim Sandoval did not share his ability
to predict behavior and actions.

The irony of that last statement would quickly become clear to Ron Cordoba.

ARNIM SANDOVAL CAN *still taste her lips on his.*
When his wife departed to visit family, she kissed him good-bye and he remembers that her lips tasted salty since she had been crying. He wonders belatedly if she had a sense that she would not be coming back.

He has told Arthur Penn why the world despises Americans. He is not certain what he had been hoping for. Some sort of realization on Penn's part? A mea culpa? A reassessment of American policies? No. Instead he receives a lengthy lecture on the glories of America because free exchange of ideas is so highly valued. Penn has no concept. No clue. He does not realize that he has just condemned his country with his own words. That it is the imposition of those ideas upon others, and the utter chaos and divisiveness caused by this love of totally uncontrolled speech, that serves to make America the great enemy it is of so many other countries. He has virtually admitted it: American arrogance dictates that the American way is the best, and heaven help any who disagree. How can any rational individual help but despise a country such as that?

Penn does not understand. He will never understand. None of them will ever understand.

Arnim Sandoval also does not understand. Much has happened to him. He spent an eternity in darkness. He has been reborn. He is in a place he can barely comprehend, encountering individuals he does not understand, facing circumstances that no rational man can be expected to accept.

Yet he does.

In some distant part of his mind, there is screaming and confusion and bewilderment at all that has happened to him, but that part of his mind is far, far away. Indeed, he truly has been reborn, and whenever he looks at the woman who had birthed him, it all makes infinite sense. He does not understand why that should be, but it is. He feels closer to her than he ever has to any woman. To any person. At first she had seemed to be the instrument of his punish-

ment; instead she is now the woman who delivered him. Who has made him great, taken him to new levels. He has been stripped down to the purity of his essence. There is his hatred. And there is her. Nothing else matters.

He sees her injured. He sees her angry. And that is all the trigger that is needed for the hatred he bears to rise up, great and glorious and terrifying to behold. He will physically reflect what he has become. He will become greatness incarnate. It will please her. It will fulfill him.

How many times has Penn and his ilk, horrified in witnessing the retaliation that comes as a result of their own actions, called him a monster? More times than he can count.

And Americans . . . so smug . . . so certain they're always right . . .

Let them be right this time. Let them take joy in their accuracy, for all the good it will do them.

RON CORDOBA HAD the distinct impression that, had Sandoval not done anything . . . if he'd just stood there . . . an enraged Gilgamesh would have torn into the hated Arthur Penn. He might well have caught Arthur flat-footed, although Ron might well have gotten an "Arthur, look out!" into play. For that matter, Arthur himself was no slouch. He might have anticipated the attack himself and adjusted for it.

But Sandoval did not choose to stand there. For Sandoval was apparently of the opinion (which Ron did not share) that Gilgamesh was going to take this matter in stride. That he was indeed going to turn Arthur loose, give up full control of the land, freely share the healing qualities of the Grail with whoever wanted it, in a way that would not make them eternally dependent on his good graces.

So Sandoval obviously decided to take action.

Once upon a time, that decision would have meant very little unless Sandoval happened to be armed or with men under his command, neither of which was the case here. But that was an earlier time. This was the present. A present where Arnim Sandoval had spent apparently eight months in the belly of the beast . . .

As a result, before Gilgamesh could match his own thoughts to actions, he was surprised by an animalistic roar from behind him that wasn't coming from Miss Basil nor from Enkidu.

It was coming from Sandoval. His back twisted, spasmed, and suddenly two small wings burst out of the back of his shirt. They were gray and flapping piteously, but they were there and they were real. He snapped his head back and forth, like a large cat shaking off water, and his body began to distort and distend. There was a rapid-fire series of cracking noises that sounded like firecrackers until Ron realized that it was bones breaking.

Now all of Sandoval's skin had turned that same slate gray, and his eyes were angled and slitted and a combination of yellow with flecks of emerald green. He stretched up and out, his clothes ripping, his neck elongating, his arms growing, his fingers extending and becoming taloned even as his legs shrunk and merged with the lower half of his rapidly growing body. There was a loud thud as his body reoriented itself to its new form and shape, thumping onto the floor in a display of thick, heavy coils.

Flinging his arms out to either side, Arnim Sandoval—transformed into a towering twenty-foot-long young Basilisk—let out a shattering scream that gave a preview of what billions of souls screeching protests in hell over their fate must have sounded like.

And Ron heard Percival mutter, "Well, *this* can't be good."

CHAPTRE
THE TWENTY-FOURTH

✝

ARTHUR PENN, NEE Pendragon, never lost his cool. Never came close. He did, however, take a step back to assess the situation, and was not ecstatic with what he saw.

Gilgamesh whirled and faced Miss Basil, who was staggering to her feet, nursing the wound to her head. "What have you done, woman?" he demanded. "*What have you done?*"

She gestured grandly and said, "I've given birth. Isn't he grand?" Miss Basil regarded the thrashing, roaring form of Sandoval and cooed, "My biological clock was ticking. I felt the need to reproduce, and Arnim was prime material for me. He's glorious, isn't he? He will dispose of Arthur, of Percival, of all of them—"

There was a blur of steel so fast that Miss Basil neither saw it coming, nor anticipated it. She was still in the middle of a word when the great scimitar cut through the air and her neck and the air again without slowing. The force of the blow sent her head flying across the room and ricocheting off the far wall like a handball. Miss Basil's body remained

standing for a moment, as if trying to register the fact that
its head was gone, and then it slumped forward, shifting in
form even as it did, so that although it was a woman's body
that slumped forward, it was a mass of headless coils that
actually hit the ground. Blue ichor seeped out of the top of
the body where the head was missing. Obviously there were
limits, even to the healing power of the Grail land. Either
that, thought Arthur, or the Holy Grail wanted no part of
the unholy Basilisk.

Insanely, Gilgamesh turned and bellowed at the lifeless
head of Miss Basil, which had rolled back across the floor
and come to a halt at his feet. *"Were you under the impression
I could not attend to them myself? Is that how far you think I'd
fallen? Is that how little you think of me?"*

"I hope you're not expecting her to hold up her end of
the conversation," said Merlin.

His comment was lost in the collective screams of the
people of the island, who had had more than enough. They
were practically stampeding one another in their efforts to
get as far away as possible from the monstrous insanity they
were witnessing. It was a terrible distraction to Arthur, and
he did everything he could to screen it out. He had other
things to attend to. Quickly he shoved Gwen toward Ron
and Nellie, taking up a station that placed himself between
his wife and the undulating form of Sandoval. *"Get Gwen
out of here!"* he bellowed.

"But Arthur—!"

He shoved her away, and he was not gentle about it,
although he was careful enough to push her right toward
Ron so that he caught her. He braced himself, readying
himself for the onslaught that was to come.

Sandoval did not appear to notice or even care about the
pandemonium unleashed around him. Instead his attention
was entirely focused upon Arthur, and the king of Camelot
brought Excalibur up as Sandoval the Basilisk leaped
through the air, propelled by his small but effective wings.

But anticipating the sweep of the blade, the Basilisk

slammed his coils down, skidded, and brought the lower half of his body up and around, knocking Arthur off his feet. The king went down, still holding Excalibur, but he landed hard on his right elbow and pain shot through his arm. Above him the creature was unleashing an ear-splitting screech, and he had the horrible feeling that he wasn't going to be able to bring the sword around fast enough.

And suddenly the Basilisk was gone.

Well, not gone, but off to one side. For Enkidu had vaulted the distance and slammed into the Basilisk's upper section. He roared defiance right in the Basilisk's face, sounding for all the world like the angriest lion on the face of the earth, and his head speared forward and his jaws slammed together. The only thing that prevented him from biting the Basilisk's head off was that the monster was a hair quicker, his head darting barely out of the way. The Basilisk screeched back at him, and then Percival was there behind him, swinging his sword around and trying to drive the blade through the creature's lower half, hoping to bisect his body.

It didn't work. The scales that covered him were far too strong. Excalibur would have been able to dispatch him, as could Gilgamesh's blade, but there was nothing particularly magical about Percival's weapon. The Basilisk registered that something was crashing up against his body, but not much beyond that.

As if thrilled to finally have a foe worthy of his capabilities, Enkidu hacked and slashed at the creature's face with his claws and teeth while Percival continued to hammer at him. The Basilisk didn't know which way to look first, moving first one way and then the other, hissing and spitting the entire time.

Arthur saw, from the corner of his eye, Gwen being hustled away by Ron and Nellie, and she was crying out Arthur's name. His heart went out to her, but there was nothing she could do at this point except try and get as far away from the scene of the chaos as possible.

Then he heard Gilgamesh bellowing stridently above the screaming and pandemonium and battle. *"I have given no one permission to leave! Stay where you are! You will listen to me! You will obey me!"* But no one was listening or obeying. It was total insanity, and not even the High King could get anyone's attention. He was becoming aware of his helplessness in the face of such discord, and it was clearly not sitting well with him. His eyes were wild with fury, the veins distending on his head. Arthur would not have been the least bit surprised at that point if Gilgamesh himself had transformed into a monster.

But Arthur could afford to give no more consideration to Gilgamesh's particular situation. Instead he had one of his knights, an unexpected ally, and a monster to concern himself with.

"Don't look the creature in the eyes!" Arthur shouted above the din. He wasn't sure if the newly-created Basilisk fully comprehended how to use its devastating visual abilities, but there was no point in taking a chance. He glanced around desperately to try and see where Merlin was, on the chance that the sawed-off sorcerer would be able to contribute in some way to the melee despite his lack of power. But Merlin was nowhere to be seen.

Arthur scrambled to his feet, holding the mighty Excalibur firmly, and started toward the thrashing three-way battle before him, and suddenly Gilgamesh was blocking his path. "Help me or get out of my way," said Arthur brusquely.

"There *is* a third option," Gilgamesh informed him.

He was smiling.

That struck Arthur as dangerous, and suddenly Gilgamesh's sword was flashing toward him with the same speed that had so effortlessly dispatched Miss Basil.

Madness! Utter madness! Arthur thought, because what sort of mind would actually seek to challenge him, battle him when other, greater foes obviously loomed. But Gilgamesh didn't seem to give a damn about the Basilisk. All his attention was upon Arthur, and Arthur barely brought Excalibur up to deflect the scimitar as it lashed toward him.

When the two blades connected, it was as if thunder and lightning had struck in opposition to each other instead of operating in uniformity. The impact ran the length of Arthur's arms and into his shoulders, and his teeth rattled and his vision blurred. Everything was happening so quickly that he did not have time to consider who his opponent was or what he was being faced with. All he was trying to do at that moment was survive.

Anger began to sweep through him. Anger that he was being subjected to this, anger that someone with such phenomenal power at his disposal, such a capacity for accomplishing great things, was throwing it away in such pointless, selfish endeavors. And then he realized that, in his own way, he had been just as selfish, and the anger was directed as much at himself as it was at Gilgamesh. He saw the capacity for greatness in himself that he had shunted aside, and saw the dark distortion of that capacity in Gilgamesh, who had gone in the totally opposite direction.

He saw it all clearly. And the fact was that Gilgamesh did not see it . . . that Gilgamesh, so much older than he . . . was not the least bit wiser.

*T*HE HIGH KING *is confident in his victory. This will all still be salvageable.*

Then he looks into the eyes of Pendragon, eyes seething with controlled fury, and for just a moment, his confidence wavers.

It is a moment . . . but it is enough.

*E*XCALIBUR SWUNG DOWN, around, and up and caught the scimitar just at the base of the blade, near the hilt.

And the blade that had—according to Gilgamesh—been the personal possession of the lord of the underworld, the blade that had laid low demons and enabled him to rescue his greatest companion from oblivion . . .

The blade shattered.

As Excalibur let out a sound that could have been a howl of triumph, the blade of the scimitar broke into a dozen pieces, flying every which way. Arthur ducked back, shielding his face and narrowly avoiding getting a shard in the eye. The Basilisk was not quite as lucky, as several of the larger pieces embedded themselves in him. Sandoval screamed from the unexpected pain, his body snapping around, shaking off both Enkidu and Percival in his paroxysms.

*N*OT POSSIBLE . . . *NOT possible* . . .
The High King stares at the shattered weapon in his hands. His mind is overloading, unable to cope. This cannot be happening. The blade cannot be destroyed. It is a blade of the gods. The possessions of gods are as inviolable, as unkillable, as gods themselves.

Gods are all powerful. The only thing that can thwart the will or efforts of gods are beings who are similarly gifted and divine.

Gods cannot be defeated by humans. And Pendragon, for all his skills, for all his long life, is still human.

His blade cannot be greater.

He cannot be greater.

Because the High King is the standard against which all greatness is measured.

He charges the Pendragon, but the whirling, glowing blade Arthur wields is too quick. He lunges to the left, and there is a cut on the High King's arm, and to the right, and now a slice across his chest. Pendragon barely seems to move, and yet the damnable blade is right there, blocking the path, creating an impenetrable shield of biting, vicious magical steel.

Again and again he moves toward Arthur, and Gilgamesh is the High King, a tower of muscle and strength such as never has walked the earth before or since. If he were able to get his hands upon Arthur, he has no doubt that he could snap the Pendragon like a twig. But Arthur might as well be a hundred miles away for all the success that Gilgamesh has at getting to him. And now the High King is bleeding from a dozen wounds, and each one individually is nothing major, but together they are starting to drain him of his vitality. And Arthur does not seem the least bit tired or perturbed or even challenged. He is looking at the High King with pity. Pity.

If Arthur is greater than he . . . then he is nothing.

He cannot be nothing.

He is two-thirds god . . . one-third man . . .

This cannot be happening . . .

Nothing . . .

He is nothing . . .

The worship placed upon him, bestowed upon him. . . . if he is nothing . . . it is all meaningless. His life is meaningless. He is meaningless.

The useless weapon slips from his hand, clatters to the floor.

He knows what he must do now.

ARTHUR WAS DIVIDING his attention between Gilgamesh in front of him, and the struggle between the Basilisk, Percival, and Enkidu behind him. They were holding their own, that much was certain, but he longed to get over there and aid them, for he was certain that Excalibur could settle this business once and for all.

"Gilgamesh!" he cried out. "End this conflict! Restore yourself to the heroism I know is yours to achieve!"

THE PENDRAGON IS speaking to him. The words are little more than faint buzzing. He goes to one knee, places his hand flat upon the floor. His body trembles. For an instant he is utterly empty, a vacuum for power to rush into, and then it comes.

He will be great again. He will destroy the Pendragon, he will

*still have the weapon, he will have it all, it cannot and will not
end in this manner.*

"**S**IT DOWN!" SHOUTED Ron Cordoba, who had just
about had it.

They were at least five hundred feet away from Gilgamesh's residence. All around them, island people were either
running to distance themselves further, or milling about in
confusion, bereft of a clue as to how they should proceed.
They were so accustomed to Gilgamesh doing their thinking
for them that they were clueless how to proceed without
him. It was a gorgeous day, the sun shining, birds singing.
It would have been positively idyllic if it weren't for all the
screaming and roaring and sounds like gigantic monsters
and warriors from a bygone age trying to kill one another.

Gwen had been struggling against Ron, trying to run
back into the palace, but Ron swung her around and sent
her sitting down, hard, on the ground. Nellie dropped down
beside her, looking up at Ron angrily. "You didn't have to
do that!"

"Tell me," Ron said.

"Tell you what?"

"What Baumann had on you."

Nellie paled slightly, and Gwen said defensively, "Why
in hell should that matter now?"

"Because," Ron told her, "I have a sneaking suspicion that
I'm not going to make it through this, and I don't want to
die in ignorance!" He turned to Nellie. "Maybe you feel you
don't owe me anything, but I kind of think you owe me
that much at least! Now spill it!"

Nellie looked to Gwen for help and support, but found
none there. "I have to admit, I'm curious myself," said
Gwen. "I trusted you implicitly, Nellie. You betrayed me.
If you have the slightest fragment of hope that we'll remain
on speaking terms after all this is done—since I, unlike Ron,
believe we're going to survive—you'll tell me."

She looked from Gwen's face to Ron's and back again, and then let out a tremulous sigh.

"We were lovers," she said.

Gwen made a face. "You and Baumann?"

"No." She squared her shoulders and said, "You and me."

She stared at Nellie for a moment, and then let out a confused laugh. "What the hell are you talking about? I never . . ." She looked to Ron. "We never . . . that's . . . it's ridiculous . . ."

"Do you remember college? Lance's twenty-first birthday?" In an FYI manner she said to Ron, "Lance was her old boyfriend. Abusive little shit. But when he turned twenty-one, Gwen asked what he wanted for his birthday, and all he wanted was a three-way with another woman." Without looking at Gwen, she said, "Is it coming back to you?"

Ron cast his eye over to Gwen. There was no blood in her face, only her red lips providing any sort of color compared to the whiteness that remained. "Oh . . . my God . . . but . . . but her name was . . . I . . ."

"You can't remember." When Gwen shook her head, Nellie just nodded. "Yeah, well . . . you were pretty stoned that night, so I'm not all that surprised. Then again, I was going through some bullshit phase at the time and just kept calling myself 'Sunrider,' so even if you'd remembered, it wouldn't have meant anything. But Lance remembered. And Lance took pictures. And saved them. And early on in the mayoral race, Lance went to Baumann with a couple of them. Because he hated you so much that he wanted to do whatever he could to torpedo your romance and Arthur's chances as mayor. And then Lance disappeared. Which weakened the story somewhat, but not completely. Baumann still had the photographs. But you know what?" She laughed bitterly at the recollection. "He liked you guys. He really did. He felt you'd be good for New York. So he kept his mouth shut. And then, when you became First Lady and he saw pictures of me with you, he contacted me. And I figured, if it had been bad with those pictures seeing print back in the mayoral days, how much worse would it have been with you as First Lady. Think how it would have looked, how it would have been portrayed . . ."

"I can see the headlines," murmured Ron. " 'First Lady Hires Lesbian Lover.' "

"*But I didn't know!*" Gwen cried out. "My God, in college I experimented with all kinds of . . . and Lance, he . . . I mean . . . I was a different person back then . . ."

"Which isn't to be confused with a thousand years ago, when you were a different person entirely," said Nellie with bitter humor. "So you see, Gwen . . . I was protecting you as much as anyone."

"And now he's dead. And the story died with him. And Arthur's out of the White House, so there's nothing at stake . . ." Gwen looked stunned at it all. "Nellie . . . I . . ."

"Yeah?"

She stared at her. "Was I good?"

Nellie held out her hand, palm flat, and wavered it from side to side. "Eh."

"Bitch," said Gwen, ten seconds before she keeled over.

*T*HE POWER COMES *rushing into the High King, and it seems to call to him, to ask him why he has waited for so long, why he has ignored it all this time.*

He has no words of apology, but then he owes it nothing. He is the power unto himself. He is the High King, he is Gilgamesh, two-thirds god and one-third man, he is the legend incarnate, and his will be done, on earth as it is in heaven . . .

*A*RTHUR FELT A strange, almost elastic feeling, as if the world around him were being stretched out of its normal shape and configuration. Trying to distance himself from Gilgamesh, lest he be helpless while in a confused state, he stumbled backward, unsure of where he was or what was happening. He saw Percival and even Enkidu lurching about as well. Enkidu looked the most disoriented, and Arthur wasn't surprised. Enkidu was a being utterly in tune with nature. If nature itself was out of whack, Enkidu would be at a loss.

Something warned him at the last instant, and he threw himself frantically to one side. The Basilisk sailed right over him, arms outstretched, hissing and spitting, and landing on the far side of the room.

And suddenly the ground seemed to go right out from under him. There was a low, distant rumbling, as if the island itself were being torn asunder, and then pieces of marble began to fall from overhead. Loud cracks reported from overhead, and there was even more rumbling as the ground bucked under his feet like an angry bronco.

Gilgamesh was still crouched upon the floor, suffused with an incandescent glow running up his arms, permeating his entire form. He wasn't looking at Arthur or Percival or even the Basilisk. All his attention was focused inward, and he was smiling with the demented contentment that only a true madman could display.

Arthur reached out almost blindly, grabbed an arm, and was relieved to discover it was Percival's. He shouted, "Go! Let's go!" and didn't wait for Percival to respond. Instead he ran toward the closest exit, which, as it happened, was a large hole in the wall that had not been there moments earlier. More debris was crumbling from above, and Arthur desperately swung Excalibur over his head in broad strokes, hoping to knock away whatever pieces of rubble might be falling down upon them. And then they were through and in the open air, except he could see that the forest and the trees were disintegrating, the green and lush vegetation all over the island beginning to wilt and blacken. Birds were tumbling headlong out of the trees and making odd little popping noises, as if they were lightbulbs that were shattering upon striking the ground, and their tiny bodies would break apart and scatter away as bits of dust.

In the distance he saw the people of the island screaming,

shaking their heads desperately, clutching at the ground as it was drawn away from beneath their feet. As the verdant terrain disappeared, it left behind it lifeless and unfriendly sheets of rock with tiny little tufts of grass sticking out here and there.

And the animals, the animals in the forest, gods, they were keeling over as well. Arthur heard rabbits scream, and he had never known they were capable of doing such a thing, but obviously they were, as the little furballs let out shrieks of such utter terror that they sounded like so many human children being menaced.

And the deer, and the other creatures, all crumbling away. Arthur saw it all.

And the people of Pus Island saw it as well.

Which was about when Arthur put two and two together. Apparently the people did, too, because they started screaming and clutching at their faces, their bodies, falling upon the rock and calling Gilgamesh's name and begging and pleading with him to just give them another chance, that they would live up to what he expected them to be and please, oh please . . .

Their skin began to draw taut, their hair started whitening. There was terror in their eyes, and they clutched at themselves as if their bodies were traitors.

There was a horrific roar and for a heartbeat, Arthur thought it was the Basilisk hauling itself from the debris, for the noise did not sound like anything capable of being issued by a human throat. Then rock and rubble were shoved aside, and there stood Gilgamesh, a look of smug determination on his face, and in his hand was the most remarkable sword that Arthur had ever seen. It glittered gold, and obviously it was not solid gold, for that would have been far too soft. It would also have been horrifically heavy, but that didn't seem as if it was going to stop him.

Furthermore the blade was long and jagged, looking for all the world like a lightning bolt. It throbbed with inner power.

Many times had Arthur heard the phrase, "His terrible swift sword," and how it "loosed the fateful lightning." It had always struck him as more than just a poetic turn of phrase. It seemed, in his imaginings, to be based on something.

Now he knew just what it was it was based upon. It was this frightful blade, this weapon that—if Gilgamesh was to be believed—had existed in some shape or other since the dawn of creation. Many forms did it have, apparently, for its magic was so potent that one incarnation was simply incapable of holding it.

"It is the power of life and death," Gilgamesh said with reverence, as if he were reading Arthur's mind . . . and for all Arthur Penn knew, he was. "Pure and simple, that is what the Grail power boiled down to. In its shape as the cup, it gives life. In its incarnation as the land, it maintains it. And as the sword . . ." and his voice dropped and was low and frightful, "it takes it."

He swept the sword through the air once, and the air seemed to back away from it, afraid to come in contact with it.

Percival stepped forward, his sword at the ready. "Highness, let me . . ."

"No," Arthur said flatly. "It would cut you down in a heartbeat."

"But . . ." He looked at Arthur with such longing. "It's the Grail."

And Arthur knew right then, right there, what Percival intended to do. The Grail had given him life eternal. Now one strike from it could end that life . . . and it was a concept that Percival was not the least opposed to.

"No," he said again, and this time there was even more to the authority of the command. "If you love me as your liege, if you value your vows to me, you will not do it."

"Highness . . ." There was urgency to his voice, mounting desperation. "Don't you see . . . ?"

"Yes. I see. And I am ordering you to live."

Percival's eyes glittered with what amounted to momentary hatred, and then, just as quickly, it was gone, and he bowed his head. "I serve at the pleasure of the King," he intoned, and there was no hint of mockery in his voice, although there was most definitely sadness and some resignation.

Arthur nodded once, accepting the reluctant vow of fealty, and then he looked around. He saw the people of the island stumbling about, confused and frightened and aging. He turned and looked in Gwen's direction and knew what he would see there. Sure enough, she was upon the ground, limp as a rag doll, and there was agony in the faces of Ron Cordoba and Nellie Porter.

"Look about you, Gilgamesh!" Arthur cried out, trying to suppress the sheer agony in his soul and not succeeding particularly well. "Look at what you have wrought! It's not too late! Let go that which you have fought so hard to hold onto, for it was never yours to have in the first place."

*T*HE HIGH KING *hears his words, even as the voice of the Grail sings to him. His arms tremble. He feels drunk with power.*

He sees Enkidu. He sees his beast brother, standing ten feet away.

"Enkidu," he says softly, and his voice vibrates, barely recognizable as himself. "To my side."

Enkidu looks at him with endless pity . . . and then slowly walks toward him. He stands but three feet away, and looks at his beloved Gilgamesh.

"You are my brother. You are my greatest love," Enkidu says softly. "And I cannot bear to see what you have become . . . and cannot bear to walk away from you."

And he throws himself upon the upraised sword.

The shock of the impact barely registers upon Gilgamesh as the sword splits Enkidu's chest. His beast brother convulses once, his head pitches back, and he trembles but does not cry out. Gilgamesh hears a voice screaming Enkidu's name, realizes that it's his own voice, and still allows it to continue as Enkidu's blood pours down over the hilt of the sword, bathing it in red. The sword glows ever brighter, drinking it in, and Gilgamesh yanks it from Enkidu's chest, tearing the tawny fur, cracking ribs and spilling some of the great heart upon the ground.

The Pendragon is saying something to him. He does not hear it. He stares at the blood upon the sword, the heart on the ground, and then picks up the piece of the heart . . . and eats it. It has been many, many centuries since he has done such a thing. Usually such organs are tough, almost impossible to chew, and must be quickly swallowed. But not Enkidu's. It is astoundingly soft, almost melting upon his tongue, and great hot tears pour down Gilgamesh's face as the soul of the one creature in the world he loved more than himself merges with his.

And he hears a second heartbeat in conjunction with his own.

And he sees himself for the first time with true clarity. Sees himself for what he is, and what he could have been.

And then he forgets.

And he attacks.

CHAPTRE
THE TWENTY-FIFTH

✝

ARTHUR STOOD FROZEN by the scene, but snapped from his paralysis as Gilgamesh came at him.

The entire moment seemed to be playing out in slow motion, and even though Arthur felt as if he had plenty of time as he brought Excalibur up to a defensive position, a part of him knew that he had reacted faster than he ever had before. A half a second at most, and then the Grail sword slammed into Excalibur.

They felt it . . .

. . . in Portugal.

And Brazil, and Argentina. Up into Mexico, and higher, and the San Andreas fault shifted, and buildings rocked, and when the second blow came, even more powerful than the first, people ran screaming in Peking as the ground buckled beneath them, and in the Himalayas there were avalanches, and every single animal in the Amazon Rain Forest capable of producing a sound screamed at the top of its throat, while every animal that could not simply froze in its tracks, a good ten percent of them dropping dead right there, and when the swords clashed together a third time, they got seismic readings at a station in the North Pole that they could not explain no matter how many months they studied it, and then came the fourth crash of the blades that existed beyond time, beyond magic, beyond human comprehension, and ten years later astronomers working for SETI, the Search for Extra-Terrestrial Life, monitoring broadcasts in endless hope of making some sort of contact, would practically faint in excitement upon receiving the very first broadcast from a star light-years away, and it would take them another five years to translate the communication which they would eventually decipher as, "*What the* fuck *was* that?"

And at the source of the conflict, the effects upon the island around them were no less catastrophic.

The ground, already bereft of the influence of the Grail, began to shatter. People were running, screaming, slamming into one another, looking at one another's faces in horror as they continued to age, and suddenly that was the least of their problems as the island cracked apart beneath their very feet. The ocean around them, which had been calm moments before, suddenly reared up and came smashing through the newly created rents. People were trying to find higher ground, but there was no higher ground because all of it was crumbling, all the buildings, the small mountains, all of it coming apart. Far beneath them tectonic plates shifted and bucked, and again and again the swords came together, unleashing power that was beyond the comprehension of either of the combatants. It was as if the very soul of the earth, dormant and resting for centuries, turned over in its bed and demanded to know what that godawful noise and clanging was, and—once having determined the origin—decided that the best thing to do would be to silence the ruckus once and for all.

Arthur risked a glance in Gwen's direction. He saw Percival cradling Gwen's unmoving body in his arms, saw Nellie scream and almost tumble into a newly created crevice and then Ron reached out, grabbed her, prevented her from falling in, and suddenly they were washed away by a tidal blast of water. Arthur cried out Gwen's name, and then there was Gilgamesh, the sword flashing, and Arthur deflected it, but only just. The ground was crumbling beneath his feet, and he saw a small, rocky shoal and leaped for it, barely making it. The terrain was dissolving faster and faster, and again came Gilgamesh, roaring with incomprehensible fury. He vaulted toward the shoal, and Arthur swung Excalibur, trying to keep Gilgamesh back. It didn't work. Gilgamesh deflected the thrust and then he and Arthur were both on a piece of land that couldn't have been more than ten feet across.

Arthur saw the first of the bodies. Islanders, crushed, floating past, and they were still aging even though they were already dead, and Gilgamesh didn't care. Arthur didn't want to see if Gwen or Percival or the others were floating past. Nothing seemed to matter. It had all gone wrong: terribly, hideously wrong, and there still was Gilgamesh, swinging the sword, and Arthur barely managed to keep it from cleaving him in half.

"*You've learned nothing in this! Nothing!*" shouted Arthur, soaked to the skin, his hair hanging in his face.

"I've learned to hate you," Gilgamesh shot back. "For now, that will suffice."

"*We could have been friends!*"

Gilgamesh shook his head vigorously, and was about to say something else when the water suddenly vomited up a scaly engine of destruction.

The Basilisk that had once been Arnim Sandoval roared up out of the water, his jaws extended, his eyes hot with hatred, and Arthur, who had been watching Gilgamesh, was caught unaware as the Basilisk came in from his blind side. One of the coils slammed into Arthur, and the King of the Britons went down onto his back, the air knocked out of him.

"*At last!*" howled Sandoval, and his head speared toward Arthur.

*   *   *

*T*HE HIGH KING *is filled with fury. After all that he has gone through, all that he has endured, this . . . this creature . . . seeks to interfere?*

Intolerable. Utterly intolerable.

Such as this monster is not worthy of snatching the High King's victory from him.

"*G*ET AWAY FROM *him*!" shouted Gilgamesh, even as he swung the sword in a vicious arc that would have easily killed the Basilisk in one stroke, had the Basilisk been there when it came into contact.

But the Basilisk was not there, for he was young and quick and still feeling the full strength of his new form flooding through him. He dodged the killing stroke with no effort, and there was plenty of him to go around as he brought his back coils down upon Arthur's wrist, immobilizing his sword arm. Arthur grunted in frustration as the Basilisk kept the mighty Excalibur pinned, and turned his attention upon Gilgamesh.

"You slew she who bore me. Who gave me new life, new purpose," said the Basilisk. The waves were coming up higher, pounding upon the shoal, but the Basilisk took no notice of them. "You must be made to pay for that."

And he locked eyes with Gilgamesh, and the full power of his gaze swelled up within him, and drove itself into Gilgamesh.

*A*ND THE HEART *and soul of his beast brother rises up against the insidious power of the young Basilisk and protects him to some degree, but the fears are still there just the same, the fears that the Basilisk's terrible abilities are able to bring to the surface like no other, and for just an instant, every single thing* *that the Pendragon has said to him makes perfect and complete sense.*

And that is the single greatest horror that the High King can ever know.

GILGAMESH CRIED OUT even as he fought down the terror and swung the sword. And again the Basilisk avoided its arc, and he brought his head around and sunk his fangs deep into Gilgamesh's wrist, freezing it for just a second. But a second was all the Basilisk required, and he twisted the powerful muscles of his body and the Grail sword was suddenly out of his hand, flying through the air. But the twist had pulled the coils off position, and Arthur yanked his hand free and Excalibur with it.

"*Wart! Grab it!*"

It was Merlin's voice that shouted through the air and above the roar of the waves, and Arthur looked and saw but didn't quite believe it.

A boat was rolling toward them through the water. It was the size of several yachts, made entirely of wood, with a great sail atop it, blasted forward by the winds that had come up from nowhere, unleashed as part of the elemental forces that the blades had aroused. At the helm, gripping a steering wheel and guiding the vessel toward them, was Ziusura, and Merlin was at the prow . . .

And next to him was Percival. And Nellie and Ron . . . and Gwen, still in Percival's arms, for a knight would never, ever let the queen slip from his keeping while there was still breath within him. Her head was slumped back, but there was the slightest rising of her chest even though death was coming for her. Arthur could practically see the dark horseman galloping toward her, his scythe poised . . .

The sword! The Grail!

"*Gwen!*" screamed Arthur, and the sword tumbled toward the water.

And the Basilisk had Gilgamesh. For Gilgamesh was still

stunned by the loss of the sword, and by whatever he had seen in the Basilisk's eyes. The terrible creature had its coils around him now, and Arthur stood frozen.

The sword hit the water, but the hilt snagged on an upraised piece of rock. It sat there, tantalizingly, mockingly. If it slid off the rock, it was going to sink in a heartbeat to a watery grave hundreds of feet below. It would never be found, and even if it was, it would be far, far too late for Gwen, who Arthur could see even at this distance was ghastly white.

And there was Gilgamesh, the first of the legends, a being who had trod centuries and inspired civilization, in the grip of a creature that was evil and venomous and wasn't worthy, just as Gilgamesh had said, not worthy of taking the life of such a man. Presuming, of course, that he could, and Arthur very much suspected that it was possible. Gilgamesh, who— however suspect the motives—had just saved Arthur from a quick death at the hands of the Basilisk, and was now about to die in exchange.

I'll do both! Do both! Quickly, move quickly, you can accomplish both aims, just hurry, Arthur, damn you, hurry!

Arthur screamed out a cry of challenge and rage, and charged. He had never moved faster in his life.

It was not fast enough.

*T*HE HIGH KING, *slayer of gods and the animals of gods, sees his end in the awful eyes of this beast, his head held immobile by the mighty hands, a blast of foul air from its mouth billowing into his face, his eyes stinging from the stench of poison. Something within him is cracking under the press of the coils, and then it breaks, and it may well be that he is bleeding within. He coughs up blood, and there is pressure behind his eyes, and suddenly the gleaming sword of Excalibur is there. It cleaves through the Basilisk's right arm, and the creature lets out a screech as the arm falls to the ground. It whirls, facing the new threat, and the Pendragon's blade is a blur.*

And the High King sees it all. He sees the ship, sees the body of Pendragon's mate, sees the Grail sword about to sink, for it all happens in an instant, and sees that Pendragon could have allowed him to die, just die at the hands of the creature, while striving to snag the Grail sword. But his instinct, one king for another, has caught him up, and Excalibur is a whirl of death, like a bladed tornado, and the Basilisk does not know where to look first. In a heartbeat it no longer matters, for Arthur's blade slices home and the creature's skull is cleaved straight down the middle, falling to either side as blood spurts upward in a geyser.

And the ground crumbles beneath them.

ARTHUR BARELY HAD time to register that the Basilisk was in its death throes when he suddenly found himself treading water. His grip on Excalibur was still firm, but then he saw a quick glitter of gold and the Grail sword was gone. His soul cried out in agony, and even though he knew there was no chance, Arthur dove under the water, kicking desperately toward it. But it was falling away too fast, too fast, and Arthur swam as hard as he could, losing track of how far down he'd gone, of how much time had passed, and the sword was descending even faster, into the murk and mire, and then it was gone from sight. Even the inner incandescence of the sword was insufficient to serve as any sort of guiding illumination.

His lungs were burning, and for a moment Arthur considered simply opening his mouth and letting the water fill him. And then he saw Gwen in his mind's eye, asked himself if it was what she would want, and without hesitation kicked upward toward what he thought was the surface.

But it was too far to go, much too far, and he felt the pounding growing in his chest. He knew beyond any question he was not going to make it, there was simply no way, and he thought, *I'm sorry, Gwen, I tried,* just as his head broke the water. He gasped reflexively and the ocean water poured into his lungs. He coughed violently, and that brought in even more water, and then he started to sink again.

That was when arms came around him on either side, pulling him to the surface once more. He looked around in confusion and was dumbfounded to see Ron Cordoba bobbing up and down in the water with him, holding him securely under the arms.

"*I've got him!*" he shouted somewhat unnecessarily, and the boat was coming right toward them. For an instant Arthur was concerned it was going to run them over, sending both of them to the bottom of the ocean, but then Percival was stretching toward them from the deck. Ron reached up and Percival snagged him, hauling them up, and moments later they were both safe upon the deck of the ship.

Arthur sank to the deck, gasping for air, Ron next to him. Excalibur lay on the deck between them. "You had to go and leave your Secret Service men behind. Just had to, didn't you?" muttered Ron. Arthur clapped him on the back, shaking his head at the insanity of it all.

"Nice boat," he commented to Ziusura.

Ziusura shrugged. "When you've survived one flood, you tend to be prepared for any eventuality."

And then Arthur saw Gwen lying on the deck. Merlin was next to her, her head cradled in his lap, staring at her forelornly.

Arthur scrambled toward him and looked down at Gwen in misery. "I . . . I thought I could do both . . ." he said. "Save them both . . ."

"It's all right, Arthur," Merlin said softly.

But Arthur shook his head. "No. It's not all right. I should have let him die. After what he did . . . all he did . . . all he was . . ."

"You didn't try to save him because of what he was," Merlin said. "You tried to save him for what he could have been. Your instincts were right . . . even if the outcome wasn't."

Arthur tried to suppress a sob, and failed, and it felt unmanly, but he didn't care anymore. He clutched Gwen's hand, and it was growing cold, so cold.

"I'm so sorry," he whispered, but it sounded pathetic and hollow.

That was when he heard Nellie scream, "*Look!*" and Ron was saying, "*Oh, my God,*" and Ziusura muttered an oath in a tongue unspoken for centuries.

Arthur clambered to his feet and ran toward the edge of the boat. He looked where they were pointing, and he couldn't believe it.

A hand was emerging from the water, a bronzed, male hand. It was holding the Grail sword, glittering against the darkened sky.

"Hard about!" shouted Arthur, and Ziusura was already steering in that direction. They came toward the sword, and the hand flung it. It sailed through the air and Arthur reached up and caught it. He gasped at the weight. Gilgamesh had hardly seemed slowed by it, but Arthur could barely hold it. "Pull him up!" Arthur called. "Get Gilgamesh! Get—"

But Ziusura was shaking his head very slowly and sadly. "I don't believe that's how the High King wants his story to end."

For a heartbeat, Arthur saw Gilgamesh's face, looking up from beneath the surface. And he saw exhaustion and sadness . . . but also satisfaction. And then a trail of air bubbles expelled from between his lips, and he sank. It seemed forever that Arthur stared at the spot, waiting for Gilgamesh to resurface, but there was nothing except the stillness of the now-calming waters.

"Highness," came Percival's voice softly from next to him. Arthur turned then and handed the sword to Percival. The Moor grunted slightly at the heft and even laughed softly. He held the blade flat across his hands, and whispered, "I hated you for so long. But, God . . . it's good to see you again."

And then it was the Cup.

There was no flash of light, no sudden release of power. It was just right there, in his hands. Arthur stared at it in wonderment. The last time he'd seen it was a thousand years ago, when it had saved him from the wounds inflicted by his bastard son. But it looked just as he remembered it, graceful and pure.

Ziusura had a flask at his hip, and quickly he poured some water from it into the Cup. Arthur held it reverently, barely daring to hope, and then he crossed quickly to Gwen.

She looked ghastly. He wasn't even sure if she was alive. The ugly wound from the assassin's bullet had returned in her head. He knelt and Merlin angled her head up as Arthur pried her lips open. He poured the water into her mouth and then, for good measure, on the wound itself.

There was a hissing from where the water came in contact with the wound, and then Gwen let out a shriek, her eyes snapping open, and she sat up and looked around in bewilderment.

Arthur sobbed out her name and, handing the Grail to Merlin, threw his arms around Gwen and cried into her shoulder. All thoughts of unmanliness in the shedding of tears were long gone as endless gratitude swept through him.

Gwen said something, her voice muffled against his body. He pulled back, looked at her with eyes glistening. She was about to repeat her question, but then she saw the Grail and awe filled her face. "Is . . . that it?" she asked.

"Yes."

"Can I . . . ?"

He handed it to her and she held it. "It's . . ."

"What?"

"It's . . ." Her voice trembled. "It's the most beautiful thing I've ever seen. That anyone's ever seen. Isn't it?"

And he touched her cheek and whispered, "The second most."

*   *   *

H E EXISTS IN *twilight. He does not know if he is alive or dead. But Enkidu is with him, and for the first time in all his life, he is no longer afraid.*

The High King is happy . . .

New York Times bestselling author
Peter David

Knight Life

**"ARTHURIAN LEGEND GETS ANOTHER
KICK IN THE PANTS."
—*PUBLISHERS WEEKLY* (STARRED)**

King Arthur, the once and future king, has been
called forth by the wizard Merlin to lead a land in
turmoil—the United States of America. But with no
throne to sit upon, Arthur must run for elected office,
starting with the mayorship of New York City.

**"A FUN SPIN ON THAT MARK TWAIN CLASSIC.
A MIX OF CLASSIC ARTHURIAN FICTION AND
SATIRIC COMMENTARY ABOUT THE NATURE OF
TODAY'S POLITICS. ENGAGING."
—*MONROE NEWS-STAR***

**"FRESH AND VERY FUNNY."
—*BOOKLIST***

Available wherever books are sold or
to order call 1-800-788-6262

A861

Penguin Group (USA) Inc. Online

What will you be reading tomorrow?

Tom Clancy, Patricia Cornwell, W.E.B. Griffin,
Nora Roberts, William Gibson, Robin Cook,
Brian Jacques, Catherine Coulter, Stephen King,
Dean Koontz, Ken Follett, Clive Cussler,
Eric Jerome Dickey, John Sandford,
Terry McMillan...

You'll find them all at
http://www.penguin.com.

Read excerpts and newsletters, find tour
schedules, enter contests...

Subscribe to Penguin Group (USA) Inc. Newsletters
and get an exclusive inside look
at exciting new titles and the authors you love
long before everyone else does.

PENGUIN GROUP (USA) INC. NEWS
http://www.penguin.com/news